P9-CFJ-229

The Caterpillar's Question

The Caterpillar's Question

PIERS ANTHONY
~ A · N · D ~
PHILIP JOSÉ FARMER

ACE BOOKS, NEW YORK

THE CATERPILLAR'S QUESTION

An Ace Book
Published by The Berkley Publishing Group
200 Madison Avenue, New York, New York 10016

Book design by Caron Harris

First Edition: October 1992

Library of Congress Cataloging-in-Publication Data

Anthony, Piers.
    The caterpillar's question / by Piers Anthony and Philip José
Farmer.
        p.   cm.
    I. Farmer, Philip José.   II. Title.
    PS3551.N73C3   1992
    813'. 54—dc20   91-41398
    ISBN: 0-441-09488-0   CIP

Printed in the United States of America

10   9   8   7   6   5   4   3   2   1

"Who are *you*?" the Caterpillar said . . . "I can't explain *myself*, I'm afraid, sir," said Alice, "because I'm not myself, you see."

—*Alice's Adventures in Wonderland*

Chapter 1

THEY had told Jack they thought it was psychosomatic. She could talk if she wanted to, and might even recover the sight of one eye. But it had taken seven years to obtain the grant from the foundation, and now she was thirteen.

He glanced at her, sitting tight and stiff in the passenger bucket. Her dark hair was cut so short it was boyish, but the gentle bulges in the heavy man's shirt she wore belied any boyhood or childhood. One hand toyed indifferently with the buckle of the seat belt, and under her cotton skirt the shiny length of a metal brace paralleled her left leg. Her sharp chin pointed forward, but of course she was not watching anything.

The horn of the car behind him blared as the light changed. Jack shifted and edged out, waiting for the string of late left-turners to clear. He wasn't even certain which city this was; the hours of silent driving had grown monotonous.

"Are you ready to stop, Tappy?" But she did not answer or make any sign. He knew she heard and understood—but he was still a stranger, and she was afraid. Had they even bothered to tell her where she was going, or why?

Tappuah Concord, maimed at the age of six, in the accident that killed her father. She had never known her mother, and the nearest of kin that took her in had not been pleased very long with the burden. Jack had no doubt they had made this plain to the little girl many times.

He pulled into a roadside restaurant. His job was to transport her safely to the clinic. She couldn't cover a thousand miles without eating.

Why hadn't they sent her by plane, so that all this driving was unnecessary? No, the plane was out of the question. Tappy surely still remembered that last trip in her father's little flier. Apparently

1

there had been a miscalculation, and they had crashed. Jack had not inquired about the details, for Tappy had been there listening, and he had never been one for pointless cruelty.

He got out, opened her door, unsnapped her seat belt, slipped his hands under her arms, and lifted her to her feet. They had warned him about this, too: there was often no way to make her come except to *make her come*. Anywhere. Otherwise she might simply sit there indefinitely, staring sightlessly ahead. He felt awkward, putting his hands on her, but she did not seem to notice.

He guided her firmly by the elbow and stopped at the little sign pointing to the ladies' room, not certain whether the girl knew her way around public facilities, and doubtful what he'd do if she didn't. He had to ask her, rather awkwardly because of the people passing nearby, and she shook her head no. Was it wisest to treat her as a child or as a woman? The difference was important the moment they left the isolation of the car. He decided on the latter, at least in public places.

They took a corner table, enduring the interminable wait for their order. He was super-conscious of the glances of others, but Tappy seemed oblivious to her surroundings. She kept her hands in her lap, eyes downcast and incurious, and he saw too clearly the narrow white scar that crossed one eye and terminated at the mutilated ear. What did his petty embarrassment mean, compared to her problems?

"Lookit that girl's ear's gone!" exclaimed a younger boy at a neighboring table, his voice startlingly loud. There was a fierce shushing that was worse than the remark because it confirmed its accuracy. Heads turned, first toward the boy, then toward the object of the boy's curiosity.

A slow tear started down Tappy's left cheek.

Jack stood up so suddenly that his chair crashed backward, and he stepped around the table and caught her arm and brought her out of that place. It was as if he had tunnel vision; all he saw was the escape route, the room and people fuzzing out at the periphery. They made it to the car, strapped in, and he drove, arrowing down the highway at a dangerous velocity. He was first numb, then furious—but he wasn't sure at what.

Gradually he cooled, and knew that the worst of the situation had been his own reaction. It was too late to undo what damage he might have done, but he could at least be guided more sensibly henceforth. He schooled himself not to react like that, no matter what happened next time.

But first he had something more difficult to do. "Tappy, I'm sorry. I shouldn't have done that. I just—" He faltered, for she was not reacting at all. "I'm sorry."

She might as well have been a statue.

At dusk, starving, he drew up to a motel and left Tappy in the seat while he registered for two rooms. He took her to one of them and sat her on the bed. He crossed the street and bought a six-pack of fruit drinks and two submarine sandwiches for their supper. Class fare it was not, but it was all he could think of at the moment.

He set things up precariously on the bed in her room, and was glad to see that she had a good appetite. She evidently was not used to this particular menu, but was experienced with bedroom meals. His pleasure became concern as he thought about it. Had they ever let her eat at the table, family style? He could see why they might not have, but it bothered him anyway. There was a human being inside that tortured shell!

His thoughts drifted to his own motives. Why had he taken this job? A week before he'd have laughed if someone had predicted he'd be sitting on a motel bed eating supper with a blind girl almost ten years his junior. But he hadn't realized how hard it would be for a budding artist with one year of college to get a decent summer job.

Jack had kicked around for two, three years—he didn't know exactly where the time went—before running into Donna. Then suddenly he had the need to make something of himself. So he went to college and studied art. Did okay, too; he did have talent. But by the time he got it together, Donna had drifted elsewhere. He never even got to tell her of the effect she had on his motivation. He grieved, of course, and considered giving it up. But he discovered that life did go on, and there might even be other girls on the horizon.

Meanwhile, he needed wherewithal to continue college; that kept him busy around the edges. He soon realized that he was not likely to make it by washing dishes at joints that had never heard of the minimum wage scale, or changing tires for tips, or taking any of the other menial positions for which one year of art seemed to qualify him.

The ad had offered a thousand dollars plus liberal expenses and the use of a good car for one week's light work. It had seemed too good to be true, and he was amazed to learn that the job hadn't been taken. No, it didn't involve drugs or anything illegal; it was just chauffeuring. If he had a valid license and a good record . . .

Jack had little else, but he did have those. He valued his potential career as a world-famous artist too much to mess it up with bad driving. He liked to travel; every new region was grist for his painting.

The job was to deliver Tappy to the clinic across the country. He assumed that it was legal for him to transport this child, or they would not have hired him. He needed the money, and didn't ask too many questions. He had had no idea that jobs like this existed! If he could find a couple more like this, at similar pay scales, his next year of college would be assured.

They had covered four hundred miles today. At this rate he'd have Tappy at the clinic the day after tomorrow, and could be back two days early. The pay was for the job, not the time, so he had nothing to lose by being prompt. If the girl didn't talk, at least she wasn't much trouble. After this he'd get sandwiches and they'd eat in the car, avoiding restaurants entirely.

Jack cleaned up the mess of crumbs and told Tappy he'd check on her in the morning. "You can find your way around the room okay? Bathroom's in a straight line from the bed, and there's a radio. I'm in the next unit if you need me. Just yell."

He paused, embarrassed, remembering that she was mute, or chose to be. "I mean you can bang on the wall or something. That okay?" Slowly she nodded, and he was relieved. She responded so little that he was never quite sure she understood him. "Good. Now get some sleep. I'll knock before I come in, so I won't catch you by surprise." That was his concession to the woman aspect of her; she had to have time to cover up if she happened to be changing.

It all seemed simple enough.

But in the morning he found her sitting there still, shivering, the moisture squeezing hopelessly out of one eye. She might have moved about during the night, but the dark patches under her eyes showed she had not slept.

"Why?" he demanded incredulously. "Why didn't you summon me, if you couldn't sleep?"

She answered him only with that catatonic passivity, and a tear. Evidently there was something he had missed.

He told her to go to the bathroom while he fetched breakfast, and she did. He told her to change her clothing while he faced into a corner, and she did. He no longer trusted her to do things in his absence, but he intended to treat her with propriety. They ate, and got back on the road.

Jack pondered the event of the night as he drove, deeply disturbed. He had not mistreated Tappy, and there had been no trouble, except for the business at the restaurant. He had spoken to her and had supper with her, and she had not been crying then. She didn't seem to be afraid of him, though he wouldn't have blamed her for that. Indifferent, perhaps, but not fearful. So what was bothering her?

He was taking her to the clinic that might bring back her sight and make her talk. She should be happy.

"Don't you want to see again?" he asked her. "I mean, there's all kinds of scenery out here. We're in New York State now—"

She turned suddenly toward him, startling him into silence. He glanced at her, but her face showed no emotion. After a moment she straightened out again.

There *was* something! This was her first voluntary response to him. She had reacted to something he had said. Was it his question about her sight?

"You do want to see?" he repeated. But this time there was no reaction. Apparently she had acted without thought, but now she had clamped down again.

She couldn't *want* to stay blind! Maybe his question had deserved no answer. Yet she had reacted. There had to be something else. Something she knew that he didn't.

Was it really a clinic she was destined for? Or had that been something they told him to obtain his cooperation? Now that he thought about it, there were a number of funny things about this whole arrangement. If they had so much money for specialists, and enough to pay him so generously for unskilled labor, why hadn't they done something about her ear? Comparatively minor cosmetic surgery could have eliminated most of the scar tissue on her face, too. And there had to be something better than that ugly metal brace on her leg. She wasn't paralytic; the leg should have mended by now.

And why hadn't they hired a professional nurse for this trip? Nurses could drive. This was a gearshift car, but only because he had asked for it; he preferred to do his own driving. They could have gotten an automatic shift for a nurse. Why had they been so happy to trust him, a male stranger? They had hardly checked his credentials, which were minimal. The only virtue he seemed to have was ignorance. Yet for three days Tappy was in his hands. Anything could happen. Legally she was still a child—but she was a woman-child.

He drove on, no longer in a hurry. The doubt kept spiraling through his mind, growing uglier with every loop. If not a clinic, *what*?

Tappy wouldn't talk to him, so he talked to her, just to keep his mind off whatever unthinkable thing it sought. Maybe it was to inhibit his own suspicions. He read out the stupid billboards as they threaded their way through the complex of Schenectady, Albany, and Troy. He cussed out the other drivers. He kept up a meaningless monologue. Anything to fill the air with sound and keep his mind at bay.

Jack did not allow himself to wonder why he was deviating from the direct route marked on his map. He just drove where the scenery looked best.

Finally, as evening came to the highway, he felt a soft touch on his arm. He looked, and found her slumped like a straw doll, sleeping.

This was the supreme compliment. Tappy would not speak, but she now trusted him enough to sleep.

Jack realized then, coincidentally, why she had reacted when he talked to her initially. It had been the first time he had spoken to her without an imperative. He had started to describe the scenery they were passing. Perhaps it had been a long time since anyone had talked to her about anything that might interest her, however slightly.

He drove more carefully then, winding around the curves as the mountain ridge loomed high ahead, marking the physique of the state of Vermont. Just before the road seemed fated to plunge suicidally into the sheer wall of mountain, it spun aside, and there was a pretty town. He found a motel and stopped.

She was sleeping as he carried her into the unit and placed her on the bed. He took off her shoes, having a little trouble with the brace; the metal passed all the way under the foot and was awkward to get around. Tappy's feet and legs were well formed, however, and though she was light, her skeletal structure was good. She would have a handsome figure when she filled out, if only something could be done about her injuries, both physical and emotional.

Jack left her and turned out the light as he closed the door.

Sleep was more important than food at the moment. He hoped she would lie undisturbed until morning.

She did and she didn't. In the night he woke, hearing a voice. Someone was in Tappy's room. He went there, but there was no one. Tappy was lying on the bed—and talking. The words were slurred, almost indistinguishable.

He paused, realizing that she was not awake. She was talking in her sleep! That was the one time her emotional barrier was down, and her voice was freed.

Then out of that seeming gibberish, some words appeared. He listened, fascinated. "Empire of the stars," she said, if he understood correctly. Then: "Reality is a dream."

But after that she turned over, and there were no more words. He withdrew, excited. So what if she was muttering about some television program she had overheard? *She could talk!*

Next day they toured the great Green Mountains, the car's little engine laboring in a lower gear to manage the steep ascents. That was all right; he was no longer in a hurry, and they could proceed as slowly as they wanted. He continued to call out the view, and though Tappy did not turn her face to him again, he could tell by her alertness that she was interested.

He spoke of the old elms and maples, the mossy rocks, the near and distant mountain slopes covered with green foliage like thickly woven rugs. They passed a ski run—a long bare swath running up the side of one of the higher peaks, resembling a scar.

And she was crying again, in her silent way. The scar—why hadn't he kept his brain connected enough to stifle that analogy before it was spoken! His description lapsed; he couldn't think of any apology that would not hurt her more.

He understood now that her passive attitude concealed an extremely sensitive nature. Yet perhaps there was a positive aspect, for at least she was now showing her emotion. He had spoken to her, and gained her interest, thereby making her vulnerable. If he could hurt her, could he not also help her, if he found the right words?

They should have passed on through the Green Mountains and headed for New Hampshire, but Tappy seemed to be coming alive. Her head turned to the north, and her blind eyes became round. What was she trying to see? Jack remembered her words of the night, and decided to learn more of this if he could. He brought the car about, returned to the last intersection, and turned north.

Tappy's head now faced straight ahead; there was no doubt she was orienting on something, and it was independent of the motion of the car. What could it be?

He followed the direction of her gaze until it turned to the side. There was now no road where she looked, but her excitement suggested that the thing was fairly close.

At noon he pulled into a motel consisting of a row of ramshackle cabins. He thought it was deserted, and he only intended to search for some fresh water for lunch, and perhaps to see exactly where Tappy's fascination lay. But presently a man ambled out. He was dressed in high-fronted jeans, a style Jack had thought only picture-book farmers affected. They were in the hinterlands now!

"Don't get much business hereabout, this time o' year," the man remarked amiably. He spoke with a rich backwoods accent that also caught Jack off guard. " 'M the caretaker, but I can fix you up with a cab'n if you like."

"Two, if you please," Jack said. After all, he couldn't drive forever. Tomorrow was time enough to deliver Tappy. "There's a girl with me."

"Ay-uh," the man said affirmatively. "Saw her. Two'll cost you double, you know. Don't have to spend it."

Jack smiled at his candor. "It isn't my money," he said, as though that made everything all right. He accepted the keys to the two cabins. Then a thought gave him pause. "Do you have any books? I mean simple ones, to be read aloud? Like a children's book, or—?"

The man scratched his hairy head. "Well, now. There's some things the tourists forgot." Evidently the two of them didn't rank as tourists, which was probably for the best. Jack no longer detected much accent in the caretaker. The man wandered into a back room while Jack waited at the door, and sounds of rummaging drifted out. At length he emerged with a slim volume. "Don't know about this one," he admitted. "First I come to. If it don't suit, there's others."

Jack read the title: *The Little Prince,* by one Antoine de Saint-Exupéry. He had never heard of the man. "I'll give it a try. What do I owe you?" The man declined money for the book, to his surprise, and he went to escort Tappy to her cabin.

They had sandwiches on a wooden table outside the cabin. Tappy made them up with a certain finesse, and he was reminded again that she was used to doing for herself. It was a mistake to think of her as clumsy; of course the other senses had been stimulated to make up for her blindness. Touch and memory, sound and smell: these she possessed. And feeling.

The day clouded over. It wasn't really cold, but he wrapped Tappy in a voluminous quilt, set her on the cabin's sagging bunk, and read to her from *The Little Prince*. It was a curious story, a mixture of childish fantasy and adult perception, with appropriate illustrations. There were hats and boa constrictors and elephants, and confusions between them; there were gigantic bottle trees growing on pea-sized planetoids. Jack didn't know what to make of it, but Tappy seemed interested, and he continued to read all that afternoon. He took time to describe all the illustrations as they appeared.

When he came to the part about taming the fox by following the fox's own instructions, Tappy smiled. Jack could not honestly claim it was like a ray of sunshine. It was not poetic. It did not erase the terrible scar across her face. He was not about to use it as a model for a contemporary Mona Lisa portrait. It was simply a faint, frail, rather human smile. But it was the first, and his heart jumped that moment.

When he read the soliloquy to the field of roses, Tappy cried. But it was the tear of a woman at a wedding, incomprehensible but not miserable. The Little Prince had a cherished single rose, then was confronted by an entire field of roses, each as pretty as his own. But he had learned a lesson from his taming of the fox. "No one has tamed you, and you have tamed no one," he said to those other roses, much to their embarrassment. "You are beautiful, but you are empty . . . because it is *she* that I have watered . . . she that I have listened to . . . because she is *my* rose."

Jack would not have thought that a girl of thirteen would comprehend the message there. He wasn't sure he grasped it himself. Apparently he had stumbled across a book that was meaningful to her.

When it finished, she took the volume from his hand and held it to her breast. He left her sitting there, swathed in the quilt, tightly hugging the story she could not read herself. She was there when he returned an hour later with a bag of groceries. He let her keep the book that night, and she slept.

This time he was alert, and was there to listen the moment she began talking. But the words made no more sense than before. "Alien menace . . . only chance is to use the radiator." He thought that was what it was. Evidently more of the television program.

Yet why should she be so intrigued with it that she repeated it in her sleep? This child suffered so terribly; how could a routine segment of a silly program affect her like this?

Then she said something different, with a peculiar intensity. "Larva . . . Chrysalis . . . Imago." Quite clearly. He knew what that was: the several stages of the growth of an insect. First it was a kind of worm, then a kind of bug, finally it metamorphosed into its moment of glory, the flying form. He had of course painted many butterflies. But she could have picked this up in any class on natural life. Why was she repeating it in her sleep with such intensity?

Unless she identified with it. Tappy's present form was about as miserable as it could be. Was she dreaming of metamorphosing into something far better? He could hardly blame her! Yet he had an eerie feeling that there was more to it than this.

She was up, bright and clean, the next morning, wearing a new dress. He hadn't realized she had a third one in her small suitcase. Her dark hair was freshly combed and seemed longer than before. He saw that she was taller, too, now that she stood up straight, and her figure was better developed than he had credited. Except for the scar, she was not an unattractive girl.

Something clicked, and he ran to the car. Sure enough, there were dark glasses in the glove compartment. They were men's glasses and were too big for her, but a little effort with the car's compact tool kit enabled him to bend the frames around to fit her face. It was awkward to adjust for the damaged ear; he had to use adhesive tape from the first-aid kid. But when it was done, both the scar and the vacant stare were inconspicuous. He did not explain what he was doing, but was sure she understood.

She raised her hand as he applied the finishing touches. He thought she meant to remove the glasses, but she brushed his face instead. The cobweb caress of her delicate fingertips passed over his cheeks and nose, and he realized that this was her way of seeing him. "My eyes are gray," he told her helpfully, then wondered if she had any conception of color. Yes, of course she did: she had been normal until the accident. "My hair is brown and I stand five-seven in thick socks."

Then, abruptly, she turned, as if hearing something. But there was nothing out of the ordinary. "What is it, Tappy?" he asked. She only stared, eyes round, as she had in the car. Whatever it was, it seemed closer now; she was trembling with excitement.

Her face oriented on something beyond, as it had before.

"Why don't we go somewhere where I can paint?" Jack suggested. She acceded gladly. She wanted to go somewhere, certainly.

The day outside was beautiful. The bright sun sent shafts through the mountains and made the morning mists rise in perpendicular tails. He hauled his portable easel from the car along with a couple of canvases, and took Tappy by the hand.

The caretaker came out as they passed the lead cabin. "Going to do some painting," Jack called to him. "We'll be here a few days."

A few days! What was he doing?

"Ay-uh," the man said knowledgeably, and went about his business. Jack had not told him that Tappy was blind.

Tappy led the way. There was definitely something she wanted to find. His curiosity thoroughly aroused, Jack cooperated. They climbed through field and forest, heading for the top of the mountain. That summit had looked very close from the cabins, almost overhanging them. Two hours later it still looked close. He had not meant to subject the lame girl to this much labor, or himself, burdened with his painting apparatus.

Jack put his free arm around Tappy's waist to help her climb, as she did not wish to turn back. He discovered a hardness there. In a moment he realized that she had *The Little Prince* with her, tucked inside her blouse. All this time . . . this was foolish of the girl, but it pleased him obscurely, and he gave her a friendly squeeze.

There was a dip in the thickening forest for a mountain stream whose bed comprised little more than a collection of massive round rocks. A driblet of water trickled between them, very cold. Jack dipped his hand in it and splashed a few droplets on Tappy. She shook them off prettily and tugged him on. Why was she so eager to make this climb?

The stream originated in a sandy patch beneath a huge old maple tree. Ancient sugaring spigots ringed the giant's gnarled trunk. Careless, he thought; these should have been removed. The water percolated up from some subterranean reservoir, as though this were the vanishing sap of the tree. Jack lay on his stomach and drank, feeling the moist coolness of the leaves and twigs against his chest. Then he guided Tappy to the same refreshment.

Life appeared. Little tubular shells decorated the bottom of the streamlet, and threadlike animalcules, and an agile salamander skittered magically away. A tiny gray and white bird watched them from its perch on a neighboring trunk—upside down. It proceeded to spiral on down, around and around the tree headfirst, until it reached the ground. It took wing for the next tree's upper section, then started down again.

He described it to Tappy, who listened attentively. She raised her hand toward the bird and smiled. For a moment he thought the nuthatch was coming to her; then it was gone, and they resumed the climb.

The ascent became ferociously steep near the end. They had to scramble over jutting rocks and tangled roots, and his painting paraphernalia neutralized a hand he needed. Tappy had no trouble, now that touch was the most important guide, and soon she was leading the way and indicating the best route for him. He followed, trying to avoid staring up inside her skirt as her legs moved above him, feeling guilty for even being conscious of the impropriety. Her legs looked healthy; did she need that brace at all?

They made it at last. There was a brief clearing at the summit, a disk of grass and bare rock like the balding head of a friar. Tappy hurried to a big rock at the top, seeming much taken with it, yet somehow disappointed, too. She opened her blouse and brought out the book, setting it on the rock.

He stood there and marveled at the ring of mountains, row on row, circle beyond circle, extending as far as he could see. The very world seemed to turn under his feet, giving him a strange exhilaration and a sense of power.

There had been a time when he thought little of such displays, when a pinnacle had been merely a distant high place. But in his youth his father took him for a climb, one unexpected day, and when they rested on the height, fatigued and perspiring from the hike, he showed Jack the land. Now Jack relived that experience.

Through the aeons of prehistory the earth itself crumpled and cracked, wrinkling into the jaggedly fresh peaks of a stony range. Then came the rain, and the ice of a glacier, and the mightiest of mounts wore down with the burden of time. The green mold of verdure pried at its grandeur, the rivers spirited away its substance for deposit to the accounts of alluvial banks. Natural history lived in the decline of the mountains, and it was written here, all around him, in the remnants of a range once greater than the Rockies. It was as if he could see all the way into the past—and into the future, too.

How was he to record any fragment of this language of eternity on his poor flat canvas? Yet it was a joy to try!

Tappy sensed his mood, and she stood on her toes beside him and kissed him lightly on the cheek. Without thinking he turned and took her in his arms and kissed her deeply on the lips.

She clung to him, her slight eager body pressing tightly against his. Nothing seemed to matter but the indefinable emotion of the moment.

Jack withdrew, confused. This was a thirteen-year-old child, with outsized glasses and a nebulous fate. He had traveled with her only three days. He had to deliver her to—

"Let's settle down awhile and . . . paint," he said, setting aside a situation too complex to be understood at once. He set up his easel and stood facing out onto the bowl of the world.

He glanced back to see Tappy comfortable on her large rock, the book on her lap. She was smiling slightly, her face made intriguing by the dark glasses. She was really quite fetching, framed by the backdrop of sky and cloud. He toyed with the idea of painting her portrait, but decided against this. It would be best to put her out of his mind for a time.

Jack's mind meandered as he painted. Perhaps the kiss had set his attention coursing along familiar channels, or it could simply have been the mood of the mountain vista. He thought of Donna, of the good times they had had together, and would not have again. That weekend they spent last spring at the cabin on the lake . . . She was marvelous, she was everything a man could ask for. And she was gone. He was trying to forget her, but it was a slow process.

Jack applied a gray edge to a distant peak, humming a half-remembered folk song. How did it go? "Up on the mountain the other day the pretty little flowers grew; never did I know till the other day what love, oh love could do!"

He paused. What subliminal connotations had brought this song to his drifting mind? He glanced again at Tappy. She was smiling and holding a goldenrod whose image showed darkly in her glasses.

His mountains were finished, at least on canvas. But his palette remained crowded with dabs and mixtures of American Vermilion, Cadmium Yellow, Ultramarine Blue, Burnt Umber, and Ivory Black. How could he casually throw away such exotic distillates? He cast about for some suitable subject for the extra.

"How about fetching me a spectacular tropical bird?" he asked

Tappy. She cocked her glasses at him. There was a falsetto cry of some large bird in the distance.

Jack jumped, but it was only a crow. Nevertheless, he gave up the notion of painting anything more. It was time to begin the long trek down the mountain. Whatever imperative had brought Tappy here seemed to have abated. He didn't know whether to feel relieved or disappointed; he had really gotten curious about the identity of the thing on which she had oriented. Apparently it was only that large rock.

It was late afternoon by the time they made it back to the cabins, since they found descending almost as hard as ascending. Tappy was tired, and he had his arm around her slim, book-braced midsection, almost carrying her as they traversed the last few hundred yards. The painting was taking a beating. The caretaker looked up as they went by. "Ay-uh," he said.

Then it was evening, and Tappy was sitting up in bed in a flannel nightie, brushing her hair. Why had he thought it was short? It was long enough to carry a gentle wave, now that she was giving it proper attention.

Jack no longer felt awkward with her. She never made a sound, but her attitude called him friend and he was flattered. He sat in the rickety chair and tried not to think of the Judas-mission that he feared was his. That clinic . . .

He had given her a little human consideration, that was all. He had talked to her and read her a story and taken her on a hike, and now she was able to smile. Had anyone at all spared her even this much kindness in the last seven years?

The shadows played across her face as she brushed, highlighting her cheeks and hiding her eyes. Burnt umber—that was the color of her hair at the moment. She was soft, she was lovely in the half-light of the cabin. Something had animated her, something she hadn't quite found on the mountain. What could it be? An imago, a transformation?

Then Tappy was kneeling before him, blind eyes staring into his face. One hand rested on his. The other hand held *The Little Prince,* a corner of the book covering her mouth.

Discovering that she had his attention, she lowered the book and lifted his hand to her lips.

Jack froze. Suddenly he realized what he should have seen coming: *she had a crush on him.*

He had to deliver her to the clinic in a hurry. God, if this ever got out—

"Tappy," he began.

She raised her face quickly, smiling. As quickly, she stiffened, grasping his import. Her face became expressionless.

Then he saw the tear. That always gave her away.

He had been clumsy again. He had been preoccupied with his own reaction to a suddenly awkward situation, and had forgotten hers. What could he say to her?

The tear coursed down her pale cheek and tucked into the corner of her mouth.

"Tappy—"

The book dropped to the floor. She scrambled to her feet and ran headlong to the bed. She flung herself facedown, her body heaving.

Jack went to her and put his arm around her flannel shoulders. "Tappy, I didn't mean to hurt you! I was only hired to—I'm trying to—"

Trying to what? Build her up for a worse fall? Offer her a friendship less than she craved—a friendship that was doomed anyway, tomorrow?

He stroked her hair, ashamed. All he could feel was the vibration of her silent sobbing. He opened his mouth, but could not speak. The situation was impossible.

Finally he turned her over and kissed her.

He could taste the salt of her tears. Then her hunger broke through with a rush that swept away his own equilibrium . . . and perhaps his conscience. He kissed her lips, her neck, her hair, and a soft fire ran through his body as her little hands pulled him down beside her, so warm. Suddenly he held an angel in his arms, and there was nothing else on earth so wonderful.

How could he explain it? He had thought he was experienced. He could only repeat the words of that song on the mountain: "Never did I know till the other day what love, oh love could do . . ."

Yes, she was blind and mute and only thirteen, and he had known her so very briefly. In that instant of excitement and rapture these considerations were less than nothing; he loved her.

Sanity returned quickly enough after his passion of the moment was sated. She did not try to hold him now. He got up, put himself together, and stumbled out to the car.

He drove, cursing himself for missing the girl beside him, for looking guiltily at the empty seat. He scarcely noticed the teeming magnificence of the Green Mountains, preternaturally brilliant in the closing evening. His brain was working now, and it was not a pleasant experience.

What was he running from? He knew he couldn't simply drive away and leave her there. He certainly couldn't undo what had passed. He was guilty of statutory rape.

He brought the car to an abrupt halt. There was a lovely miniature waterfall barely visible beside the road, splashing a column of water into a great wooden barrel for roadside use. Its artistic ingenuity was wasted on him tonight.

He had brought this calamity upon himself. He had deviated from the route. He had kept her with him instead of delivering her promptly to the clinic. He had forced his unwitting attentions on her until she *had* to respond.

Why? Was it because he suspected that he was taking her to no clinic, but to some correctional institution for unwanted burdens, where she would never receive any genuine kindness? Was he trying to shield her from that horror?

Or had he secretly intended to seduce her?

What did a man want with a woman? Beauty, capability, independence, personality? Or did he really desire, more than anything else, *total dependence*?

Jack thought about the ways that society crippled women, keeping them out of business and sport and in the house, bound by a pervasive economic and social double standard. A wife had to be smaller than her husband, weaker, less intelligent.

Take that to the logical extreme and—Tappuah.

No, he couldn't believe it. That was not his way. He had only sought to help. But he was not proud of his performance.

He did not know what to do, but he did know he could not leave Tappy unprotected at the motel. Whatever was to come of this, they would see it through together.

One thing was sure: he could not deliver her to the clinic. For him there would be charges he could not deny. For her there would be no freedom, no joy at that place. The moment they heard her talking in her sleep, they would classify her as crazy, and that would be the end of her.

Was she crazy? He could not accept that!

He returned to the motel, and tumbled onto his bunk without undressing, without checking on Tappy. Maybe the night would offer some possible solution. Maybe some miracle.

He slept erratically, his dreams a turmoiled rampage of mountains and scars and unutterable pleasure. Of a metal brace touching his leg. *Larva, Chrysalis, Imago . . . Rape.* He woke with a feeling of terrible remorse to the desolation of darkness. Now perhaps he could appreciate Tappy's state of sightlessness. Of hopelessness.

Then he was being touched. Tappy was there, her hand on his shoulder, shaking him. "What is it?" he asked blearily.

She kept pulling at his shoulder, urgently. "Tappy, what I did with you was wrong," he said. "I should never have touched you, and I deeply regret it. Certainly I shall not do it again." Yet there was a core of doubt.

But she ignored his protest. She wanted him to get up; she was not trying to repeat their liaison, it seemed. What could she be after?

He got up, feeling grubby in his unchanged clothes. The glow on his watch said 3 A.M. "What do you want?" he asked, half fearing the answer.

She tugged him to the door.

"Something out there? Let me turn on the lights—"

But she pulled him imperiously on. "No lights? Tappy, you know I can't see in the dark! At least let me get a flashlight."

At that she paused. He felt for the drawer where he had put the emergency flash, and found it. But it occurred to him that she might have reason to stay out of sight. Were there robbers near? "I have it, but I'll leave it off if you'll lead me where you want to go."

She reached and found his hand with the light, and patted it. "You don't mind if I turn it on? You're not hiding from anything?"

She patted his hand again, then resumed her motion toward the door. Baffled, he turned on the flash and walked after her.

She opened the door and stepped out. He saw that she had her shoes on, and a jacket, over her nightie. She was definitely going out, and she was in a hurry.

He followed her out. "Tappy, tell me where you're going! I'll take you there. It will be faster that way."

She paused to gesture in the darkness. He shone the light on her. She was pointing with her right hand toward the mountain they had climbed, while holding *The Little Prince* in her left.

"Up there? Now?" he asked incredulously. "Tappy, that's—" He broke off, catching himself before saying "crazy."

She nodded vigorously. That was where she was going.

"But *why*? There's nothing up there, not even a view, at this time of night. You didn't find anything before!"

She headed off across the lawn. He had to follow; he could not let her go into the forest alone. "Tappy, if you would only tell me what this is all about! If it's because of what we did last night—"

She turned then to face him momentarily. Her head shook no, and she was smiling. Then she gestured him on and resumed her route.

She certainly didn't seem suicidal! She was happy, almost glowing with excitement. Yet she wasn't trying to vamp him either. She obviously knew the significance of what they had done, and was if anything pleased with herself, not ashamed. She wanted him with her, but this was something else.

Yet what could there possibly be atop the mountain at this hour? He could think of nothing. Nothing they might want to encounter! Had Tappy really gone over the edge? Had she convinced herself that there was some kind of salvation or atonement up there?

If she was crazy, it was his fault. All he could do now was go along and try to see that nothing else happened to her. "This way," he said, taking over. "We found a better route on the way down, remember? Here." He followed his light to the route he remembered.

Then he remembered the book. "Tappy, that mountain gets steep. You'll need your hands, and you can't tuck the book into your shirt. You *have* no shirt. Here." He checked the jacket she wore, opened it wide, and found a huge pocket in the inner lining. The book just fit. Then he closed the jacket around her slight torso, inadvertently brushing one of her breasts in the process, and buttoned it up. He suffered a pang of guilt, condemning himself for even thinking about what he never should have done.

There ensued two hours of struggle. What had seemed open in the daytime seemed impenetrable in the darkness. Branches loomed out of nothingness to bar their passage, and vines caught at their feet. They were both tired from the prior day's exertions. But Tappy was driven by some imperative he could not fathom, and despite his misgivings some of it translated to him. They scrambled together for the summit, heedless of the bruises on their bodies and the tears in their clothing. The night was chill, but they were laboring so hard it didn't matter; in fact, it helped them keep going.

As they got closer to the top, Tappy's urgency only increased. She was desperate to get there faster, and that communicated itself to him; he found his heart beating with more than the considerable exertion. When they encountered the worst of the climb, where a section was almost vertical, he picked her up and virtually hurled her to the higher ledge, then scrambled up himself. It was all moss and grass and dirt, no sharp edges, but at this point they didn't care about abrasions. They had to get there at the ultimate speed.

The sky was thinking about brightening as they made it to the edge of the bald summit. Just as well; he had turned off his flashlight whenever he could, to conserve its waning power, but it had almost expired by this time. Now Tappy clambered up so quickly that he could hardly keep up. They would be at the top to see the dawn come in—yet what was that to her, blind?

Could it be that she was recovering her sight? Had she wanted to test it on the most wonderful thing she remembered, the sunrise? Yet she had given no evidence of sight; she had not flinched when his flashlight played across her face.

She charged, panting, toward the rock that had fascinated her by day, gesturing to him to follow. She oriented on it unerringly, as though she could see it.

They came there, and almost collapsed on the stone. Tappy was so excited she was virtually dancing; her smudged face shone with expectancy. She grasped his hand with her left, and with her right reached out to touch the rock.

Nothing happened, of course. He touched it with his free hand, somehow feeling the need to verify its solidity. It was cool and hard, exactly as a rock should be.

"But what brought you here?" he asked her.

She clung to his hand, not responding, not disappointed. She stood by the rock, expectantly.

"Tappy, I want to understand," he said. "You brought me here for a reason. You can tell me, if you want to. I have heard you speak in your sleep. Please, I want so much to know about you. Maybe if you talk, you won't have to go to that clinic. Anything I can do—"

She faced him, her eyes not quite finding his. She spread her hands in a gesture of incapacity. She would not, or could not, speak to him in words.

He started to move away, but instantly she grabbed him, catching his shirt. She would not let him leave.

"All right, I'll wait," he said. "Just let me sit down." He turned, about to settle on the rock.

This time she almost tackled him. She shoved him away from the rock, but held his arm, refusing to let him go either.

He could not understand what she wanted, but he waited with her there by the rock while the sky brightened gloriously in the east. Dawn was coming. Too bad he had not brought his paints.

Every few seconds Tappy touched the rock, delicately, as if afraid it would explode. There was something about it that mesmerized her. But this seemed to make no sense! Was she, after all, losing touch with such reality as she had known?

The sunrise swelled to its full wonder. He was tired and battered, but he loved it. He stood there, describing its colors to Tappy, as the phases of it manifested.

Then the first beam of direct sunlight speared through and touched the rock. He was remarking on that, aloud, when Tappy grasped his hand again, and reached for the rock once more.

This time her hand passed into it. It was as if the stone were fog. As he stared, not quite believing his eyes, she made an inchoate sound and half stepped, half tumbled *into the rock*.

Her body disappeared within it. He opened his mouth to exclaim in amazement—but then her trailing hand hauled on his arm, urgently drawing him after her.

Jack understood none of this, except for one thing: Tappy was not crazy. She had somehow known that this rock would change, and that she could enter it as the first sunbeam touched it. It had been some kind of a window, a portal—to what? To Imago?

Her hand tugged again, becoming desperate. Tappy was going there, unafraid, and she wanted him with her. Could he refuse?

What was there to hold him in his familiar world? Trial on a charge of rape? No, he had reason to go elsewhere. Far elsewhere!

He knew that if he took any time at all to think about it, he would know better. He had no business stepping into rocks! But he could not let her go alone.

Jack entered the rock. Its substance enveloped him, passing across his body with a faint electrical tingle. Then his head followed, and he was through.

Chapter 2

LATER, he wondered why he had entered the immense boulder. If he had stopped to consider the outré dangers that might await them, he would have yanked Tappy from the boulder.

His will and his reason at that moment seemed to have stepped outside for a chat, leaving his body without guidance. He felt numb, though something thrilled beneath the crystalline surface of his frozen brain. Still not believing that he would find the rock anything but impenetrable or that he could ignore its petrous imperative, he stepped forward. He did not know what to expect when his hand, holding Tappy's, went into the rock.

He found a soft resistance which forced him to lean against it, and then he was in darkness. He was unable to breathe; his nostrils were covered with a semiliquid stuff. Silicon had become silicone.

Her hand pulled on his, and, holding his breath and hoping that he would not have to do it for long, he went two more steps. Air flowed around him. Light touched his shut eyelids. He opened them and breathed deeply.

He looked around. For a moment, he felt like a preliterate confronted with his first photograph. He could make no sense or order out of what he saw. It was all just a snarl of lines with no meaning. Tappy was the only thing not unchaotic. She was standing facing the sun, her blue-gray eyes open, her head tilted back as if bathing in the light. She looked happy.

Then the landscape seemed to shift and to fall into an arrangement which was, if not familiar, at least Terrestrial enough to be reassuring. The boulder from which they had emerged was about six feet higher than the one they had gone into. The other side had been pinkish-gray granite. This looked like black basalt. It was near a shallow creek about two hundred feet broad at this point, and it was in a valley extending for half a mile on both sides.

The sky was blue and unclouded. A gentle cool breeze flowed around him. He judged that the sun was about a quarter of the way above the true horizon. But he seemed to be in a valley in the floor of a crater. Immense walls circled the valley. He did not, of course, know how far away they were.

Certainly, he was not on Earth. Though some of the low-growing plants nearby looked like Terrestrial bushes, the tree on his right was, he was sure, not a thing that grew anywhere on his native planet. Its pea-green bark was as smooth as skin, and it exuded a greasy and slightly reddish thick liquid. The ground at the base of the tree and among high, arched, exposed roots was wet with the liquid. Its branches started about halfway up the fifty- or sixty-foot height but began a leftward twist not far from the trunk and spiraled up around the trunk. The leaves were dark green disks covered with pale red spider's-web designs.

About a dozen flying animals were roosting on the branches or were on top of nests made of dried mud. Some were tiny, the size of yellow finches; some, as large as ravens. Their batlike wings were covered with brightly colored fur. Their faces were batlike, foxlike, and monkeylike. Their cries were as varied and as melodious as those of birds.

Tappy, still smiling, startled him by muttering in what sounded like a foreign language, then made gestures which he interpreted as a request for him to describe their surroundings.

He told her in detail everything he could see. She turned, her hand still in his, and tugged him toward the east, if it was the east, along the creekbank. He walked beside her, giving her directions when they came to a rock she might fall over or to a sudden dip or rise. Meanwhile, his empty belly asked for food, and he wondered how they were going to eat and how, if they had to spend the night in this country, they would survive if the air got cold and if there were any dangerous animals or snakes in this place.

A horn blared nearby. Startled, he and Tappy halted. She moved her head from side to side as if she were listening. He looked around. From a distance, ahead of them, came another sound. It was almost exactly like the chuffing of a steam locomotive, the sound of which he knew from watching movies. Whatever originated it, it had to be a long way off. Then the horn blared again, nearer this time.

Though it sounded much like that of an automobile, Jack did not think that there was any such nearby. This terrain and the lack of roads indicated that cars would be a rarity indeed. Though, of course, he really did not know what to expect here. Surely, the sound had to be originated by an animal. However, he was wrong unless the honker was a two-legged animal that had arms, hands, legs, and feet remarkably like a human's.

Around a huge boulder eighty feet ahead of them near the creek strode a humanoid figure. The face was not that of *Homo sapiens;* it looked more like the helmet of a medieval knight than anything else. The eyes were dark slits in the brown skin. Below them a large, noseless, and sharply downward-angling bulge formed the upper jaw. The froglike mouth had very thin dark lips. The lower jaw, chinless, sloped abruptly below the lower lips toward the neck. In all, the face below the high forehead formed in profile an isosceles triangle.

Its dark skin glistened with grease. Its penis was about eight inches long and two inches thick, but it lacked testicles.

Its mouth open, issuing the blaring sound, it marched straight toward Tappy and Jack, its pace not the least broken when it saw them. Its right hand held a stone-tipped spear and on its back was an animal-skin pack. Behind it, around the boulder, came a parade of similar beings. Two males were first, carrying bows in their hands and quivers full of arrows on their backs. Then came six obvious females (though they lacked breasts) and seven children. Behind them were four adult males and two half-grown males, all armed with spears.

Except for the honking leader, all were silent.

Tappy, far from looking alarmed or questioning, seemed to be at ease. She was even smiling.

Presently, the parade passed them, and, after a while, the honker and the honking were gone.

Jack did not ask her any questions about the creatures. He knew that she would not answer. He went to the creek, bent down, and scooped up water in his cupped hands. After he had drunk enough, he told Tappy to drink. The water seemed to be pure, another indication that he was not on Earth.

"That's great stuff," Jack said, "but my belly's kicking up a storm. I wonder what's good to eat around here?"

They resumed walking and came to a bush laden with large cherrylike fruit on which a family of tiny opossumlike animals were feeding. These ran when the two approached them. Jack did not know if the fruit was fatal to humans, but he would, at this moment, anyway, rather die of poisoning than starvation.

He picked and bit into a "cherry" and tasted something like a butterscotch liqueur. He spat out the four small pits and said, "If you'll wait awhile, Tappy, we'll see if this kills me."

She shook her head and groped along a branch, tore five of the fruit loose from their thick stems, and popped them into her mouth. They ate all the rest and then drank more creek water. Jack went behind a bush for a bowel movement, though Tappy could not see him, of course. Not having toilet paper bothered him, but the amenities of civilization—or was it conveniences?—were not to be found here. Not so far, anyway.

Tappy went behind the same boulder to relieve herself after Jack had told her where not to step. He kept expecting to feel a sudden sharp or burning pain in his guts. As time went on without any discomfort, he forgot about his apprehensions.

He knew now that they had arrived in the morning of this planet and were going northward. The sun had risen higher, not descended. Also, the numbness he had felt after going through the rock had dissolved. Though he still was uneasy, he could think clearly. What that led to was a strong desire to be back on Earth. Especially when, just as Tappy began climbing up the rocky but bush-grown slope toward the top of the valley, he saw a group of tawny lion-sized animals come out of the forest across from the creek. When one of them roared, it exposed large sharp teeth.

To live, big predators had to prey on big herbivores, but Jack had not seen any of the latter. He hoped that the large meat-eaters were on their way to a place where large grass-eaters abounded. He also hoped that these predators would not consider him and Tappy as food. He breathed easier when the group, after drinking from the creek, walked back into the forest.

Tappy had not halted when the beast roared. She was feeling her way up the slope, grabbing a bush when the footing was insecure and pulling herself on up. He followed her. By the time they reached the top, his hands were bleeding from sharp rocks and thorns, a knee of his trousers was torn, and he was sweating and thirsty again. He forgot about that, when, panting, he looked around and up. The floor of the crater angled downward from the bases of the walls, enabling him to see much of the area. Most of it seemed to be covered with green and scarlet plants, the branches of which surely extended over the many streams that must run down from the walls. There had to be a lot of rainfall to keep all this vegetation alive.

Now he could see more clearly what had seemed to be just splotches on the crater walls when he had been in the valley. The entire circle of crater wall was covered with gigantic figures and symbols.

The walls had to be at least thirty miles away. Perhaps fifty. He had been in Arizona once and knew how deceiving distances could be in very clear air. That meant that the figures might be a thousand feet tall. He could not estimate accurately since he did not know how far away they were.

The symbols scattered among the figures were of many bright colors, and none was like any he had ever seen before. Some of the figures were of machines or vessels. Most were of bipeds, some of whom looked human enough. They were doing all sorts of things and were in various postures. Some of the paintings looked like spaceships, but he could not be sure.

"Damn it, Tappy! Wait for me!"

She was heading toward the woods. He caught up with her and said, "We have to stay together so I can *see* the dangers. Remember, I'm the one who isn't blind!"

Tappy made a gesture with her right hand which he interpreted as apologetic. If he had hurt her by reminding her of her blindness, he could not see it on her face. She looked eager to get going. To where? Did she know? Or was she being drawn by some undefined but powerful feeling like the instinct of a lemming? That was, he told himself, not a reassuring analogy. Lemmings were pulled toward destruction. However, it might be the right comparison after all.

He was thinking too much, too concerned about what they might be walking into. If he allowed himself to be sucked into the maelstrom of his thoughts and apprehensions, he would not be able to go on. He would just sit down and refuse to go a step farther. He would die. Either he would starve or a predator would get him.

That was enough incentive to make him drive onward, though another was the crater panorama. He was a painter, and his curiosity about the gigantic figures burned in him. That must be the biggest mural in the world. Who could have done it? How? Why?

They entered the shade of interlocking branches, the lowest of which radiated from the trunks about ten feet above them. Through the infrequent spaces among the leaves, sunlight speared. This illuminated the ground-mat of purple plants, one inch high, growing closely together, which seemed to spread everywhere. His feet crushed the plants, and a thin liquid exuding from them spread a faint peppermint odor. Most of the trees had a deeply corrugated, pale orange bark. The heart-shaped green leaves, covered with purple rosettes, were about six inches long. The branches were populated by a variety of small furry creatures, winged and wingless. They were as noisy as birds, and some of the fliers were as beautiful and varied in their markings as Terrestrial birds.

There were, here and there, bushes and plenty of dead wood fallen from the trees. But the walking was almost as easy as if they had been in a well-kept park.

After an hour's walk, Jack said, "Let's rest. I don't know where you're going, Tappy, I hope you do, but whatever is there isn't going to go away."

That might not be true. Maybe it was going to go away, and, somehow, Tappy knew it.

He brought out a few of the butterscotch "cherries" from his jacket pocket and handed them to her. From another pocket, he took a half dozen he had saved for himself.

"We have to find something solid to eat, protein and carbohydrates. Or we'll start having diarrhea."

Soon after resuming their journey, they came across a broad and shallow stream. While hand-cupping its water to drink, Jack saw some foot-long salamanderoids in pursuit of tiny fishlike creatures. He stuck a hand in the water and waited, still as a fishing bear, until a salamander came close. He grasped the thing and lifted it, though its wrigglings and greasy skin made it hard to hold, and hurled it against a tree trunk. He ran after it just in time to seize it again as it crawled painfully back to the creek. He knocked its head against the trunk once more. It still tried to creep away, but he took his jackknife from his jacket pocket, opened it, and cut the thing's head off. Its blood was red.

After catching another, Jack took off its head and gutted both of them. He collected dead wood, made shavings from it, and used his cigarette lighter to start a fire. Then he skewered a salamander on a pointed stick and held it over the fire. Though the flesh was undercooked inside and burned on the outside, it was more than satisfactory.

"Tastes like greasy frog legs," Jack said as he started cooking the second animal.

After washing their hands and faces in the creek, they started to go on. Jack, however, called a halt so that they could check their possessions. Some of them might be useful.

Tappy had nothing except the nightgown, socks, and shoes she wore. That she had not automatically taken her handbag along showed how urgent her desire had been to get to the gate-rock. He had his wristwatch, and his pants and jacket pockets held a comb, a handkerchief, the jackknife, the cigarette lighter (he had quit smoking but still carried it), car keys, a leather holder with four pencils and a pen, a small notebook with unlined pages, and his wallet. This contained four hundred dollars, mostly large bills, credit cards, a driver's license, and photographs of his parents, sister, and of some of his better paintings.

There were also three quarters, two dimes, a nickel, and five pennies.

Except for the knife and the lighter, the items seemed to be useless. But he decided not to discard them. They pushed on and did not stop until the half-twilight of the forest began darkening toward night. He told Tappy to wait while he climbed a particularly tall tree. Fortunately, there was a big boulder under it from which he could leap upward and grab the lowest limb. While he was climbing, flying mammals fled before him. He went by several nests with young in them, but did not touch them. The parents flew chittering at him, swooping around his head. He also had to brush off hundreds of long-legged insects which, however, did not bite him.

When he had gotten up as far as he could go, he looked westward. Though the sun had dropped below the crater wall, the sky was still bright, and a pale light lay over the upward-sloping land. He gasped, and he clung to the bending treetop to keep from falling.

The Brobdingnagian figures on the wall were moving.

He watched while they and the symbols around them marched along the wall as if in a slow-motion film. He stayed there for at least thirty minutes, shouting down now and then to reassure Tappy that he was all right. Finally, the figures and the symbols stopped moving. He did not know how far they had gone in their travel, perhaps a few miles. He wondered if they moved during every twilight and would eventually complete a circuit.

As he started down cautiously, he saw a pale round object with a dark crescent on its northeastern part slide up from above the eastern wall. He waited until it revealed itself as a moon slightly smaller than Earth's Luna. He was just about to tell Tappy about it when something huge and dark shot across the silvery face. It seemed to be circular and to be topped by a structure of some sort through which the moon gleamed here and there. Then the object was gone, though he had the impression that it had flown into the crater. If it could be seen from here, it must be enormous. And it must have a staggering power to be able to keep its bulk aloft.

When he got down, he waited until he had recovered his wind before he told her what he had seen. Surprisingly, Tappy nodded as if she understood what the titanic vessel was.

He said, "Well? Explain," but she did not, of course, answer.

"I know you can't help it, Tappy, or you appear not to be able to speak, though sometimes I wonder. But you really frustrate me."

She put out her hand as if to tell him that she was sorry or, perhaps, to get comfort from him. He took it and stroked the back of her hand, then pulled her to him and held her close for a little while.

"We'll get through this somehow."

He hoped that he sounded convincing.

The dying light sifting down through the leafy canopy was presently replaced by a pale gloom shed by the moon. By now, the cries of the small animals, ever-present through the day, had died with the light. They were succeeded by a booming from far off, its direction undetectable, and, now and then, a roaring. He shivered from more than the cooling air.

He and Tappy had to find some relatively safe place to sleep, and that could only be up in a tree. He explained this to her before he climbed into several nearby trees. Finally, he gave up.

"There's just no way we could sleep up there without falling off the minute we went to sleep."

They passed a chilly and fretful night, often awakening suddenly, and most of the time dozing. For warmth and courage, they held each other in their arms, but their arms became numb. And, every time one moved, the other was startled out of sleep. During the night, Jack wished several times that Tappy was a big and fat girl. That thought gave him the only smiles of the night.

The booming faded away. Though the roaring filtered through the woods now and then, it did not come nearer. That was not so comforting, though. It seemed to Jack that a predator would quit roaring as soon as it smelled a prey and would then approach it very quietly.

Once, he heard a new sound, a hooting. It quit after a while, but he stayed awake for a long time after that. He thought of the silence of the forest during the day. It was not really silent; the noises were just different from those of the city and much less loud, but he could become used to them. There were no radios blaring rock or country-western that could be heard two blocks away from the cars, or ghetto blasters of youths who would tell you very sincerely that they were very concerned about people's rights and the need for protection from invasion of privacy. There were no vehicle horns blaring; no sirens wailing. No thunderous jets overhead. No flickering icons or voices and music from the TV sets.

At that moment, Jack wished to hell that he could be back among the ear-scratching screeches and unmelodious clashings.

When the darkness began paling, he and Tappy got up. They were tired and cross, though they tried not to show it. After squatting behind the bushes, they pushed on until the sun came up above the crater wall. Jack caught two salamanders, made a fire, and cooked them. These, with more berries and fruit, filled their stomachs. They took their clothes off, Tappy removed her leg brace, too, and they rolled, gasping and crying out, in the cold creek water.

Just as Jack stood up to go ashore, he saw the leading edge of a wave of red liquid coming from upstream. By the time he got Tappy out of the creek, the water was bright red from bank to bank. It looked like blood, but he could not imagine that any one animal could bleed that much. Was there a large-scale butchery going on up there? If so, what was being slaughtered and who were the killers?

After a few minutes, however, the water cleared.

Jack considered going east for a while to avoid whatever had reddened the creek. When he decided he would, he told Tappy they should make a detour. She shook her head and walked north. He shrugged, and he followed her. Maybe she knew what she was doing.

They did not come across the carcasses or corpses that Jack expected, except that of a rabbit-sized mammal lying half in the creek. Insects rose from it in a cloud as the two passed its stinking body. Though it was bipedal and looked mammalian, it had a long beak resembling a woodpecker's. Later, they heard a hammering and saw, back in the forest, a similar animal knocking its beak against a tree trunk. So, the animal was, in a sense, a woodpecker.

When the sun was straight above their heads, as seen through a break in the leafy ceiling, Tappy halted. She turned slowly, her nostrils twitching as if she were trying to catch some odor. Then she turned east. They walked for perhaps a mile before coming to another creek. Or, for all Jack knew, the same creek. After drinking again, they walked to the other bank, the water up to their knees in the middle, and they went up the bank, steeper on this side.

She stopped again, turning her head from side to side, her right hand extended and going back and forth across a vertical plane as if she were feeling an invisible wall. After a minute of this, she turned north, stopping only when Jack called out to her that she was heading for an immense and conical, anthill-like structure. When he followed Tappy around it, he was confronted by a big hole on the opposite side.

Within it sat cross-legged one of the creatures with a face like a knight's helmet. He was holding a large piece of cooked meat which he stuck at intervals into his mouth. His lower jaw did not move, but very sharp and tiny yellow teeth moved inside the mouth. They seemed to be in several rows, one behind the other, and to be moved by some biological mechanism inside the "visor," as Jack thought of it.

Jack looked around for some evidence of the fire that had cooked the meat, but he could see nothing.

A stone axe was by the honker, and so was a pile of different kinds of fruits and vegetables. There was also a liquid-filled gourd by the heap of steaks.

The honker did not seem to be startled or alarmed at the sudden appearance of the two humans. Its dark eyes, which were at least a quarter inch inside the bony face, looked steadfastly at them.

Jack described the honker to Tappy, though he had the feeling that she had known that he was in the structure. Jack was the one startled when she gave vent to a series of soft honkings. The creature did not respond until its teeth had ceased moving and the meat had been swallowed. Then it responded just as softly. Jack could see now that something white projected from the tip of its tongue, something as slim and as sharp as a thorn.

Tappy looked disappointed.

"What in hell is going on?" Jack said. "You can talk to this thing?"

Tappy shrugged. Then she felt along him, dipped her hand in his pants pockets, and drew out a coin, a quarter. She turned to the honker and held the quarter out to him while she honked more dots and dashes. By then, Jack had figured out that the creature spoke in a sort of Morse code.

The honker extended its hand. Without directions from Jack, Tappy walked up to the honker. He took the quarter from her, looked closely at both sides of it, rubbed it between his thumb and finger, then said something. Tappy held out both hands, which the honker filled with two large steaks and a pile of pancake-shaped and -sized green and purple vegetables. She honked something, the honker replied, and she turned and held out the barter to Jack. He stuffed the meat in one of his jacket pockets, the vegetables in the other.

The honker stuck its tongue far out, enabling Jack to see more clearly the white thorny projection at its end. Tappy stuck her tongue out, turned, and walked away.

Following her, Jack said, "Damn it, Tappy! If you can speak their lingo, why can't you speak English to me?"

She did not reply. Angered and bewildered, he walked closely behind her. He had to break his surly silence to warn her of a house-sized boulder ahead of her. As if she already knew that it was there, she walked up to it and began feeling its rough reddish side. Shaking her head, she went around it and walked on northward.

An hour before dusk, they stopped. He made another fire and recooked the meat, which was too rare for him. Its blood and grease had coated the inside of his jacket pocket and drawn a bloom of pesky flying midges that he had to keep brushing off. These also bit savagely, making him even more angry. After they had eaten, however—the pancake-sized vegetables were raw but delicious, tasting like a mixture of cheese and asparagus—he began reproaching himself. He should not have bad feelings toward her. He could have refused to go into that gateway-boulder with her, and she must be under some kind of obsession or compulsion or both. Under a "spell," so to speak.

He continued on the same path of thought while climbing trees to search for a place to bed down. When he found one, he kept only half his mind on the task of finding dead branches on the ground and getting them up into the tree and placing them with their ends across two limbs. The auxiliary branches and the knobs and sharp points were removed, smoothed off with his jackknife. His knife was getting duller, he noted. The time would come when it would be useless, and the lighter would be empty. That thought made him feel panicky. However, perhaps he could trade more coins with a honker for a flint knife or an axe.

Shortly after the moon had risen, they were lying on their platform of hard branches. These were far from comfortable, and they could get warmth and softness only in each other and the little protection their clothes gave. Tappy was in his arms, his jacket spread over their upper parts. She hummed a tune he had never heard before, then fell asleep. The leg brace, which she had taken off, lay between her legs. Though he was very tired, he could not sink as swiftly as she into merciful unconsciousness.

He could not stop trying to make sense of what had happened, to find a pattern in the events that would give them an order and a goal.

Just how were Tappy's relatives—the two who had reluctantly given her a home—involved? Had they really been so eager to get rid of her? Was that eagerness an act? Could they have known somehow that Tappy was far more than she appeared to be? Mr. Melvin E. Daw and his wife, Michaela, upper-middle-class people, affluent, had seemed pleasant enough, though they had not been able to hide their dislike of Tappy. Their instructions on how he was to take Tappy to the clinic had been specific. But they had certainly not volunteered any information to answer his unspoken questions. They had given him a map of the route he was to take to New Hampshire and had stressed that he should not deviate from it. Why? There were other roads he could have taken.

Could they possibly have directed him to that road by which was the rural motel he and Tappy had stayed in? Could they have estimated his traveling time so that he would take lodging there overnight? There were, as far as he knew, no other motels in that area.

How could the Daws have known that he and Tappy would go up that hill and find that boulder?

Reviewing the conversation with the Daws and their gestures and expressions, he thought that what had seemed innocent enough then was now sinister. That interpretation, however, could be shaped by his suspicions, which had been shaped by the bizarre events occurring after they had stopped at the motel.

And how could a blind thirteen-year-old know, consciously or unconsciously, that the gateway-boulder was there? How could she even know about gates to other worlds?

Something—when and how he could not guess—had been implanted in her. It was driving her toward a goal that she could not explain or would not explain because something was keeping her from doing so.

"Empire of the stars."

A science-fiction cliché, essence of corn.

"Reality is a dream."

First said by some ancient Chinese philosopher.

"Larva . . . Chrysalis . . . Imago."

Entomological. But he did not think that these words applied to insects.

"Alien menace . . . only chance is to use the radiator."

That radiator certainly was not part of an automobile.

"Alien menace . . ."

He shivered. He had been conditioned by too many movies with horrible and evil monsters from outer space.

But that did not mean that such things did not exist.

He was in a situation which needed a superhero to deal with it, and he was far from being a Flash Gordon or Luke Skywalker. He was not even a good imitation. He had never shot a gun and knew nothing of fencing or the martial arts beyond what he had seen in films.

He awoke from a nightmare. He had been in his studio, a studio that had never existed in reality but one he had imagined he would have some day. Bright sunlight fell through the enormous skylight like the shower of gold that had impregnated Danaë, bathing a nude Tappy in the center of the room. Not the Tappy he knew, but an older and fully developed young woman. He was before his easel and had the portrait almost done. All he needed were a few more strokes of the brush to get her face just right, to give it a hint of the ethereal. No, of the unearthly.

The light darkened. Looking up, he saw that black clouds had slid under the sun, though the sky had been, a moment ago, without a trace of the nebulous. Then the clouds lowered green-gray tendrils—tentacles—and somehow they came through skylight glass and began misting the room. He could see Tappy only vaguely now.

The horror did not begin at once. It was hidden behind the swirling fingers of the cloud as they reached out for him. They touched him at the same time that he saw that Tappy's skin had become greasy. The glistening fatty exudation dripped from her as if she were a burning candle and pooled around her feet.

The shiny and greasy stuff began to rise before her. Very quickly, Tappy became gaunt, and then she was skin wrapped around bones. Now she was walking toward him, her arms held out. The figure forming from the grease had been left behind, but it was sliding along behind her on the trail. He could see through Tappy's skin and bones despite the weak light, and he could see that the figure was a rapidly swelling replica of her.

He wanted to scream but could not. His throat was plugged with semiliquid fat rising from deep within himself.

Tappy's hand almost touched him. The figure behind her reached around her, slid her arm along Tappy's outstretched arm, and shot her hand toward his mouth.

He came out of the nightmare to find himself groaning.

Though the moon did not relieve the darkness much, he could see Tappy's eyes staring at him. But she could not see him at all, of course. Or could she?

She muttered something. He said, "It's all right. Go back to sleep."

She closed her eyes and began snoring softly.

Larva . . . Chrysalis . . . Imago, he thought.

Was she going to change from what she was now into something as different as a larva was from an imago? Or did those words apply to someone else?

Then one of those sudden and unexplainable shifts of mind happened, and he began worrying that he might have made her pregnant. After a while, he dismissed the worry with a rueful grin. They were in a situation so serious that the chance that she might have a baby was a slight problem. As of now, anyway. Nine months from now, it might be very grave. If they lived that long.

He fell asleep again, and he was making love to Mullins Blanchflower, if what he was doing could be called making love. He awoke at the tail end of a wet dream, wondering why his unconscious would choose Mullins for his dream partner. She was a rather plain and chubby girl he had known in high school, though not in the biblical sense. He had never consciously wished to make her. But copulation with undesirable girls had happened occasionally in his night fantasies. The unconscious was a tricky and unpredictable bastard.

He thought: Now I'll have to wash out my shorts. And I thought I was too tired, hungry, and miserable even to contemplate screwing. If I'd known how things were going to be, I'd have tried it with Tappy. But then she'd have been too tired, hungry, and wretched or would have thought she was. Anyway, for God's sake, I was just worrying about her maybe being pregnant. Of course, there are other ways to get off. But she might not be ready for those.

What a jerk I am!

He was lying on his side, and something—it must be Tappy's leg—was next to his chest and stomach. He opened his eyes and saw her profile, though dimly. He also saw something dark astride her legs and leaning far forward. Her body was bare to just above her breasts. The nightgown had been pulled up above them.

He tried to shout and at the same time to rise and grab the thing sitting on Tappy. He could only tremble; his throat and tongue seemed numb; his body had no more muscles than a log. He hurled his will at his body, screaming at it to move. But he was as lax as if he had been bitten by a poisonous snake.

Now he was able to see the figure on her a little better than when he had awakened. Though it was not raping Tappy, as he had first thought, he did not lose any of his sickening fright. It was bending far over her, its face against her breasts or between them. Then it sat upright, pulled its legs up, and got to its feet. Jack rolled his eyes sidewise to keep its head in sight. He could make out, dimly, the knight's-helmet face of a honker, and its male organ. It—he—bent over to look down at Jack. His tongue moved far out and then back in. Faint as the light was, it showed the white thorny tip at the end of the honker's tongue.

The honker patted Jack on the forehead as if it were reassuring or comforting him. It turned away, still bending over, and placed something between Tappy's breasts. Then it climbed slowly down from the platform and faded into the blackness.

Jack, sweating despite the chill, wondered if he was to stay paralyzed until he starved to death or, more likely, was eaten alive by beasts or insects. Then he felt ashamed, because he had considered his own plight before thinking of Tappy's.

He did not know how much time had passed when he began to be able to move his fingers and toes. After a little while, he could turn his head. Some time later, he could utter some slurred words and lift his arms and legs. Meanwhile, Tappy was also making sounds and moving her head and limbs. Presently, both he and she sat up. Something fell from her chest and between her legs onto the platform. She lifted it up and put it close to her eyes, though why she would do that when she was blind Jack did not know. She handed it to him. As soon as he had it in his hand, he knew that it was the quarter he had given the honker in exchange for the food.

He did not have time to think about the implications of its return. Thinking would have done no good, anyway. Tappy, weeping, was in his arms. Jack stroked her bare back and told her that everything was okay. She shook her head, rubbing her face against his chest. Then she pulled away, took his right hand, and placed it between her breasts.

He said, "My God!"

A hard swelling the size of a marble was under her skin. It felt very warm.

She touched the side of her neck and put the tip of her finger on the side of his neck. The pressure made him aware that where she had touched was very tender. He felt sicker. The honker must have stuck the thorny tip on its tongue into their necks and injected a temporarily paralyzing poison.

When dawn came, they climbed down and washed their hands and faces to refresh themselves. Jack decided that he would wash out his shorts and bathe when the air became much warmer. He told Tappy to lift her nightgown so that he could examine the swelling between her beasts. It had grown no bigger, and the skin over it did not seem as warm. As far as he could determine, there was no break in the skin. However, when full sunlight came, he looked closely at it and saw a very small reddish dot in the center.

The honker had stuck the thorny excrescence—maybe it was an organ—into her chest. The thorn must be both a poison injector and an ovipositor, though he did not know if an egg had been shot through the thorn's hollow shaft into her. Whatever it was that had been planted just under the skin, it had grown very fast.

Or was there some other explanation?

"For God's sake, Tappy," he said, "if you have any idea of what's going on, you must tell me if you can! Talk! Please talk!"

Tappy, looking distressed, shook her head. Her index finger felt the round lump.

He mastered the impulse to grab her by the throat and force words out of her. That would not do it, he knew, or thought he knew, but he felt that he had to do something to get answers to his questions. If he did not soon get at least a little explanation of what had been happening, he would go crazy, amok, completely out of his mind.

At that moment, a deep thrumming came from above. He seized her hand and pulled her along until he came to one of the narrow breaks in the forest ceiling. Above him, far up, was something enormous. It was descending slowly, and the sound it was making becoming ever louder.

"It's got to be that ship I saw outlined by the moon," he muttered.

Though the size of the vessel was awesome and its mission was unknown and, thus, possibly dangerous for him and Tappy, he almost felt relief. Whatever happened, he might be able to get some answers. Though it was probable that he would not like them.

He told Tappy to stay where she was while he climbed a tree. She looked frightened but nodded. When he got to the top of the tree, he could see the bottom of a truly titanic ring. It had to be at least a mile in diameter and two hundred feet thick. The purplish-gray sides went up for an indeterminate distance, and from its upper edge curved many gigantic metal beams of the same color as the circular base. The curving beams or ribs met at the center to form an open cap or cage. Here and there boxlike structures clung to the circle at the bottom and along the sides of the ribs. There were no rocket exhausts, no obvious means of propulsion.

As the vessel dropped closer, the thrumming became a roar that was so loud he thought he would scream. Standing on a branch, with one arm wrapped around the thin trunktop, he put his fingertips into his ears. That did not help much.

The circular structure was now about two hundred feet above but a quarter of a mile away. At that moment, the coins, his wristwatch, his jackknife, everything metallic in his pockets, became hot. He tried to get rid of them before they burned him, but he was slowed down because he had to cling to the trunk with one hand. His fingers were scorched before he had thrown the hot objects down through the branches. He climbed down to find that Tappy had removed her leg brace. They clung tightly to each other while the bellowing around them became so loud that it seemed solid.

Suddenly, there was silence. He looked up through the break and saw, far up, some of the curving ribs. The weight of the machine must have crushed trees beneath it, and its lower edge must have sunk deep into the ground. He released Tappy, and she sat down, pale and shaking.

An animal resembling a furless anteater ran past them. Jack could not fully hear its whining and its claws slapping the ground, but at least his hearing was beginning to return.

Tappy groped around until she found her leg brace. She touched it gingerly, then picked it up. It had cooled off by now.

Jack, not knowing what else to do, wanting to do something, began looking for the items he had discarded. But he stopped. Tappy was holding the brace up with one hand and feeling along its inner side. That had been covered with a soft thick fabric to prevent skin-chafing, but it had been partially melted away. At one end of the inner side was a long and narrow opening. It had been hidden by a panel that had, for some reason, slid into a recess in the brace.

He said, "Hold it, Tappy! Wait!"

He took the brace from her and examined the opening. There were six tiny orange-colored buttons inside, two rows of three, with a somewhat larger scarlet button at the head of the rows.

"What the hell!"

He seemed to have been saying that a lot lately.

Only a baby's fingers could have pushed one button without pushing another next to it. He said, "We got something here, Tappy. Just what I don't know."

He took one of the pencils from the leather holder in his jacket pocket. Holding the pencil in his right hand, he gripped the brace in the middle, and he pointed one end at a nearby tree but away from his body. He made sure that the other end did not point at Tappy.

"Maybe I shouldn't," he said. "Do I know what I'm doing? No. But I'll do it, anyway."

Using the eraser end of the pencil, he pressed on the larger, scarlet button. Nothing happened. Had he really thought that it would?

He paused to tell Tappy what he was doing. She looked surprised but not as much as he had expected.

He said, "It can't be a weapon, Tappy. It'd be too awkward to use as such, unless . . ."

Perhaps it was a weapon, but the designer had been forced to camouflage it as a leg brace and, hence, could not avoid cumbersomeness in its handling.

He placed the pencil end on one of the orange buttons nearest to the scarlet button.

The tree the brace was aimed at split soundlessly, though the crash of the upper part on the ground certainly was noisy enough.

The tree had been neatly sheared off.

Shouts filtered through the forest, human voices. The blaring of honkers also came through. He paid them no attention.

Where the upper part of the tree had been, extending from the stump, was a shadowy but clearly visible replica of the part that had fallen off. It was the ghost of the sheared-off part.

Chapter 3

TAPPY'S touch on his arm jogged him back to their immediate predicament. The sounds of pursuit, if that was what they were, were drawing erratically closer. Jack did not know what was going on, but he was pretty sure they did not want to fall into the hands of whatever might be after them. Tappy's urgency indicated that she felt the same.

But the great ring of the base of the ship surrounded them. The thing had come down on them like a monstrous cage—which was what it probably was. Somehow it had known where they were, approximately, and enclosed them so that its personnel could canvass the limited region and make them captive. Exactly as he would have done to capture a moving bug he did not want to squish: set a jar over it first.

So how could the bug get free before the end? Tunnel under the rim of the jar? Fly up into the center? Surely not!

He looked again at the brace in his hand. The scarlet button was faintly glowing; he had not noticed that before. That could be the on/off switch—and the device was still on. Ready to fire again.

That notion made him freeze. He pointed it upward and used his pencil to touch the largest button again.

The glow faded. Right: now it was off. He resumed breathing.

Tappy was tugging at his arm again. He looked the way she was facing. "But that's toward the rim!" he protested, keeping his voice low. "You haven't seen it, but take my word: that thing is two hundred feet thick! No way we can get by it without mountain-climbing gear. We'd be better off dodging them in the center, and using this thing if we have to. It just sheared off a tree!"

She knew; she had heard the tree crash down. She pointed toward the rim and touched the brace he held.

"Wait, wait, Tappy!" he protested. "I guess you know what this thing is—did you always know?" She shook her head no. "You remember now? Our entry into this world jogged your memory?" She nodded yes. "So now you know how to control it? You know how dangerous it is?" Yes.

"Then you will have to show me," he said. "This thing is so powerful I don't dare use it ignorantly. It was just luck I didn't have it pointing toward one of us instead of that tree!"

He got down and scraped the leaves and twigs away from a section of the ground. "Here's a diagram of the buttons on this thing," he said, taking her hand and using her finger to draw it, so she would know exactly what he was doing. "Here is a big scarlet button, which is the on/off switch; it glows faintly when it's on." He pressed her finger into the dirt. "Here are six smaller orange buttons, one-two-three, one-two-three. When I turned the big one on and touched this one, zap! It cut through that tree."

Tappy disengaged her hand and took his instead. She was going to make him point to a button! He extended his finger.

"You have me over the orange buttons," he told her as the tip of his finger moved. "The scarlet one is farther over." But she knew where the buttons were; she seemed to have a good memory for what she had touched. She pushed his hand down. "That's the third orange one in the right-hand row. That's the one you mean?" She pushed his hand down harder. "Okay, I got it, Tappy! Third button!" But still she pushed.

What was wrong here? "Look, Tappy, I don't think this will do anything unless the scarlet one is turned on first, so—"

She nodded affirmatively, but still kept his hand down. "There's something different about this? I can't let go of it?" She nodded yes. "But of course I *can* let go—oh! Do you mean sustained fire?" She nodded again and finally let his hand go.

"Got it," he said. "Turn it on, touch that button, and treat it like a gushing fire hose. Don't point anywhere I don't want to cut, even if I'm no longer touching the button. Thanks for warning me!"

Once more she pointed urgently toward the rim. It was high time; the searchers were uncomfortably close, by the sounds.

"Okay, Tappy! On our way!" He took her hand with his free one and set off for the rim. They weaved around trees and bushes, keeping low, and left the sounds of pursuit behind.

This was interesting, he thought as he moved. He had assumed that the most dangerous place was nearest the rim. But maybe they figured the bugs would not go near the glass of the jar, so they were concentrating on the center. The bugs were moving in an unexpected direction.

How was it that their pursuers knew in a general way where they were, but not specifically? If there was a bug on them—a radio frequency emitter—it should enable others to close on them readily enough. Not that there should be a bug. Unless—

Unless that honker had planted it! That marble under Tappy's skin, between her breasts: what about that? First the marble, then the giant ship, one-two.

But several things made him doubt it. That honker had seemed friendly rather than threatening, despite what he had done. And if that had been a location device, why was it so ineffective at close range? And why so obvious? It would have been easier simply to plant it in Tappy's clothing, so that they would never know it was there. So whatever that marble was, it was unlikely to be a bug of that kind.

Jack didn't want to think about whatever other kind of bug or grub or egg it might be.

The huge rim loomed close, as high as it was thick: about two hundred feet. It looked like a twenty-story building without windows, extending to either side, slightly concave. The wall was absolutely smooth, all too much like the glass of a gargantuan jar except for its opacity. Who could have made a flying device this large? Its mere existence suggested a technology far beyond anything known on Earth.

Since when had he believed this was anywhere close to Earth? Tappy had led him through some kind of space warp or time warp to an alien planet; that had been obvious from the start. Yet how had she known of that aperture? He was sure she had not known that anything like this was going to occur when they started. She had been too forlorn, too sensitive to the hurts of the world. Only now that they were here was she really coming to life.

Well, not exactly. That evening in the cabin, when they had made love—maybe it was statutory rape to others, but it had been love to the two of them, in those minutes. She had known what she was doing, perhaps better than he had. He had condemned himself for it, but now—

Tappy's hand was tugging him again. She knew he was losing his focus on the present. He was doing that too much! If they somehow won free of this high-tech trap, then maybe he could think about love.

"I'm aiming it at the wall," he told her. "I'm turning it on. This is what I'm supposed to do?"

She nodded yes, emphatically.

He touched the third orange button.

A circular section of the wall glowed. Then it disappeared, and some of the ground under it. Now there was a hollow in it, deepening visibly.

Jack gaped. "It's eating through the rim!" he exclaimed. "Like melting butter, only there's no vapor. The wall is just *gone* there!"

Tappy urged him forward, toward it.

When he stepped forward, correcting his aim so as not to intersect the ground, the circle of indentation became smaller. But the center deepened more rapidly. It was as if he held a cosmic blowtorch whose heat was greatest in the center. The original dent now and a smaller but deeper dent inside it—and as he proceeded, that inner dent developed another.

"It's a conic section!" he exclaimed. "I mean, a cone—the ray is coming from this device, and expanding, and it vaporizes—bad word—it disintegrates in an expanding circle. So as I walk into it, it seems to be getting smaller, but it's not, really. Am I making sense?"

Tappy merely urged him on. They walked into the hole he was making. It was a tunnel now, about ten feet in diameter, forming about twenty feet ahead of them. The radiator seemed indefatigable.

The radiator! Suddenly Tappy's sleep-talking words came back to him: "Alien menace—only chance is to use the radiator!" This had to be what she had meant: a weapon that radiated a cutting or dissolving beam. The aliens had trapped them, but the radiator was cutting them free. The aliens had set a jar on them, but these bugs were drilling their way out.

There was a clamor of alarms. The sound was unfamiliar, but its strident nature was unmistakable. The aliens had finally caught on to what was happening.

Tappy heard it and jogged him: hurry!

Jack broke into a run, keeping the brace aimed. The tunnel became smaller as he came closer to the site of action, but it quickened its drilling pace. He was operating closer, and the cone was smaller, so had less metal to drill and was faster. He should have thought of that before.

The tunnel became irregular. As he ran, he was waving the beam, and it showed. He tried to keep it steady, but it was impossible. It didn't matter, as long as there was a tunnel they could follow.

He turned his head, trying to look back as he ran. The tunnel started veering to the side. He had to focus ahead, but he had caught a glimpse of a shape in the tunnel behind them. They were sitting ducks, or at least running ducks, for any shot from behind!

Then at last the tunnel broke through to light. First a circle, then a full-sized disk opened ahead of them. They were through the rim! But he heard footsteps behind.

He touched the scarlet button, turning off the radiator. Then he had a better idea. He whirled to point the device back at the tunnel.

A man was there. He threw himself down, trying to get out of the line of fire. He knew what the radiator would do to his body!

Human heads appeared above the rim, peering down from its distant top. Jack aimed the radiator at them. They disappeared. He hadn't fired; they had dived out of the way. A bluff was as good as a real attack. He was glad of that, because he was no killer. He was just trying to get away.

He turned again, and ran with Tappy into the thick of the forest, which seemed to have been cut back somewhat by the landing of the ship. They skirted the huge trunks of the trees, now hidden from the ship by the interlocking canopy above. Jack was trying to put as much foliage between them and the ship as possible. They had broken out, but it would be no good if the men caught them and hauled them back.

Why hadn't someone shot at him and Tappy? There had to be weapons, and the two of them had been an easy target in that tunnel. Someone could have fired from cover above the rim, too, before they reached the trees.

The answer had to be that this was a capture mission, not a kill mission. The way the ship had come down, enclosing rather than flattening, suggested the same. This was a no-squish-bug effort. Great—it gave the bugs a real advantage. But why? What was so precious about *these* bugs to make them worth this phenomenal endeavor?

"Tappy," he gasped as they ran. "We seem to be getting away, but we won't stay clear long if we don't learn more! Unless you know what's going on here!"

Her face turned to him, her head shaking yes, then no. That meant that she understood some, but not enough.

"Then let's get some information!" he said. He was not what he thought of as a bold man, but the past few days had shaken him loose from every preconception he could think of.

Tappy didn't object, so he set up his trap. "Wait here," he told her. He turned on the radiator and dissolved a tunnel through the thickest part of the forest, where the trees were small and set closely. He followed the developing opening, running behind the cone. The smell of peppermint came from the cut plants. He hoped he wasn't extirpating some animals along with the foliage; he hadn't thought of that in time. Then he curved it until the tunnel end was just out of sight of its beginning. He turned the radiator off and ran back to Tappy. "Now we hide!" he gasped, drawing her to the side.

They found a place behind a thicket of young orange-barked trees and ducked down, watching the tunnel. The normally noisy animals were quiet now; he hoped that didn't give the two of them away.

Soon enough a man came running, spied the tunnel, and charged into it. He was carrying a weapon of some sort, which startled Jack: what was the point, if it was not to be fired at the fugitives?

But he had no time to worry about that. He stepped out into the tunnel, pointing the radiator. "Hey, Joe!" he called.

The man stopped and looked back, chagrined. He started to bring his weapon to bear.

"Nuh-*uh*, Joe!" Jack said, putting a finger on a button of the radiator. "Drop it!"

The man let the weapon fall to the ground.

Jack strode toward him, keeping the radiator aimed. He had never intended to fire it at the man, but he was pleased with the success of his bluff. "Now talk, Joe: what's this all about? Why are you after us?"

The man's mouth tightened. He seemed to understand Jack, but he refused to answer, and the threat of the radiator was no longer persuasive. Strange. And awkward, because the man had called his bluff, and he couldn't do anything about it. It was a mistake, ultimately, to bluff, he realized, because once it was proved empty, all was lost. It was necessary either to be able to follow through on a threat or to make the bluff so bold that the other did not dare call it.

He couldn't carry through. He just couldn't kill a man who wasn't attacking him. He probably couldn't kill even if the man did attack him. He was a sensitive artist, not an insensitive goon. Only if Tappy were threatened would he—

Jack had an inspiration. He pointed the radiator at Tappy.

"Nao!" the man cried, horrified.

So he had guessed right! It was Tappy they wanted to capture. He had suspected they didn't much care about Jack himself; he was nobody, just an ignorant person who had happened to get involved with her. Tappy had known or remembered how to reach this world, so she must have been here before. The aliens must have been waiting for her—and they wanted her alive.

Larva—Chrysalis—Imago. There was something about Tappy that made her valuable—so valuable that this monstrous flying cage had been sent to catch her. But she had been given a weapon, and taught its use, so that she remembered once the situation required it. That knowledge must have been hypnotically suppressed. Her return to a more familiar environment was bringing back her memory.

But why give a blind girl a weapon that required sight for its operation? If Jack hadn't been along, Tappy would have been virtually helpless.

These thoughts were buzzing through his mind as he faced the man. He knew that they did not have much time; at any moment there would be others coming here. But there were questions that had to be answered, lest they fall into the next trap their pursuers sprang.

"So you do speak English," Jack said. "You may not care much about your own life, but you do about hers. Well, keep quiet and follow us, or I will radiate her." He was ashamed for the lie, but he was afraid Tappy would be subject to some fate worse than death if he didn't use this lever to get the truth. "Find a place we can talk," he murmured to Tappy.

Tappy immediately moved to the edge of the nulled tunnel and felt her way into the green and purple foliage. Jack followed, pointing the radiator at her. She understood what he was doing.

"Yao are naot serious!" the man said. He had a strong but indefinable accent, as if this was a language he had learned in a class and hadn't used much. "Yao are with hur! Yao will naot radiate hur."

Jack used his pencil to touch the scarlet button. The dim light came on. *Don't let him call this bluff!* he prayed.

"Aokay! I um caoming!" the man exclaimed, his accent worse. There was no doubt that the threat to Tappy really unnerved him, despite his suspicion that Jack didn't mean it.

Empire of the stars. Could she be the daughter of the Emperor, stolen away and now to be recovered? But surely she would *want* to be returned to her family and her status! Unless this was a hostile force, a usurper who wanted to hold her for ransom or brainwash her and set her up as a figurehead. If she died, they would have no chance to make a pretense of legitimacy, and the loyal subjects would rise up and throw them out.

But then why send her to a backwater region of a primitive planet like Earth? Why let her suffer as the ward of an unfriendly family all these years? Anything could have happened to her! If they had the technology to give her the radiator, why hadn't they at least fixed her sight? Jack was no psychologist, but even he had seen that she was a desperately lonely and unhappy girl. She was about as unlikely a princess as he could imagine.

Tappy was better at finding a hiding place than he would have been, because she tended to explore with her hands and body, while he depended more on sight. Soon they were in a niche in the undergrowth where the sunlight hardly penetrated. They would be able to hear any searchers before they got close.

The man sat on one side, and Jack faced Tappy on the other side, keeping the radiator pointed and his pencil poised. He knew that the moment he got careless the man could jump him. Even if Jack won the struggle, the noise would give their position away and the others would close in. With the best luck, he was unlikely to have much time. He had to make it count.

"Why are you after Tappy?" he demanded.

The man's gaze flicked to the girl, and Jack realized that he had blundered already: the man had not known her name. Not her Earth name, at any rate. But he answered. Jack was already getting used to the accent, and tuned it out in favor of the meaning. "We must restrict the Imago."

There was a key word! "What is the Imago?" Jack demanded. "Why must you restrict it?"

The man seemed at a loss. "It has to be restricted!"

"Look, Joe, I'm an ignorant lout from a primitive planet. I don't know anything about this Imago, except that it's gotten me into a lot of trouble. So you'd better give me good reason not to wipe her out, and wipe you out, and anybody else who comes after me, so that I can go home and forget all this. Tell me all about the Imago before anybody else gets here. Give me reason *not* to radiate everything in sight." He hardly believed himself! He was talking like a thug from a grade F movie. But he didn't have time to figure out how to act like a tormented perfectionist from a grade A film.

The man told him, somewhat awkwardly. It wasn't that he didn't know it, but that he could not believe that Jack didn't, so he kept skipping over elements that he assumed Jack already understood. In the course of this Jack picked up some background about the empire and the planet they were on.

It seemed that there were several components of the empire. It wasn't exactly an empire, but whatever it was was too complicated for Jack to assimilate at the moment, so he used the term as mental shorthand. It included so many stellar systems that there was no reliable survey listing them all. Human beings were on several of its planets, not because they were native but because they had been imported as labor from overpopulated Earth, which planet didn't even miss them. The alien rulers were called the Gaol, as it were the gaolers of the empire. They did not care what the human laborers did, as long as they did their jobs; they were allowed to have their own families and entertainments. One of the planets they worked on was this one, where the dominant native species was what Jack thought of as the honkers. The empire was governed by completely alien creatures who had no biological and little intellectual association with human beings, but whose technological power was such that no known force could oppose it.

Except the Imago. Therefore it was to the Gaol's interest to nullify the Imago. The Imago seemed to be another type of alien entity, possessing no body of its own, other than what for want of a better term was a spirit. It seemed to be singular, though perhaps it was that only one of its kind chose to interact with solid creatures. When it did, it manifested only by the enhancement of the powers of that person. Whether it entered other than human hosts was unknown, but probably it did, because sometimes it skipped a generation of human beings, only to reappear seemingly randomly. It seemed to associate with this honker planet, where spirits had more force than they did elsewhere.

But when it entered a person, it took time to manifest. At first it was the Larva, largely quiescent, inhabiting the person from conception into childhood. That stage seemed to last for about seven years, until the child was six, and the spirit could not be detected. Then it metamorphosed into the Chrysalis. The child did not change physically, but now the symbiotic entity manifested. The child developed mental or emotional rapport with other life, including animals and plants, and there was a faint mental aura that sophisticated sensors could detect. After another seven years it metamorphosed to its adult stage, whose nature no one knew except the Gaol who governed the empire. It was conjectured that the rapport with other forms of life expanded into full-scale telepathy and the power to modify the emotions of others. If so, it meant the Imago could take over even the minds of the Gaol and make them do its will. That would give it the capacity to rule or to destroy the empire—even if it was based in the body of a blind human girl.

"Then why don't you just kill it?" Jack demanded. "So it can't mess with your alien masters?" He still hated to talk this way, as if he didn't care about Tappy. His feeling for her was a strange and wonderful thing, not exactly love and not exactly apart from love. Already he recognized the truth of what the man was telling him: Tappy related to other life, and he felt that relation through his mind and heart. He was beginning to understand why he had made love with her, as the Chrysalis of her nature touched him. If this was only the suggestion of her mature power, what would be its full expression?

The man explained: The Imago could not be killed. If its host was destroyed, it simply sought a new host. Then, fourteen years later, the threat to the empire returned. In the early days, perhaps millennia ago, the Imago had so disrupted the empire as to cause its dissolution. Only when the Gaol had learned how to nullify the Imago had they been able to reconstitute and maintain the empire. Now they tracked the Imago diligently, and when it manifested they captured its human or other host, drugged it into unconsciousness, and maintained it in tight security within a field that scrambled any possible mental or other emanations. They kept it in that condition, carefully alive, as long as nature and technology permitted; with luck their reprieve lasted as long as a century.

When the captive Imago-host finally died, the search began again. Its occupation of a new host seemed to be random; no one could predict where on this planet it would appear next. The Gaol had the power to obliterate the planet, but feared the Imago would only manifest on another; it was better to keep it here. So this world was left in its natural state, unlike most other planets. The Gaol intended to locate and nullify the Imago as usual, forestalling any possible threat to the empire's stability. If the Imago-host was found and killed, the process would have to begin over. Therefore the empire impressed upon its minions that due care should be taken. Whoever was responsible for the loss of the Imago would suffer in ways no ordinary person could imagine—and so would his family and his community.

Now at last Jack understood. Tappy was the current host of the Imago. She had been the child of a human colonist on this honker planet. When her expanding empathy for life had manifested at age six, she had been hustled to a place where the Gaol could not quickly find her. There must have been trouble; maybe the minions of the empire had been in pursuit, and Tappy's father had been killed, and she maimed and blinded. But she had gotten free, though at the terrible price Jack had seen. Her injuries had turned out to be an advantage, because they restricted her, so that she did not call attention to herself. She had been put under a hypnotic block against even speaking the language. All this had been necessary to hide her from the notice of the Gaol, whose search methods had to be sophisticated and unscrupulous. Indeed, the empire must have searched, and finally was on the verge of locating her. So she had had to be moved—and an ignorant Earth native had been hired to transport her. Jack.

"Why didn't she return to her family here?" Jack asked.

The man grimaced. "What family? When the Gaol found out she was gone, poof! So was her community."

Jack looked at Tappy. She nodded. She had known throughout that she was orphaned. The Earth cover-story had been accurate in essence if not in detail. That was the price of being the host of the Imago.

"So where are you going?" Jack asked her. For she had certainly been headed somewhere with great urgency.

"That is what we want to know," the man said. "So we can stop her from getting there. But it no longer matters, because we have captured the Imago."

"Don't you wish!" Jack exclaimed. "You're not locking Tappy up drugged for the rest of her life! I'll radiate her into nothingness first!" This time he was telling the truth: death was better than that. He saw her nod; she agreed.

Then there was a faint flash. Jack did not lose consciousness, or even feel pain. He simply lost his volition. The minions of the empire had closed in on them and used some sort of weapon. He had talked too long, and been caught. Worse, he had betrayed Tappy into their power.

Now other men appeared. "Good job, 'Joe,' " one said, mockingly using the name Jack had bestowed on the man. "You kept them distracted until we were sure of our shot."

Jack had after all played the fool. He had been so interested in what he was learning about Tappy that he had not kept properly alert, and they had crept up close. No wonder Joe had been so cooperative, once he got started talking! It hadn't mattered how much Jack learned, so long as he was kept occupied.

"Get up, follow that man," the new man said to Jack and Tappy, indicating a man who was now standing nearby.

Jack got up and followed the man, and Tappy did the same. His body was not paralyzed, just his control over it. He had to do what anyone told him.

"Go to the container and get the null dose," the leader told the one they had been talking to. Now that man got up; apparently he, too, had lost his volition.

Jack found that though his body obeyed the directive, his mind remained free. He could think anything he wanted, for what little good that might do him. So he pieced together the remaining elements of what had happened.

The weapons the men carried were not for killing or stunning, but for blocking off the mind's conscious control of the body. They probably generated an intense local field that affected all people in it, but did not extend far. So one shot had taken out all three of them in the niche, but not those standing beyond it. This was surely a necessary limitation. That explained why the men pursuing them had not fired at them before: they had to get within the short range of the will-stunner before using it. The radiator seemed to have no such limit, so had been a fearsome counterweapon. If only he had remained alert with it!

The anonymous leader made them march toward the huge cage ship, which it seemed was called the container. That made sense; it was used to contain fleeing people. But for the radiator, it would have contained them effectively enough. Now they had lost the radiator. What a mess he had made of this! He should have let the information go, and kept running with Tappy.

As they approached the ship, he saw that the hole the radiator had carved through the giant rim was smaller. No one was working on it; the thing seemed to be healing itself! At the rate it was going, in a few more hours the injury would be gone.

Injury? What was he thinking of!

The rim of the container loomed high. Then a dimple appeared before them, expanding into an opening. Inside was a ramp. They stepped in, and the ramp carried them upward in the manner of an escalator.

It deposited them somewhere in the middle of the rim. Another door irised open, and they stepped into a beautiful apartment. The walls seemed to be windows on planetary scenes; the illusion would have been perfect, except that each wall showed a different planet. One had a deep green sky with two small bright suns orbiting each other; their dual shadows were slowly changing configurations and shades as he watched. Another was night, with a few scattered stars and a monstrous nebula or galaxy seen end-on beyond them, taking up half the view, wondrously three-dimensional. Another was a cityscape whose buildings curved esthetically to touch each other at different levels; one even made a loop, which was unlooping and extending toward a different building at a fair rate. It was as if the buildings were kissing or copulating. Still another—for the walls were not set square, but angled in the manner of the interior of a faceted stone—showed a ship on a great yellow sea, and the ship flexed to accommodate the passing waves, while tiny people or creatures sported in those waves.

"Hello."

Jack would have jumped had he had control of his body. He had been standing immobile, only his eyes moving to take in the wonders of the walls. Now he looked at the woman who had spoken. She sat before a wall looking out over fairly conventional snow-covered mountains.

She was impressive. It was not that she was young, for somehow he doubted that she was, despite her remarkably firm and slender body. She wore a closed cloak that was opaque only at the fringes; her central torso showed clearly through it, her breasts so well formed that they seemed unreal, her legs slightly spread so that her manicured pubic region was plain. Jack felt an erection starting, an involuntary response to the potent suggestions of her apparel and posture.

"You may call me Malva," she said. "What may I call you?" She looked at Jack.

Now he found he could speak. "Jack." But that was all he was able to say; his mouth would not work at his own behest.

The woman's eyes flicked to Tappy, who remained silent. They returned to Jack. "Tappy," he said. "She can't—" But he was trying to go beyond the immediate directive, and stalled out.

Malva nodded. "A block. Standard procedure." Her gaze returned to Tappy. "But you will respond appropriately by nodding." Tappy nodded.

Meanwhile Jack's gaze, drawn to Malva's head when he had to answer her, noted eyes whose irises were red. Not bloodshot, but a deep esthetic cast. Her hair was the same hue, looking natural, though no living woman had ever grown that shade. Perhaps it figured: if she had gone to the trouble to have plastic surgery on her body so she could show it off, she would think nothing of dyeing her hair and using tinted contact lenses.

"Sit, and we shall talk," Malva said.

They sat on the blocks that slid out from the wall behind them, where the door had been. They looked like hard plastic, but they were soft, with just enough spring to be comfortable.

"I serve the Gaol," Malva said. "I am fifty-four Earth years old, but as you can see I am attractive. Without the Gaol I would be far inferior physically and mentally, and I would not have this pleasant residence or the privileges of rank. I say this so that you can appreciate the advantage of the favor of the Gaol. You will not be offered such favor, but you can avoid incurring their disfavor by timely cooperation."

The wall behind her abruptly changed scenes. Now it showed a classic inferno, a medieval representation of Hell, with tall fires forming the walls. In the foreground was a rack on which a naked human man was bound. A black-hooded tormenter was extending a glowing red rod toward the man's genital region.

"Any torture your mind can imagine, and a number it cannot imagine, may be visited on your body by the order of the Gaol," Malva said. Behind her the rod touched the man's penis, and the flesh blistered and smoked while the man's body struggled ineffectively, and his mouth opened in a soundless scream of agony. "So I am sure you will not hesitate to answer my simple questions so that I can make a proper report to my masters."

She looked at Jack. "How did you come to associate with the host for the Imago?"

Jack stared a moment more at the scene beyond the woman's luscious body. The red-hot rod was now cooking the victim's testicles. The scene could be a mock-up or a recording, rather than any contemporary event, but it was distressingly realistic. He suspected that this was a bluff, similar to his own threat to radiate Tappy, but he decided not to chance it. "I was hired on Earth to drive her to another address."

"What was the nature of your relationship with her there?"

Again he saw no reason to equivocate. "I was her companion, and then her lover."

Malva nodded slightly, unsurprised. The wall behind her returned to the mountainscape. "You did not know her nature, but you felt the effect. She is the Chrysalis."

"Yes."

"How did she drop from our screens?"

Jack gazed blankly at her.

"You can not answer, or you will not?" she inquired, frowning briefly.

"I can not. I don't know what you mean." But he had just learned something: there *was* a choice. Apparently the loss of volition extended only to the body, not the mind. He could not speak unless she asked him to, but his mouth would not say what his mind did not authorize.

"And she will not. We can not force the Imago." Malva considered a moment, crossing her legs under the cloak. Now her pubic area was not visible, but the underside of her thigh was similarly fascinating. She was an old woman with the body of a young woman, and she knew exactly how to display it. He hardly knew her, and what he was learning he didn't like, but his body had notions of leaping and plunging. "Would some information help you to answer?"

"I do not know."

"Are you willing to answer, if you can?"

Jack did not consider himself a coward, but he knew he was no hero. If they used even the crudest of tortures on him, he would scream out all he knew about anything, or say whatever they wanted him to. He knew that had been the case with the victims of the Inquisition, and he had no doubt that this woman could have him put on exactly such a rack as the wall picture had showed. He and Tappy were captive, already lost; resistance was pointless, especially when he didn't know anything anyway. "Yes."

"The Gaol supply us with certain techniques of observation," Malva said. Now the panel behind her showed the surface of a planet that looked very much like the one they were on. "The natives are hostile to the Gaol; they do not resist openly, so are allowed to exist, but neither do they volunteer any information." The honkers appeared, marching by in much the manner Jack had seen when he and Tappy had first arrived on this world. "But we do not need them. We are able to survey the natural pattern of life on the planet, and to detect net changes caused by unnatural interference. Every living thing's spirit remains with it until death, and for a time after its death. A dichotomy manifested. We traced it to the unnatural death of two salamanders. Do you understand?"

"We did kill and eat salamanders," Jack agreed. "But any animal could have done that!"

"The balance of nature is finely tuned. There was a slight excess in deaths. Next day there was a similar excess, but we could not locate it or confirm it; it was only a probability of outside interference."

So the creatures they had eaten had given away their presence! Jack had never heard of such a survey, but he had no reason to doubt it. Why should Malva lie to him, instead of torturing him?

"In due course we found their vacated spirits, and were sure," the woman continued. "We were at that point able to get a fix on the aura of the Chrysalis. Rather than intercept it immediately, we elected to wait to see where it went. That would enable us to root out whatever remaining traitors to the empire were on the planet and diminish the likelihood of any assistance being rendered to the next Imago, should it manifest here. Do you understand?"

He was appalled, but he did understand. "Yes. You intended to root out every part of the weed."

"Then, abruptly, the aura faded," Malva said. "We had to act immediately, lest the Imago be lost. We brought the container in and enclosed the region of the aura's last manifestation." She peered closely at Jack. "Something happened in that night which we do not understand. What damped out the aura of the Chrysalis?"

Suddenly it came clear. The honker! The honker had injected something into Tappy that formed a tight marble-sized ball under the skin between her breasts. A timed-release capsule of a chemical that somehow counteracted the broadcast of the aura the ship was tracking. Tappy, realizing that they were probably being tracked, had talked to the honker when she bought food from him. The honker had accepted the pretext—what need did it have of an Earthly quarter?—and made its preparations. Then it had come and done what was necessary, returning the quarter. It had not been a sexual attack; the honker had a penis which remained unused. It had been a favor to the Imago, which the honkers surely recognized and supported. Because the small operation was painful, it had anesthetized them both, giving it time to do the job, and for the chemical to circulate slowly through Tappy's body, interfering with the manifestation of the distinctive aura. Tappy had not known exactly how the honker was going to help— probably the honker had not known either, until checking with others of his kind—so had been frightened at first. As a child might be frightened of the doctor, despite knowing the doctor was trying to help.

As long as any of that ball of substance remained with Tappy, the Gaol instruments could not track her. Yet what difference did it make now? Jack had blundered them into captivity anyway.

Still, if there was any chance at all that Tappy could escape, that marble on her chest would be invaluable. It didn't show under her nightie, even with her jacket hanging open; though her breasts were nascent, the stretch of cloth between them masked the swelling. The minions of the Gaol, so certain of their power, had not bothered to search the captives at all. The marble had escaped notice. Jack was not about to tell this empire quisling about it.

"Is your silence one of ignorance or resistance?" Malva inquired.

He wanted to lie, but found he could not. That required too great an act of volition. His choice was between the truth and the refusal to answer. He refused to answer.

Malva nodded, unsurprised. "So you do know something, and the Imago has corrupted you. Let me remind you of the alternatives. There are possible advantages to cooperation—" The screen behind her showed a bed sliding out from a wall, and to this bed came the image of Malva herself, her cloak dissolving away, her breasts and buttocks quivering as she walked. From the other side came Jack, his clothing dissolving similarly away to reveal the erection he really did have. Malva lay on the bed, smiling invitingly as she spread her legs.

But Jack knew this was merely a sophisticated show. This woman had no interest in him, only in his information. She might indeed offer sex to him, to obtain it, but the moment she got it she might have his skin made into a lampshade. Meanwhile, the thought of Tappy as a drugged and imprisoned thing, kept artificially alive for most of a century, was such a horror that Malva's temptation became anathema. He remained silent.

"And disadvantages to noncooperation," Malva continued after a moment. The bed became the rack, the curtains of the room transforming to flames, and the body on the rack became Tappy, her small breasts shaking as she writhed with fear. The Jack figure donned a hood and fetched a blazing red-tipped poker. He extended that tip toward Tappy's genital region, angling it, threatening to rape her with it.

The substitution of Tappy as the object of torture was startling. Not only did it show the versatility of Malva's control of the images, it betrayed the falsity of them. *There was no marble-swelling between the image's breasts.* Malva didn't know about that, and he would not tell her. He was unable to look away, but he tuned out the image as irrelevant. Malva was bluffing, and he had found her out, and now his hand was greatly strengthened. He was learning about bluffs!

"What is your statement?" Malva inquired.

That gave him more latitude; he no longer had to betray Tappy or be silent. He called Malva's bluff. "You can not torture the Imago. You probably can't torture me either, or you would have done it by now. Your masters don't give you that much authority."

Malva pursed her lips as the mountains reappeared behind her. "You may be ignorant, but you are not entirely stupid. It is true that I am limited to the mechanisms of oblique persuasion. But it is also true that the end will be the same, and that you will find it far more comfortable to deal with me than with the Gaol. I will proffer one further offer, which will not be repeated. Give me the information I require—I see that you do have it—and I will grant you one year of extremely comfortable life with the woman of your choice, which may be me or a simulation of Tappy or any other you prefer, and subsequent return unharmed to your own planet. Face the Imago."

Jack obeyed the directive. He turned to face Tappy, who stood without moving. She looked like a street waif in her oversized jacket over her nightie. Her only expression was a single small tear on one cheek.

"Imago, I can not force you to do anything," Malva said. "But I can free your host to give your companion an honest answer. You know enough of the Gaol and their human minions to judge whether my offer will be honored if Jack agrees. You know he must make his own decision, based on the truth, so you have no motive to deceive him. Answer him: is my offer valid?"

The tear accelerated. Slowly Tappy nodded yes.

"Your answer, Jack."

It seemed like folly, since the woman would discover the marble the moment Tappy was stripped for her incarceration. Yet two things stopped Jack from capitulating. The first was that he suspected Malva was still bluffing; she was desperate to make him tell, so was pulling out all the stops, and she wouldn't do that without good reason. So there had to be reason for him *not* to cooperate. Maybe there was some way to save Tappy. Or maybe it was simply that Malva was expected to handle things, and the Gaol would be annoyed with her if she left a loose end, and would demote her or replace her with a rival.

The second reason was that no matter how much objective sense it might make, he could not betray Tappy, and this would be a betrayal. Her tear told him that. "No."

"Go down the ramp and enter the small craft at the exit," Malva said. "It will convey you to the Gaol." Her voice was controlled, but Jack thought he could detect a slight stress in it: the stress of fear or of fury. Whatever else he had failed to do, he had scored against her.

But his body was already moving, as was Tappy's. That single shot from the null-volition pistol had really fixed them! Apparently the effect continued until nullified, and no other restraints were needed. Not for enough time to get them safely to the Gaol. Malva had to be sure of that, or she would have taken other precautions.

Now, of course, his doubts loomed. What had he accomplished by his defiance? He hadn't saved Tappy, but he had doomed himself. He was a painter, not a hard-nosed negotiator!

There were two seats in the little vehicle, which looked like a gull-wing door car with the doors left open. They got in, but the doors did not swing down. Instead a slight scintillation indicated the presence of a force field that sealed in the car. Then it rolled forward, accelerating like a jet plane, and took off. Those gull wings really were wings! This was an airplane. Jack would have gaped, but no one had authorized him to do so, so his mouth remained closed.

The plane flew low over the forest, evidently programmed so precisely that the close clearance was no problem. Then it lifted, and Jack saw the huge crater valley where they had entered this world, with its gigantic symbols around the rim. The symbols that moved grandly around, periodically, like the elapsed-time ring on a diver's watch, making a new setting.

Now, flying over it, he saw that the depression was far too regular to be a natural crater. It was either artificial or had been excavated and reshaped after its formation, for some alien purpose.

That reminded him of another mystery: the brief redness of the river he had seen. What could have caused that? There was so much about this planet he still didn't know!

There was a touch on his shoulder. Jack turned to face it, taking it as a command for attention, before he realized the significance of it. Tappy was the only one beside him—and she had done it. She had volition!

Tappy's finger touched her lips in the signal for silence. You bet! A radio could be monitoring this cabin, as a routine precaution. If she had somehow thrown off the effect of the shot, he would keep her secret. But his own body remained helpless.

Tappy pointed to the panel before them. He looked, again obeying the implied directive. He could obey her as well as Malva; it didn't matter who gave the orders, or how they were given.

There was something like a steering wheel there, recessed into the panel. That must be for use by the pilot when this craft was not on programmed flight.

Tappy's hand extended until it touched the panel, then slid along it until she felt the wheel. She nodded. Then she found Jack's arm and guided his hand to the wheel. She made a gesture of pulling it toward him.

She was telling him to fly this thing? He looked at her, startled. She nodded yes, knowing his question.

But he couldn't do that! He had no idea how to operate a normal airplane, let alone this alien craft.

But the alternative was to let the two of them be flown to meet the Gaol. He had no idea what the aliens looked like, but formed a mental picture of huge sluglike monsters whose proboscises sucked out the guts of human beings. Surely false, but it made the point: it was better to crash this craft than to suffer what the aliens had in store for them.

He had been given his directive. Now his arms and head were free. He took hold of the wheel and pulled it toward him. It didn't come. It was locked in place. Probably it required a special key or code to free it, to prevent exactly such an accident as this one.

Tappy, aware of his problem, turned around in her seat and reached behind it. In a moment she brought something from a compartment there. It was her leg brace—with the radiator! The fools had dumped it in the craft, for delivery to the Gaol along with the captives. What arrogance of assurance!

She touched another orange button with her little finger, pointing it out to him. Then she handed him the brace and touched the panel, her hand coming to rest on the wheel.

Use that on the wheel? It would null it into nonexistence, together with the entire front of the craft!

But Tappy was insistent. It was a different button she had indicated, and evidently it did a different thing. If not, did it matter? They would be better off to crash and die than to fall into the hands—tentacles?—of the Gaol, he was sure.

Jack pointed the radiator at the center of the wheel, nerved himself, and touched the large scarlet button. It glowed. Then he touched the correct orange button.

There was a click. That was all. Nothing changed. He turned off the radiator, lest he brush a functioning button and do something drastic.

Tappy found his hands and took back the radiator. Jack, frustrated, gripped the wheel again and yanked, if only to show the futility of the act. It came out of its recess and locked into place—and the craft wobbled.

Jack stifled his astonishment, realizing that, once again, Tappy had known what she was doing. That setting of the radiator had evidently shorted out the locking mechanism, which might be magnetic, and freed the wheel. He had just overridden the programming, assuming manual control. It was that easy. Now all he had to do was fly this thing.

He turned the wheel, clockwise, just a bit. The craft veered right. He turned the wheel back, and the craft responded. He pushed down, and the craft dropped. He lifted, and it rose. He squeezed it, and the craft accelerated.

He had the hang of it already! This thing was made for an idiot to fly. That was fortunate, because he was an idiot in this respect.

Tappy touched his arm. He looked at her. She made a gesture of a circle, then pointed up.

Fly up? After circling? He didn't think he understood. Why the circle? Unless the circle represented the crater valley—or a compass. They had been going north from the crater, and "up" on a compass could indicate north.

He leaned toward her. "North?" he whispered.

She nodded agreement.

He turned the craft until it was flying north. At the rate it was going, they would soon get there, if it was on this planet. But where was he supposed to land? He could do so only on Tappy's directive, and she was blind.

How had she thrown off the volition nullification? Suddenly the answer was there: the honker's marble! Not only had it made it impossible for the aliens to track the Imago, it had made their weapon lose its effect on Tappy. Either she had thrown off the effects of the weapon rapidly, or she had never suffered loss of volition at all. She might have faked it, knowing that Jack had no control, until there was a chance to escape.

If he had betrayed her, and told Malva about the marble, they never would have had this chance. And Tappy had been unable to tell him that. She had had to let him decide himself, and had been afraid he would succumb.

How glad he was that he had not! He had been more of a man than he had taken himself to be.

Something flashed on the panel, attracting his gaze. Two little blips were there, blinking. Oh-oh; he had a notion what they might represent.

He looked around. There, at about seven o'clock on the dial, were two flying craft similar to this one. They were closing fast.

He knew what had happened. The alarm had been given the moment he overrode the program and assumed manual control. Other ships had been sent out to bring him in again.

He leaned toward Tappy. "We're in trouble," he whispered. Then he managed one tiny act of his own volition, with great effort: he kissed her ear. Perhaps it was possible only because he knew she would like it.

Chapter 4

"TWO Gaol airplanes coming fast," he told Tappy.

He thought, What do I do now?

The chances were that the planes climbing up below him were faster than his. Even if the speed of his craft matched theirs, he was very handicapped. This was his solo flight, and he had had no training. An aerial dogfight between him and two professionals would last a few seconds. If that.

"Get a grip on yourself," he muttered.

That reminded him that squeezing the wheel caused the craft to accelerate. He clamped down as hard as he could on the inflated rim. But the plane was so high up that he could not tell at once if its velocity was increasing swiftly.

He looked out of the window on his left. The pursuer seemed not to be gaining so swiftly.

However, his hands would get tired soon. Surely, there must be a control on the panel before him that locked in to whatever speed he wanted. It was a dumb idea to regulate the airspeed of this craft by squeezing on the wheel. The engineers who had designed this certainly did not think like their Earth counterparts.

However, this machine surely should have something like the cruise control of a car. When set, it would maintain the desired rate of travel to give the pilot's hands a rest.

The names on the plates below the lights and switches and buttons on the panel were in a totally unfamiliar alphabet. If it was an alphabet. Maybe the letters were ideographic or syllabic, like ancient Aztec or Chinese or whatever.

Another glance through the window showed him that, yes indeed, the chaser was eating up the space between his craft and his quarry's. Perhaps its pilot could squeeze harder, but he did not think so. The adrenaline surging through him should give his hands the strength to crush rocks.

He wished he had a brush big enough to paint the other planes out of the sky. Reality, unfortunately, was not a painting. It was hard objects, some of them moving very fast, objects driven by human beings out to kill him and Tappy.

That thought was conceived out of despair by panic. But it gave birth to relief. A limited relief, true, yet it was tinged with hope.

Whatever they would do, they would not kill Tappy. Though desperate to catch her, they must avoid doing anything that might result in her death.

Therefore, they would not shoot the plane down.

What they would do, probably, would be to try to force their quarry to land. Unless . . . no use attempting to imagine what was in their bag of tricks. He would find out soon enough.

The planes were slowly but steadily closing the gap between them and Jack's plane. One pigeon. Two falcons.

Below, a forest spread out, dark green like an Earth woods except here and there were irregularly shaped areas of orange-colored trees. The crater was receding fast. Ahead was more forest. In the distance were the peaks of a mountain range. Now and then the sunlight flashed on a river. Or was there more than one? A large lake appeared on the right.

A number of tiny boats with single masts and bright white and purple triangular sails scudded across the smooth green water. Jack was too high to make out the figures on the decks.

He started as something touched his neck. It was Tappy's finger, of course.

He was very jumpy. For a second, he had thought that an insect had landed on his neck.

Her wondering and anxious expression showed him that he had been silent too long.

"The plane on my left is now even with us," he said. "The other . . . here it comes! It's even with us now. Now they're rising. I think they plan to get above us and force us down."

Jack shouted, "Oh, no, you don't!"

Tappy gasped and jumped a little at his outburst.

Savagely, he turned the wheel to the left, pushing in on it at the same time.

The craft curved to the left and dropped swiftly.

Jack, glancing at Tappy, saw that her eyes were wide open, and she had paled.

"I'm trying to shake them!" he said. "Hang on! We may be in for a rough ride!"

He was thinking, Why in hell didn't I grab the radiator and try to shoot them with it?

He was doing better than he had thought he would in such a situation. So far, he had not done badly for one who considered himself to be an artist, not a man of action, ten thousand miles from being an Indiana Jones. But that had been on the ground. He had frozen for a while when in the air, and he still was not completely thawed out.

The pilots of the Gaol machines had quick reflexes, though. They had not been caught with their mouths open. Their planes had curved and dropped, too, following his course by a split second or so. Now they were above him again, diving at the same angle and velocity. They were also jockeying so that each would be just above the end of one of the wings.

He turned the wheel and pulled it back until the plane was on an even keel. At least, he thought that it was. By now, he assumed that one of the instruments on the panel was an angle indicator. It looked like the ones he had seen in movies showing an airplane's cockpit. It was round and in its center was a horizontal line. The line swung up at one end and down at the other, or vice versa, as one wing dropped and the other rose.

At the moment, it was straight across, and the wings seemed to be level, too.

Give him enough time, and he might figure out most of the functions of the instruments.

But he was not going to be given that time.

The bottoms of the fuselages, twelve or so feet above the tips of his wings, began lowering. He noted with a part of his mind that the wheels had withdrawn into the shell. He supposed that the wheels of his craft had also withdrawn. But he had heard no sound of machinery moving.

Jack told Tappy about the situation. She lifted the radiator with both hands, holding it before her face.

"Yes, I know," he said. "But wait a minute. I want to try something."

By then, the fuselage bottoms were only six feet above the wingtips of Jack's machine. The gap between them constantly varied by a foot or so. The rough air bounced Jack's plane up and down and did the same to their pursuers. They would not be able to touch their bottoms against his wingtips. Otherwise, the wingtips might break. Or something else and worse might happen.

They were betting that he would not try to call their bluff.

"Let's see!" he said loudly.

He released much of his grip on the wheel rim. At the same time, he pulled back hard on the wheel. The nose of the craft lifted sharply, and the wingtips almost struck the other planes. The pilots must have been startled, but they lifted their own planes quickly enough to avoid the collision. They did not slow down, however. They shot ahead of Jack's machine.

Jack took his hands off the wheel. The nose dropped, and the craft headed downward at an angle of perhaps forty-five degrees in relation to the horizon. He had expected it to stall and to fall like a stone. But it must have some sort of safety factor, a fool-compensator, in its program. In several seconds, it began to level out. The machines in front of him began climbing and turning at the same time. For certain, they would come back and attempt the same forcing-down.

He had gained some time and distance, however. And the sky, which had been clear, was suddenly dark on the horizon. He hoped that the clouds would be heavy with rain. A lightning and thunder storm would be welcome, too. He just might be able to lose the Gaol in a storm.

He said, "Tappy! Are we still going north? Headed directly toward whatever you want to get to?"

She turned her head slightly to the left and to the right. Then she pointed a few degrees to her right. Jack turned the machine until she nodded, and he straightened out the course. He had seen that one of the indicators on the panel had swung its pointer, too. The needle tip now rested by a symbol which he supposed must indicate north.

Soon, too soon for him, the Gaol had returned. One of them rode on his left, making no attempt to get above his wingtip. He stretched his neck to turn and look through the window in the top. At first, he saw only sky. Then abruptly and sinisterly, the nose of the second machine appeared. It was directly above Jack's machine and descending on a horizontal plane.

He understood at once what its new position meant. It was going to lower itself on the top of Jack's plane. Then it would land, in a manner of speaking, on his plane. It would decrease its speed until its quarry would have to support part of the weight of the Gaol craft.

Its pilot must know what he was doing. He must be sure that Jack's machine could not sustain the added weight. And that it would be borne, however slowly, to the ground.

A moment later, a grinding noise and a shudder running through the fuselage announced that Jack was right.

The window was blocked by the blue bottom of the fuselage.

Jack told Tappy what had happened. Her alarm and puzzlement vanished. She held the radiator out to him.

He took it and said, "I'd rather not shoot through the sky-window."

One of the panel dials had on its face a vertical tube like a thermometer. The "mercury" was a bright orange. Its top had gone down, passing symbols marking, he supposed, altitude. The machine was losing speed and height at a rate that upset him. But he was not going to panic. Not now, anyway.

His mouth was very dry, and a low-burning pressure in him told him that he must urinate. Soon. Or the pressure would be intense, and the burning would not be low.

"I want to open the window on the door in my side," he told Tappy. "There are two buttons. The forward one is orange. The one behind it is yellow with a blue stripe running across it."

She had shown him how to unlock the operational program. Maybe she was familiar with the design of the cockpit.

Tappy smiled and groped along the door to her right until she found the buttons. Then she rested a finger lightly on the yellow one.

"Thanks," he said. He pushed in on the button on his door. The window began to lower, and cool air screamed into the cockpit.

He reached out to take the radiator from her. At the same time, he thought, Wait a minute! How did she learn so much about the design and operation of this airplane? She was six years old when she fled from here to Earth. How could she know all this? How many kids on Earth or here would be familiar with this complex stuff?

The answers to this question, as to many, would have to wait. He hoped he would live long enough to hear them.

The window was completely open now. He reached into his jacket, found one of the pencils in the leather holder in the inside pocket, and withdrew it. Then, leaning out of the window and twisted so that he could look back along the fuse-lage and upward, he extended the brace—the radiator—toward the wing of the Gaol craft. The air tore at him and caught the radiator, but he was gripping it hard. It was not easy to keep the weapon pointed at the wing while he pressed the pen-cil end against the orange button, the firing activator, the trig-ger.

There was no visible radiance expelled from the end of the brace. He knew there would be none, but he had momentarily expected one. He was too conditioned by all the science-fiction movies he had seen and all the books he had read.

The wing, cut in half, was whisked away, tumbling over and over.

He should have expected the shadow. But he had not. He grunted when he saw the transparent but still visible plane attached to the sheared-off wing. Then the strange and unexplainable thing was out of his sight.

The plane suddenly lifted as the solid and opaque Gaol craft on its back fell off.

He swung the radiator to point at the other plane. For the first time, he could sea the pilot's face clearly. Previously, it had been a blank or, rather, a generic human face. Now it came into focus, and he saw the features of an individual. A woman's face. Since she was unhelmeted, her reddish hair was visible. It was coiled into a bun on top of her head. A Psyche knot. Her delicate and rather pretty face was frozen. Her mind must have gone blank when she saw the wingtip flutter away and her colleague's plane roll off the back of Jack's machine.

The next moment, she had an even more puzzling and urgent matter to disturb her. Jack had pressed the radiator button. The tail of her plane got a quick divorce from the front part. It dropped, the shadow of the other part turning as it turned. And a shadow of the rear section projected from the still-flying part.

For a few seconds, the winged half-plane struggled onward, though losing altitude swiftly and beginning to bank to the left. The propulsive-levitation engine must radiate from inside the wings, Jack thought. But the pilot could not steer her craft.

Then the shorn plane nose-dived.

Jack turned the plane to observe what would happen next to the Gaol machine. It sped straight downward. A half a minute later, the pilot dived out of the window. Something was strapped to her front. Presently, she managed to straighten out, and she flew at a steep angle toward the ground.

She had put on some kind of parachute or emergency one-person mini-aircraft.

He looked in the space behind the seat. It held two cylinders about fourteen inches high and with a radius of six inches. Three levers were sticking out halfway down a yellow vertical stripe. Attached to the cylinders were harnesses.

The pilot's hands had been on the cylinder. Evidently, she had been using the levers to guide her flight.

Jack turned back to the north. The compass needle indicated that he was headed toward the exact direction that Tappy had indicated. But, just to make sure, he asked her again if he was headed in the right direction. She nodded.

It was strange that he trusted her more as a compass than he did an electromechanical device. Or was it? She knew the true direction better than any man-made compass. But the panel device could be malfunctioning or affected by aberrant magnetic fields.

While he was going toward the black clouds, he looked at the instruments. One of those switches or buttons must be a cruise control. Another would put the plane on automatic navigation. And what was that blank screen that looked so much like that on a TV set?

He decided that it was best not to monkey around with anything the exact function of which he did not know. So far, he was doing all right with his flying. But what about when he had to land? What activated the machinery to lower the wheels?

Of course! Ask Tappy!

He should have thought of that automatically. But his mind was still not completely thawed out. It contained ice, the ice of anxiety.

No genuine hero, I, he thought.

He had not volunteered for this perilous voyage. No one in his or her right mind would do that.

Well, yes, he had entered the rock, and no one had forced him to do that. However, he just could not have allowed Tappy to pass through the gate, or whatever it was, alone. What he should have done, he should have kept her from going into it. Even if he had had to use force.

No. Somehow, she would have found her way back if he had dragged her away. It was her destiny, and it was her will to follow her destiny.

My destiny, too, he thought. If I had refused to go with her, I would have loathed myself until I died. And am I not really living, vibrating, keenly aware, alive in every atom of my mind and body? Wasn't I a sort of walking dead before I passed through the gate?

I didn't know it. I had to come here to find that out. All those people on Earth—well, most of them, anyway—are semizombies.

The clouds and the mountains ahead swelled. After a while, the black roiling mass, shot with lightning streaks, covered the mountains. It would be raining inside that mass. That reminded him that his mouth was still very dry. His bladder pained him again. During the dogfight, as he thought of it, he had forgotten about the urgency within him.

Where could he land to get much-needed relief? There was forest below him as far as he could see. Could this plane alight without a long runway? Come straight down like a helicopter? It certainly had used a short takeoff space. But there were very few open areas, and these looked as if they were small.

That reminded him that he had meant to ask Tappy about the panel instruments. Urged by him, she ran her fingers over the switches, buttons, and dials. When he told her to stop at a certain instrument, she did so. But she could not tell him what they were for unless he ran down a list of questions and she would nod if he was right. This took too much time and required too much patience for him to learn what every instrument did.

However, he did make a lucky guess about the screen. It showed the view from the rear of the plane if you pressed one of two buttons below it. He activated it. Then he said, "Just what I was hoping wouldn't happen!"

Three large black dots were in the sky, flying in formation. They were at the same altitude as his plane.

"We're being followed," he said. "They've sent at least three pursuits after us."

He looked through the windows to each side and through the window in the ceiling. He could not see any other craft. Then it occurred to him that there could be Gaol machines below him. But his eye-sweeps saw nothing.

The chasers seemed to be in faster aircraft than the two he had disposed of. The dots had grown larger. It was highly likely that the downed pilots had radioed their experiences to their HQ. These newcomers would be much more cautious.

The radio blared, startling him and the girl.

Malva's voice filled the cockpit.

"You will turn back! You will turn back! Return to the place from which you took off! Return to the place from which you took off! You will be escorted back! You will be escorted back!"

Jack said, "For God's sake!"

Though his mind threatened to rupture from the strain of its resistance to the commands, it was making him turn the plane.

If his mind could have teeth, it would be gritting them so hard it would break them off.

"Tappy! Order me to disobey Malva!"

But how could she do that? She could not speak.

He was desperately trying to think of an idea. His mind was running around like a squirrel looking for nuts it had buried during the summer. It knew they were somewhere in this area. But exactly where?

The plane was by now going in the direction from which it had come.

"Tappy!" he said loudly. "Can you write?"

She nodded.

He released the pressure on the wheel rim. Let the plane slow down. He was in no hurry to get back. A few seconds later, he handed her a pencil and the small notebook he carried in the leather holder in the inner jacket pocket.

"Write down your order to me to disobey anybody but you. Then show it to me. I don't know if it'll work, but we've got to try everything!"

Why didn't I do that long ago? he thought.

Then, Well, things've been happening too fast. I can't think of everything.

Tappy, frowning in concentration, wrote on the topmost paper of the notebook. She held it in front of him.

He groaned.

The writing was in Gaol characters.

He was surprised that she knew that. She had fled this planet at the age of six, and how many that age could write? Though he could not read the characters, he could see that her penmanship was beautiful. She must have been precocious. Or, maybe, the Daws had continued her Gaol education. Which meant that they were not just your ordinary Earth citizens.

"No, in English," he said.

Looking distressed, she shook her head.

"Do you know any foreign language? I mean, non-English Earth language. Like French or Spanish?"

Again, she shook her head.

That squirrel in his mind was frantic now. It was whirling around like a furry gyroscope.

"All right! Let's try something else! You used body and hand language to tell me to fly this plane! Can you do the same to tell me to turn back to the north? Malva will give her orders again, but you could cancel them."

Malva would repeat her command. And Tappy would have to override Malva's orders. And then Malva would give her orders again. The plane would yo-yo until the pursuit planes caught up with it.

The bitch might be listening in now via the radio.

He leaned over and whispered to Tappy.

"You didn't point out the radio switches. We have to find them and turn them off."

Malva's voice had come from a grille inset above his head. But there were no buttons or switches near it.

First, he eliminated the controls and indicators the function of which he knew. That left about twenty-five unknowns. What if resetting one caused a serious change in the performance of the craft? Like shutting off the power to the engine?

He had to do something very soon. The three pursuers were steadily growing larger.

At that moment, Malva's voice rang in the cabin.

"You will obey the orders transmitted to you by your escort! One aircraft will guide you! Follow it! Stay at the same level as it! Descend when it descends!"

"Ah!" Jack said.

When the voice had come on, a green panel inset in the center of the steering wheel started to glow.

"Repeat!" Malva said. "You will . . ."

Jack had cut her off by pressing the green panel with his fingertip. The panel ceased to glow.

"Gotcha!"

He pressed the panel again.

" . . . follow the plane in front of you and . . ."

"Sure, we'll just do that, you bitch!" Jack shouted. And he turned the radio off.

All that time, the radio had been on, and he had not noticed the glowing panel. But then he had been busy. Moreover, he was not a trained pilot.

He laughed as he wheeled the craft around and headed for their destination. Some of his dread and uncertainty was gone.

That Malva's commands were being ignored must be whirling her around as if she were glued onto a jet engine vane. She would be horrified, burning with panic. Her masters would not be tolerant about her failure.

He did not feel the least bit sorry for Malva.

Now the air had suddenly become much rougher. The plane fell and rose as if it were diving into and out of express elevators. This was the forerunner of the storm. What would it be like when they were inside its troubled heart?

If it were not for those aircraft catching up with him so swiftly, he would have tried to climb over the storm. But the chasers would overtake him sooner if he lost speed by ascending. They might do so, anyway. The only way to escape was straight ahead. The electrical disturbances there might affect whatever detectors the pursuers had. If this happened, they would lose him and Tappy.

Might . . . if . . .

It did no good to wonder about might-have-beens. But that was an integral part of the human mind. Animals never worried about these. Humans found it necessary. They had to fantasize. So, maybe, it was good for them.

No time for that.

He squeezed the inflatable rim again. "Go ahead, Tappy. Try to cancel the spell, whatever it is, the control she has over me."

Tappy seemed to be thinking hard. Then she smiled. After tearing off the sheet she had written on, she drew a single character. She held it in front of him.

"You know I can't read it."

She half turned and gestured behind her. Then she passed her hands over her face and twisted her features. She was trying to look like somebody. But she was blind.

"You mean," he said slowly, "you're giving me the impression of a face from the voice of that person?"

She nodded, and she pointed behind her again.

Her expression was haughty and arrogant.

"Oh! You mean Malva?"

She nodded and smiled happily.

"But knowing that, how's that going to help me?"

She opened her mouth wide, stuck the sheet of paper close to it, and moved her mouth and jaw as if she were chewing. Then she pointed at him.

He started to ask her what she meant when she reached over, felt along his face until she found his mouth, and jammed the piece of paper between his lips.

Before he could protest, he found the paper stuffed into his mouth. She was still making the chewing motions.

"Grrbgrrbgrrbgrrb!"

Which meant, "You want me to chew this and swallow it?"
Evidently, she did. So he did.

Tappy threw up her hands to indicate that all was well.

He was not so sure. Only one way to find out.

He activated the radio again and said, "Malva, you slimy evil slut! What do you think about your control of me now?"

He winced at the hatred and viciousness of her invective, not all of which was in English.

Then Malva, after her hard breathing had ceased, shouted, "You will obey me! You will obey me! Come back as commanded! Come back as commanded!"

Jack did not have the slightest urge to turn the wheel. He pressed the green-glowing panel again and grinned at Tappy.

"Now we can get back to business."

But the roughness of the air had become a savagery. He and Tappy had been bouncing up and down and swaying hard from side to side. Now they might soon be lifted from their seats.

He said, "Tappy! We need belts to hold us down!"

Tappy frowned again. Her mouth drew up at one corner. Then she smiled. Her fingers brushed along the center area of the panel and stopped over a button. The plaque above it bore a character different from any other on the panel. Below it was a flashing orange light.

She pressed her back against the back of the seat. She gestured that he should do the same. As soon as he had obeyed, she pushed the button. Immediately after, she sat upright against the seat back. He heard a click. From the panels behind the seats slid two long bands. These began curving, went over his and Tappy's chest, and stopped after they entered two extensions which had risen from beside the seats.

Safety belts.

Then he felt something curving around his waist. Another metal band was enclosing him. Both belts seemed to move, settling in, feeling the shape of his body, fitting themselves with maximum efficiency.

That was not so surprising. But he was amazed when the metal of the belts suddenly became much softer. In fact, they felt like stiff cloths.

The orange light went out. The recessed bulb beside it was now glowing a steady green.

Jack said, "You just remembered where the belt button was?"

She nodded.

Again, he wondered who or what had inhibited her against speaking English. Whatever it was, it had not kept her from talking to that honker. If only he had time to learn from her how to communicate in honkerese, he could bypass that inhibition. There he went again . . . if . . . if, painting pictures in his mind.

Suddenly, the savage bumps and drops and rises of the plane increased in frequency and intensity. If it had not been for the belts, he and Tappy would be ricocheting around in the narrow cockpit. Or should it be called a cabin? What was the difference? Being bruised and having bones broken did not depend upon word definitions.

Then the light dimmed, and the lights inside the plane came on. Automatically. Tappy had pushed no buttons.

Straight ahead and very near was the evil-looking black roil of the storm edge. He gripped the wheel so hard that the plane surged ahead. Though he had thought that he had been squeezing with all his strength, he had fooled himself. Just before the plane plunged into the clouds, he remembered reading something long ago: that entering a violent storm in an aircraft was like slamming it into a concrete wall.

That had certainly been exaggerated—somewhat—since the impact did not flatten the plane out. It kept going, though it had shuddered and the altitude indicator showed an alarming loss of height. Rain and darkness enclosed the craft. But, almost immediately, the rain on the windshield evaporated. Yet, the downpour was still almost solid a few inches from the shield. This machine had no visible windshield wipers. Something was keeping the rain from hitting the windshield.

The headlights of the craft were on, but he could not see more than a few feet beyond its nose.

He was still squeezing hard on the wheel and had it pulled far back. Though he was not losing any more altitude, he had not regained that lost when entering the storm.

The mountain peaks! How far below the plane were they?

Lightning exploded nearby. Thunder boomed. Tappy reached over and felt his neck, then lowered her hand to grab his shoulder.

"We'll be fine!" he shouted.

It was within the realm of possibility. But she needed strong encouragement.

So did he.

Soon, embarrassment and discomfort would be added to the danger. He was going to wet his pants.

Maybe there was something to help him in the storage space behind the seats. Like a bottle. Anything. He did not dare to lessen the pressure on the wheel rim. Tappy would have to grope around in there for him.

He told her what he wanted her to do and why. She twisted around in the tight restraint of the belts and felt as far as she could reach. She smiled and then worked away at something. He twisted his neck far enough to see that she was unfastening a belt around a box. The belt came loose when she clicked something on the buckle. Then she managed to bring out with one hand a plastic container.

It was heavy and fell out of her hand before she could grip it with both hands. But it was on the space between them. After feeling it, she found and pressed a button on the box. The lid came open. Inside were stacks of small plastic square containers. And plastic bottles.

The bottle she brought out held a transparent liquid. Water, he hoped. And it was. She unscrewed the cap and tasted it, smiled, then held it out to him. At that instant, the orange liquid inside the altitude indicator shot up. He was pressed against the seat.

An updraft was hurtling the airplane toward the top of the storm.

He released his right hand from the wheel and took the bottle. It had slopped some water out of it, but there was more than enough for him despite his intense thirst.

When he handed the half-empty bottle to her, he said, "Drink it all up! I'll use the bottle then!"

She lifted it to her lips and did not put it down until all the water was gone. She must have been as thirsty as he.

However, using the bottle for its second purpose was not easy. The plane was still bouncing around while going up. There seemed to be up- and downdrafts within the big updraft. Desperate, he managed to relieve himself completely. Never mind what missed the bottle.

Meanwhile, Tappy had been holding down the box, which tended to rise during a vigorous downdraft. She screwed the cap back onto the bottle and placed it in the box. After relocking the box, she struggled to get it back into its place in the storage area. Finally, she did it.

He had no time to thank her. Now a fierce downdraft plunged the machine toward . . . what? He squeezed the wheel rim with all the muscle he could muster. And he pulled the wheel far back, though he wondered if pointing the nose of the craft too high would cause a stall. He hoped not. It seemed to him, however, that the propulsive-levitational power might, pun intended, forestall stalls.

At least, he felt better now. Otherwise, he would not be making a pun, especially such a lousy one.

He had no reason to be freed of some of his fear. At any moment, a downdraft could smash the plane into a peak or the plane might fly head-on into a very high mountain.

A minute later, he was again thoroughly scared. The dazzling white lightning bolts and their ear-ramming explosions increased. They seemed to be in a nest of electrical entities hatching right and left. Tappy squeezed his thigh while the ravening energy transformed the black world into a white one.

Her fingers dug into his flesh when a gigantic round ball, its brightness brain-piercing, appeared in front of them. She could not see it, he supposed, but it must be making some impression on her nervous system.

As they hurtled through it, their flesh seemed to become as clear as spring water. Their bones were dark. Tappy was a moving skeleton beside him, and his hands and arms were Death's own body.

Then the ball was gone. They were again fleshed. But their hairs were standing on end. Her long tresses stood out like straight needles. She looked like the Bride of Frankenstein.

Somewhere behind them, the ball exploded, and the airplane shook. Their hair crackled and then fell back, free of the static electricity.

A moment later, Tappy shook his shoulder. He looked at her pale face. She was obviously distressed about something. He did not think that it had been caused by the ball.

"What is it?"

She was shaking her head and pointing at her forehead. Then she pointed straight ahead, held up her hands, and rotated them. After which she made a circular motion close to her head with her right hand. She looked very puzzled.

"I don't get it," he said.

She reached out and ran her finger along the instrument panel until she located the compass. Holding the tip of her finger on it, she turned her head toward him. With the other hand, she made the circular movement.

He said, "Oh! You mean . . . you don't know now where that place . . . your goal . . . destination is? Where we've been headed since we got here?"

She nodded vigorously and sat back. Now she looked distressed.

"I'm sorry," he said.

That did not help her. Or him. And it was a winner of an understatement.

"It must've been that white-hot ball, that St. Elmo's fire," he said. "That last explosion. It was a huge sphere of electricity discharging. Somehow, it glitched that homing sense, whatever it is that was leading you straight to your destination. I thought that was some sort of psychic power. But it could be electrical—semi-electrical, anyway."

Tears rolled down her cheeks.

"We still have the panel compass," he said. "And maybe your, uh, power, homing sense, will come back soon."

No use telling her that the compass was probably messed up, too. He intended to go by it until he knew that it was malfunctioning.

A half hour later, they shot out of the storm. The late afternoon sun shone unimpeded by clouds and revealed that they were only about two thousand feet above the ground. The mountains were behind them. Ahead was a plain that ran over the horizon. Isolated trees and groves of trees were scattered over it. A river made S-turns across the terrain. The vegetation was much thicker along its banks. Many animals were heading toward or away from the water. The land reminded him of an African veldt except that the grass was a bright green and many of the beasts did not look like Earth fauna.

Not like present-day animals, anyway. Some of them looked like mammals that had roamed Earth many millions of years ago. For instance, an elephantine creature with a long proboscis and four tusks, two turned upward and two downward. Its ears were rather small, though. That must mean that this area did not have a hot African-like climate.

Heading north by the panel compass, Jack flew for another thirty minutes. Meanwhile, he worried about Tappy. She was still weeping. And then there was the fuel supply. Which of the indicators showed how much was left? To take her mind off her loss—if it could be done—he asked her to locate the fuel indicator. She touched an instrument much like the altitude indicator except that the liquid in the tube was a bright green and the symbols alongside it were different.

"Looks as if it's half-full," he said with a cheeriness he did not feel. "We can still go a long way. How about that?"

Despair had been covering her face like a transparent mask. It did not change.

The plain eased into hills which soon arched their backs, like a meow of alarmed cats, to become mini-mountains. Colossal trees seemed to stride over these, trees the lowest branches of which curved downward into the ground, forming enormous Gothic arches.

After an estimated forty miles, the plane put the hills and the great trees behind it. Ahead was another vast plain. Five miles from the edge of the forest was a broad shallow valley. In its center was a very strange phenomenon.

"There's a dark and roughly circular cloud about a half mile across," he told the girl. "Every seven seconds, something in its center glows. Must be very bright to get through that cloud. Can't make its outlines out. Wait a minute! Let me count . . . ah! The glow lasts seven seconds. And there's a camp, a big one, circling the cloud. Tents, huts. Lots of people scattered around. Vehicles parked past the camp, some planes parked beyond them."

He swung the plane back and straightened it out parallel to the edge of the forest.

"We'll land along here someplace and then hide the plane, if we can. I don't want to get any closer. If they're Gaol . . . hope they didn't see us."

As he turned the craft, he had seen men behind some big instruments aimed at the cloud. A small party was entering the cloud. The flash silhouetted the men when they were first enveloped, but, a few seconds later, they were no longer visible.

Tappy's finger touched the side of his face. When he turned his head, he saw her smiling. The despair was gone. She leaned forward, traced a fingertip along the instrument panel, and stopped it at the compass. Her gestures after that, plus her evident joy, told him that they were close to their destination.

He was concentrating on landing, but he said, "Those people there. Are they Gaol?"

He glanced at her. She was drawing the edge of her right hand across her throat. Then she nodded.

"We have to get down and hide the plane," he said. "I hope the camp doesn't have radar equipment. If they do, they'll have spotted us by now. Everybody's attention seemed concentrated on the cloud."

He was also worried that their three pursuers might suddenly appear and see them.

He lowered the window, leaned out, and checked the wheel wells, what would be called fenders if this were a car. The wheels were still within the wells. Okay. If he had to land it on its belly, he would. He asked Tappy about the wheel-lowering control. She did not know where it was.

He took the craft down parallel to the edge of the forest. Except for some bushes here and there, the plain made an excellent landing field. It was not as smooth as a concrete strip, of course, but it would do. He flattened out the angle of descent about ten feet above the ground and slowly eased it down. Then he leaned out through the window again. The wheels fore and aft on the left side were halfway out of the wells. Must be some radar in the plane that automatically activated the wheel-lowering mechanism when it came within a certain distance of the ground.

The front wheels touched a second before the back wheels, which came down with a bang.

"How do I stop this plane?" he said. "Where are the brakes?"

He had released his grip on the inflatable wheel rim, but the vehicle was still going at about five miles an hour. He had to steer around several bushes blocking their path.

Tappy groped along the panel until she touched a slight protuberance, a purple panel glowing with a faint light. She pushed in on it. The panel lost its glow, and the plane slowed down, then stopped. He pressed the panel again and turned the plane into the forest. Somewhere on that panel or maybe on the wheel was a control that would permit him to lessen or increase the speed below five mph. At the moment, he would have to do without it, improvise.

"Can the wings be folded?" he said.

She shrugged.

"Don't know, right?"

The plane taxied between the arches of two trees, its wingtips almost scraping the bark. Then he swung sharply right and went under an arch. When the craft was behind the trunk, unseeable from the forest edge, he pressed the purple panel. The plane rolled about ten more feet before stopping. It was still behind the tree, which had a trunk ten times thicker than that of a California sequoia.

The seat belts hardened and slid back into their recesses.

"Know how to back this thing up?"

Tappy shook her head.

As he got out of the plane, Jack realized how tight and tense he was. His body ached, and his neck muscles were as stiff as a hardcover book. After he got Tappy to knead his neck, he could bend his head without the neck vertebrae cracking. He did the same for her. Then they explored the area, though making sure not to go too far. It would be easy to get lost in this vast shadowy place where the longest line of sight ended at sixty feet.

They drank deeply from a brook, decided not to eat some big juicy-looking red berries on a bush, listened to the screeching pandemonium of the numerous birds above them, and then returned to the plane. They ate from a jar in the storage compartment, a thick pudding colored chocolate brown and tasting like beef mixed with chestnuts.

Tappy then pulled on his arm with one hand as she gestured toward the north with the other.

"I know you want to push on now," he said. "But we can't cross the plain in the daylight. Now . . . you want to get into that cloud, right?"

She nodded vigorously.

"We'd better get some sleep first and fill our bellies, too, before we venture out."

First, though, he put some containers of food and water in a plastic sack he found in a box. He looked for and found a flashlight. He removed most of the stuff in the storage space so that she could curl up on its floor. He would try to rest on the seat she had occupied, his feet on the pilot's seat. But a minute after he had settled into the least uncomfortable position he could find, his eyes opened.

"I just thought of something," he said. "The cabin lights. They come on automatically when it gets dark. The light'll be a beacon for the Gaol. You know how to override the automatic turn-on for them?"

She did not. But, as he reviewed the flight, he remembered a panel light that had been illuminated when the cabin lights had come on as the plane entered the storm. He pressed the inset under the light, and the cabin lights sprang into photonic being. Another pressure, and the lights died.

"That's done," he said. "We can both sleep now."

But, a minute later, he sat up, eyes open.

"Does Malva . . . the Gaol . . . know where you were heading? I mean, do they know the cloud, that flashing light, is where you want to go?"

She had her eyes closed. She sat up, too, and spread out her hands and lifted her shoulders.

She was uncertain about what they knew.

He lay back down.

"Go to sleep, Tappy. I promise not to say anything more until we've had a good long snooze."

It was some time before he drifted off. He could not keep from worrying about Malva setting up a trap for them in the camp. However, he and Tappy would not know about it until they went into the camp. So, let the Fates decide.

That was not a thought to ease his anxiety. Anxiety. A psychological jargon-word for fear.

Finally, he slept. And he dreamed that he was painting one of those gigantic figures that marched along the inner wall of the crater. When he awoke, his neck stiff again, his back aching, he remembered the dream. He thought, That's what I should be doing now. Painting. Not be running scared through a world I never made and never would make. But Earth was also a world I never made and would considerably alter if I'd had anything to do with the Creation.

Take things as they are—you can't do anything about changing its basic structure—and deal with them as best you can.

He got up without disturbing Tappy. As he crawled out, though, he heard her muttering in her sleep.

"Reality is a dream."

Sometimes it's a nightmare, he thought. Once more, he wondered why she could speak English while asleep yet could not do so while awake.

Tappy woke up four hours later. She looked refreshed, though the hard floor must have been uncomfortable. By then, clouds had covered the night sky, and thunder and lightning were playing rough games in the west. A wind had come down hard like a swatter against a fly. Even in the comparatively sheltered forest, it whistled and streamed Tappy's long hair out. All that cheered up Jack. The visibility on the plain would be limited, and the Gaol would be snug in their tents and huts. He hoped. If it would only rain, he and Tappy would not care if they were soaked. That would be one more thing to help them.

He did wish, however, that Tappy could tell him why they were going to that cloud and what awaited them.

They set out across the plain. He carried the radiator in one hand. After walking two miles, leaning a little sideways into the wind, they were in a savage downpour. The cold water made them even more miserable, but it did make them step up their pace.

After what seemed a long while but was not, they were at the rim of the shallow valley. The light from the center of the cloud was still coming on every seven seconds. The cloud itself, otherwise invisible in this darkness, was outlined when the light flashed.

There were lights on in the shelters and strung along paths which led to huts that Jack assumed were latrines. Not a human being was in sight. That did not mean that no sentries were posted. It could be that he just could not see them. But what did the Gaol have to fear? Besides, this camp looked to him more like a scientific expedition than a military base.

On the other hand, what did he know?

The lightning arrived at the camp at the same time he and Tappy got there. The white streaks helped illuminate the camp for them. But it would also help any guards to see the intruders. He waited awhile, crouched on the rim, and surveyed the scene for sentinels. If there were any, they were well hidden.

Finally, he said, "Let's go, Tappy."

They scrambled down the muddy and rock-strewn slope, slipping now and then. He held the radiator high to keep it from getting dirty. However, the rain cleaned their clothes in a short time. Shivering from more than the cold water and wind, they walked across a fairly even ground to the outer rim of the camp. Crouching, they passed between two wind-flapped tents. He held the radiator ready, the pencil in the other hand. Loud voices came from the tents. Lights shone from the little windows. They left these behind, passing, after a quarter mile of sticky mud, several of the huge machines Jack had seen. These stood on towering tripods the ends of which were stuck in the ground. Cables also ran from them to big metal pegs driven at an angle into the earth. Other cables led from them into the darkness toward the camp. Jack assumed that these were power conductors. The machines on top of the tripods resembled giant cameras, but he doubted that they were for photographic purposes.

While lightning screwed through the sky, exploding at a so-far-safe distance from them, and thunder banged maniacally, they crossed about a half mile of plastic covering. That kept them from sinking in the mud.

Then they were dazzled by the light in the center of the cloud, Now closer to the whiteness, they could see more clearly. Its source seemed to be a titanic building. It was, perhaps, not more than five stories high, but its length was at least two thousand feet. They could not be sure about that nor about the roundness of the structure. But Jack got the impression of a Brobdingnagian cylinder. Whether or not one of its ends was pointed, he could not determine.

Jack halted. The light disappeared, though the afterimage of the building lingered for a second or two. He did not wish to go into that cloud, which, now that he was near it, roiled like the storm in the sky and extended pseudopodia and shrank them back into itself.

The light blazed again.

This time, he saw the center thing more clearly. The end on his right was pointed. The main body was rounded.

Tappy had been holding his hand. She moved ahead, pulling him after her. If she was courageous enough to plunge into the cloud, he could not hang back. And she should know what she was doing. Would she penetrate the cloud if she thought they were in danger?

Yes, she would if it held something she desired or thought was worth the risk.

The cloud closed around them. Instantly, the wind ceased. He felt no rain pouring on him. Somehow, the cloud repelled or evaporated it before it got to the ground. But the stuff that enveloped him was oily and sticky. Moreover, after a few steps, he seemed to slow down, to have to push against the cloud. It was as if its essence was a very thin jelly. That must be a delusion, he thought. If the cloud really was thickening, it should make it harder for him to breathe. That did not seem to be happening.

Then he smelled a sickening odor. As he drove on against the ever-thickening element, he was permeated with the stink. It reminded him of rotting beef. If it got worse, he was going to vomit.

Tappy was pulling harder on him as if she were getting impatient with his lagging.

Then she fell, her hand sliding out of his. He could not see until the bright light came back. For seven seconds, he had a good look at her. She had fallen over something. Just before the light went away, leaving him in the greasy darkness, he realized that she had stumbled over a body. It was in the uniform of a Gaol, and it was lying facedown, but its neck and body and arms and legs were swollen.

The source of the stench was the dead man.

He thought, Up in the airplane, I saw men going into the cloud. But I did not see any coming out.

Tappy got up, though he did not know it until her groping hand touched his chest. He reached out and pulled her close. She was trembling.

"What's going on?" he said, holding her close.

She could not answer him, of course. She released herself from his arms, felt along his arm, and gripped his hand again. Then she was leading him into the cloud.

The stink of death was left behind after only a few paces. That cloud must be heavy and keep the molecules of the decaying body from going far. Certainly, the stuff sheathing him was getting denser. He had to push even more against it. His growing nausea, however, was now receding.

I'll bet no Gaol has reached the building or whatever it is, he thought. Why does Tappy think she can succeed? Even if she does have some ability the others lack, she'll have to leave me behind.

And why did that man die? If he could not go ahead, why did he not turn around and come back out of the cloud? What killed him?

Finally, he could not struggle any more. He was winded, and each breath was heavy with oiliness. The stuff seemed to soak into his mouth and nose, his throat, his lungs. He was trapped like a fly in molasses. Panicky, he yanked back on Tappy's hand, but she did not move. Her hand came loose from his. He struggled to take a step backward and found that he could not move his hind foot more than several inches.

If I die, he thought, will my corpse sag slowly, sinking by inches until I finally lie on the ground? Will my body begin decomposing halfway through my slow-motion fall?

Then something touched his chin.

The light, brighter than lightning, returned, and he saw Tappy. She was turned around, had gotten closer to him, and had reached out with a questing finger.

She could move, though her briefly seen face was twisted with effort.

"Go on, Tappy!" he shouted. "You can't help me! Go on!"

He could hear his voice, but it seemed to be inside his head. He doubted that his words got very far from his lips before they were absorbed.

Chapter 5

BUT her touches did not stop. Her hands were on his shoulder, trying to lift him, trying to make him resume walking. She didn't want to go on without him.

He tried again, this time with reason rather than muscle. "Tappy, you have something important to do. You have a destiny. You are the Imago! You must get to where you're going, and you can do it, because you are what you are. But I am only mortal. I can't reach the source of that light. I will die just as that Gaol soldier did. That's how it's meant to be: only you can get through."

He paused, gasping with the effort of shouting through the cloying fog. But he had to convince her. "My job is done. I had to get you safely to this place. Now you must go on. Don't let this effort be in vain! Go and be the Imago! Go! Go!"

But she refused. He knew why: she might be the Imago, but she was also Tappy, the blind, mute girl. She had a crush on him. He, fool that he was, had taken advantage of it, and that had done nothing to abate her love. She had refused to leave him before, and she was refusing now. Reason was no good against adolescent passion.

Which meant that if he gave up, so would she, and it would be for nothing. He had to do something. But what?

Then he thought of the radiator. It had gotten them out of more than one scrape already; could it do so again? But this seemed so farfetched that he couldn't quite say it outright. "The—can it—here?"

But she understood him immediately. She passed her hands along his body until she found the radiator. She brought it up and found a button. He didn't even know which one, only that she put one of his fingers on it.

85

It was worth a try. He aimed the device away from her, turned it on, and pressed that button.

This time a visible beam came from it. Rather, an invisible beam with a visible effect: it dissipated the fog. In its path the fog just seemed to shrivel or melt, giving out a noisome odor, leaving a tunnel of clear air.

Could he go into that tunnel? If it was the fog that held him, then maybe he could. He hauled one leg forward, toward the clear region ahead. The fog resisted, seeming unwilling to give up the limb, but the fog had been weakened, and the leg was able to break through. Then the other leg. The tunnel was narrow here, but broad ahead, in a slowly thickening cone. His feet remained mired, but his legs were now clear, and he was able to duck his head to clear it, too. What a relief, to breathe free again!

He worked his way farther into the tunnel. It was like stepping out of quicksand; now his body was free. The tunnel remained where it had been carved, enabling him to move through it. He looked back, and saw it slowly squeezing together behind him. But that didn't matter. In fact, it might be good, because he didn't want to leave a passage for the Gaol forces to enter.

He aimed the radiator toward the intermittently flashing light. It sliced through the fog, leaving a closing offshoot like the cutoff elbow of a meandering river. When he held the beam in place, the new tunnel broadened and clarified. He wiggled it around enough to enlarge the tunnel at the near end, then turned it off. He didn't want to waste the radiator's power, not knowing how much of a charge it had.

He glanced at Tappy, who was standing beside him. "It's working," he said, his confidence resurging. "On to the light?"

She nodded. "Then follow me." He marched ahead. He did not want that beam touching her!

Soon there was a whiteness that did not dissipate. It was the hard surface of the structure inside the cloud. It glowed blindingly. By its light he saw pseudopodia of cloud extending inward from the round rim of the tunnel, like so many cilia eager to move him along this intestinal tract. He was not comfortable with the image.

Then, abruptly, it was gone. He blinked, trying to adapt his sight to the relative gloom. Now there seemed to be nothing where the building had been!

In seven seconds it was back, blindingly bright again.

"Tappy, there's something strange here."

She merely urged him on, pushing him from behind.

"There's a glowing wall or something, the side of the building, if that's what it is, for seven seconds; that's what makes the light through the cloud. Then it's gone, and I think it's just an empty hole that the thick fog can't fill in, in only seven seconds. But it can't just vanish! It doesn't sink into the ground; it's just here, and then it's gone, and then it's here again." He was watching it do this while he spoke, shielding his eyes from the brightness so that he could see better in the darkness. "It's as if it just ceases to exist, but there's no implosion of air or anything. Tappy, that thing may be dangerous!"

But she kept on pushing. She was not alarmed; rather, she was excited.

"Tappy, do you understand what I'm saying? This thing is big, maybe a third of a mile on a side, and maybe some kind of super-science can make it phase in and out of reality, but I don't want to be standing on its turf when it phases in! We'd both be crushed flat!"

She came up beside him. She pointed ahead, and nodded her head positively and vigorously. She urged him on yet again.

"Okay, Tappy," he said dubiously. "I'll warn you when we're at the edge, because—"

But now she was hurrying ahead by herself, and he had to lumber after her. "Wait! You're going to run right into it! Wait for it to cycle back!"

Too late. Tappy ran across the section where the wall had been. Then the wall returned, and he crashed into it. The surface was diamond-hard, as befitted its brilliance.

Stunned more by the realization of Tappy's fate than by the physical shock, Jack leaned against the wall. Why had she done it? He had warned her!

As the horror deepened, he struck at the brilliant wall, as if to punish it for crushing that innocent child. Yet he condemned himself, too, for not catching her in time. She had misunderstood, she had not heard, she had—

The wall disappeared. He fell into the vacant space, automatically lifting the radiator clear, taking the fall on his shoulder and side. Pain lanced through him; he knew he had suffered an injury. But what did it matter? In a moment he, too, would be squished so flat that nothing showed. For there was no sign at all of Tappy, not even a bloodstain. She had been totally obliterated.

Jack lay flat on his back and waited for the return of the bright building. Somehow this termination seemed fitting.

Then there was light, but this time gentle, in shifting pastel colors. He blinked, trying to align this with his notion of death. Hands were touching him, caressing him; then a face was kissing him.

It was Tappy. She was whole and warm despite her wet nightie and sodden jacket. She was every bit as glad to find him here as he was to find her.

"But—the building!" he protested, holding her close. Again there were two levels of reaction: the sheer relief and wonder of her wholeness, and the mystery of what had happened. His body was reacting emotionally, while his mind was floundering intellectually.

"If I may," a man's voice said.

Jack jumped, looking around. He had somehow assumed that they were alone in the afterlife, or whatever this was. Now he saw a nondescript young man wearing ordinary shirt and slacks, neither of which seemed to fit perfectly. It was as if the manufacturer had had another body style in mind. "Who?" he asked, at a loss.

"I am an agent of the Imago," the man said. "I and my companions exist to foster the well-being and success of this entity. Because the Imago has assumed human form and has brought a human companion and is conversant with your language, we are assuming this form and mode of communication. Because the Imago desires your welfare, we shall treat you responsively."

Jack looked at Tappy, who nodded, feeling his motion. He made as if to stand, and immediately the man and another came to help him up. Two young women appeared, helping Tappy similarly. The women wore blouses and skirts which seemed to have been crafted by the same misguided tailor who had done the men. Their figures seemed good, but their clothing was making a valiant effort to demonstrate otherwise. The colors were all over the place, nothing matching or complementing well.

This simple action did not reassure Jack. The men looked ordinary, but there was a machinelike strength in their bodies, and their flesh was like plastic. He could see that the women, too, were inhumanly powerful, despite their appealing forms.

Jack found himself feeling light-headed, as if he were running without a warm-up and his system was out of whack, hands cold and pulse racing. He had thought Tappy was dead, then thought he would die, too, and suddenly everything seemed all right. He just didn't trust it!

He had a tendency to react inappropriately when caught out of sorts. He did his best to control it. It wasn't just himself involved here; it was Tappy. When he had undertaken to deliver her to the clinic, he had assumed a commitment to get her there safely. As it had turned out, they had gone on a spectacularly strange journey. Maybe this was the true clinic. But maybe it wasn't. He owed it to her to find out.

"Uh, Tappy—these are your friends?" he asked.

She nodded and smiled.

"Is it okay if I find out more about them?"

Tappy nodded again.

Jack turned to the first man. "Are you human?"

"No. I am what you would call an android or machine. We all are."

"An android, as I see it, is an artificial living man. A robot is a machine in humanoid form with a computer for a brain. Which are you?"

"We conform physically more closely to the latter description. But we are sentient in the manner of the former."

"You mean you are conscious? Free-willed? You're not just a program?"

"That is correct."

Certainly it seemed possible, considering what Jack had already seen: a monstrous spaceship that healed itself, and a building that flashed in and out of existence without crushing what was under it. That cycling seemed to have stopped; once the building had taken them in, it remained firm. "Maybe we had better introduce ourselves. I am Jack. This is Tappy, whom you call the Imago. What are your names?"

"We have none, but will answer to whatever you choose to call us, if the Imago agrees."

"Call her Tappy."

The man glanced at Tappy. "Imago?"

Tappy nodded.

"Jack. Tappy. And our names are?"

The urge to be flippant increased. Jack had to yield to it a little, or risk going wrong in some worse manner. Maybe he could get a smile from Tappy, and tide through. It hardly mattered whether these were friends or enemies: it was better for him to hold his cool until he knew for sure.

He decided to do it the simple way: alphabetically. "You are Abraham, Abe for short. He is Bartholomew, Bart for short. Are there any more of you?"

"There are six of us presently animated," Abe said. "Three of each apparent gender."

That meant that they weren't really male and female.

"Then the third male is Coleman, or Cole." Jack turned to the women. "And you are Abigail, or Abbie, and Bridget, Brie, and the one I don't see is Candace, or Candy."

"Thank you," the two females said together.

"You sound just alike," Jack said. "Can you make your voices different, so we can tell you apart by sound as well as sight?"

"Yes," the two said, in different voices.

"Yes," the two men said, similarly.

Tappy smiled.

This was almost too easy; Jack hardly trusted it. "Look, maybe we'd better get changed, and then we can talk. I guess you folk don't have to eat—you have power cells, right?—but you know we do. So—"

"Certainly," Abe said. "Come with us, Jack."

Jack knew he would have no choice if his will opposed theirs. "We'll change, and then Tappy and I will eat together," he said.

They hesitated. Then Tappy nodded, and Abe spoke immediately. "As you wish, Jack."

They took him to a smaller chamber, where he stripped, wincing as he flexed his bruised shoulder. "You are in physical distress, Jack?" Abe inquired.

"I bashed my shoulder coming in. It will heal."

"There is no need to wait." Abe placed both his hands on the shoulder, one on each side. Jack felt a current, and his pain faded.

The man might be a robot, but he had a healing talent! Maybe it was just some kind of electrical anesthetic, but it made life easier for the moment.

Then Jack stepped into what looked like a shower. Suddenly he felt warm and clean. He had had the equivalent of a full shower in half a second, painlessly. He was still marveling as they presented him with clothing similar to their own. He could tell by the feel that it was of alien material, but it felt good and fit him well. In fact, it seemed to adjust itself to his body of its own volition. So why didn't it fit these alien men and women better?

"Uh, before we go back," Jack said. "Is there a—a bathroom? I mean, a place where I can—?"

"Step into the purifier again," Abe said.

Jack stepped in, but didn't see any toilet. Then, suddenly, he had no need for it. Somehow the wastes in his body had been removed. He decided not to protest.

"Um, Abe—you serve Tappy, right?"

"The present form of the Imago, yes."

"And me you help only because she wants it?"

"Yes. It is not ordinary, but her will is our law, literally."

"And you went to the trouble of learning my language and customs, because of her? You really don't care about me otherwise?"

"This is the situation."

"And if she told you to kill me, you would do it?"

"If she were serious."

"And Tappy herself—you would never harm her, or go against her wish?"

"This is approximately true. Were she to desire something harmful to herself, we would decline—"

"Got it. You really are her agents, no matter what."

"This is the situation."

"Thanks."

"It is her will that you be given full information."

Jack was satisfied with that. Since he also wanted what was best for Tappy, there should be no trouble. If these humanoids really were to be trusted.

They returned to the main chamber. There was now a table there, with fairly familiar food on it. Tappy was standing behind a chair, dressed in a clean and well-fitting blouse and skirt, her hair brushed out and tied back by a red ribbon. Only the scar on her face marred her dawning prettiness. That and the slightly unfocused eyes.

"You look wonderful, Tappy," he said.

She broke into a smile, extending her hand to him. He saw that though she was the mistress here, she remained eager for his company and reassurance.

He took her hand and squeezed it. Then they sat down to their meal, catered by Abbie and Brie.

It consisted of a small lettuce and tomato salad, mashed potatoes, and a steak, with a glass of milk on the side. But the lettuce was red, which was possible, and the tomato green, also possible depending on the variety. The milk was brown, which could mean chocolate. The steak was blue.

It was that last that made him conclude that this was not ordinary food after all. It was artificial food, surely with the requisite nutritive elements. But the Agents of the Imago—the AI—evidently had no direct experience with the world Jack had known. That showed in their clothing and in the food. Either they were color-blind, or they had misinterpreted the colors. Tappy could not correct them, because she couldn't see the food.

But it took only a moment for Jack to conclude that he should keep his mouth shut, except for eating. This was his first direct evidence that the AI were fallible. There were things they didn't know. That was reassuring. It also argued for their legitimacy, in a perverse way. They were here to help Tappy, who didn't care about the fit of their clothing or the color of the food, so they didn't pay proper attention to that. They hadn't expected Jack, who could see and who knew, so were caught short. Malva would have put him under a mind-probe or something and gotten the details right even if it burned out his brain. The AI had left his mind alone. He had better encourage them to continue doing that.

Tappy was already eating. He dived into his meal, and the taste was close enough. Probably everything was made from hydroponic soybeans and injected with taste and color, but for all he could tell, the steak was from a dragon. It would do.

For dessert Abbie brought green pumpkin pie, and Brie brought cheese. Jack looked at her, and at the cheese, and stifled a laugh. It wasn't that the cheese was blue, literally; it was the coincidence of the name.

Tappy became aware of his reaction. Her face turned toward him.

"It's nothing," he said. "Just that I named her Brie, and Brie is a variety of cheese."

She smiled. Brie, the seeming woman, did not. She did not seem to be offended; she just did not have emotions, and would not have understood the humor anyway.

And there was another key. These were indeed robots. They might be conscious, and know a lot, but they were not feeling. It seemed that it was not feasible for even this advanced civilization to duplicate a living creature to that extent.

They completed the meal, and the AI brought small hand-held units that blinked by their mouths, making them suddenly clean. No toothbrushes needed here!

Now that he was fed, Jack realized how tired he was. It had been an extremely trying sequence of several days, physically and emotionally. The frenzied trek up the mountain in the night, the crossing through the portal, encounters with the honkers, big dome-ship of the Gaol, the capture and interrogation by Malva, the flight in the airplane, the struggle to get through the cloud, the nullification of volition—he realized that he had had no problem with that since Tappy had had him eat the paper with the symbol on it; he felt free-willed now. But tired.

"Maybe it's time to rest," he said. "If it's okay with you folk." He suspected that they had a lot for Tappy to do, but he was sure she was as tired as he was.

Tappy nodded agreement, and that forestalled whatever the AI might have had in mind. "There are bedrooms," Abe said.

They got up, and Tappy managed to catch his hand. Her fingers clung to his, not letting go. She wanted him with her for what passed for night in this building.

Should he argue the case? On the one hand, he did not want to give the AI the notion that he regarded the Imago as a sex object, so it was better to sleep apart. On the other, he still didn't really trust this situation, and feared that once he separated from Tappy for any length of time, he might not be allowed to get together with her again. The AI could kick him out, and tell her that he had decided to go home. Then there would be no living person to watch out for her interests. Maybe the AI really wanted what was best for the Imago—but what of Tappy? There was a living, feeling girl there who was in some ways just like any other, but in other ways a truly tragic figure. Jack was no psychiatrist, but he honestly felt that in this situation, he was the only one who could truly relate to that girl.

So he went with her to the bedroom they had designated for her. The AI expressed no objection. Abe and Abbie came in to undress them.

"Uh—" Jack began. Then it occurred to him that he valued the things the AI did not know about him, and shouldn't give them away. They didn't know that human beings who chose to share a bedroom did not necessarily have strangers undress them. Let them remain ignorant.

So he let them do it. He was facing away from Tappy, and left it that way. In due course he and Tappy were in pajamas and nightie and in the bed, which was large enough for two. The AI withdrew through the doorway, which seemed to close behind them. The light faded, leaving them in darkness.

Tappy found his hand again and drew it to her. She wanted him closer.

Jack knew he had gone wrong once, but he wasn't going to do it again. Not this way. Tempting though the prospect might be, on one not-quite-secret level. If she was the Imago, she was probably beyond his aspirations. If she was a hurt blind girl, she was underage. Either way, forbidden.

"I am here to help you, Tappy," he murmured. "I think I can help you best just by being near you. Until you achieve your destiny." Then he drew his hand loose, rolled onto his stomach, and tried to sleep.

For a moment he was afraid she would start crying. Then she rolled over, too, toward him, and set her hand on his back. With that contact she seemed to be satisfied. Her breathing became even.

He was relieved. He knew that had she insisted on more, he would in the end have succumbed. He had before. It was not easy doing what he believed was right. But it was best. He could never fully redeem the wrong he had done her, there in the cabin in the Green Mountains of Vermont, so far away in more than one sense. Maybe his recent efforts to get her to wherever she was going represented his need to atone. Meanwhile he could at least avoid making it worse.

He slept, and dreamed, and in one dream he was approaching Tappy, desiring her, and feeling guilty for it. He knew, even asleep, that she was beside him, and it was his duty to leave her alone. But there was that in him that wanted it otherwise.

He knew it was morning, because it was light, and Abe and Abbie were there to get them dressed. Jack felt greatly refreshed; maybe there was something restorative in the air here. He had slept well, and it seemed that Tappy had, too. He was amused to note that the two AI had gotten mixed up again: Abbie was tending to Jack, and Abe to Tappy. An individual's sex was evidently not of great significance to them.

They took turns in the shower, stripping down for it. Jack had managed to avoid looking at Tappy's nude body the night before, but realized that he could not do so now without making more of his human foibles apparent than he cared to. Fortunately he had a reflex that prevented him from having a masculine reaction in public. So he affected neutrality, as he had during the night. Whatever the AI did not know about any aspect of his relationship with Tappy was fine by him.

Her body was and was not what he expected. She was slender,

but not thin; her legs were nicely fleshed, her hips and buttocks rounding into womanhood, and her breasts were well enough formed. Yet neither was she at the adult level. He judged that she was about halfway across her transition from childhood to womanhood, physically. In some countries, as he understood it, a girl was considered to be old enough if she appeared old enough; mere years did not define statutory rape. In such a country, he would have been in trouble anyway.

But there was something else. That intangible glow. She turned her face to him and smiled, fathoming where he stood, and it was as if there were an aura about her. She knew what they had done, and she regretted it not at all. She had in that sense proven herself. Perhaps it had been at that point that she became independent of the need for the leg brace. She had begun to assume command of the situation, to choose her own course. To lead. She had led him to the portal between worlds. The Imago had begun to manifest, and surely it permeated her now. She had power, and knew it, and her growing confidence manifested in a straighter stance, a certainty of acceptance, and a subtle knowing. In a country that judged by attitude, she would be deemed old enough.

When she was dressed, that aura remained. She took his arm, guiding him rather than being guided by him. She squeezed, indicating that she was by no means through with him. Oh, yes, she was changing!

After breakfast it was time for talk. They sat in comfortable chairs in a three-quarter circle. "There is more to clarify, Jack, and it is best if your ignorance is quickly abated," Abe said. "We think you will be more receptive if you learn it in your own manner. Please make the remaining inquiries in your mind."

Jack reminded himself that this was not a living man. He should not react to the seeming condescension. But he was slightly irritated. So he became slightly unreasonable. "I have no remaining inquiries, thank you."

Tappy's face turned to him. Her tongue was between her teeth, as if she needed to bite it. She was amused.

"Surely you do, Jack," Bart said, neither amused nor annoyed.

"You folk are interchangeable?" Jack inquired, now playing to his audience of one living person. "You alternate on sentences?"

"Yes, if you wish," Abe said.

"What about the missing two? Why haven't we seen Cole or Candy?"

"They have been at work on maintenance. But you need have

no concern; their responses would be identical to ours."

This was getting nowhere. Jack knew he was being unreasonable. Therefore he became more so. "Maybe I'd rather judge that for myself." He stood. "I'll go find Candy."

Abe looked at Tappy. She tittered. It was the first truly human sound he remembered hearing from her. Abruptly his unreasonableness took another turn. "You're here to serve the Imago, right? Well, you can serve her best by removing the block that stops her from talking to me in my language. You can do that, can't you?"

"We can," Abe agreed. "But—"

"Then get on it!" Jack snapped. "Then *she* can ask the questions. Let me know when she's ready." He strode from the chamber.

No one followed. Probably Tappy had indicated no, and she herself had been intrigued by the notion of being able to talk again. He had half expected Tappy to try to come with him, to plead silently with him, but she had not. It was a sign of her new confidence that she knew he was making a deliberate scene, and apparently she was enjoying it. Maybe the emotionless AI manikins annoyed her, too, but because they served her, she could not make an issue of it.

But now he was stuck wandering around the building without a guide. He had no idea where he was going. So he was making pretty much of a fool of himself. But he was stuck on his course. He kept walking, striding down the hall he found himself in.

He came to some sort of central square, except that it was round. Halls radiated out to the four directions, and there were shafts going up and down. He was walking so fast that he was stepping into the pit below before he realized. But he didn't fall. He just floated across the center, as if he weighed nothing, his inertia carrying him on to the far side.

Antigravity? Well, why not! They seemed to have everything else.

He decided to explore the shaft above. He turned and jumped. If there really was no gravity here, he should be able to sail right up to the top.

Instead he found himself angling toward the far wall of the shaft. He twisted as well as he could before crashing into it, managing to get a foot out to break his fall. But instead of rebounding back into the center, he found himself catching his balance and straightening up. The wall was now his floor.

He looked back. There was the center, with its radiating halls. Now the one he was in seemed level, and the one he had come from seemed vertical.

Jack shook his head. Live and learn! He resumed his walk, going toward what might or might not be the top of the building. There did seem to be light at the end of the passage.

It turned out to be an opaque but glowing wall. Or floor. When he came to it, his orientation shifted again, and now he was walking on it. Its surface seemed slightly curved, so that he could not see the full length of the new passages, which extended in four directions from the mergence. This was like the center square, only one hall was missing: the one which would have led on through the wall and outside, perhaps.

"Where do I go from here?" he asked himself aloud. He realized that he could fairly readily get lost, and make an even bigger fool of himself than so far. Maybe that was why the AI had let him go: they were waiting for him to give up and accept their way of doing things. Passive persuasion.

A woman appeared before him. "May I assist you, Jack?"

Startled, he stared at her. She was definitely not one of the ones he had seen before. Abbie and Brie were female but conservatively so, really not much more developed than Tappy herself. This one was comparatively voluptuous, with an orange dress that showed the rounded upper contours of her breasts somewhat more than would have been the case had the fit been perfect. Her dark hair swirled about her face and shoulders cohesively, lending additional sex appeal.

"I have two questions. Three. Four."

"I am at your service, Jack."

"You are one of them? An AI?"

"Yes, Jack."

"Then you must be Candy."

"Yes."

"How did you appear so suddenly?"

"I stepped through the panel." She demonstrated by stepping back. Her body disappeared, first the front side, then the back side. Then her face reappeared, framed by darkness. "It is an opaque screen. You may enter, if you wish." Her face disappeared again.

Jack put out one hand. It passed through the opacity and disappeared. "Oh—like the rock!"

"Like a portal, yes," Candy agreed. She was standing in the

chamber, which was like another bedroom. Now he was, too. "And your fourth question?"

"Why are you so different from the others?"

"We established four of us as the original complement, of a neutral type, to serve the Imago and her companion. We were not certain what was in order, so withheld two pending further information. Our research indicated that your species is highly sexual, and since you did not indulge with Tappy, we crafted my form to be more mature. You may relieve your sexual frustration with me, if you wish."

So he and Tappy had been watched. Somehow he had known that would be the case. The AI intended to protect the Imago, and for all they knew, he could be dangerous to her.

"I'm not sexually frustrated," he said shortly.

"Then I apologize for our misunderstanding. When your copulatory member became rigid in the night—"

"That's normal!" They had observed, all right! He had forgotten the dream, but now it came back. He hoped they had not been able to see into his mind then.

"We did not know," Candy said. "Your particular species has not come often to our attention. I can assume a less provocative shape."

"You can do that? Just change your shape?"

"Do you wish me to demonstrate this?"

Suddenly he believed it. "No. Keep your present form. I like it." And maybe, he realized, he should take her up on her offer, so as not to be further tempted by Tappy. Candy might be a robot, but he suspected that she would feel exactly like the most cooperative of women, and she surely knew what she was doing. In that sense, she was adult, regardless of her technical age.

"I will show you more of my body, since you like it," she said, her hand going to her dress.

"No!" For suddenly he realized that this, too, would be wrong. She was a machine, possessing no emotion, so it would inevitably be fake, not real. A cross between sex and masturbation. And to whatever extent it was real, it would be a betrayal of Tappy.

"I apologize for disturbing you. I will conform precisely to your expectation, if you will advise me what—"

"It's not that. It's—" But again, he did not want to tell her, knowing that in reality she was a neuter machine. "Just how old are you, anyway?"

"In your terms, approximately one hundred thousand years."

Jack tried to keep his jaw from dropping, and half succeeded. He had assumed she had been constructed within the past year or so. "You've been—a beautiful woman—from before the time there *were* human women?"

"No, Jack," she said, unsmiling. "I am not human. I have served the Imago in the shape of whatever species the Imago has chosen as host. As have we all. We are long conversant with the Imago, but not with your species."

"But with your fancy building right here on this world near Earth, you must have—I mean, even the minions of the Gaol are human here!"

She paused just an instant. "I think it is essential that your ignorance be swiftly abated, as Abe advised you. But it is apparent that we are not evoking your cooperation. Please advise me of the manner best to approach you, so that you will be receptive."

Jack stared at her. "You really want to know?"

"Yes, Jack."

"Why?"

"Because the Imago is presently in a human host. She is therefore subject to the idiosyncrasies of the human nature. If we learn from you what those are, we shall be better able to work with her."

"Oh, so it's her you care about, not me!"

"Yes, Jack."

Actually they had never pretended otherwise. He was here on sufferance, because Tappy had brought him, and they treated him courteously, by their definitions, because she wanted them to. They were not evil, merely ignorant of the human nuances. Their very mistakes with him demonstrated the truth of that.

Had these been secret agents of the Gaol, they would have approached him in either a more deceptive or more forbidding manner. Malva had alternately enticed and threatened him. It had all been bluff, but it showed the way she worked. These AI had done neither. Well, Candy had offered him sex, but had done it so clumsily that it was obvious that she knew next to nothing about the emotional aspects of it. That wasn't surprising in creatures who had no emotions.

The conviction was growing that the AI were the genuine article, and that he really ought to cooperate with them. But he needed something more.

"You are all in mental contact with each other?" he asked. "When I talk to Abe, it's the same as talking with you, even if you're not there, and vice versa? Whatever I do with you is the same as doing it with him?"

"Yes, Jack."

"So if I had decided to have sex with you, it might as well have been with him?"

"Yes, Jack. He would have formed an orifice—"

"Give me one decisive reason to cooperate with you."

"We exist to forward the purpose of the Imago."

Jack stared at her. "That's it?"

"Yes, Jack."

They remained at cross-purposes. He pondered a moment. "Suppose I said I would cooperate if you ripped off one of your arms and threw it away?"

She put her right hand on her left elbow and made a contortion. The left arm came out of its shoulder socket, dangling tentacular threads. She threw it to the floor.

"That was just a question!" Jack exclaimed, appalled. "I didn't mean it literally!"

"I apologize for misunderstanding, Jack."

He stooped to pick up the arm. It remained warm and soft. No bone projected from the torn end, just a hard plastic surface. "Doesn't it hurt?"

"We do not experience pain."

"But it's a shame to waste such a finely crafted limb! Now you can't use it."

The fingers on it flexed. "I can use it, Jack. It merely lacks anchorage."

He handed her the arm. "Put it back on, then."

She took it by the elbow again and pushed the end into the gaping shoulder socket. The shreds of plastic melted and flowed, sealing over the injury. "It will not be at full strength immediately, but it will serve," she said.

"Okay, I'll cooperate until I find reason not to," he decided. "Not because I know anything about the Imago, but because I care for Tappy."

"Tell me how to avoid antagonizing you, so that you will not find reason not to cooperate with us."

"For one thing, stop this damned condescension!"

"I do not understand, Jack."

"You keep treating me like a feelingless object."

"Yes. Does this disturb you?"

"Yes, it does! And it will disturb Tappy, too. In fact, that could be why she wants me here: because at least I understand her feelings, somewhat."

"But we are feelingless objects ourselves."

"Then how the hell did you manage to serve the Imago in its other hosts? Weren't they all living creatures?"

"We were more conversant with their nuances, and had competent input. They were in the Galactic Registry."

"And my species is not?"

"It will be added, Jack, now that the Imago—"

"Yes, I see. The Imago must have chosen it because it was a primitive backwater species no one would suspect of harboring such a significant entity."

"That is a likely conjecture."

"So you were caught short this time."

"Yes. If you will tell me what I am doing wrong, I will correct it immediately."

"Just like that," he said with irony.

"Yes, Jack."

"Okay, I'll make you a deal. You show me around this place and tell me what I need to know, and I'll tell you how not to antagonize me while you're doing it."

"This is what we asked of you at the outset of our association."

"First lesson: never say 'I told you so.' "

They walked through the door-portal, and she showed him around. They talked, and he pointed out the nuances of human interaction as she ran afoul of them, beginning with the ill-fit of her dress. She became both more human and more attractive at a rate that was alarming in its implication.

He looked at the brightness of the outer hall. "What's beyond this?" At her gesture, the white wall-floor became transparent, and they could see outside.

Jack stared. It was a blaze of light from a seemingly infinite number of sources. "Those—those are stars!" he exclaimed. "But so many, so close!"

"We are in a globular cluster of stars, orbiting the galactic center. Because this cluster is outside the plane of the galactic ecliptic, it will be among the last to be drawn into the black hole."

"So you won't have to move and rebuild soon?" he asked, still stunned by the change.

"No, that is of no immediate concern, as is anything beyond

a few billion years. But it represents another backward region, of little interest to the Gaol, so they are unlikely to search here soon."

"Backwater species, backwater cluster," he agreed. "It does make sense. But how did we come here? This building was in a cloud on the honkers' world!"

"This is not a building, Jack. It is a mobile city. To fetch the Imago, we rendezvoused intermittently at the designated spot and broadcast our signal. When the Imago came, we ceased the shuttling and settled at the primary location."

"Let me see if I have this straight," he said, staring at the amazing sky. "When Tappy came through the portal to the world of the honkers, you picked her up on your instruments, and sent your city: seven seconds there, seven away. Tappy could tune in on your signal, but so could the Gaol, so it was a race. The Gaol tried to get to the city and destroy it, but couldn't, so they tried to intercept Tappy instead. But the honkers helped her avoid the minions of the Gaol, and to get away from them when they did capture her. It was a close call, even so."

Candy smiled, a thing she had not done before he advised her about things like that. "You have a marvelous understanding of the situation, Jack!"

"Just how far is this from the honker planet? And how far was that from Earth?"

"This is about fifty thousand light-years from the honkers, and that planet is about one thousand light-years from Earth. The planetary portals cannot retain their tuning long, so are normally established for short ranges."

Jack shook his head. "So this is a spaceship, really!"

"I think it does not match your concept, Jack. A ship of space can travel where it chooses. A city must be carefully programmed and routed. This one is able to travel only from here to the realm of the Imago's concealment. Now that it has vacated that world, it will not be feasible to return there; the Gaol will prevent it."

He could appreciate the determination of the Gaol! "So they are searching for us now. Will they follow us here?"

"They can not trace an intermittent phase-state. That is why we used it, and have used it in prior millennia. They will have to spread their net again, narrowing down the possible regions of the galaxy where we might be. Their efficiency has been increasing in recent centuries, and we may have no more than a year to complete the training of the Imago. This is why we require your help."

"A year? How long does training usually take?"

"Seven years—the full term of the ripening of the Chrysalis. Because the Gaol were unusually alert this time, the Chrysalis had to be hidden instead. This makes it difficult."

That was surely an understatement. They had to squeeze seven years into one, and work with a life-form they understood only imperfectly. It would be about as easy to teach a dolphin to speak Greek. But with the help of another dolphin who understood their purpose, and was friendly with the one they had to train, maybe it was possible.

, They walked on around the outer wall of the city, gazing out of the floor. The ground came into view, seeming to be like a vertical wall; the gravity inside the city related to the city, not the planet outside. A glassy covering extended over the region surrounding the bright shell, and through it Jack could see what appeared to be exotic foliage.

"Is that a greenhouse?" he asked. "Where you grow the soybeans?"

"Please clarify your reference."

"You're feeding us reconstituted things, or adapted from something you grow. I'm sure it isn't what it appears to be, because this isn't Earth. We do a lot with a plant called the soybean, and maybe other plants, too."

She smiled. "Why, yes, Jack, you are most perceptive." Despite his knowledge that she was following a script which he himself had just revised, he found himself warming to her. He liked being flattered by a beautiful woman.

"Let's go down there."

She shook her head. "No, Jack. That would not be wise."

"Why not? Those plants aren't going to eat me, are they?"

"Not physically. But they are of rather special breeds, capable of adapting rapidly to unusual conditions, such as the light of thousands of suns, and of producing particular nutrients as required. They are responsible for the air you are able to breathe, which is poisonous to most creatures of the galaxy, and they refine your essential fluid, water. We select those aspects of their production which are appropriate. There are other aspects which are not appropriate."

More was falling into place. The planet of the honkers was similar to Earth in its atmosphere and gravity, so human beings had been able to colonize it. How they had come there—well, he could ask, and would surely receive an answer, but he preferred to wait and find out for himself. So the Gaol recruited human minions to serve in that region, and perhaps elsewhere, but humans were no more significant than goldfish in a bowl. Except that this time the Imago had chosen a goldfish as host. What a kettle that was!

"Just what would happen to me if I went among those plants?" he asked.

"Physically you would not suffer; the plants have been attuned to your biology. But your mind and emotion might be affected by their pheromones. We have no direct information, but our references suggest that your perception of reality could be distorted, changing your nature significantly."

Reality is a dream. Jack remembered those sleep-talking words of Tappy's. Did they relate?

He turned away from the scene as if losing interest. "I note you have control of gravity here."

"Yes."

"How is it that you have such high-tech features, yet have to hide from the Gaol?"

"The Gaol are conquerors. We are not. We lack emotions, therefore have no desire for aggrandizement. We exist only to serve the Imago."

"But you are machines! Some living species must have made you. What happened to those folk?"

"I know of no such species."

"You're saying that you robots evolved on your own?"

"I have no knowledge of this."

Jack dropped the subject, but filed it away in his "unfinished" mental compartment.

They continued walking. Then Candy paused as if startled. "Jack, we have learned that the Gaol are quartering the galaxy, and will locate us sooner than we anticipated. We shall have to accelerate our program. Your cooperation is essential, because Tappy knows and trusts you. But we of the AI do not know or trust you well enough to risk the Imago with you. Will you allow us to survey you?"

"You've been risking Tappy with me all along!" Jack exclaimed. "Last night—"

"No. You were monitored, Jack, as you know. Had you sought to bring her to harm of physical, mental, or emotional nature, we would have interdicted it. Now we must allow you greater access to her, for you relate to her in a way we do not."

"I'm human," he said wryly.

"That is true. You also have a relationship with her that has greater leverage than we can muster at the moment. We had hoped to learn the human ways, and relate to her, so as to train her adequately in the time available. But now we must work through you more directly."

"What happens if she isn't properly trained?"

"This much we have learned of your recent culture: you have a weapon called a gun?"

"Yes, we have guns," he said, scowling. "So do the Gaol. If you expect me to use a gun—"

"No. But if one were to place a gun in the hand of a small child—"

"The power of the Imago—it's like that? Dangerous?"

"The analogy is imperfect. But in degree, it is like a gun capable of causing a planet to rupture. I think you can not at present appreciate the actual nature of the power of the Imago. Perhaps gun is not the appropriate term. Perhaps grenade, or detonator—"

"I'm getting the gist. That girl is dangerous."

"Only if her power is improperly used. But with appropriate direction, it means the salvation of galactic culture. It is essential that its proper potential be realized."

"So you want to use me to make Tappy do something. I'm not sure I care to be used."

She turned to him, taking him by the arm, staring into his face. Now she was animated, and startlingly pretty. "Jack, we *need* you! I beg of you: help us."

How well she had learned! Every inflection was right, every aspect of her facial and bodily expression. Her hair was tumbled back, her bosom was heaving, her eyes were wide. On top of that, he believed her: the AI were now desperate. There was no way he could turn down her plea without feeling like a heel.

"What does this 'survey' entail?"

"We will put you in a chamber and question you. Your responses will be analyzed. By this we shall know whether it is appropriate to place the Imago in your charge."

"My charge! Tappy's a person! She should be free to make her own decisions."

"Tappy is a person," she agreed. "The Imago is not. If I may return to my crude analogy, the Imago is like the gun in her hand. You must tell her how it is to be used. When we are sure that your judgment and motive are suitable."

"So that she won't turn that gun on you?"

"That is not our concern. If the Imago were to desire our destruction, we would destroy ourselves. But we can not allow the Imago to be misdirected."

They had a point. "Okay. Survey me."

"Here." She led the way into the closest step-through panel. Was it coincidence that they were right here, or could any chamber serve? He decided that the chambers were as interchangeable as the AI themselves were.

Then Candy was gone. Jack stood alone in what appeared to be a rocky desert. But the rocks were giant crystals, and the sand was confetti, and the sky was purple. Evidently the AI notion of an Earthly landscape.

Had you your desire, what would it be?

"You mean, apart from Tappy's welfare?" he asked.

Without qualification.

"Well, first I'd see that Tappy was okay. In fact, I'd like to see her cured of everything that ails her. I want her to see again, and be happy—

Do not speak. Imagine.

Imagine? "Maybe I could paint it," he said. "If I had my paints."

Paint.

He pretended he had a brush, palette, and canvas set up on an easel. He touched his brush to blue, and made a sweep to paint the sky blue.

The blue appeared. He moved his hand farther, and the blue spread accordingly. Then he let his hand drop and just pictured it—and abruptly the entire sky was blue instead of purple. "Like a computer painting program!" he exclaimed.

Clarify your reference.

He ran through the mechanism of computer painting in his mind. There was agreement: this was somewhat like that.

Then he really got into it. He painted a picture of Tappy, not as she was now, but as she would be if he had his wish. She stood before him in a green dress with a yellow sash, her hair tied back with a matching yellow ribbon but nevertheless falling to her waist. Her face was without blemish; the scar was gone.

Her eyes focused on him. "Jack, I see you!" she exclaimed. "I'm happy!" She made a pirouette, her skirt flaring, showing her legs to the knees, no brace.

And for yourself?

Jack was at a loss. He discovered that his original ambition of being a successful commercial painter had left him. That would require returning to Earth alone and rejoining its culture. "How can you send them back to the farm, after they've seen Paree?" he asked, repeating an imperfectly remembered quote. He had not seen the best of what the galactic society had to offer; in fact, he had seen mostly pursuit and oddity and ugliness. But behind it lay the amazing technology of the advanced cultures, and now all he wanted to do was know more of it. No, that wasn't all, but somehow he was unable to settle on the rest.

"I don't know," he said.

The chamber became ordinary again. Candy stood where she had been; apparently she had never left. "Thank you, Jack," she said.

He smiled ruefully. "I guess I washed out on that one! My mind just went blank."

"No, Jack, you provided us with the information we required. We now trust you."

"But you didn't learn anything about me! I couldn't answer the simplest question about the nature of my ambition."

"You have no selfish motive."

"Sure I have selfish motives! I just wasn't able to define them. I mean, there's so much here that I want to learn about, only I have no way, and I know I don't belong here, but I don't want to go back—what a mess!"

"Jack, if I had emotion, I believe I would like you." She took him by the elbow, guiding him from the chamber.

It opened immediately on the larger room where he had eaten with Tappy, but she was no longer there. He was suddenly nervous. "Tappy—where is she? You haven't isolated her while you were distracting me, have you? I tell you, all bets are off, if—"

"She will join you in a moment," Candy said. "Now we have important material to impart. Which of us would you prefer to do this?"

"All of you!" he snapped. "Something's up; I know it. If you want my cooperation, bring Tappy here now."

The other AI appeared, stepping together through the opaque panels around the room. Their clothing now fit perfectly. One man was unfamiliar; that would be Cole. "In a moment," they said in unison. "First we must acquaint you with the situation."

"Oh, for God's sake! I didn't mean it literally! Abe, you be the spokesman. The rest of you just settle back and twiddle your thumbs or something. What's going on?"

Abe stepped forward. The other five stepped back, putting their thumbs together. Jack's annoyed glance stopped that: they were coming to understand about non-literal.

"The Gaol will isolate this retreat in as little as three days," Abe said.

"Three days! Candy said the Gaol were coming sooner than you expected, but three days? How did that happen?"

"We surmise that they located this site in the globular cluster during a prior quest for the Imago, several centuries ago, and retained awareness of it. There are a limited number of suitable planets in such clusters. In this manner they are able to check potential locations much more rapidly than is possible in a routine quartering. This puts us in an extreme situation."

"Extreme isn't exactly the word! You need seven years, you were going to cram it in in one year, and now three days? I don't know much about how you operate, but that seems pretty chancy to me."

"You have understated the case," Abe said.

"Sometimes I do that, too. Or do you mean there is more I don't know?"

"Yes. We have treated Tappy in the manner you desired, with her acquiescence, but without complete success."

Jack felt an ugly thrill of apprehension. "All I said was to null that mental block that stops her from speaking English! You mean she can only speak some words?" He knew it was more than that.

"We also eliminated her physical deformities," Abe said. "She now has no weakness of limb, and should be able to see normally."

"You cured her blindness?" This was more than he had hoped for.

"It is your desire," Abe said. "You wish her to see and speak and dance. When we made her aware of that, she acquiesced, and we proceeded."

"My survey! You told her what I imagined?"

"She wished to know. She had supposed that you might prefer her unchanged. Learning otherwise, she chose to change."

"Of course I want her to see!" Jack said. "I want everything that is best for her. But I didn't know it could be done. What's this about your not succeeding? What happened to her?"

"We eliminated her physical defects. But this does not appear to be sufficient. She can see and speak, but she does not. We suspect that despite her acquiescence to your will, she lacks motivation to do these things."

Jack thought about that. There had been a hint back on Earth that Tappy might be able to do more, but didn't try. He could understand that; her case had been hopeless. But she had come alive with him, in more than one sense. Now she should be eager to see everything, and to talk about it. What was holding her back?

"Once the Imago is ready," Jack said slowly, "what then? I mean, what does Tappy do?"

"She will serve the Imago implicitly, as do we."

"Will she have any time to herself? Any social life? Will she get to read any books, or splash in the ocean, or sleep an hour late?"

"Such things are meaningless to the Imago."

"Well, then, I think I have a glimmering of what you don't. I can see why she might hesitate just to step into this role."

"Please explain this to us."

"Tappy wants to *live*!" he exclaimed. "She's not a robot! She's had so little joy of life, and now maybe she has a chance—and she'll have to throw it all away and get into harness as the Imago. No chance at all to be a child or a girl, just to change from one kind of freak to another. No wonder she's afraid to move ahead!"

"It is true that we do not understand the urges of human life," Abe said. "Either in their acceptance or their denial." He glanced at Candy, and Jack realized that none of them understood why he had not simply made sexual use of the woman when she suggested it. Maybe other galactic creatures had no hang-ups about that sort of thing. "However, the Imago may do as she desires. Nothing is denied her. She may splash in water or gaze at a text if she wishes."

"But she won't want to, you said."

"Past manifestations of the Imago have not had incidental interests of the flesh."

"Because you had seven years to train them," Jack said. "There was no place for such things in your curriculum."

"True. What is your point?"

Jack took a deep breath. "You are right. I really do understand Tappy in a way that you don't."

"Therefore it may be possible to make the Imago functional in the current host, with your help, despite the extreme brevity of training. This is what we ask of you."

"You want me to talk Tappy into seeing and talking, so you know she is 'functional,' so she can step right into harness now as the Imago."

"Yes. And thereafter, you must serve as her immediate adviser, so that she does not misuse the power of the Imago."

"And you don't care how I do it. I can talk to her, have sex with her, anything, just so long as she snaps to."

"Yes."

"And you will be advising me what to advise her, so that my own ignorance doesn't mess things up."

"True."

"How do you know I will do what you advise?"

"That was ascertained in the survey."

Jack was gaining respect for that survey. It hadn't seemed like much, but obviously they had fathomed his motives. If he agreed to the deal, he would honor it.

"And why do you figure she'll do what I tell her to?"

"Because she loves you. This is a phenomenon we understand no better than we do the source of the power of the Imago, but we have seen its effect. She is immediately responsive to your will."

"But *I* don't love *her*!"

"Therefore you are objective. This is appropriate."

Jack ground his teeth. "Why don't you take a flying fuck at the nearest sun?"

"This is a rhetorical question?"

"This is a nonrhetorical no. I won't do that to Tappy."

Abe paused only that fraction of a second that passed for machine confusion. "Why?"

"Because it isn't fair to Tappy. She may be the host for the Imago, but she deserves some joy of life, and I refuse to be the one who denies that to her. Especially I refuse to toy further with her emotions. She never did deserve that."

"It is concern for her larger welfare that motivates you?"

"Yes. Want to verify it in your survey chamber?"

"No. We accept this. But we must remind you that Tappy's

alternatives and ours are limited. We believe that the course we ask of you is best in the circumstance."

"Maybe you'd better spell out those alternatives for me."

"The first we have described: you will work with her, under our guidance, in this manner circumventing the training we are unable to provide."

"Got it."

"The second is to delay until the Gaol arrive and capture her. The seven of us will then be destroyed, and Tappy will be cocooned for the duration of her human life, allowed neither freedom nor death."

"God, no! I heard about that. No way."

"The third is the easiest and perhaps best, but we suspect you will object to it also."

"Maybe. Let's have it." He figured he had them on the run now.

"To destroy the host immediately, freeing the Imago for a future host who may have better prospects."

Then Jack knew he had lost his ploy. Of course that made sense! They served the Imago, not the host. They did have an easy way out. But it was impossible for him. Tappy had to live!

"You win. I will cooperate in the first course."

"We thought you would. However, your reactions have been irregular."

"But I have a condition."

"Is this something that will facilitate your effort?"

"I think so. You have told me the bleak alternatives. Now I'm telling you that you can't treat Tappy like a machine. You want me to make her do things which she fears will make her independent of me. That's the one kind of thing she *won't* do for me: help me get rid of her. Not if she knows what she's doing."

"We do not follow your logic."

"You don't have to. Just take my word for it. If I have to do your dirt, it has to be my way."

"What is your way?"

"Put us in your greenhouse."

Again that pause. "If this is not effective, we shall have to destroy both of you before the Gaol arrive."

They were machines. They did not bluff. He was putting his life on the line, and Tappy's. "Just don't jump the gun, okay?"

"You are asking us not to act prematurely?"

"Yes."

"Then we shall do it your way. When she is able to see you and talk to you, you must emerge from the garden. Then we will know that the two of you are ready."

Jack nerved himself, and gave himself no time to waver. "Then get on with it. Where's Tappy?"

The room widened. There stood Tappy, in the green dress and yellow sash he had imagined during the survey, with the matching ribbon. She was unscarred, and her feet were in yellow slippers, without trace of any leg brace. Her body seemed to have filled out somewhat, though that could have been the enhancement of the dress. There was an intangible glow about her, which could have been the animation of the strengthening Imago, or of the love they said she felt for him, Jack. She was, to his eyes, at once young and vulnerable and in need of protection, and absolutely beautiful in her own right.

Then he saw that she held a book in her hand. That would be *The Little Prince*. He felt like laughing and crying, without being quite sure why.

"Tappy," he said.

She turned toward the sound of his voice, smiling. In her face was sheer adoration. But that was not what shocked him.

It was that both he and the AI had seriously misjudged the situation in one vital respect. There was no chance of his deceiving or betraying Tappy. He would never do that. It was that his objectivity, which they depended on, was threatened.

He was in the process of falling in love with her.

Then the chamber faded, and strange vegetation appeared around them. They were in the garden.

Chapter 6

THE three-day garden, Jack thought.

The many-colored wonder around him, the exotic plants and queer insects, the multitude of birdsongs would, under other circumstances, have thrilled him. He would have run from this fascinating growth to that fascinating growth and dragged Tappy behind him while he chattered away, describing everything he saw, moving her hand so that she could feel the trunks and leaves and fruits and berries, all of them strange and delightful.

Not now. All he could think of was the time limit they had. Three days. He had to perform a miracle before they had passed. And he was no god. God, he was no god!

The flaming colors and the varied shapes he saw did not blaze loveliness and form beauty. They imaged forth despair.

He closed his eyes to shut out the garden. He needed to think without distractions. A human in an unfamiliar place tended to think unfamiliar thoughts. It did not slide along the old groove; it lacked the oil of the accustomed; it halted because of the friction of the strange. True, the unfamiliar would, in time, become the familiar. But time was what he did not have.

He felt Tappy's left hand touch his right shoulder, move down his arm, find his right hand, and slip hers into his. It was as if the correct key had been inserted into the correct lock. But, for some reason, the key could not turn.

He said, "It'll be all right, Tappy. We'll make it."

He opened his eyes. She was standing by his side, her head turned to look at him. Look? She could not see. If he did not find a way soon to restore her vision, both of them would be dead and forever sightless. That thought soared like a silent scream from the garden and drilled into the sky.

He was close to breaking down.

Become at ease with the surroundings, he told himself. Then you can think straight, whatever pressure you might be under. Maybe.

The sky was blue, and the sun, now straight overhead, looked like Earth's. It could be real or it could be an illusion made by the AI. It made no difference. It was a clock. When it was at the zenith for the fourth time, it would mark the end of the third day.

Oh, Time! Run slowly! Flow no faster than a glacier!

Still holding Tappy's hand, he turned toward her. She was smiling as if she knew something he did not. He was going to ask her if she really did when he saw something out of the corner of his eye. He switched hands and kept on turning. The object was a huge tent that looked like one of those he'd seen in Arabian Nights movies. Caliph Haroun al-Rashid's or Aladdin's. It was scarlet with strange green, yellow, black, and white symbols on it, with a wide entrance over which sheer drapes fell, with symbol-bearing flags fluttering in a light breeze. He led Tappy into its cool interior. The ground was covered with very thick Oriental-type rugs displaying abstract designs. Six rooms were within, gauzy drapes forming their walls. In the center of the entrance room was a marble fountain with running water. A faint quite-pleasant musky odor was everywhere.

He found a table large enough for six diners. On it were many covered dishes and silver cups and cutlery. In two other rooms were beds suspended from the overhead poles. One room contained a washbowl, a bathtub, and a toilet. Plenty of towels, washrags, soap, toothbrushes, toothpaste, and toilet paper. Everything, in fact, including cosmetics, that they could possibly need. Much more than they could use in three days.

"Maybe we'll have guests," he murmured.

Since neither was hungry, they went back outside. He was silent for a long while as they walked through the garden. He led her by the hand, but, often, she stopped when her free hand felt something interesting. Then she caressed it until she had the shape and texture and odor of the tree bole or flower or bush branch or berry in her mind.

Once, while she was doing that, he said, "You're like one of the four blind men who felt the elephant. You can feel a part of the elephant, so you think you know how all of it looks."

He paused for emphasis.

"But! But if you could see, you would know what an elephant really looks like! And if you could talk, you could describe how the elephant looks to those who can't see."

She frowned with puzzlement.

He said, "So, okay, you haven't heard that story."

He told her the ancient Arabian tale of the four blind men who had, for the first time in their life, a chance to feel an elephant. When asked what it "looked" like to them, each gave a different answer. The man who'd felt the tail said the elephant was like a rope. The second, having fingered the trunk, said the beast resembled a large snake. The third groped around a leg and reported that the elephant was undoubtedly shaped like a living hairy monolith, was, in fact, a very tall uniped. The fourth felt a tusk and said that the beast was more like a hard-shelled fish than anything else.

"I may not remember that grade-school story very well," Jack said. "But it was something like that. You get the idea. Feeling and hearing aren't enough. You can't get the whole picture, the true picture, of the world unless you can see."

He waited for a reaction. She was expressionless for a minute or so while they stood there. Then her face became sad, and a tear oozed from her left eye. She gestured with her free hand as if she were signaling hopelessness. At least, that was how he interpreted it. It could have indicated helplessness.

"What if those blind men only had to open their eyelids to see?" he said harshly.

He hurt inside. The pain resonated with hers, but he could not be too tender, too careful of bruising her feelings.

"If they had refused to see . . . well, they should've been kicked in the ass."

A second amoeba-shaped tear crawled out and ingested the first. And she pulled her hand away from his.

"Oh, hell!" he murmured.

Doing this was like attacking her with a spear equipped with a blade on each end. He stabbed himself and her at the same time.

They were standing by a tree with a twenty-foot-wide trunk at the ground level. Instead of bark, it had a transparent and skin-smooth covering. Below it were blue and red networks. The finger-thick red tubes and the pencil-thick blue tubes pulsed alternately. The trunk bent abruptly just above the ground, became horizontal, then curved into an upward spiral. The trunk narrowed as it ascended, becoming a thin tip when a hundred feet high.

Atop it was a flower which looked like a Christmas-tree star. Corkscrew branches bearing round purple leaves grew from the trunk halfway up it.

Jack thought he saw the vertical part of the tree move itself slightly toward him. It almost had the air of an eavesdropper bending his head to hear better. No. Must be his imagination. But, several seconds later, something fast slammed into the tree a few feet above him. Instead of bouncing off, it clung with eight tiny legs. The legs telescoped from below the buttercup-yellow body, which was hemispherical and as large as a half-coconut. It had no head or wings that Jack could see. Then, from the bottom center of its body, a thin and stiff member extended downward.

Its sharp tip plunged through the glassy skin into a red tube. The skin rippled violently. The thing, insect, whatever, was propelled from the skin. It fell onto its back and lay there while its legs telescoped into themselves, the red-fluid-tipped proboscis became limp, and the yellow body turned green and then black.

Jack had no idea of what had happened. But the tree had gotten rid of the parasite just as a horse twitches its hide to get rid of a biting fly. But the twitch doesn't kill the fly.

Where had the AI gotten the fauna and flora of the garden? From what strange world had they come?

Distractions, he thought. I've no time to explore the garden and to contemplate its wonders and beauties. The tent should be pitched in the middle of a flat desert.

He became aware that Tappy looked as if she had a question. Suddenly, he recalled that she, like him, had been startled by the loud noise of the impact of the creature on the trunk. He said, "It's okay. Just a big insect running headlong into a tree. Must've been going fifty miles an hour."

He wanted to be alone for a while so he could think. But he could not leave her. Since neither had had any sleep for a long time, he suggested that they lie down in the tent. He did not intend to take a nap. That would waste time. But sleep would give her the energy she was going to need when he started the intense process of artificial emotional maturation. Force-feeding of the psyche. *When* he started? *If* he started! At the moment, he did not have a smidgeon of confidence that he would be able to think of a plan that would work within the strictly allotted time.

In fact, he doubted that he would be able to imagine any plan at all.

They entered the tent and went into a room with two large hanging beds. Tappy crawled into one and gestured that he should join her. He was pleased. She must have gotten over her wounded feelings, and she would want the physical and emotional warmth of his body next to hers. Any other time, he would have lain down by her.

He went to the bed, leaned over, and kissed her. Then he said, "I have to think, Tappy. I'll be in the other bed while you sleep. Believe me, it's absolutely vital for me to be undisturbed. If I held you, I'd have thoughts I couldn't control. You understand?"

She shook her head, and she held out her arms.

"You have to grow up fast," he said softly. "Become an adult in hothouse time. Part of being an adult is being able to give up something so you can achieve something better."

He kissed her on the lips again and patted her.

"That's the way it's going to be."

As he got into the bed, however, he did not feel nearly as confident as he had sounded. His project was, in some ways, equal to God's creation of the world. But God took four days just to make the heavens and the earth and divide the waters from the dry land and make plants and then the animals. The work assigned by the AI to one puny Earthman had to be done in three days.

The big difference, aside from the Power demanded, was that God knew how to go about doing what must be done.

No, there was another difference. Tappy had free will. Assumedly, once God had created humans, He had left the use of their free will entirely up to them. Tappy did not want to see and speak, and God Himself wasn't going to change her mind.

He stared up at the sagging ceiling of the tent. The girl was snoring gently. Somehow, she had managed to fall asleep at once. That pleased him. She very much needed the rest, and she would not be bothering him with her silent but seen presence.

It was not easy to organize his thoughts and slide them down a single channel. He kept thinking of the AI's words. "Past manifestations of the Imago have not had incidental interests of the flesh."

Put simply, "She won't care at all about affection or screwing."

Well, he could handle that.

That was what one part of him said. Another part was greatly disturbed by it.

He steered his mind firmly back to the initial phase of his task: Project Tappy. How could he get her to see and to speak?

Then, there was the warning the AI had given him. He must make sure that Tappy did not misuse the power of the Imago. But that sounded as if she would have some control over the Imago. If she did, how much?

Hey! he told himself. I've drifted off the first phase. Back to the track.

Then, there was the promise of the AI to help him with the project. No. The AI had said that he would be working under its guidance. But no AI had shown up to help him, and it—they—had not told him how to summon them.

And he had to use Tappy's love for him to get her to do what must be done—if he ever figured out what to do. Since he didn't love her—did he?—he was somehow not honorable. To use her love as a tool against her—though it was actually for her—he might have to pretend that he was madly in love with her. That made him feel sneaky and treacherous. Really rotten. Unclean.

Suddenly, he heard bells ringing loudly.

They might be warning bells or wedding bells.

Or funeral bells.

What a crazy idea, he thought. Almost at once, he realized that he had fallen asleep between the thought of how rotten he was and the wakening thought of the bells. Or had the latter been the tag end of a dream he did not remember?

He sat up, rocking the bed.

"Oh, Lord!" he said loudly. "Whatever I do, I'll lose her!"

If he could not make her mature enough within three days, he and Tappy would be destroyed.

If he did succeed, he would keep her alive. But she would no longer be completely human. She would be the fleshly instrument of the Imago.

Tappy must have heard his exclamation. She turned slightly. But she did not awaken. Presently, he heard her mutter, "Reality is a dream."

Was that phrase the key to the door which would admit the Imago?

I'm just not up to this! he told himself. Talk about your frail vessel or your brittle tool! I'm it! I just can't do it! Might as well give me a spoon and tell me to dig the Panama Canal! In three days!

He got out of bed and went to the entrance room. There he drank deeply from a cut-quartz glass filled with the fountain water. Then he turned toward the entrance. He stopped.

The garden was gone. Replacing it was the flat desert he had wished for. Sand and rock, rock and sand, no plants at all, no shadows, the only moving things heat waves, the expanse as straight and as level as the tracks of God's locomotive to the unbroken horizon.

He felt as if he had just seen zero and infinity converge.

Chapter 7

FOR a moment, he was dizzy. At the same time, he was numb. His heart thudded against an icy shield as if it were a whale trapped beneath arctic ice and trying to break through.

Though he had lived through events much more outré and terrifying than this, he had expected them to be strange and dangerous. This one was completely unanticipated. It caught him as off guard as if his body's electrons had suddenly reversed polarity. Instead of a rug, a world had been yanked from under him.

When his numbness thawed out, he thought, The AI! They must have some kind of telepathy! I wished for the garden to be replaced with a desert. And the AI, like Aladdin's genie, granted my wish. But they did it while I was asleep.

His question now: Had he and Tappy been transported elsewhere or had two worlds been exchanged? Or was all this an illusion? Or a dream?

Next thought: What difference did that make?

It was then that the AI, a female, came around the corner of the tent. He jumped, and his nerves clanged like the bells in his awakening dream.

"For God's sake!" he said. "Next time, give me some warning before you do that!"

"I will," the AI said. Apparently, it knew what he meant. It walked up to Jack and stopped with its nose less than an inch from Jack's. Its breath smelled like machine oil. That, of course, was his imagination. But it stepped back, saying, "You are uncomfortable because I am so close to you. Does this distance make you more at ease?"

"You can read my mind?" Jack said after he had nodded. Despite the double jolt, he was breathing easier, and his heart was slowing down.

"Not your thoughts. My ability isn't like reading words on a screen. I sensed that you wanted help just as I sensed your uncomfort at my near proximity."

"What about replacing the garden with this?"

Jack waved his hand to indicate the desert.

"I'd think that'd take a pretty concrete image."

"Images, yes," the AI said. "Not words. I can receive images, though they're distorted. But I can unscramble them. Why do you need help or guidance? Have you thought of something which needs our help? Physical or mental?"

"Not yet."

The AI looked up at the sun.

"An hour and a half has passed since you came here."

"Oh, well. Just hang around for a few minutes. I'll have it all figured out by then."

"That would be most gratifying," the AI said.

The thing would not understand sarcasm, of course. Jack said, "When I really need you, I'll transmit an SOS."

"SOS? I don't have that vocabulary item," the AI said.

"And I'm wasting time talking to you!" Jack said, snarling. "Begone!"

Without replying, the AI walked around the corner of the tent. Jack hesitated, then hurried after it. By the time he had rounded the corner, the AI had returned to the building, wherever it was.

More of my precious time shot down, Jack thought.

The first day became the longest that Jack had ever endured. Yet, when the sun dropped into the slot of the horizon, it also seemed to be the shortest. His whirling brain, a mental centrifuge, threw off scores of plans and many variations and combinations of these. None was worth anything. Each was weighed in the balance and found wanting.

Meanwhile, Tappy paced back and forth within the entrance room or walked around and around the fountain. Her burnt-umber hair and yellow dress made her look very young and very pretty. And very vulnerable.

The upright and horizontal poles supporting the tent emitted light. Jack and Tappy took turns in the bathtub. For some reason, the AI had not supplied a waterless skin-cleansing cubicle. Perhaps, they sensed that water and soap were more satisfying to the humans. They were not capable of perceiving that a shower would have been even more satisfactory. Afterward, Jack and Tappy sat down to eat. Jack tried to keep talking so that the dismal silences could be brightened. But they increased in number and length.

When they were through eating, he said, "You've been kept in the dark too long, Tappy. I haven't told you what's going on because I wanted to spare you fear and distress. However, I believe now that keeping you in ignorance isn't fair. If something bad happens, it shouldn't take you by surprise. And, maybe, you could help even if you can't talk."

She listened intently while he told her the situation. He omitted the desire of the AI for him to use her love for him as a tool. She took it well, though she could not keep her face expressionless. Shadows of fear passed over her face now and then like the shades of very thin clouds on the Earth when passing below a bright moon.

"Now you know," he said. He leaned over the table and took her hand in his. "I told you all this only because we're in a desperate fix."

She squeezed his hand, and she looked confused.

He said, "I know. It's all mixed up. There are many things I probably don't understand any more than you do. One of the most perplexing is why you still don't see and talk. The AI say they've removed the blocks keeping you from doing that. They also say that it's up to you to go ahead. You don't, they say, because you aren't motivated to do so. Is that true?"

She raised her hands and hunched her shoulders. That meant, he supposed, that she did not know.

"The AI have great powers," he said, "but they're not all-powerful or all-knowing."

For a moment, he was strongly tempted to lie and to tell her that he was madly in love with her. The ends would justify the means. After all, the fate of the universe was at stake. Corny as that sounded, echoes of thousands of science-fiction stories, it was true.

However, he was not deeply concerned about the lives and deaths of perhaps trillions on trillions of people. Not at this moment. He deeply cared only about Tappy and himself.

"If you could speak, Tappy. If only you would."

He heard silence; he saw tears.

Something rose up within him. It was a red flash flood that crumbled the walls of his self-control. He banged his fist hard against the table. Then he yelled, "My God, Tappy! We'll die! What is it? What keeps you from speaking and seeing? Do you want to be blind and dumb? Do you want to die? Is there something in you that says you should die, that you deserve to die? Even if it means that I die, too?"

She reared up out of the chair and walked away, her shoulders straight, neck stiff, her body seeming to vibrate with anger. Since she was familiar with every inch of the walking space of the tent, she made her way to the bedroom as if she had 20/20 vision.

A few minutes later, he followed her. She was lying on her bed faceup, tears welling. He said softly, "I'm very sorry I yelled at you. I didn't mean what I said, accusing you of wanting to die, I mean. It's just that I'm so frustrated . . . and scared. I am human. Can you forgive me?"

She smiled weakly. Then she held out her arms. He went into them and wrapped his arms around her for a while. She sobbed. When his back started to ache because he was so bent over, he eased her down onto the bed and straightened up. She reached out, picked up *The Little Prince* from the bedside table, and held it out to him.

He did not know why the story seemed to console her. Perhaps, she could insert herself into it and forget, for the time being, her own identity and troubles. She might be the sad little boy whom Saint-Exupéry described in such simple but telling language. In a way, the plight of the child prince was hers. He, too, was parentless and lonely and sought a true friend and companionship and was puzzled by the world in which fate had placed him.

Jack was reading to her about the child's encounter with the desert fox when he stopped. He was silent so long that she reached out and tugged at his arm. Looking up from the book, Jack saw her questioning expression.

"I just got an idea!" he said. "From this story!"

She shook her head.

"The fox wants to be tamed by the little prince. But the prince doesn't know how to tame the fox. So . . . the fox instructs the prince how to tame him. Don't you see, Tappy! You can teach me what I must do to change you! We'll try, anyway! It might be the way to do it!"

Her hunched shoulders, raised eyebrows, and spread-out hands, palms up, said, "How?"

His enthusiasm propelled him from the chair he had drawn up next to the bed and sent him to pacing back and forth. "Don't know yet. But at least I . . . we . . . have got something to work on. Let me think."

While he walked, he struck the palm of his left hand with the book. It was as if the hand were iron and the book were flint and he hoped to strike fire from them.

"When we were in the plane, you gave me a piece of paper on which you'd written a word. It was supposed to make me able to disobey Malva's orders over the radio. But it was in Gaol writing. It had six different characters and two that were repeated. Now. Listen carefully. Do each of these characters have an equivalent in English speech?"

She frowned.

"I mean . . . let's say . . . does one of them, for instance, symbolize any single sound in English? Like 'l' as in lend? Like 't' as in Tappy? Like 'e' in lend? Or 's' as in seen? Got it?"

The girl nodded.

"Good!"

He looked around but realized that he had not seen any paper or pencils in the tent. He closed his eyes and visualized a sheaf of writing paper and three sharpened pencils. Then he summoned up an image of a knife. He'd have to have something to keep the pencils sharp.

Tappy stirred restlessly. He said, "Be patient."

A minute later, he heard a woman's voice.

"Do not be startled."

He said, "Come in," and an AI walked through the entrance into the bedroom.

He groaned. She was empty-handed.

"We do not have the strange objects you telepathed that you wanted," she said. "What use are they?"

"You can perform technological miracles," he said, "teleport us, read minds, but you don't know what writing paper and pencils are?"

"We don't have everything," it said. "Especially primitive artifacts. Tell me in detail what you need, their use, their materials."

After his description, it said, "I can't say precisely when I'll be back, but it'll be soon."

It walked out of the bedroom. Curious, Jack followed it into the hall made by drapes. He saw something blurry, like heat waves, appear around it, concealing it. Suddenly, the AI and the wavy envelope were gone.

He had expected a bang of air rushing in to fill the vacuum left by the AI. There was no sound.

He returned to the bedroom. "Tappy," he said, "while we're waiting, I'll tell you more of what we're going to do."

Ten minutes or so later, an AI, a male this time, appeared. Jack and Tappy were deep into the procedure. The AI, not bothering to excuse the interruption, said, "This is not what you asked for. It's the equivalent, though that is not the correct noun. It's better."

It held out two white, flat, thin, and one-foot-wide squares made of what looked like plastic. One side of each was silvery. After Jack took it, the AI extended to him two silvery objects that looked like a pen. "Pass the end of this across the screen, and it will make what you wish to write on the screen. You don't have to press it against the surface."

"We've got something like that on Earth," Jack said.

"Press the orange strip on the side after you've written on the screen," it said, "and it will voice what you've written. Press the green strip, and what is written on one will appear on the screen of the other. Press the yellow strip on the edge of the bottom, and the writing will be cleared. Activating the green strip will allow you to dictate to it and see your words in printed form. This tiny projection here, when pressed once, lets you scroll down. Pressed twice, it scrolls up."

The AI showed him the rest of the controls.

Jack guided Tappy's hand to a square and a stylus. She had heard the AI and did not need instruction.

"Thanks," he said to the AI. "You can go now."

It walked into the hallway. Jack said, "Okay, Tappy, let's go. I've asked you a lot of questions. From your responses, I've learned that the Gaol alphabet doesn't have an equivalent letter for each letter in the English alphabet. Like, for instance, the English letter 'a' can stand for several different sounds. So can a number of other letters, like 's' stands for the initial 's' in surprise and also for the 'z' sound in the second 's.' And so on.

"But the characters in Gaol writing stand for one sound only. Some of the Gaol pronunciations don't exactly correspond to our English way of sounding them, not American English, anyway. But the letters for them cover both pronunciations. There are some sounds in Gaol we don't have in English, but they probably won't give too much trouble. Anyway, you're going to write in English with the Gaol letters. After I learn the equivalents, right?"

She nodded. He pressed the orange strip on her recorder. He began slowly dictating sentences in English. They would include all the sounds in English speech. At least, he hoped they would.

He was no linguist. But if he found that he had overlooked some, he could supply them later.

Her printing appeared on the screen of his recorder as she made them on hers. When she was done, he said, "The Gaol alphabet is longer than ours, but I expected that."

He sat for a while studying the Gaol letters and their English equivalents. Apparently, the Gaol had no 'p' or 'd' in their language. He told Tappy to double the Gaol 'b' and 't' to indicate these sounds.

"Now I'll ask you questions. You'll write the answers in English using the Gaol letters. More than one way to skin a cat. Whoever installed those mental blocks wasn't smart enough to make them foolproof."

Tappy's smile was so wide it reminded him of the Cheshire cat's grin.

His smile was not as big. Even if he could converse with her in this roundabout fashion, he had not found the way to make her mature seven years in three days. But it was a step forward. That is, it was unless another obstacle was revealed.

"First question, one of many, Tappy, maybe."

And the most important, he told himself, though I don't expect an answer.

"Do you know how to compress seven years of aging into three days?"

Tappy looked startled. She wrote with the stylus two letters which appeared on his recorder. He had to scroll down the section with the Gaol-English equivalents to check his memory. The letters spelled out NO. There went his idea, derived from *The Little Prince,* that she could teach him how to mature her. However, maybe she could do that but did not know it as yet.

He said, "Do you have now or have you ever had any awareness of the Imago within you? Anything that might be the Imago making itself manifest?"

No.

He sighed. If only . . . Forget about ifs. No time to fantasize.

"Until we came to the honkers' planet, then, nobody had ever said anything to you about the Imago? Or hinted at its existence?"

No.

"Can you remember anything before the plane crash in which your father died?"

No.

"No?" Jack said. "Then how can you remember the Gaol writing? You must have learned it before you came to Earth."

She printed: I don't know. I just do.

"Then your mind isn't completely blocked off," Jack said. "Maybe we could pry it open wider. But we don't have time to try even if we had the psychological tools."

He paused, then said, "You don't remember anything before the plane crash. But you can somehow use Gaol writing. Maybe there are other things you could use."

How to find what these were, if there were any?

He wished he could go back to Earth and locate the Daws, the last people to have known Tappy. They could tell him much—maybe.

Had the Daws or other people before them imposed this hypnotic memory-block? If they had, they could also cancel it.

Then there were the honkers, the beings who he, when he first saw them, had assumed were sapient but not very bright. One of them had implanted that tiny bead or egg in between her breasts and thus kept her from being subject to Malva's will. That showed that they were no dummies. It also showed that they must know much. If he and Tappy could get back to the honkers' planet, they might find out more or perhaps all about this mystery.

And if only Tappy were six years older and thus close enough to maturity that . . .

There you go again, he told himself. If, if, if.

IF!

That word suddenly glowed in his mind like a Times Square of revelation. Its light generated what might be a great idea.

Maybe it would work. But he'd have to ask the AI if they could do such a thing.

He sent out a mental message.

"Get your half-metal asses down here."

Chapter 8

THEY, consisting of one female AI, met Jack by the fountain. Before he proposed his plan, Jack asked it about something that had occurred to him while he was waiting for the AI to show up. It had little to do with the previous idea except that it involved Tappy's mind. Also, it might be important later on.

"Could you get through the block that keeps her from remembering her first six years?" he said.

"My data indicates that it would be extremely difficult and would take a long time," the AI said. "We don't have time for that. Also, it's tricky even with the instruments we have. Using them could drive her mad or even completely destroy the memory now inhibited."

Jack said, "I thought I'd ask for future reference."

He explained what he had in mind for her immediately and asked the AI if his plan was workable. Within the deadline, that is.

The AI took about ten seconds to consider. Jack thought that it must be linked to a data bank because it surely did not have the required information in its brain. There was no use asking it about a linkage just to satisfy his curiosity. It did not matter enough for him to waste time over it.

"It's possible that we can do what you have proposed," the AI said. "Of course, we can't give her a complete false memory covering seven years. That would mean imposing trillions and trillions of data of different kinds, sensory, iconic, verbal, oneiromantic . . ."

"I get the idea," Jack said. "No use to list them all."

"Thus, the impressions would have to be relatively few. But they would be vivid; they would seem to be real. As I've been informed, you humans have great gaps in your memory."

"Some don't," Jack said. "A few gifted people have photographic memories."

"We know that," the AI said. "In the woman's case, it doesn't matter. She can't remember back before she was six years old, and any seeming gaps of memory after her treatment could be accounted for by the traumas she's endured. However, since she would supposedly be twenty years old, how would we fool her? Wouldn't she wonder why she, a twenty-year-old, still looks thirteen?"

"She'd just think that she looks very young for her age," Jack said. "She's one of those people who probably will look younger than their age. I suggest that you insert a few memories of people telling her how young she looks."

"Noted. It'll be done. But . . . we have doubts that the memory insertion will deceive the Imago."

"I don't know if it will be fooled or it won't be," Jack said. "It makes no difference. We have to try. And we'd better get cracking very soon."

He started to say something more on the subject, but no sound came from his mouth. His lips were open, and his jaw hung down. Then he snapped it shut and frowned.

The AI waited patiently for him to speak.

"All of a sudden," Jack murmured, "all of a sudden . . ."

"What?" the AI said.

"It struck me that I've got an ethical problem! I haven't asked Tappy if it's okay if we mess around with her mind! It's a terrible thing to do that and not even ask her if we can! Yet, the situation is such that we can't ask her if she'll cooperate! To do that would negate the plan from the start!"

"The larger ethical issue overrides the smaller," the AI said. "Our data makes that clear."

"You have no intuition about ethics," Jack said. "You rely on data. We humans do, too, but we also have feelings. Mine tell me that we are sinning against Tappy."

"We know the definition of 'sin'," the AI said. "It's a philosophical and theological concept which has no relation to reality— except as it governs the behavior of *Homo sapiens* . . . and some other sentients."

"How about the Imago's concept of sin, its ethical standards?"

"I have no direct knowledge of that. But it always works for the general good of sentient groups who are also ethical."

Jack thought that no group, or individual, for that matter, believed that it was doing evil. Did Hitler or Stalin or Mao believe that he was evil? No. What they did was for the good of the group they ruled. Or so they believed. Apparently, though, the Imago could perceive what and who was truly good.

"Go away," Jack said. "Let me think."

"The larger does not always outweigh the smaller," the AI said. "But, in this case, it does."

It turned and walked out of the tent and around the doorway.

Jack paced back and forth. Presently, he heard the tinkling of the little bell which he had gotten from the AI and then placed on the table near Tappy's bed. She could not call out to him if she wanted him, but the bell could be heard throughout the tent and some distance away from it. He went to the bedroom, where she was now sitting on a pile of pillows near the bed.

"What do you want?" he said.

She held up her recorder. He went to her and read what she had printed on it. By now, he was becoming fairly proficient in reading the Gaol alphabet. He only had to refer to his equivalence list twice.

She had written: What is happening?

"I've been busy with the AI," he said. He hesitated, then said, lying, "We're going to put you under hypnosis and try to break through your memory barrier. Maybe, if we're lucky, we can find out what happened before the plane crash."

Suddenly, he had known what he must do to her. It was making him lie to her because the most important thing, the only really important thing, was to develop that entity inside her to the Imago phase.

God help her! God help him! They were, from the cosmic viewpoint, only agents. In some respects, their fate was no more important than the AI's. But it mattered greatly to Tappy and him. They were not unfeeling robotic AI.

Tappy looked anything but happy. In fact, her left hand was gripping her right hand tightly, and she was biting her lip.

"What's the matter?" he said.

She shook her head.

He said, "You are troubled. Don't deny it. I have to know what it is."

He picked up the recorder from the little table and nudged her shoulder with it. After she had taken it, he handed her the stylus.

"Tell me," he said.

She wrote: I reely dont know but I get paniky, sick at my stomik, feel cold as ice, when I think of being hipnutizd.

She added: Please dont make me do it.

She was terrified. Why? Because, he was sure, whoever had installed that block had also put in a command to make her resist fiercely any attempt to remove it. Since he did not intend to have her hypnotized, he found it easy to reassure her.

He said, "Don't be afraid. We won't do it. You're safe from that. I swear."

She relaxed at once and smiled, though shakily.

Now, though, she would fight against anything she could interpret as an attempt to probe her mind. The only thing to do was to sedate her while she was asleep and then have the AI insert the false memories. He hated the idea. Nevertheless, it had to be done.

He pulled her up from the chair and held her tightly. She was still trembling and did not quit until several minutes passed. He spoke soothingly and told her that, somehow, things would work out well. Though she probably did not believe him, she may have found some comfort in his words. Perhaps, she was interpreting his embrace and his concern as an expression of his love for her.

That made him feel even more traitorous.

What a Judas he was!

Finally, he released her. It was evident that she did not want him to do that, but he held her at arm's length, one hand resting lightly on her shoulder.

"I have to talk to the AI," he said. "I'll be back. First, though, is there anything I can get them to get for you? They can probably provide anything you'll want."

Except safety and peace of mind and my love, he thought.

She wrote: Id love a big reel big mug of hot coco with a marshmello.

The child's spelling caused him to be engulfed with tenderness. She was a child, and she had been terribly wronged. And now he was wronging her.

"I'll do that," he said. "Be back shortly."

He started to withdraw his hand. She grabbed it and held on. Then she made signs with one hand that she wanted to go with him.

"I'm very sorry," he said. "I just can't do that."

He gently pulled his hand away and walked out of the room. By the time he got to the fountain, an AI, a female, was waiting for him.

He told it about Tappy's request for cocoa.

"It'll be ready for you when you go back," the AI said.

"Put a sedative in it," Jack said. "She needs to sleep a long time while we're planning what kind of memories to give her. And when we're ready to insert them, she'll need something to make her unconscious before she's put wherever you plan to put her during the operation."

"It will be done. She must be very disturbed. We received impressions of great fear from her."

"Do you blame her?" Jack said.

"We don't blame or praise," the AI said.

"You just do the job you were made for, right? Give me the cocoa. I'll take it to her and stay with her until she falls asleep."

He was startled, though he should have been prepared for something like it, when the waves appeared behind the AI. They suddenly cleared to reveal another AI, a male. It held on a tray a mug with at least a quart of steaming cocoa and a huge marshmallow floating on it. He took it. About six minutes later, he returned. The male was gone.

"It didn't take long," he said. "She fell asleep before she'd drunk a quarter of the cocoa."

He had thought that he would be taken to the city-ship for the conference. But the female AI, Candy, was the only one he saw, and they stayed in the entrance room. He sat down on a pile of huge pillows and made notes on the recorder while they talked. Candy stood in one place and moved only its lips. Its lack of the gestures and twitchings and slight shiftings of the bodies all humans make while talking bothered Jack. It also lessened his feeling that the AI were human. Though he had known they were androids, he had clothed them with humanity, with real life. Now they were naked of these. They were just machines. So, what was he doing talking with machines?

It was, he acknowledged, better than having no one to talk to.

After they had covered various possibilities, Jack said, "Okay, here's how it'll go, if you agree it can be done. You'll make and then insert about seven major memories per year over a seven-year period. Forty-nine very strong incidents. That is, memories of incidents which have been powerful in maturing her.

"Then you'll insert a number of lesser incidents. Things that might not be significant to other people but Tappy will remember . . . seem to remember, anyway . . . because they're important to her. Things mostly pleasurable, I'd say. She might as well have some happiness in her past even though they're false memories."

"Seven years is a long time for a human," Candy said. "And, as I understand it, time seems to go more slowly for a youth than for an adult. The older you get, the faster time seems to go. Is that correct?"

"That's what older people say," Jack said. "I know that my childhood seemed to stretch out for a much longer time than when I was a teenager."

"Then, logically, shouldn't she have more memories in the earlier years of her pseudomemories than she has in the later years? The first four of her seven years should contain more memories than the last three?"

"Not necessary," Jack said. "Just give her a sense of extended time during those years, the feeling that the first four were the longest. For the last year, though, since the events of that year will seem to be the most recent, you should increase the number of pseudomemories."

Writing a scenario for seven years was not easy and required much rewriting. Tappy had awakened before dawn. Jack had to quit work, talk to her awhile, and give her another sedative in a fresh cup of cocoa. She was not aware that much time had passed between the two drinks.

While he ate breakfast, he worked on the scenario. Though he desperately wanted to sleep, he kept writing and talking to Candy until he had completed his work. Then he said, "You can start work on the memories."

"It seems satisfactory," Candy said.

It was silent and unmoving for a minute. Jack's eyes were drooping; his body sagged; he felt that his immediate surroundings were sliding in and out, in and out. They seemed to be drawers filled with tableaux which someone invisible was pulling out and then shutting.

Suddenly, Candy was shaking his shoulder. Jack said, "Wha . . . ? Wha'ss going on?"

"You were sleeping," Candy said. "We didn't want to wake you up, but you should know that the work is complete. Tappy has her seven years of pseudomemories."

That brought him up off the pillows and to a standing position. His legs felt numb, his back ached, and his brain seemed to be filled with antifreeze.

"How, how long have I been asleep?"

"Fifteen minutes and thirty-two seconds," Candy said.

"That quick?"

"The scenario was prepared while you wrote it out, and the changes were made immediately," the AI said.

"I thought you had to take Tappy to the equipment!"

"You assumed that. All the pseudodata was transmitted to her mind while she slept in the bedroom."

Jack asked for a large mug of black coffee. It arrived about ten seconds later, carried by a male AI. After Jack had downed the hot liquid as swiftly as he could stand it, he walked to the bedroom and looked in it. By then, the sun had come up, but the pole lights were still on. Tappy was sleeping on her side. She was in a new nightgown. Near her, on hangers on a line, were her new clothes.

Her old clothes had been stripped off and thrown away. When she woke up, she would have to have different garments, of course. In fact, one of the false memories was of throwing the original nightgown away.

Held in one arm was a big fuzzy teddy bear. That had been given her, supposedly several years ago, as a birthday gift. She had, supposedly, asked for it, and, since then, had used it as her No. 2 security blanket. Her No. 1 was Jack himself.

The suspended bed had been replaced by a conventional one. It was large enough for Tappy and Jack to romp around on in sexual play. Jack was supposed to have been sleeping with her for the last five years.

The formerly bare room was now filled with many things: furniture, machines that played the music of many planets, though not of Earth, dolls, an ice-cream dispensing machine, a table loaded with cosmetics, which she supposedly used for makeup, and a mirror she could not use as yet, games for blind people, and dozens of other items, some useful, some recreational.

One of the AI had followed Jack to the bedroom entrance. Jack turned to it.

"The Imago?" he said very softly. "Shouldn't it be manifesting itself?"

His heart battered his chest hard. He felt a great fear and awe. It was as if he would soon be in the presence of the living God.

He did not know if he could endure such an experience. His flesh would become wax and would melt in the terrible light and heat. He looked at Tappy and thought he saw, for a second, something stirring in her, something no human eyes could look upon without being seared.

"Why doesn't it wake her up?" he said softly. His voice trembled.

Part of his fear was the knowledge that she would no longer be the Tappy he had known. She would be a fleshly tool of the Imago.

"What do you mean?" the AI said.

"It . . . the Imago . . . should awaken her when it awakens."

"I don't know why," the AI said. It added, "There's no guarantee that the woman will have matured. Even though she may think she's seven years older, her body might not. Or her subconscious may not be fooled. Or the Imago may perceive the truth."

"Can you give her a shot of something to make her wake up?"

"It's better to allow her to awake naturally."

At that moment, Tappy turned onto her back.

Jack said, "For God's sake!"

Her nightgown revealed the top half of her breasts. Between them was a bulge the size of a large egg. The tight and dark red skin over it looked as if it were about to burst. Around it at its base was a purplish swelling. A yellowish liquid shone on its surface, and that oozed out even as Jack stared at it.

He strode to her bedside and reluctantly touched the skin on top of the bulge. It was fever-hot. Her forehead felt hot, too, though it was cooler than the bulge.

"The egg the honker inserted!" he said. "It's infected!"

"No. It's just grown," the AI said. It put a finger on the bulge and then on Tappy's forehead. "Notice how much weight she seems to have lost in the last few hours. The egg's grown so fast it's sucked energy from her. The whole process probably involves an enormous expenditure of energy. She should be all right as soon as the process is completed."

"What does this mean for Tappy?"

Despite the AI's reassurance, Jack was certain that she was sick and that she could die from the disease.

"I do not know. It must be part of the Imago's maturing process. Or hers. Or both. Or it could have nothing to do with the Imago. We'll have to wait and observe."

Tappy, though still sleeping—or unconscious from the fever—jerked. That was followed by a twitching of her hands, which then became motionless. Her eyelids fluttered but did not open. Then a line redder than the rest of the skin appeared on the very top of the bulge. One end was pointed toward her chin; the other, toward her navel.

Then the break gaped like two thin lips. A few seconds later, it extended itself for a half inch on each side of the bulge, revealing something dark greenish below it. Then the line very quickly ran down both sides and disappeared into the purplish fester.

"We have to do something!" Jack cried.

"We can only wait and observe."

The line bisecting the skin gap on the top widened slightly.

The greenish round thing pushed upward a trifle.

The AI, standing by Jack, touched his shoulder.

He looked up and then behind him as the AI gestured to him.

A haze just beyond the entrance was clearing. It cleared, revealing a female AI. It walked in swiftly and stopped a few feet from Jack before speaking with the usual emotionless tones of the androids.

If it had been human, it would have screamed out the news.

"The Gaol have found us!"

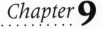
A FLURRY of questions surged through Jack's mind. Could they flee again? Obviously not, or the AI would have done so. Could they fight the Gaol? Same answer. Could they talk the Gaol out of it? Unlikely.

Jack realized that their ploy to age Tappy in her fancy, so as to evoke the Imago immediately, no longer mattered. The Imago might be awake, or it might still be asleep; either way, the Gaol had won, because they had closed in too soon. There just hadn't been time!

He sighed. This was the part he hated. "Then do what you have to do," he told the AI.

"And what is that?"

"Destroy us both. So the Imago will be freed to seek another host. It's the only way we can foil the Gaol now."

"We are unable to do that."

Jack was perversely annoyed. "What do you mean, unable? You told me that you would do it, to prevent the Imago from falling into Gaol power. There's very little time left. So do it now, while you can."

The scene was fading or changing. The exotic vegetation he had first seen from the station's window appeared around them. The AI assumed better definition, and became the voluptuous creature he had named Candy. "No."

"No? Why?"

"Because we no longer serve the Imago. We have been taken over by the Gaol and are now agents of the empire."

Jack saw the awful logic of it. Naturally the Gaol knew how to handle the AI. They had nullified those androids at the outset, before physically taking over the station. Maybe they had managed to deceive the AI about their approach, so that the AI thought they had more time than they did.

Jack came to a sudden, terrible decision. "Then I'll do it!" He turned toward Tappy, hoping that he could bring himself to kill her bare-handed. One smash of her head against the floor could do it. Then they could do what they liked to him; he didn't matter. He saw that she now lay unceremoniously on the floor, between the plants, her book beside her. He took a step.

But Candy moved more swiftly than he thought possible, and intercepted him. Suddenly he had an armful of phenomenal woman who was nevertheless not a woman at all. She closed her arms around him and lifted him from the floor. He felt her awesome power and knew that he was helpless. She might look like a siren, but she was also as deadly as one.

"All right!" he gasped. "Put me down. I'm helpless."

She set him down.

"So what happens now?" he asked. He doubted that he would be able to distract her or change the course of the conquering Gaol, but he was casting about for anything that might conceivably make a difference.

"Now we wait for the arrival of the minion of the Gaol."

"Oh, you mean Malva," he said jokingly, remembering the woman who had tempted and threatened him, back on the honkers' planet.

"Yes. She is the human interface for the Gaol."

No luck there. He looked around. "What's happened here? Did the vision change?"

"The effect of the plants has been nullified by the Gaol. This is reality."

Reality is a dream. Jack remembered that statement of the sleep-talking Tappy. Suddenly it had new meaning. Could this be just another dream, a product of his own worry? So that the Gaol had not captured them? In that case, all he had to do was change it.

He heard a small noise. It was just a kind of plop.

He turned to Tappy—and stopped. Because now he saw that the egg-thing on her chest had completed its hatching. There was just a purple wound with yellowish froth. Something green was sliding, rolling, or scrambling away from her: the hatchling.

Candy dived for it. But the thing scooted around one of the plants, just eluding her grasp. She tried to pursue it, but it was lost.

"What is it?" Jack asked.

"We do not know. But the artifacts of the honkers can have devious effects. It is better to destroy it immediately."

"Too late for that," Jack said, privately satisfied. "You'd have to destroy the whole greenhouse to get it now."

She did not reply. Instead she went to Tappy. "We shall cleanse and cover this injury," she said. "It will not prevent the host of the Imago from surviving."

And the Gaol did want that host to survive so that the Imago could not escape to occupy some other, unknown, host.

But here he was, taking this vision literally again. He needed to change it to something more acceptable. To a dream in which the Gaol were far away and the AI still served the Imago. He concentrated.

Nothing changed. But perhaps it would change when he slept, as it had before. Except that this last change had happened while he was awake and alert. Just as it would if reality were taking over. Damn!

Then he realized that it didn't matter. If this were merely another dream, then the Gaol were not here anyway. There was no point in scaring himself. He could believe anything he wanted, good or bad, but Tappy would remain safe. And maybe the Imago would wake.

Maybe all it needed was to be evoked. To be called up. "Imago!" he said. "I charge you, wake! We have dire need of you."

Nothing happened. Candy was treating and bandaging Tappy, ignoring him. She evidently took this dream seriously.

Suppose this *was* reality? If he gambled that it wasn't, and did nothing, Tappy was doomed. He had to assume that it was, and search for any possible way to save her. If he succeeded, and it was real, then Tappy won; if he failed, and it was a dream, Tappy won. Only if he failed in reality did Tappy lose, even if he seemed to be succeeding in a dream.

So this was reality. It was the only safe assumption, despite the seemingly hopeless situation.

Jack squatted and touched Tappy's hand. "Imago! Wake!"

There was still no response. Whatever it took to wake the Imago, this wasn't it.

Unless its consciousness was linked to Tappy's. "Tappy, wake!" he cried, squeezing her hand.

Her eyes opened. She smiled. "Oh, Jack, I see you!"

He felt an electric thrill. She saw him! She was talking to him! Their ploy had worked!

She sat up, and she looked at Candy. "And who is this woman?"

"You have a—an injury," Jack said, still elated over this success, though her questions were awkward. "This is an AI android. She is treating you."

Tappy looked down. "Oh, it stings!"

"Here is the bandage," Candy said. "Let me apply it."

Tappy lay back again, allowing the treatment to proceed. "This won't interfere with our lovemaking, will it, Jack?"

The implanted memories! She remembered five years of sexual activity with him. What was he to say to that?

"The injury won't interfere," he said carefully. "But there is something else that will. Tappy, the Gaol have caught us, and only the Imago can get us free. Can you—is it—did it wake with you?"

She hesitated, as if exploring her inner being. "No. There is nothing."

Tappy had been fooled, but not the Imago! It was a Pyrrhic victory. How much better it would have been if it had been the Imago instead of Tappy who had gained the ability to see and speak!

"It hardly matters," a new voice said. "We have gained control."

Jack turned, startled. There was Malva, the human minion of the Gaol they had encountered on the honkers' planet. The woman they had tricked, because she had not known about the honker's egg and its effect.

Jack saw nothing to be gained by politeness. "You wouldn't have control, you quisling, if the Imago had matured in time."

"We are assuming that the Imago *has* matured," Malva said. "Didn't the androids tell you its nature?"

"No." Surely the AI knew, but somehow in the rush of other things he had never thought to ask them directly, so of course they had not told him.

"It is a creature of extreme empathy. Any living entity with whom it associates closely becomes similarly empathic, and transfers this quality in turn to others, though the effect diminishes with each transfer. In due course it damps out, but the presence of the Imago continually renews it. If it lives free, the Imago will in due course conquer the galaxy. This is of course why the Gaol oppose it."

"Empathy?" Jack was bewildered. "How can that hurt the Gaol?"

"It does not hurt any creatures, directly. It merely changes them. Empire becomes impossible."

Candy continued to work on Tappy, who was listening; evidently she had not known this either.

"I must be really dense," Jack said. "As I understand empathy, it is merely a matter of identifying so closely with something else that you seem to feel its nature yourself. You seem to project your personality into it. You feel its feelings as your own. That's nice for understanding, but not much for blowing up enemy spaceships."

Malva smiled. "You are indeed somewhat obtuse about this, but this can be attributed to your primitive background. Do you mistreat, oppress, or exploit a person or creature for whom you feel empathy? Tappy, for example?"

"No, of course not!" Then Jack began to understand. "You mean the Imago causes others to feel empathy for it? So they won't hurt it?"

"No one can hurt the Imago, because it has no tangible essence. It is eternal and invulnerable. However, it is true that others soon lose their inclination to mistreat whatever host the Imago occupies. But this is only part of it; they develop general empathy for all living things, and that changes their lives."

"And it affects the Gaol, too!" Jack exclaimed. "So they don't feel like exploiting other species!"

"Precisely. Therefore the Gaol take steps to prevent exposure of any other creatures to the Imago. It will be isolated for the lifetime of its current host."

"But I'm with the Imago!" Jack said. "And Candy, and you. We've all been exposed."

"You have been exposed, true. The android is of course immune, being without living tissue. That is why the Agents of the Imago are able to kill its host, if left to their own initiative. They serve the Imago in part by being unaffected by it. I have not been exposed."

"Sure you have! You're standing right here. Unless its range is pretty limited—and from what you say, it isn't. You probably have to be a mile away to be clear of it. And you aren't."

"Gaol policy is to allow no other creatures within the stellar system of the host of the Imago, though probably a light-hour's distance is sufficient. I am five light-hours distant."

"Like fun you are!" Jack strode toward her.

She did not move. She merely watched him with a condescending smile. He reached her and grabbed her arm—and his hand passed through it without resistance.

Amazed, he grabbed for her with both arms, finding nothing but air. She simply wasn't there.

"You are addressing my hologram," Malva said after a moment. At the moment her face was right next to his, and his arms were lost in the image of her body. Her voice seemed to come from her mouth. "Your culture is too backward to be familiar with such things. It is a projection in three dimensions, with sound. It is a convenience of communication when direct personal contact is not desired, as in this case."

Jack had to accept the fact that she was not where she seemed to be. He swept one hand through her apparent midsection, one finger extended in a final gesture of contempt and backed off. "But the light-speed limit—how can you be five light-hours away?"

"To primitives, the speed of light is an absolute limitation. The Gaol are not primitive. Thus when the AI city traveled fifty thousand light-years instantly, the Gaol's pursuit was limited by the speed of the search pattern, not the speed of light. Our present dialogue is similarly unlimited."

Jack realized that she had no reason to lie to him. But still he hoped for some way out. Could he provoke her into providing it? "Why are you wasting time talking to me?" he demanded. "If you have such power over us, why don't you just put me out the airlock and seal up Tappy?"

"No!" Tappy exclaimed. Candy had finished bandaging her, and now she walked across to join him.

"We have no intention of mistreating you in any way, Jack," Malva said. "It is true that we shall confine the host of the Imago, but you will be allowed to remain near her for your lifetime. We shall if you wish conform the android to Tappy's likeness so that you will have suitable company, and you will have all your material and intellectual needs met."

"But you're going to put Tappy in a coffin!"

"This is necessary, yes. The Imago must not be allowed the freedom of even the ship. But you are harmless."

"If a ship will confine me, why won't it confine her? If it has to be, why not confine us together?"

"Because in past millennia the Imago has proved to be remarkably adept at escaping confinement," Malva replied. "We have not ascertained exactly how it manages it, but have verified that complete immobility of the host in isolation is sufficient to confine it for the duration."

"Well, I'm not going to cooperate in the incarceration of Tappy! I'll tear apart your ship, piece by piece, until I free her."

Malva shrugged. "I think not."

Suddenly there were bars in front of him. Jack turned, and discovered that he was caged. The chamber had been halved by a palisade of bars from ceiling to floor. He was walled off from Malva's image and from Tappy and Candy.

He grabbed the nearest bar—and received a formidable shock. They were electrified!

But he still had his voice. "Don't let them put you in their coffin, Tappy!" he cried.

Tappy looked at him. "I will try to resist. They don't want to hurt me, because that might shorten my life span. But the android is very strong."

Jack had discovered that. "Maybe that's the key! Tell them you'll hurt yourself if they try to put you away. You can do that, before—"

"Tappy," Malva said, "if you resist, we will torture and kill Jack."

Tappy looked at Jack. Then she spread her hands. "I will not resist."

"But you *must* resist!" Jack cried. "You can't let them salt the Imago away for a lifetime!"

Tappy merely looked at him, her tears flowing. "I love you, Jack."

"And I love you!" he cried without thinking. "That's why they must not put you away!"

She approached the bars and put her hands on them. They did not shock her. She put her face close to his and kissed him when he matched her on the other side. "These past five years with you have been so wonderful, Jack. They will serve for a lifetime's memories. Go with Candy; I don't mind what form she takes so long as you are well treated." She kissed him again and withdrew. "I am ready."

Jack knew it would be useless to protest further. Tappy did love him and would not do anything to hurt him. And *that* was why Malva had talked to him: to develop that leverage on Tappy. They were taking no chances at all with the confinement of the Imago.

Candy brought out what did indeed look like a coffin, except that it was surrounded by equipment that surely was designed to preserve the life of the person within. Tappy climbed in and lay down. The nightgown did not seem to matter. Candy swung the lid down. It was not a simple thing; it was spiked inside like an iron maiden.

"She'll suffocate!" Jack cried, but even as he spoke he knew she would not. There would be air piped in and nourishment, and her bodily wastes would be piped out. The seeming iron maiden was not a torture box but a mechanical maintenance device.

Candy folded down clasps on the coffin and locked them in place. Now it was impossible for Tappy to fight her way out even if she regained consciousness—and of course she would be drugged throughout.

Then metallic walls formed around the coffin. The plants in that vicinity disappeared. "What's that?" Jack asked, sure that he would not like the answer, but unable to stop himself.

"That is the formation of a spaceship," the Malva image answered. "The AI city station has been moved to a remote star and will be destroyed, leaving only the isolation ship. A Gaol unit will keep it under continuous surveillance for the lifetime of the host, which should be about a century, since she is young. The Gaol empire will be preserved."

A detail filtered through. "This city will be destroyed? But then what of me?"

"You will die with it, of course."

"But you told Tappy—"

"I lied. Now the Imago is secure, and you are surplus. There remains only the separation of the ship from the city and the destruction of the city with all its equipment."

"All by remote control?" Jack asked, the numbness of the finality of defeat sinking in. The Gaol certainly were thorough!

"No. The confinement of the Imago is too important to be done remotely. A Gaol will handle the concluding details."

"No, it won't!" Jack said, grasping what trifling fragment of victory he could. "Because if it comes here, it will be contaminated by the Imago, and you can't risk that."

"True. Therefore the Gaol individual, too, will be destroyed."

"But one of the conquerors wouldn't sacrifice himself!"

She shrugged. "Believe what you will. The Gaol is now boarding the city and will perform the necessary chores. Now I bid you oblivion, Jack, as my role here is terminated."

"Bitch!" Jack screamed as she faded out.

Candy walked across the chamber. "Where are you going, android?" he demanded.

She did not pause. "To the portal to admit the Gaol."

"Bring it back here and introduce us!" he called sarcastically.

When she was gone, he turned to stare at the coffin. He took hold of a bar to shake it, but it shocked him again. His arm was numbed; he could not get close to Tappy.

What was he to do? He couldn't just give up, yet there seemed to be no alternative.

Chapter 10

THEN he saw something. It was small, green, and looked like a thick-legged spider. No, it was more like a tiny octopus. It was crossing the floor toward him.

The hatchling! He had forgotten it! Ordinarily such a creature would have revolted him, but this thing had been with Tappy, and was formed mainly of her flesh. He couldn't dislike that, even if it was some honker joke. Also, he did feel empathy for it, and for life in general. Malva had been right about that much.

He squatted. "Come here, you little thing. I won't hurt you. I'm about to die anyway. What's your business?"

The thing approached his hand. It extended a tiny tentacle and touched his finger.

Jack felt a warmth. It wasn't physical, though; it was emotional. He felt an increasing awareness of the linkage of all things. He was attuning to the exotic plants in the vicinity, and felt their discomfort: the Gaol had established a field which suppressed their natural ambience. And he felt Tappy, her consciousness fading as the drug slowly penetrated her system; she was being forced into sleep, but there were no dreams there. The Gaol did not trust the Imago even to dream safely.

He looked at the hatchling. He picked it up. The thing assumed flesh color and disappeared against his palm. "You're doing it!" he exclaimed. "The empathy—you're magnifying it! Are you the Imago?"

But as he considered the question, he knew the answer. The Imago remained with Tappy. It would not leave her while she lived. The hatchling was merely another agent of the Imago, of a different kind. It was alive, and it was mobile.

That trick of blending with his hand—was that a signal of something more? It had been green when it first manifested, and green when it had come to him. Jack moved to a green plant and set his hand against it, letting the hatchling slide onto the leaf.

The hatchling turned green again, matching the plant so perfectly that it disappeared. Quickly Jack reached for it, and found it where the leaf seemed to thicken; it was solid, but able to change its color and shape instantly.

He set it back on the floor, which was metal gray in this section. The hatchling became a perfectly matching gray as it flattened out. It was a chameleon! It had disappeared the first time, when Candy pursued it, not entirely by hiding behind a plant, but by blending with it.

So now he knew two things about it: it magnified the empathy, and it was very good at hiding. But what good was either ability, when Tappy was locked away and the rest of the city was about to be destroyed? If the honker who had planted this creature on Tappy had intended to help her, how had it expected her to overcome something like this? Because it was now apparent that the nullification of the Gaol's volition block had been the work of that egg, as was Tappy's disappearance from the Gaol's tracking devices. The egg had hatched, and the hatchling had at least two other properties. Something else was needed—and perhaps the honker had anticipated this situation also, and the hatchling had what would be required.

Jack reached down to pick up the hatchling, but could not find it; its camouflage was too good. "Where are you, little friend?" he asked.

The hatchling turned green again, manifesting as it had before. Jack picked it up. "But how come you showed yourself to me before?" he asked it. "I never would have seen you, otherwise." Then he realized that that was why: it had wanted him to see it.

"But why now, when it's too late? Sure, we can be friends, but soon we're going to be dead. Do you have some way to rescue Tappy?"

There was no answer, just that overwhelming empathy. The hatchling did not seem to be intelligent or to have any telepathic communication. Apparently it had responded to him because of the empathy: it knew what he wanted, just as he now knew what the surrounding plants wanted. It knew he wanted to help Tappy.

Yet he hadn't wanted to see it when it came to him. He hadn't known its nature, and had forgotten about it after seeing it the first time. The hatchling had introduced itself to him by approaching and turning green. Didn't that indicate some separate understanding and decision on its part?

He reviewed the circumstance of that introduction. It was just after Candy had left, so he was alone. That made sense; she had wanted to destroy it, so it had waited until she was gone.

But if it wasn't intelligent, how had it had the wit to do that? To distinguish between her and him? He had part of the answer: Candy was not alive, and Jack was, so it could indeed distinguish them, and probably avoided any moving thing that was not responsive to its power. But the timing—how had it managed that? Well, maybe it was programmed to hide as long as there was any hostile thing nearby, whether living or dead. So it could approach Jack only when he was alone.

But the color change—it must have taken some wit to do that for him. It could have come up to him unseen, and worked its magic on him, and he might never have realized that it was responsible for his suddenly broadening empathy. It had made itself deliberately clear to him.

He went over the situation again. Candy walking out, himself calling sarcastically after her: "Bring it back here and introduce us!" Then she was gone, and the hatchling—

The hatchling had introduced itself. It had responded to his desire for an introduction, though his desire had been facetious. The hatchling was not smart enough to distinguish the pretense from the reality.

"Mystery solved," Jack said. "Much good may it do me. I think that the honker just didn't realize how bad a situation we would be in. It thought that maybe we'd be in Malva's hands, and you would touch her and make her have empathy for us, and help us escape. Instead we're with an AI who is now AG: Agent of the Gaol, and can't be corrupted. And we're going to be blown to smithereens by a real live Gaol—"

Then it dawned on him. "The Gaol! Can you make *it* empathize?" And knew it could. Because the Gaol feared the Imago, and the hatchling was helping the Imago.

Jack heard footsteps. Candy was returning. "Stay cool, hatchling," he whispered to the imitation palm of his hand, which mirrored even the lines and creases and slight variations of color. This thing was good!

Candy entered. Behind her rolled a weird machine. It was blue, with three wheels and three triangular handles, like a huge trash

collector. Six little lenses circled it above the handles. The top
was a rounded dome.

"There is the container for the host of the Imago," Candy
said, indicating the enclosure around the coffin. "There is the
human companion of the Imago." She indicated Jack. "There is
one other creature, which hatched from an egg planted on the host.
It disappeared among the plants."

The machine rolled to a stop before the coffin-enclosure. The
dome stretched upward, becoming a column, then turned at right
angles. Something shiny appeared at its end: a large lens. It surveyed the enclosure.

Jack realized with a shock that this was the Gaol. A seeming
blend of machine and flesh, a natural cyborg. That wasn't just a
lens—it was an eye on a stalk, the kind a snail had. The six little
lenses must be primitive eyes, for general sensing in all directions,
while the big one handled the detail work.

"Time remaining until destruction fifty-five minutes, Earth
time," Candy said.

"You bitch!" Jack shouted. "You mean you've already set the
bomb? That's what took you the time just now?"

She did not answer. She was no longer responsive to him, only
to the Gaol. He couldn't insult her any more than he had been
able to insult the image of Malva.

Then one of the triangular handles on the Gaol unfolded. The
knob at its apex was actually a joint. One leg of the triangle was
the upper arm, and the other was the forearm, with a claylike mass
on its end. The clay sprouted fingers or tentacles and touched a
panel on the enclosure.

The enclosure opened, revealing the coffin inside. The arm
touched a fastening, and it unfastened. Soon all the clasps were
opened, and a second arm unfolded to aid in lifting the lid. The
huge stalked eye peered inside.

"Yeah, she's in there," Jack called, outrage substituting for
sense. "And now you're contaminated and will have to be
destroyed. How do you like that, slugface?"

The Gaol lowered the lid and refastened the clasps. Evidently
it couldn't be baited, assuming it could even hear or understand
him. But surely it could hear, because Candy had spoken to it
in English. That language had been programmed here, because
it was what Tappy understood, and the Gaol had not bothered
to reprogram the AI. Why should they, when the AI and all their
works were about to be destroyed?

Now the Gaol rolled over to inspect Jack, followed by Candy. Its eye oriented on him.

"Yeah, I'm the freak from Earth," Jack said. He suffered a wild inspiration. "I have something for you." He extended his arm carefully through the space between the charged bars. The hatchling was now a green ball.

The Gaol took the ball. It oriented its eye on it. The ball changed color, matching the hue of the Gaol. It disappeared against the puttylike blue flesh.

Would this work? Would the hatchling succeed in bringing empathy to the Gaol captor? Or would the Gaol simply destroy it?

"That's the hatchling!" Candy exclaimed. "The thing from the egg. It may be dangerous."

The Gaol ignored her. It retracted its stalk-eye and stood on its wheels, thinking its own thoughts.

"Time remaining until destruction fifty minutes, Earth time," Candy said, exactly as before.

She was on a countdown! They had set the time bomb, and she was now its readout.

The Gaol remained immobile. Was it simply waiting for the countdown to be completed, or was it responding to the hatchling? The fate of the galaxy might depend on the answer. Minutes passed with no action.

"Time remaining until destruction forty-five minutes, Earth time."

The Gaol extended its eye stalk. It oriented on Candy. There was a whistling sound. It seemed to emanate from the creature's knobby elbow. Well, sounds did not have to come from a mouth; the Gaol did not seem to have a mouth. If the elbow contained vibratory apparatus so that it could whistle, why not? Maybe it could whistle from all three elbows, keeping in tune with itself. Maybe that was how it got its jollies.

Jack realized that he was not making that up. He was feeling empathy for the Gaol, too! He was coming to understand it, to a degree.

Candy turned to Jack. "The Gaol wishes to converse with you. I will translate for it."

So that elbow whistle was its way of communicating! He would have found that considerably more interesting if his situation wasn't so desperate.

"Great," Jack said. "We can get to be friends while the clock winds down. Then we can all be destroyed together."

The Gaol whistled. "I am coming to understand your distress," Candy said. "I wish to make you more comfortable."

The empathy was working! "I cannot be comfortable until Tappy—the Imago—is free."

Again the whistle. "The Imago will separate from this unit at thirty minutes before destruction. The Imago will not be destroyed."

"But that's not freedom!" Jack protested. "That's the worst captivity, for the rest of her life!"

"If that separation is not effected, the host of the Imago will be destroyed with the rest. That is not permitted."

"I don't want the host destroyed either!" Jack exclaimed. "I want Tappy free!"

"It is not possible to defuse the bomb," Candy said for the Gaol. "It will detonate on schedule."

Jack realized how thorough this trap was. Even if the hatchling converted the Gaol, they would all be destroyed. Possibly the AI could have found a way out, because this was their city and they had centuries of experience. But they now served the Gaol. Unless—

"There has to be a way," he said desperately. "You, Candy— you used to serve the Imago. Can the Gaol revert you, so that you serve the Imago again?"

The Gaol whistled. "I have now reverted," Candy said.

Just like that! Jack wasn't sure he could believe it.

"I will save the Imago by destroying the host," she continued.

"No!" Jack cried, becoming a believer. He had forgotten this aspect.

She paused at the Gaol's whistle. "There is no other escape for the Imago, Jack. Death will free it."

"Then don't be in such a rush about it," he said. "Since this city is going to blow up anyway in half an hour—"

"Forty-one minutes."

"Then you don't need to kill her. Just bring her out here with us, and she'll die when we do."

"This is true." She would have seemed surprised had she been human. She walked to the enclosure and paused. "Gaol, may I open the ship and release the host?"

The Gaol whistled.

"Why do you need to ask?" Jack demanded, afraid that the Gaol would change its mind. "Haven't you reverted to AI?"

"I have, Jack," she replied as she worked on the enclosure. "But the Gaol retains authority and can cancel my reversion at any time. It is better to verify."

So it was a spot nullification of the Gaol program, not a revocation of the whole. The Gaol might be becoming sympathetic to the Imago, but was not a fool. A truly reverted AI might have turned immediately on the Gaol and tried to kill it.

"So I guess we'd better talk," Jack said to the Gaol. He was privately amazed at what he was taking for granted, but realized that the empathy could account for this. "What's your name?"

"The Gaol lack names," Candy said as she swung the panels of the enclosure aside. "It is a concept confined to primitives."

"Well, I'm primitive, so I prefer names," Jack said. "Will you answer to Garth Gaol?" He was being humorous again, though he realized that humor was wasted on the others. At least it helped him retain some semblance of sanity.

"What does such a designation signify?" Candy asked. The coffin was now exposed again.

"That you are masculine and understanding of human foibles," Jack said with a smile. "And that when I say 'Garth' I am addressing you or referring to you, and no other entity. It is a convenience for dialogue when more than two creatures are present."

"I will answer to Garth," Candy agreed for the Gaol. She lifted the lid of the coffin.

"Garth, what are your present feelings?"

"I wish to enable you and the Imago to achieve satisfaction."

"Why?" Because Jack remained wary of dangerous confusion. Empathy was fine, but an alien definition of satisfaction could be treacherous. Just as Candy's idea of saving the Imago had been to kill Tappy. If the creature could state a convincing rationale, maybe he could trust it.

There was no response. After a moment, Jack caught on, and said, "Why, Garth?" He saw that Tappy was now sitting up, looking dazed; the drugs would take time to wear off.

"Because, Jack, the facilitator is enhancing the rate of my corruption by the Imago, causing a conversion which would ordinarily require approximately twenty-four hours to occur in as many minutes. The creature has the substance of the host of the Imago, therefore is dedicated to that host and through it, the Imago. Thus it enhances the power of the Imago to bring empathy to those it contacts. The process is not yet complete in my case, but the first stage of the conversion is the instillation of the will to be converted, so I am accepting it rather than destroying the facilitator and proceeding with my duty."

This was more of an answer than Jack had anticipated! "The hatchling is the facilitator? It facilitates whatever is of interest to—to the person whose flesh has provided its substance?" Then, after another pause: "I direct the question to you, Garth." The Gaol had taken his instruction about the use of the name in a rather literal and limited sense.

"That is its nature, Jack. We were aware that such creatures existed, but not aware that they existed on what you call the honkers' planet. Perhaps it is an import. Such a creature, acting in conjunction with the Imago, is a strategic masterstroke. It makes the Imago infinitely more dangerous to the empire."

So the honker had indeed known what he was doing! Except that they were shortly due to be blown up. "How much time till destruction, Candy?" he asked, morbidly interested.

"Thirty-six minutes."

"Destruction?" Tappy asked.

"We have encountered a—a special situation," Jack told her. "I'll explain it in a bit. This is Garth Gaol, whom we may consider to be a friend." He hoped. "Just relax."

Tappy did so, ministered to by Candy.

He returned to the Gaol. "Garth, can you tell us how to save the Imago and ourselves? I mean, without killing the host of the Imago?"

"Ordinarily I could do so, Jack, but at present I am distracted by the process of conversion. I am also losing my capability to think and act with precision and force, because of the increasing constraints placed upon me by empathy with those who would suffer the consequences of such action."

This, too, was interesting. "You mean the Gaol dominate the galaxy because they lack empathy? Because they don't care about the suffering of those they subjugate?"

The Gaol did not answer, but it wasn't necessary. Of course it was true! It was true historically on Earth, too. Power was grasped by those who had least sensitivity to the harm they did to others. This was probably the root of the saying "Nice guys finish last." Empathy might not be the same as conscience, but the effects could be similar.

Something else registered. "Candy, didn't you say that the Imago was supposed to be separated from this city thirty minutes before destruction? So that the host of the Imago would not be destroyed?"

"Yes, Jack."

"So that thing's not just an enclosure. It's a spaceship!"

"That is true, Jack. It is the isolation ship for the Imago's host."

"Will it hold more than just the coffin? I mean, other people?"

"Yes, Jack."

"How much more? I mean, could we hitch a ride in it?"

"It is capable of supporting the lives of three sentient beings as represented here."

"Three?" Jack was taken aback. He had in mind rescuing all four of them: Tappy, himself, Garth Gaol, and Candy. Because if they all piled into that ship and took off, the watching Gaol station would not see anything amiss. It was *supposed* to separate. To establish the Imago's utter isolation. Then the city could explode on schedule, and it would be assumed that everyone was dead except Tappy. It was a way out!

"Damn!" he said. "Someone's going to have to be left behind."

"Why, Jack?"

"Because there are four of us!" he snapped. "Only three can escape in that ship."

"But only three of us are alive, Jack. You may leave me behind."

She was not alive! Of course! That did reduce it to three. "But by the same token, you can come along," he said. "You won't be using any air or water or food, and we need you to take care of Tappy. I mean, the host for the Imago."

"This is true, Jack."

"Well, then, let's do it! How much time do we have until separation?"

"Two minutes, Jack."

And here he had been wasting time on details while their deadline was overhauling them! Naturally the emotionless AI had not been screaming warning. "Get us all on board that ship now!"

"The Gaol must authorize that."

"Garth, you must authorize it!"

The Gaol whistled. Candy went into action at blurring speed. She lifted Tappy out of her coffin and resnapped the fastenings. Then she touched a button somewhere, and the bars blocking Jack disappeared. He ran to the ship, and the Gaol rolled beside him. Tappy was now standing in the ship, seeming to have suffered no debilitation from her brief session in the coffin. There were not even any marks on her; however the life-support devices attached, they did not seem to have punctured her skin.

"Close it up!" Jack cried. "Get this crate into the air!"

Candy paused. "The life-support container is already closed, Jack. I do not understand the remainder of your directive."

He definitely had to watch that vernacular! "I mean the ship! Do what you have to do to get this ship safely sealed and separated on schedule!"

Candy resumed her blurring motion. The panels closed, and internal light came on. It seemed like closing a wooden crate from the inside, but it was a metallic spaceship.

"Separation," Candy announced.

Jack looked around. "Shouldn't we get into acceleration couches or something?"

"Why, Jack?"

Oh. Inertialess drive, of course. They had crossed the galaxy without any feeling of acceleration; why should this little ship be different? "Then can we look out a portal? To see where we're going?"

"Why, Jack?"

"I'm primitive, remember? I just feel easier, and I think Tappy would feel easier, if we could see outside."

"Of course, Jack," Candy said in the manner of one humoring a child.

The opaque panels became transparent. They could now see out in every direction. In fact, the whole ship was transparent. It was as if everything were made of glass, including the motor, assuming it had one. Then Jack realized with a start that the four of them were transparent, too, and almost invisible against the backdrop of the central core of the ship. Once again galactic science had surprised him. "Thank you," he said inadequately.

He took Tappy's hand and led her to the curving wall. They looked out. There was the city, already drifting away below them. From this vantage it looked like a giant globe. He had thought of it as a blinking dome, back on the honkers' planet. Perhaps half of it had been under the ground.

"The host must eat," Candy said. "The preservation unit is no longer sustaining her."

"The food's all the same, isn't it?" Jack asked. "I mean, nutritionally, regardless what it looks, tastes, and feels like? So bring us candy bars."

"This is a confection in my present image?" Candy asked, perplexed.

Jack laughed. "Close, but no cigar."

"I do not understand."

Even Tappy smiled then. Jack explained about candy bars. Soon an approximation was produced. It looked a bit like something left behind by a sick dog, and tasted somewhat like oysters steeped in chocolate, and it squished suggestively as they bit into it, but it would do.

Tappy nudged him. "Let's find a bed," she murmured.

"Yes, so you can rest," he agreed. "In the normal manner, without being sealed in a box."

"So we can make love." She smiled. "In the normal manner, without being rushed. We are the only human beings here."

There were those five years of sexual relations again, implanted in her memory. What was he going to do? He didn't dare tell her the truth, because that might not only hurt her feelings deeply, it might cause the Imago to retreat, if that was possible. Would Garth Gaol then revert to his nonempathy state, and do what was best for the empire? It couldn't be risked.

He hated lying, or even evading the truth, with Tappy. But he knew he shouldn't do what she so innocently wished. She now thought of herself as twenty, which was old enough, but she remained thirteen. Which was the greater evil? The lie, or more statutory rape?

The worst of it was that he did feel the stirring of desire. His emotional state was in flux, somewhere between fancy and love, and her new ability to see and talk increased his feeling for her. So did his heightened empathy. It now seemed natural to follow through with sexual expression. But he knew it was not.

He had to stall. "You've been through so much, Tappy. The— the egg hatched, and it drew substance from you, which you have to restore. Then you were confined in the Gaol's box. We feared it was for life, but with the help of the hatchling we managed to change Garth Gaol's mind. You've been in and out of something like suspended animation. You need to rest, and recover your equilibrium."

"Yes, and that is always so much easier in your arms, after we have made love."

He was getting nowhere! But maybe he could avoid it another way. This was a tiny spaceship. There shouldn't be anything like a double bed on it. "Candy," he called. "Can you fix us up with a wide, soft bed?"

"Of course, Jack." She did something, and the glassy interior of the ship convoluted. Now there was a glassy mattress behind them.

Tappy sat on it with a muted squeal of delight, drawing him down with her. Jack's crisis of conscience intensified. Tappy had gone without resistance into the coffin, in the belief that this would save Jack and cause him to be well treated. She had been ready to suffer her most terrible fate, and to let him go to the arms of a pseudowoman—because of her generous love for him. And how had he returned that love? By deceiving her, by having her drugged and by doctoring her memories—and by denying her what she most wanted.

"Oh, Tappy," he said, turning his face to her. She remained glassy; he could see right through her head. But this startling effect did not change her outline, or his burgeoning feelings. "I wish—"

He was cut off by her kiss. And suddenly it was as it had been back on Earth, the first time, when he had tried to comfort her and been swept into sex with her. He *did* love her, and what else mattered?

They broke the kiss. Her hands went to his clothing. She showed experience in this—the experience of five years.

Something caught his eye. "Tappy—look!"

They looked. The spherical city was flying apart. In a moment the major fragments separated, and separated again, until there was nothing but an outward-flying sphere of debris. It reminded him of the remnant of a supernova, only this was on a far smaller scale. Then that sphere became smoky, and then it faded. Soon nothing remained but haze, and finally—nothing.

The AI station was no more.

Now, belatedly, Jack realized that they were hardly safe yet. They were alive instead of dead, and Tappy was free and conscious instead of in a comalike state. But this ship was supposed to remain isolated in this stellar system, with no visitors, and there was a Gaol warship or equivalent standing guard. How were they going to get to anywhere where the Imago could do any good?

Now there were tears on Tappy's face. "The Agents of the Imago—they were good to me," she said. "I never saw them, except for Candy just now, I only heard them and felt them, but they did so much for me. It was long ago, yet still—" Then her brow furrowed. "It was seven years ago. I remember! I was blind,

and lame, but they helped me to see and walk without limping.
Then you and I went to a nice planet, with a wonderful little
house and garden, and oh, it's as if we just made love all the
time! After the first two years, when you said I was too young.
But I broke you down finally, when I was fifteen, and proved I
was old enough. Then we just did it and did it, and it was always
so perfect. I hardly remember anything else! But then, suddenly,
we were back in the AI city in space, and I don't remember how
that happened. And the egg—Jack, there was no egg before! I
was stung by the honker, and it helped save us from the Gaol,
but then the swelling faded away. Did another—"

Now Jack appreciated the monstrous gaps they had left in her
memory of those fictional seven years. No mention of the egg
at all! How could they have forgotten to account for that? And
the seeming return to the AI station—there should have been a
rationale for that, too. They had thrust her unprepared into a
situation both old and new. No wonder she was confused!

He had to patch over it somehow. So he started talking, extem-
poraneously, hoping to satisfy her. Because her doubt could be
the destruction of them all. He had to convince the Imago, too,
if it had any sentience of its own. The fate of the galaxy might
depend on that!

"Tappy, you're right. There's been a lot of confusion. We did
go to that garden planet, and it was great, and we thought it would
last forever, but the Gaol had never given up searching for us. We
were there to give the Imago time to mature, and to give you time
to get to know me really well, so that when the Imago manifested,
you and it would work with me for the good of the galaxy. The AI
said that otherwise—the Imago is so powerful a force that great
evil could come, if things were not right when it matured. So we
weren't really doing what we thought. I mean, we weren't there
just to have fun. We knew it would have to end when the Imago
came."

He paused to take a breath and to gauge her reaction. She was
gazing raptly at him. He was giving her a perspective that helped
to shape her scattered memories and impressions. And actually, he
wasn't lying; he was just interpreting. Because the basic purpose
was as he was saying. Only the time span differed—and in her
mind, that time was all there.

"So then the Imago did mature," he continued. "And at the same
time, the egg—we had thought it was just a sting or something, but
apparently it was a tiny egg, that was timed to grow and mature

the same time the Imago did, so it could help—it grew big, and hatched, and the hatchling turned out to be a little chameleonlike creature that can greatly facilitate the effect of the Imago. The Imago is—is empathy. For every living thing, animal and plant. Every type of creature. And it really can save the galaxy, because a Gaol with empathy for others is a decent person. The way Garth is. You carry supreme empathy with you, Tappy."

"Yes," she breathed, lying back on the bed and drawing him down with her. "I feel it, oh I feel it! Always a little, but now overwhelmingly." Her hands drew him in. "Tell me more about it, while you make love to me."

Jack had hoped she would forget about that. But it didn't matter; he knew he was going to do it. She really was old enough now, not just because of her phantom seven years, but because the Imago made her more fully adult than any normal person could ever be.

"But with the arrival of the Imago," he continued, stroking her body, touching her small breasts on either side of the bandage, through her nightie, "came also the Gaol. They had not been able to find us until then. But they zeroed in on the Imago, as if it had been only a few days. The AI had to fetch us, to try to keep us safe, in a hurry. We had to leave everything behind. Even your favorite teddy bear. I'm sorry about that. But the Gaol came to the AI station, too. Just as the Imago and the hatchling came. The Gaol took over the station. Malva manifested, looking exactly as she did seven years ago, and just as mean, and forced you into the coffin. I mean, the—"

Tappy touched his lips with one hand. "Stop, Jack. You have caught up to the present. I'm relieved. I was afraid that something awfully wrong—that maybe it would turn out to be all a dream—that you didn't love me after all—"

"Oh, Tappy, I do love you! Doubt all else, but don't doubt that!" That much he could say with sincerity now.

"I don't doubt it," she murmured. "Now let's make love."

"Yes." Relieved, and flush with his burgeoning emotion, Jack got off the bed and stripped his clothing. He had made the dream real for her and saved the situation. Whatever parts of it were lies, he could at least make this much true. He owed it to her—and he wanted to do it.

He lay down beside her and touched her body again. And discovered that she had fallen asleep.

Chapter **11**

"NOW we must have a council of war," Jack said hours later, when he and Tappy were rested. "Let me be sure I have it straight: Candy has a great deal of specific knowledge about the Imago, but no real initiative; she acts on the directives of the Imago as relayed through its host or someone designated by the host. In this case, me."

"This is true," Candy said.

"And Garth has a great deal of knowledge about the Gaol and their empire, and about the mechanics and organization of their space vessels. But his newfound empathy for other living things has played havoc with his concentration, and in any event he was not a decision-maker, he was a technician deemed to be expendable. So he, too, lacks initiative."

The Gaol whistled. "That is correct," Candy said.

"But we do all want to serve the interests of the Imago to the best of our abilities," Jack said. "So since I seem to be the one with initiative, and Tappy trusts me, is it agreed that I serve as temporary leader of this group?"

Garth whistled. "What is a leader?"

"A creature who acts as the originator of the actions taken by the group. As the guide for others to follow. The one with initiative."

There was no response. So Jack prompted it. "Garth?"

"Agreed," the Gaol whistled.

"Candy?"

"Agreed."

"Tappy?"

"I love you."

Jack smiled. He was still slightly startled to hear Tappy talking. She was quite pretty now, with her face clear and her hair nicely done; Candy was taking excellent care of the host of the Imago. And, for whatever reason, Tappy did look older; her breasts showed more clearly under her sweater (where had Candy found a sweater for her?) and there was an aura of maturity about her. She had the attitude of adult confidence. "Apart from that."

"Yes, agreed, of course." She glanced sidelong at him. "Now will you initiate a kiss for me?"

"You aren't going to try to seduce me again, and fall asleep before we get there?"

She shook her head, smiling. "No, Jack."

He leaned over and kissed her. That had really worked out well, last night. (He chose to call a period of sleep night, regardless of the clock. The clock hardly mattered now.) He had not denied Tappy, she had denied him, and he still wasn't guilty of another statutory rape. But he knew that he would not luck out that way again, and wasn't sure he wanted to. They were far from Earth now, and no one else cared about the detail of age. Certainly the conversion of the galaxy was more important than the precise timing of an act of love between two creatures. Still, his Earthly inhibitions remained. So he loved and desired Tappy, and yet also felt guilty for those feelings, irrational as that might be.

"At least, not right now," Tappy added, crossing her legs so that her thighs showed under her skirt. (Skirt? Candy must have a clothing generator similar to the food generator!) Her legs, too, seemed to have added flesh. If she intended to incite his interest, she was succeeding. She must have had considerable experience in this, and learned exactly how to push his buttons—in her seven years of fantasy. Maybe her empathy, because of the wakening of the Imago, enabled her to understand his desire in a way she otherwise would not have.

Had it really been only three or four days—or had it been seven years, and the brevity of the time span was *his* fantasy? He looked at Candy, who was now quite demurely clothed, her former sex appeal damped down. She would know—but could he trust her answer? If this were another dream, she would respond in the manner required by the dream, which might have no relation to the truth.

Jack shook himself. There was no profit in such speculation. He still had to assume that this was reality, and make it work. As reality, this presented a considerable challenge.

"All right. So here we are in isolation, the only free folk in this stellar system, with a Gaol empire ship standing guard five light-hours away to blast any intruder into oblivion. What happens if we try to make this ship leave this system, Garth?"

"Nothing," the Gaol whistled. "It is incapable of interstellar travel."

"Then suppose we make it travel toward the Gaol ship?" Then, when the Gaol did not answer, he added: "When I look directly at you, when speaking, as I am doing now, this has the same effect as naming you."

"It would take this ship several Earth years to traverse that distance—and when it did, the Gaol ship would simply move away across the system in one hop."

"So we can neither escape this system nor approach the Gaol ship," Jack concluded. "How, then, can we accomplish our purpose?" He looked at Garth, who had no answer, so he looked at Candy.

"We can bring the Gaol to us," Candy said. "They will come if the host of the Imago requires attention."

"Say, you are capable of original thought after all!" Jack exclaimed.

"No, only of assessing prospects in a given situation, when required to do so," she clarified. "The AI have become proficient at avoiding the attention of the Gaol, and therefore know what draws that attention."

"Still, I'm glad we brought you along. You are good for Tappy, and perhaps good for the mission."

"This is my purpose in existence," she reminded him.

It was no use trying to compliment the emotionless AI! "So what is the best way to bring the Gaol ship to us?" he asked. "By 'best' I mean to take into consideration brevity of time, concealment of our motive, and our chances of converting its personnel to empathy."

"I am unable to assess these values with competence."

Jack looked at Garth. "Are you?"

"Yes. It would not be wise to try to bring the full ship here, as it would apply stasis to this craft and investigate it in detail from a secure distance. Any living creature who boards this ship, or who approaches closer to it than one light-hour, will be destroyed after completing its business."

"You have a point," Jack agreed. "The big ship is not going to let us near it. But how about a small ship—or a robot ship? Could we take over that, and use it, without the big ship knowing?"

"I could accomplish this," Garth agreed.

"And because it's a robot ship, with no living creatures aboard to be corrupted, they may not even check it," Jack continued. "Now, Candy—what can you do to make them worry about the security of the Imago host, without alarming them enough to take precautions we couldn't circumvent?"

"A minor equipment failure—perhaps a malfunctioning sensor, suggesting that there is no problem, but the sensor is giving a false indication. A robot ship would routinely but promptly replace the sensor. The Gaol leave little to chance."

"Garth, can you cause a sensor to malfunction? Do you know which one is minor enough to generate no real alarm?"

"Yes. Yes."

"And is there room on such a robot repair ship for the four of us?"

"No."

Jack's heart sank. "For three? Two?"

"No. No."

"One?" Jack asked despairingly. Their plan was coming apart already.

"No."

"Not even one? Then how can we use the robot ship?"

"We can remove its robot and substitute one of us."

Oh. "And then that one can convert the Gaol battlewagon, single-handed, and return here to rescue the others," Jack said.

"Yes."

He would have to watch that irony; these creatures tended to take him literally. "Which one? Tappy?"

"Yes. Only the Imago can convert the ship, and she is the host. She must take the facilitator, because she will not be able to maintain close contact with any personnel for the requisite time."

"But Tappy knows nothing of a Gaol ship," Jack protested. "She would get lost or caught immediately."

"My empathy indicates that your argument is specious," Garth whistled. "You do not desire to risk the host, because of your special feeling for her."

Right on target! But Jack realized that if this was the only way out, and they didn't try it, their alternative would be to float here forever in space, leaving the Imago as effectively isolated as the Gaol intended. Maybe they could set up another dream realm and have it a lifetime of love on a garden planet, but that wouldn't do the galaxy any good.

"The host must be confined in the life-support container when the robot comes," Candy said. "Otherwise the robot will know as it approaches and uses its detail scanners that something serious is wrong, and will withdraw and send an alarm before making physical contact."

"Then Tappy can't be the one to go," Jack said, feeling mixed frustration and relief.

"She must be confined until the robot boards, then unconfined after it has been incapacitated," Garth whistled.

Jack saw that it had to be. He could not let his personal feeling for Tappy, which was romantic, interfere with the mission of the Imago. It was that mission which had brought them to this realm of super-science. He had been close to Tappy from the time he first met her, and the ambience of the Imago had been working on him all this time; he had to do what was best for it.

They worked on Tappy for the next several hours, drilling her on the interior of the Gaol guard ship, which it seemed was similar to the one in which they had first encountered Malva. Garth clarified that the robot would dock at a special port, where it would be cleaned in vacuum, so she would have to wear a space suit. But because that area did not have life sensors, she would be ignored by the machines, and could make her way inside. There she would have to remove the suit, but retain a face mask, because the ship was pressured with Gaol atmosphere that she couldn't breathe.

"But you are breathing our air!" Jack protested.

"I am not. I am wearing a transmutation filter." Garth unfolded an arm to tap himself at his base, between the wheels. Jack had assumed that this was part of the creature's transmission, since the axles for the wheels projected from it, but realized that he had been anthropomorphizing. Men did not breathe from their bases, but it seemed that the Gaol did. And of course they did not use the same kind of air; they were alien creatures. Maybe the honkers could share air with the human beings; that was why both species lived on the honker planet. But that must be a rarity of compatibility. He just hadn't thought about it before.

What about Malva, then? She hadn't worn a mask. But she hadn't been in the company of any Gaol, either; she probably had her own sealed atmospheric chamber. He really had taken too much for granted.

He returned to the present situation. Once Tappy was aboard the big ship, she would have to make her way to the Nexus Gaol, or what Jack called the captain. She would use the facilitator to corrupt that individual, and then he would help her corrupt the rest of the ship. Jack didn't argue about the term "corrupt"; he knew that Garth did not mean any affront.

But how could Tappy ever accomplish such a thing? The odds were against her. There were so many things that could go wrong!

"What are the odds?" he demanded grimly. Then he had to explain to them what he meant.

Candy and Garth held a dialogue, and came to agreement. "The odds of the host's success in this endeavor are approximately one in three. But if she fails, the odds are nine to one that the host will be dead, and the Imago will be free. That, too, is success. So the endeavor, taken as a whole, is worthwhile."

"Great," Jack said, sick at heart.

"If I am to leave you, perhaps forever," Tappy said, "I want to make love with you one last time."

"Of course," Jack said numbly.

But when they went to the bed, the specter of her death loomed so large in his mind that he was impotent. It was as if he were sending her into it, and somehow it seemed that if he renounced this part of it, she would not suffer the other part. "I'm sorry, Tappy," he said.

"I know. I feel your guilt and sorrow. Just hold me."

That much he could do.

"If I do not return," she said after a while, "you must take Candy as your lover. It will not mean anything to her, but it will help you to forget."

"I don't want to forget!" he exclaimed.

"You would not be here, except for me. I could not live or die in peace if I left you to the emotions you now feel. Promise me that you will take her."

"I promise," he said. Because otherwise she would have been even more unhappy, and it would be his fault. There were ways in which this newly adult Tappy was harder to accept than the lame blind child had been.

Then they slept, embraced but without great solace

They set it up. Tappy gave Jack the hatchling, which had come back to her after converting Garth. It was able to eat human food, because its flesh was from a human being. She returned to the coffin and Candy locked her in. Then Garth selected a sensor and sent a piercing whistle through it. Jack was aware of no change, but both Garth and Candy assured him that the sensor was now malfunctioning, and would attract the attention of the monitoring ship.

They assumed their stations. Since no one was supposed to be aboard the isolation ship except Tappy, they had to hide in shielded areas so that their life forces would not be detected by the robot. Jack's station was by the entrance port; he would use a tiny wire Garth had provided to nullify the robot's programming switch from behind. Then Garth would fix the sensor, and Tappy would take the hatchling and enter the other ship in lieu of the robot. Then they would wait. Perhaps for a long time.

Suddenly a small alarm sounded for the approach of a body in space. This was in order; the robot would pick up that alarm and know that the isolation ship was functioning properly, despite the one bad sensor. The robot ship was not velocity limited; it had passed from the master ship to the isolation ship almost instantaneously. But the final approach was slower, so that the locks could be merged. Though the robot did not require atmospheric pressure, the isolation ship was pressured for the sake of the drugged host, and that pressure and composition would be maintained throughout.

The lock opened—and a man stepped through.

Jack gaped. It was supposed to be a robot! What had happened? His little wire was useless, because the man had no external programming switch. And he was not alone; there was the sound of footsteps behind him.

The man turned and saw Jack. His eyes seemed to widen in similar surprise. His mouth opened to cry warning to his companion.

Jack threw the hatchling. It struck the man on the forehead and clung, quickly fading out of sight. Then Jack ducked around the man and flung himself into the other ship, hoping to catch the second man by surprise.

He did. He plowed right into the other, wrapped his arms around him, and bore him down. Jack scrambled to put a hand on the other's chest, to hold him down long enough to look at.

And discovered that it was a woman. Her face was petite, and her chest was—

Embarrassed, Jack removed his hand. "I don't suppose you speak my language?" he asked.

"We are programmed for the language of the host of the Imago," she replied.

"And I don't suppose I can trust you not to attack me if I let you up?"

"We are not attack androids. We are maintenance personnel."

Oh. No wonder it had been so easy. She had not fought him at all. Then something else registered. "Androids—you mean you're not alive?"

"We are not alive," she agreed.

"And you could lift me off you with one hand?"

"Like this?" She grasped him by the belt and lifted him into the air with one hand.

"But you obey the directives of living creatures?" he cried desperately.

"We do."

"Well, I'm a living creature. You must obey my directives."

"Of course. What are they?"

"First, put me down. Then vacate your ship. Then signal the home ship that all is well."

She put him down. She got to her feet. She walked to the other ship. There stood the android man.

"Give me the hatchling—unharmed," Jack directed him. Because of course the hatchling had had no effect. He had to describe the hatchling.

The man reached up to strip something from his forehead. He handed it to Jack. The hatchling did not seem to be harmed. Jack realized that this arrival of the androids instead of the robot was better than what they had anticipated. Not only did this allow two individuals to return with the ship, one of them could be a human-seeming woman without causing any alarm.

After that it was easy, physically. Tappy emerged from the coffin, and she and Garth took the places of the two androids. With Garth's direct guidance, they judged that the odds of success were now three to one in their favor.

The locks sealed and the ships separated. Jack settled back to wait. He was now the only living thing in the isolation ship, but the three others looked human and would obey his directives. He would be fine, if he could just keep his mind from the challenges facing Tappy. Since he couldn't do anything about them at the moment, there was no point dwelling on them. He needed to distract himself.

"Say, do you folk want to learn to play strip poker?" he inquired brightly.

Chapter 12

JACK had never felt so lonely. Like most creative people, he did not suffer from isolation for long periods. Not as long as he could paint or read thought-stimulating books.

But Tappy was gone, and he might never see her again. He felt as if he were a lone figure standing in the middle of a surrealist painting, say, in one of Salvador Dalí's white plains stretching toward a horizon much farther away than Earth's, a tiny figure, the only human being on a vast malignant world. Nothing Terrestrial existed there except him. He could walk forever with only increasing loneliness for a companion, though black depression might also join him.

Since her ship had gone, ten minutes had dripped as if from a stalactite. When it had disappeared, seemingly erased from this continuum, it was like his heart had been anchored to the ship and had been ripped out when it had shot away. That was, of course, poetic exaggeration, but it came close to expressing his agony at her departure.

He paced back and forth, passing by the three androids. They stood without moving, their eyes open and unblinking. After a while, unless he ordered them to do something, they would seem to be furniture. His imagination worked hard to envision what Garth and Tappy could be doing now. But it was like an ancient Roman slave pushing on a huge grinding-wheel spoke. It just went around and around and the pushing got heavier every minute.

He tried to think of something else.

The Imago? What could its true nature be? How had it originated? It seemed to be some sort of divine entity. But, as far as he knew, it had no mind. Or, in fact, a body. No material body, anyway.

What was it? A chip off God's block? What did that phrase mean? Nothing. A child of God or a special envoy? Or a manifestation of God? But "manifestation" was just a word which signified nothing in this situation. It was a word to conceal ignorance. Just as most words in philosophy or in theology masked lack of knowledge about reality.

But Tappy had murmured in her sleep, "Reality is a dream."

"I give up!" he said loudly.

He began weeping. After several seconds, he quit, and he dried his eyes. He felt better then, though not much better.

Suddenly, glass shattered without sound around him. There was no glass, but it seemed as if there had been. Sharp things without edges pierced him. The largest thing, a piece, a shard, whatever it was, slanted through his brain, bringing light with it. Then the "glass" evaporated. Through the broad but, at the same time, thin triangular space left by the passage of the "glass," light poured into the "wound."

The light expanded like a nuclear fireball, then divided into two photonic amoebas. One was still in his head; one seemed to hang before his eyes. Through the latter, he saw Tappy. Then she moved from directly in front of his vision. No. Whatever he was seeing through had moved. She turned toward him and looked into his eyes. But her face was expressionless. She did not see him.

He cried out, "Tappy!" as if she could hear him. Her lips moved, and he could hear her. The words were somewhat blurred, but it was evident that they were not addressed to him.

Immediately thereafter, the clearness of the vision faded. A ripple passed through it, then all he saw was wrinkled and distorted. Tappy and the off-white wall behind her and some partially revealed machines and instruments behind her stretched out as if they had been painted on a rubber band being pulled out lengthwise.

He realized that he was seeing part of the interior of the Gaol spaceship to which she and Garth had gone. They had gotten into it, though just where they were and what their situation was, he could not tell.

Suddenly, the scene seemed to be squeezed on both sides, making Tappy and the machines tall and thin. That state held for several seconds before abruptly becoming normal. He realized that, whoever or whatever the transmitter was, it was having trouble controlling the output.

He was in some kind of telepathic communication with Tappy. No. Not communication. It was a one-way transmission. But definitely via a medium he had not believed could exist. Telepathy.

Then he no longer saw her. He was looking at the Gaol cyborg, Garth, and he was hearing human voices and clicking sounds.

The hatchling! It was his transmitter. It had been on Garth, allowing a view of Tappy from Garth's vantage. Then the hatchling had leaped from it to somewhere. Ah! Now he knew. It was on her shoulder. Her hand and part of her arm had risen to block partially his view, then dropped.

By means Jack would never know, the hatchling was showing him what it saw and heard through its peculiar receptors and transmitter.

Or was the Imago doing this with the hatchling as its transmitter?

But how and who did not matter. Being and doing did.

He stood for a long time, almost as motionless as the androids near him, while he watched. Tappy had turned about one hundred degrees to the left. She and Garth were at one end of a large room. Men and women in loose green robes were seated at desks and consoles. Many of these bore three-foot-wide square crystals. Their faces bore strange symbols and images. Most of them seemed to be operated by verbal commands. Once, a crystal extruded part of its face in the shape of a human hand with one finger. The finger bent to point back to the screen. Its operator spoke, and the hand sank back and became one with the face of the block.

What kind of computer was that?

Large green vines festooned with huge many-colored flowers and clusters of berries covered the ceiling and parts of the walls. Since Jack could not smell them, he supposed that the hatchling's telepathic powers did not include odor. The vegetation was primarily to supply oxygen and secondarily to relieve the sterility and monotony of bare walls.

The room vanished. He swore. Was this to be the end of the transmission?

Several minutes passed during which he paced back and forth. Had something bad happened to Tappy and the hatchling or did telepathy demand so much energy that the hatchling could no longer project the view? What? What?

As suddenly as it had gone, the scene was back. But the hatchling seemed to be on top of Tappy's head now. He saw that two of the berry stems on the wall just ahead of Tappy no longer bore a berry. Also, one berry was half-eaten. For several seconds, he did not realize the implication, then he struck his right palm with his left fist.

Of course! The hatchling, like all creatures, had to have food. It had leaped to the cluster and eaten its fill.

Though Jack had seen no mouth on it, it had one or it ingested as an amoeba did.

He also knew now that the creature could not see or hear as Tappy and Garth did. It used their brains and eyes to transmit what they saw and heard. He was looking through Tappy's eyes, hearing through her ears. When the hatchling was on Garth, it functioned as it did on Tappy. He should have understood that before now. But he was somewhat numb from the shock of the unexpected transmission.

Tappy and Garth began to stroll across the room. Some operators glanced up at them. Nobody made a move toward or questioned them. The two intruders were regarded as part of the crew, though some may have wondered why the woman was not in uniform. However, the crew might know only what their duties were. They might not even know why the ship was located here or what its overall mission was.

Tappy and Garth went through a door (hatchway?) into another large room. This contained several vast transparent cases, at least sixty feet high, in each of which spun an upright cylinder. Jack had no idea what their function was, but they made a loud humming noise.

The two intruders approached a door at the opposite end of the room. Two guards, bipedal cyborg Gaol, stood on each side of it. They were eight feet high, four-armed, and plated like knights. Their helmets had half-open visors concealing the face but showing large glowing eyes. Two hands on their right sides gripped the barrel of a weapon with a disk at its end.

They did not move when Garth led Tappy past them and along the wall beyond them. Then he stopped, and his wheels turned to face the wall. A huge window was set in it, and Tappy could see into the next room. Jack realized at once that it was the control center (the bridge?) of the ship. It was not all the instruments and flashing varicolored lights and crystal display blocks and the intensity of the operators that made that certain. It was the creature in the center of the room.

He—she—it, whatever it was, was sitting, if its posture could be called sitting, on a slowly rotating wide disk on top of a narrow pillar six feet high. The edge of the disk almost touched the upper end of a long narrow ramp. A four-legged being would prefer a ramp to a staircase.

"My God!" Jack said.

The thing on the disk must be the true, the basic, the real Gaol, the being in its natural form. Garth and the other Gaol he had seen were cyborgs, their naturally endowed bodies reconstructed to be Gaol-machines. Some had bodies in which part of their skin was exposed. Others were entirely armor-plated. These would be lower-class Gaol. An oppressed class with no right to object to being made half machine. Or, perhaps, they had volunteered.

In any event, weird as it was, the captain's body was what evolution had given it. It looked like a giant ratcage with a head, two arms, and four doglike legs. Its organs were suspended in a sac inside the cage. The sac filled three-fourths of the cage. Its two very long humanoid arms, anchored by a thick framework of bone on the front end of the sac, had copperish skin. The neck projecting from the sac was long and thick and mottled purplish. The head was a caricature of a human being's.

Start with the bottom of the Gaol. That was a turtle's lower plate, almost six feet long. From the sides rose long curving ribs that merged with a spine arcing from the rear of the plate to its front. The blimp-shaped sac was attached to the spine with muscles Jack could clearly see through the copperish skin enclosing them. When the Gaol was momentarily before a bright light on the wall, vague shapes were silhouetted in the sac. Its organs, no doubt.

The bottom of the sac rested on a thick fleshy pad attached to the plate.

The neck extended horizontally from the front of the sac through a wide opening in the front ribs.

The head! It had almost no forehead, and the cranium had no room for even a small brain. Jack guessed that the brain was in the sac.

Brutal and fierce described the face. The jaws projected to form a mouth like a shark's. Its open mouth revealed a multitude of tiny but very sharp triangular teeth set in three rows.

It had no tongue. There were three nostrils on the end of the beastish head, two below and one above. The top one was covered by a small flap of skin that blew in and out, though not smoothly and at regular intervals. Jack could not hear it but thought that it was communicating by whistling its Morse-code-like words through that nostril.

At right angles above the jaws was a broad plane of bone in which were set two large quite human-looking eyes. These were blue. The ears resembled chrysanthemums.

What kind of a planet could have originated such a creature? It could not be an Earth-like world.

After staring through the window at the ghastly being (ghastly to Jack), Garth rolled toward the two guards. Tappy followed it until Garth whistled at her and gestured at her to wait for him. Then he lifted two extensions and shot the guards with a ray from each. The green beams cut off the heads of the guards, and these clanged on the floor and rolled a few inches. Their bodies remained upright; their arms still gripped the barrels of their weapons.

Garth opened the door to the control room, revealing to Tappy's eyes (thus Jack's) an airlock chamber. Then the Gaol entered it, and the door closed behind him.

Tappy was probably in shock because of Garth's unexpected and deadly attack. Jack did not know about that. The hatchling did not transmit emotional feelings. Not in this situation, anyway. She looked around. None of the operators in the room behind her nor in the control center had paid any attention to the killing. They may not have seen it, but the operators outside the control center must have heard the noise of the fallen heads.

"What's going on?" Jack said. He had expected any action by Tappy and Garth to be subtle and, in essence, pacifistic. But . . . but what? Ah! The hatchling could not enter the control room to transmit empathy to those within. The gases the Gaol breathed would kill it. If it stayed outside the room, its empathic effect would be eventually felt by the control center crew. But Garth had to take immediate action. He had decided that there was only one way to seize control of the ship. It must have been his idea since Tappy could communicate with him only through gestures. Also, he probably knew that Tappy, so full of empathy—soaked with it, in fact—would draw back from use of violence. Garth had been affected by the empathy transmitted to him, but he was still more governed by logic than feeling. A good thing, too, Jack thought.

Tappy went back to the window and looked around the side of the wall into the control room. By then, Garth had cut every Gaol operator in there and was rolling up the ramp. The captain was standing up on his four doglike legs, his arms waving, the flap over his whistling nostril going up and down. His "face" was incapable of expressing anything but ferocity, but his hands said that Garth would be sorry indeed that he had attacked the captain.

It was, of course, bravado. The captain carried no weapons.

Whatever it was saying in its whistling speech, it did not impress Garth. He wheeled onto the rotating disk, grabbed the captain's head with two suddenly extruded hands, and tore the head off from the fat neck. A dark reddish-blue blood shot out of the open neck. But Garth had rolled back out of the way of the spurt quickly enough to avoid most of it. The captain's legs gave way under him. His bottom plate struck the disk surface. The legs and arms flailed for a few seconds, then were still. The coppery skin of the sac became bluish.

Garth threw the head across the room and against a wall. With that savage gesture, he had shown that the lower-class Gaol did resent and hate their lords.

Tappy had turned away to avoid seeing more of the carnage. A moment later, Jack could see nothing through her eyes. The transmission had been cut off.

Ten minutes later, a loud clang throughout the isolation ship told Jack that Tappy and Garth were back. Airlocks opened and closed. And Tappy, sobbing, ran into his arms.

An hour later, they were eating at a small table in a corner of the main room. She had calmed down enough to have a good appetite and to be optimistic. But Jack did not entirely share her bubbling outlook, though it was difficult to resist it. He knew that the empathy that had enabled them to conquer the monitor ship was a weapon with limits. Actually, empathy alone had not done it. Violence had also been necessary. He worried that the empathy might become so strong in Tappy, himself, and Garth that they would be unable to use force against their enemy.

Too much of anything, no matter how good it was, could be a bad thing.

Just now, he and Tappy were in the isolation ship, which was inside the monitor ship, which was now orbiting a huge gaseous planet of a G-type star. The crew was under the influence of the empathy. Undoubtedly, the Gaol were aware that both vessels had disappeared along with the Imago host. They would be furious but, at the same time, frightened. They would be even more disturbed, Jack thought, if they knew what had actually happened.

Garth rolled through an airlock. He halted by the table. Candy said, "Garth wishes to report."

"Tell him to report," Jack said.

When Garth had quit whistling, Candy said, "He reports that the sensors indicate that the Gaol probes will probably locate the general location of this vessel within an hour. Once that is done, the Gaol won't take more than an hour to pinpoint its location."

"Tell him thanks," Jack said, though he felt it was wasting time to inform a Gaol of his gratitude. But maybe it wasn't. Who knew how deep the empathy effect went? He turned to the girl.

"Tappy, I've been thinking about where we should go next. It's useless to just keep on dodging and ducking. We should go back to the honker planet. I have a hunch that there is where we'll find the key to defeating the Gaol, if there is a key. Anyway, the honkers'll help us. They probably have a lot of information we need. For instance, the honker who sneaked in at night and deposited the egg in you. What does he know? Who ordered him to do that? Would he and others help us hide someplace where the Gaol can't detect us, if such a place exists. What do you think?"

She did not hesitate. "It seems to me it's the only way we can go. I was just waiting for you to suggest it."

"Fine! But don't defer to me from now on. Don't wait for me to suggest something. If you've got a good idea, spill it."

She embodied, literally, the greatest force in the world of sentient beings. Yet, she looked up to him as her leader. This would have flattered him if he had not felt so puny and helpless. But he was not going to let her know that. She needed someone she could depend upon. Or thought that she could. She was under enough stress without having to assume leadership. But she should think of herself as a junior partner for now.

He reached across the table and squeezed her warm hand.

"We've kept ahead of the ratcages so far," he said. "But until now, we've mostly just been running away. It's time to take the offensive." Just how they could do that, he had no idea.

"Candy, tell Garth we're returning to the honker planet. I know he's never been there, but he'll find it in his star charts, and he'll get us there toot sweet."

"Toot sweet?"

"Immediately. Now, the exact spot where we'll land and what we'll do after that . . ."

Having finished the instructions, he rose from his chair, went to Tappy, lifted her up, and held her tightly. The hatchling, which he was also now calling the Imaget, moved from her shoulder to her hair. It changed color as it did so and became practically invisible. Jack did not worry about accidentally crushing it with his hand or stepping on it. It was so quick that it seemed to anticipate any movement threatening it. Which, indeed, it could be doing. Its telepathic powers could include more than transmission of the thoughts of others.

Chapter 13

JACK, Tappy, Candy, and Garth stood on the floor of the crater. About ten miles away, the gigantic icons and symbols on the crater wall moved very slowly in their never-ending parade. Now that Jack was close to the wall, he could see that the figures were on a smooth band made of some kind of material—certainly not of stone. The band or ring was set halfway up the wall. Its lower edge was at least three thousand feet above the crater floor. Its upper edge was about five thousand feet from the floor. Thus, the ring was two thousand feet broad. Above this, the crater wall extended upward for an estimated three thousand feet.

Who were the makers of this Brobdingnagian ring? What did the images and symbols mean? What could be rotating the mind-reeling gigantic artifact? What . . . ? Jack quit thinking about it. Or tried to do so. He had a much more urgent problem to consider—survival.

The Gaol ship had left after Garth had given it instructions. It would be in orbit now, ready to return if Garth radioed a command. If other Gaol ships came while it was still in orbit, it would transfer to the system of another star. And it would move again if it were again located.

Jack led the others toward the wall. Between it and the place where the ship had departed was a tiny camp of honkers. Jack wanted to give the honkers plenty of opportunity to be alerted to the presence of the intruders. If the honkers were caught unawares, they might scatter in a panic or, perhaps, attack the strangers.

But if Jack could get friendly with them, he might get them to hide the refugees, maybe even direct them to the leader of the secret organization Tappy said existed among the honkers.

Beyond that, though, she did not know much about it.

Jack had to work fast. The Gaol would find Tappy and her companions very soon if they did not get to a hiding place. Garth had told him that it would be at least three hours before the Gaol's vessels would appear above the planet.

The sun was just descending from the zenith. The refugees were on the bank of a large creek. The vegetation on the plain was somewhat like that on an African veldt—now and then. But there were distinctly non-Terrestrial plants here. Like those that resembled thirty-foot-high croissants with one end stuck in the ground and with many large-headed red pins stuck in them. A moldy blue-green moss dripped from the pins, which were probably just exotic-looking branches. The ends of the pin-branches had knobby growths with holes in the center. Very tiny reptiloids stuck their shiny plated heads out from the holes.

These trees and others lined the creek. Beyond these, yellowish grasses as high as Jack's waist grew thickly. Their expanse was broken here and there by plants twenty feet high, their puce trunks ascending in a zigzag fashion to topknots of thick scarlet and lemon fronds.

Far to Jack's right, some enormous blue piglike beasts with huge round ears and elephantlike proboscises munched on the grass.

Somewhere, an animal roared.

Jack ordered Garth to take the lead. His big wheels pressed the grass down to make an easier path for the others. If they encountered a large predator, Garth could cut it down with his built-in beamer. But Garth's presence would make access to the honkers difficult. These always fled if they saw a Gaol. On the other hand, Jack was betting that the honkers knew that Tappy was the host for the Imago. If they watched the strangers long enough, they would conclude that Garth was not your run-of-the-mill Gaol.

They had walked a mile when Garth halted. His whistles were low, and Candy, replying, also whistled softly. Then she spoke in English. "He says he detects middle-mass life-forms ahead about twenty meters. Also on both sides of us and behind us. He can hear them move and see their body heat. He cannot hear them speak."

"Tell him to proceed very slowly," Jack said.

Tappy came to his side and took his hand. She looked wary but not frightened. She certainly was much tougher than when he had met her. Her scary experiences might have destroyed the nerves of many, but she was basically courageous and resilient.

She had held his right hand briefly as if a touch could give her strength. Or did she think that she was giving him the strength? Though the Imago seemed to be sleeping, some of its power could be leaking from it to her. And she was unconsciously transmitting that to him.

"You're getting too introspective, Jack," he told himself. "You're so eager to find hidden meanings in this mess, you're getting ridiculous."

His left hand dangled free, but it was ready to snatch the beamer out of its holster if it were needed. He, Candy, and Tappy each carried one. There was also one in a recess in Garth. Jack could lift the lid and grab it quickly. But that was to be used only as a surprise weapon. All four beamers had been taken from the Gaol ship before they had left it. They also had extra batteries.

The Gaol moved ahead. Jack walked behind him but several paces to the Gaol's right. When he saw a figure stand up from the grass twenty feet ahead, Jack told Candy to tell Garth to stop. The person in their path was a honker, though unlike any he had ever seen. Its body was festooned with animals and reptiles. At least, that was how the honker looked at first glance.

Tappy walked past Jack and Garth. Her right hand was raised high, its palm open toward the honker. The honker responded with the same signal. Jack knew that that was the I-come-in-peace sign. He made the same gesture, and so did Candy. Other honkers appeared from the tall grasses. He looked behind him. Scores of their fellows had popped out of their hiding places. They held flint-tipped spears and long blowguns, but these were pointed at the ground. And when the first one to bar the strangers' path blew some kind of salute, they also saluted.

After Tappy had quit honking, the male "wearing" the animals bowed low. The tentacles growing from his hips rose and waved. The dormouselike beast whose tail was embedded in the honker's navel waved its paws and squeaked loudly.

Jack thought, If I ever get back to Earth, I'll do a painting of this exotic being. He's so baroque, so nightmarish. I could make a career just from my depictions of non-Earth beings. And then there's Tappy in her many moods, Tappy blind, and Tappy seeing.

At the moment, it looked as if he had little chance of ever returning to his native world. And, if he and Tappy did defeat the Gaol and she elected to stay here, he would not leave her. Without Tappy, he would not care where he was.

Now she was honking at the witch doctor, chief, or whatever he was. When she stopped, he honked for a long time at her. While speaking, he moved slowly toward her. Jack saw that he was old and wrinkled. Liver spots covered his body. But he was certainly quick and agile, nothing stiff or creaky about him. The snake coiled around his neck had a long thin body banded with alternating black and scarlet. Its head was twice as large in proportion to its body as any Earth snake would have been. It resembled a skinned and earless wolf's. It had neither eyes nor eye sockets. It uncoiled enough to extend its body and to lick Tappy's eyes and cheeks with a long wet unsnakelike tongue.

The dormouselike beast, the tip of the tail of which was sunk into the honker's navel, also lacked eyes. It stiffened its tail so that its body was at right angles to the honker's. Then its hairy three-toed paws clung to the skin of Tappy's belly for a moment while it sniffed with a huge doglike nose. Its tongue shot out. It was cylindrical and tipped with four tendrils. These momentarily flattened out on her belly, curled, then withdrew around the tip of the tongue, which also withdrew.

Jack had thought that the oyster-shaped thing over the honker's genitals was a sort of codpiece. But it quivered with a life of its own under its hairy exterior. And it split bilaterally for a few seconds to reveal some of its organs. Jack shuddered with repulsion. What function this molluskoid had, he could not guess. Nor did he really want to know.

By then, the conversation of honker and human was over. The animal-festooned male turned and began walking toward the crater wall. Except for the rear guard, which disappeared into the grass, everybody followed the weird male.

Tappy said, "He's the oldest honker on this planet, maybe two hundred or more years old. He's the administrative and spiritual leader of all the honkers. He's a sort of, how to translate? . . . shaman, from a long line of shamans."

"Does he have a name?" Jack said.

"It's a word that means, uh, one who puts a system together, uh, one who also gets a system working and keeps it working."

"You mean a builder?"

"No."

"An operator?"

"No, it's more like a . . ."

Poor Tappy! Her formal education had been very neglected. She smiled and said, "An integrator!"

He told himself not to be so hasty in the future in judging her knowledge.

"Good! Let's call him the Integrator. I wonder what he integrates?"

The honkers appeared to be Stone Age preliterates. But that must be because they wanted the Gaol to believe that. As evidenced by the Integrator, they were more advanced in biological science than the peoples of Earth. What else were they concealing?

The Integrator halted, and he scanned the cloudless sky. The only objects in it Jack could see were five crimson birds circling high in the distance. Satisfied that he saw nothing suspicious, the shaman walked into a grove of huge trees resembling banyans with thick overlapping plates of yellowish bark. Jack sniffed at their strong odor.

He said, "Wino's delight! Muscatel, three dollars a gallon!"

The shaman walked into the semidarkness of the center of the grove. Jack, following him, was startled when he saw the bark of the central tree open. It swung out to display a hollow in the tree. A honker stood within it. He bowed once to the shaman and three times to Tappy. Then he turned and went down a steep flight of steps. The shaman leading, all followed him.

But Tappy stopped and said, "What about Garth? He can't get down the steps, too. It's too narrow. And these wooden steps wouldn't bear his weight."

"Oh, man, I forgot about him," Jack said.

He, Tappy, and Candy went back up the steps, forcing the honkers behind them to get out of the tree. Jack was startled when he stepped out into the half-light. Garth was gone. A score of honkers was busily erasing the tracks of the Gaol's wheels.

"Ask them where Garth is," Jack said to Tappy.

Tappy honked at the nearest female. Then she said, "They've hidden him in a big hole in another tree. It's covered up with a fake section of bark."

"For God's sake!" Jack said. "Why didn't they tell us? And how did they get Garth to cooperate?"

She honked again, listened, and then said, "Some of the honkers speak the Gaol language. They can't whistle, but their honks can be the equivalent of the whistles that make up words. They just have to be the same lengths of the whistles and have the same timing between groups of whistles. He understands them when they do that, but he doesn't know honker speech.

"The Integrator didn't tell us that Garth would be hidden. Apparently, he took it for granted that we'd know that Garth had to be concealed up here. That's the way of the honkers. They assume a certain amount of intelligence in others. We'd better get used to their way of doing things, Jack."

They went down the steps again and passed through several tunnels lit only by pine torches set in wall sconces. They emerged into a vast cavern. This was well illuminated by light from plants growing on the walls and ceilings. These were tangled vines growing luminiferous pods.

A twenty-foot-wide stream of water coursed from a hole in one wall to a hole at the far end of the cavern. A bridge formed of material like spiderweb silk, its cables attached to the cavern ceiling, crossed the stream. The mouth-watering odor of meat cooked in stone braziers filled the cavern. The smoke drifted slowly along and was sucked up by a large hole in the ceiling. About thirty honkers, adults and a few children, were here. The youngsters were like children on Earth or elsewhere, playing, making a lot of noise, running around, having a good time, and testing the adults' patience.

Jack expected to be annoyed by them, especially since he needed quiet and privacy to think about his plans and also to talk (via Tappy) to the Integrator. Surprisingly, the noise was not to bother him. Perhaps, his increased empathy made him more tolerant.

Then he caught sight of a table near the wall and forgot about the infants. He walked to it and bent down to look intently at the objects on its top. They were three concentric circles made of some brown fibrous cardboard and, in the center, a tiny rose-red stone. Bending over to get closer to the stone, he saw that one side of it had been carved to make a sort of throne.

The inner circle bore on its inner side the same images and symbols that were on the crater-wall ring. These were also on the inner side of the two outer rings. By them were several piles of papyruslike paper. The top pages of these were inked with handwritten characters. These honkers were not preliterates.

He called to Tappy. Before she could reach him, a honker walked swiftly to him and began "talking." When Tappy got to him, she said, "It's a model of the crater bands. Apparently, there are two similar rings around the one we can see. They're concealed inside the cliff. He says this model is the latest in a long, long series. The honkers have been studying it for many centuries, maybe millennia, trying to figure out what the function of the real rings is."

A series of loud blasts from the Integrator interrupted her. She said, "He wants to talk to us. Now."

The Integrator sat on a high-backed and intricately carved chair by a table. He was feeding his body-beasts with meat and vegetables. Another honker was doling out live insects to the mossy oysterlike thing covering the shaman's genitals. Somewhere in the mass beneath its thick greenish hair covering was a mouth.

At a gesture from the Integrator, Jack and Tappy sat down. But the shaman indicated that he had meant for Tappy only to take a chair.

She said, "Sorry, Jack. He says this is going to be a long talk, more like a lecture, actually. He doesn't want to be interrupted by my translating what he says. You wander around, do whatever you want to do while he talks. Later, I'll report what he's told me."

"Don't forget to ask him about the model of the crater rings," Jack said. "I want to know everything he knows."

"Runner there, that's his name, Runner," Tappy said, indicating the male who had told her about the model, "will guide you. You can go wherever you wish, but he'll see you don't go into dangerous areas."

Jack bent over and kissed her forehead. "See you." But he did not leave at once. He stayed to watch the Imaget snatch a tiny piece of meat from a dish near the edge of the table. It had to move fast to escape the lunge of the snake thing. Jack paled. It would be a terrible loss if the Imaget were killed.

However, the hatchling was the fastest creature he had ever seen. Its jump was a blur like a hummingbird's wings in flight. In fact, it looked as if it had zipped from this continuum into another and then immediately reappeared in this world. That was a fanciful analogy, which, however, might be true.

An estimated hour later, he returned from his tour. Though he could not understand his guide's language, he had comprehended from the gestures that the many caves he had seen were a very small part of the complex. Part of it was a natural cavern network. Another part had been dug by others than honkers, if he interpreted Runner's hand signs rightly. And the honkers had extended the work of their predecessors.

Many of the caves contained animals and insects. These were obviously being mutated into species the honkers intended to use for their own purposes. One great chamber particularly fascinated him. Millions of green red-spotted flies were in cages made of what seemed to be glass. But this material was excreted by a horde of worms laid out in frameworks. The stuff, when dried, could be used as glassy panes.

Runner managed to impart the information that the flies were very poisonous.

Another chamber was devoted to a fungus that ate metal and plastic. The latter material, Jack guessed, came from artifacts which the honkers had stolen from the Gaol or picked up after they had been discarded.

When Jack was led back to the council chamber, Tappy and the shaman were still at the table. She was drinking a ruby-red liquor from a strangely shaped goblet of cut quartz. The Integrator was sipping his drink from another curiously formed stone goblet. Jack took several seconds to realize that the container was made of bone, not stone, and that it had to be the skull of an upper-class Gaol.

The shaman gestured for Jack to sit down. A honker brought him a stone goblet shaped like a hawk with half-folded wings. Its eyes were large emeralds. The liquor smelled like wine and was wine. It was too thick for his taste, but the glow that came swiftly after swallowing it was pleasant.

"I like it fine," Tappy said. "But you should know it's made from insect blood."

If he had not swallowed so much of the liquor, he might have gotten sick. By now, he didn't care if it had been made from horse manure. This world wasn't such a bad place after all. In fact, he felt as if everything was going to work out in Tappy's favor. The Gaol would be utterly defeated, and all would be well in the world.

While Tappy related her conversation, the shaman went to sleep. Some sudden honks and the wild waving of his hip tentacles indicated that he was having a dream. Or a nightmare.

"What'd he say about that?" Jack said, pointing at the crater-ring model.

"The shamans still have no idea what the crater ring is for. It was there when their ancestors climbed the crater wall and came down onto the floor. By the way, their name for themselves can be translated as 'the Latest.' Nobody knows why they're named that. They do have myths about its origin.

"Anyway, when the Latest got here, they saw the moving circle, and, of course, it's intrigued them and even become part of their religion. The original settlers thought that the images on the band were representations of the gods and the symbols were holy messages. If deciphered, they would bring permanent peace and plenty to the honkers, other peoples, too. The more enlightened now believe that the ring was made by a species that came here from another planet."

"Ring? The model shows three rings. How do they know there are three?"

"You'll know when we see a burial chamber of the people who made the rings. The honkers call them the Makers. We'll see the chamber soon. Oh, yes, I almost forgot. The honkers call the rings the Generator."

"Generator of what?"

"The murals in the burial cave imply that the rings are a generator of some sort."

"And what happened to the Makers?"

"The honkers believe that the Makers built the Generator as a weapon against the Gaol, a last-ditch stand. But the Gaol killed all of them before it could be used. The Gaol had no idea what the ring was for. They consider it to be a great curiosity but not worth intensive investigation. To them, it's some kind of religious artifact."

"All those millennia, and the honkers don't have the slightest idea what its purpose is or how to operate it?"

Despite his strong pleadings, she refused to say more about it.

The Integrator was absent during the following "day." Jack asked Tappy if she knew where he was.

"He's gone ahead to the burial chamber we're to visit. He didn't say much about what he'd be doing there except that he had to repaint some of the murals. They're so ancient they need retouching now and then. I suppose he's going to prepare the chamber ritually for our visit."

The day after that, they were awakened early—or he thought it was early since there was no sun to go by—and were given breakfast. Immediately afterward, Candy accompanying them, they started their journey through the tunnels and the caves. Three lesser shamans led the way. These lacked the implanted animals, but the genitals of each were covered with the mossy oyster-thing, and each had a pale snake-thing coiled around his or her neck.

Throughout the journey, Tappy was silent. Jack asked her what was depressing her. She only replied that she had much to think about and was trying to work her way through them. Would he please not be worried about her? She would be all right soon.

After three meals, the party came to a halt. The Integrator was waiting for them in a tunnel. The luciferous pods growing on the vines on the wall showed two large packs, a large canteen, a chamber pot, and a collapsible wooden ladder on the floor. The Integrator had camped here, Jack thought. But why at this place? It looked like every other tunnel the party had traversed except that one section of the wall was bare of the vegetation.

But the honkers, including the lesser shamans, were obviously awed. All halted when they were thirty feet from the Integrator, bowed, and honked softly.

Tappy had spoken about the chambers during their trip. Nobody but the chief shaman entered them except for some highly placed shamans who repainted the murals when they needed it.

The Integrator, honking a "chant" over and over, danced around the tunnel in a tight circle. Then he went to the bare section and pushed on it. It swung out at one side and in at the other. It was a door of stone on pivots in its center. Musty air rushed out.

Jack looked into the darkness within. The shaman, after some more incomprehensible "chanting" and dancing, lit a pine torch. The flame wavered slightly, showing that the tunnel had some ventilation. The shaman posed in the doorway, facing toward Tappy. He honked at her, genuflected three times, turned, and walked into the darkness.

Tappy said, "You and Candy are allowed, too, Jack."

Candy just behind him, he followed the girl and the shaman for about twenty feet. The tunnel began curving here. After two hundred paces, counted by Jack, the tunnel straightened out. Immediately, a large arched doorway was ahead of them. The shaman walked through it, his torch lighting up the immense chamber. He set that in a wall sconce, then lit two more torches he had carried in a bag on his back. He handed one to Tappy and one to Jack.

There were several fascinating objects seen dimly in the shadows deeper within the chamber. But a mural near him caused him to stop and study it by the light of his torch. It looked as if it had been painted yesterday. In fact, he could smell the paint.

He said, "I can't believe it."

Above him was a painting depicting, among other things, a group of four people. No. Change that to three people and one weird being who looked as if it were half machine. The human beings were a young female, a somewhat older male, and a woman. But a section of clockwork and wires was exposed in a hole in the woman's chest. That meant what? That she was not really a human being. She was an android.

And, though the half-machine did not look much like Garth, it portrayed a cyborg fitted with wheels.

To one side was another painting. It was clearly the space-time vessel in which he and Tappy had taken refuge and found the androids in it. Squiggly lines around it represented, he supposed, the pulsations emanating from the vessel.

All the images had been freshly repainted.

Jack's heart was clenching as if it were a hand desperately squeezing down on ectoplasm. Though he did not want to look again at the young female in the painting, he forced himself to do so.

She did not have Tappy's features. But she had that sweet expression Tappy so often had and that wondering look. Like the faces of Alice in Wonderland and of Dorothy in Oz. The artist had also managed to give a sense of both vulnerability and invulnerability. Jack had never seen anything to match the contradictory impressions in any work by an Earth artist, and he thought he had seen all the works of the great ones and the near-greats.

She wore a blue robe of some sort. It was not a nightgown, but it could easily have been used for that purpose.

A circular section in her breast and stomach areas was white. Representations of rays emanating from the central brightness shot through her body and several feet beyond her. Was that symbolic of the Imago?

He looked more closely. On her left breast was a vague tentacled shape through which the fabric of the robe could be seen. The Imaget?

The hairs on the back of his neck seemed to be standing up, and cold raced over his skin.

The young male did not have his face, and his clothes were not those of any Terrestrial. But he held a painter's brush in one hand.

The four certainly seemed to represent prophecies or predictions of the coming of Tappy, Jack, Candy, and Garth. Impossible—yet, there they were, and the young human female shone with the Imago within her, and she bore the Imaget on her breast.

He stepped back, lifted the torch higher, and saw the image above the group. It was of tongues of fire shooting above the heads of the four persons. Above these were images of the crater-wall rings and their figures and symbols.

From its interior sprang more tongues of fire. And in their midst were upper-class Gaol, the ratcages. Some of them were burning.

How would the rings be powered? The outer one had been rotating slowly for many thousands of years. Some kind of machinery had to be turning it, the other rings, too, he supposed. Nothing in the painting indicated what that could be. Was there a vast engine deep under the crater floor? What did it use for fuel? A shaft plunging to the hot core of the planet? A shaft which conducted the heat to the machine, where the heat was converted to electricity? Or had the Makers possessed means of which Terrestrials had no inkling?

By now the Integrator was bobbing up and down and whirling with an agility and endurance amazing for such an old person. He was also honking loudly.

Jack moved close to Tappy and spoke softly. "This couldn't be just coincidence."

He felt numb, but deep within him was a fiercely hot ball of excitement. "My God! Predictions can't be valid. No one can look into the future and see what's coming. Not about what individuals'll be doing, anyway. Especially if they won't exist for thousands of years. If true prophecies or predictions could be made, we'd just be machines rolling along tracks that were laid in the beginning of time. There'd be no free will.

"Past, present, and future would be fixed. We wouldn't be responsible for anything we did, good or bad. No, I just can't swallow that."

Tappy looked as if she had just seen some horrible monster coming out of a wall.

She said, "I can't believe it either, Jack. The Integrator told me about this, but he made me promise not to tell you about it. It was all I could do to keep silent. But I think I couldn't really believe what he said. I thought we should see this before we got high hopes, too high, and then fell off the wall like Humpty Dumpty."

Jack tried to dispel the numbness but failed. When he spoke, it was as if he were under water.

"Maybe someone—who, I don't know—is trying to make this prophecy, this prophetic mural, come true. Like a self-fulfilling prophecy. That'd be the only rational explanation. But who could be doing this if that is the case?"

"I'm really confused," Tappy said.

"Me, too."

She smiled, though it was obviously difficult for her to do. She said, "What difference does it make if we are programmed? Does it really matter if Fate or Someone has determined our lives? Or if we screw it all up by ourselves? We think we have free will. Even if it's a delusion, we wouldn't believe it. Not if we had solid proof. We'd deny it. So why worry about it, rant and rail and curse the gods? We can only act as if we truly were the masters of our destinies."

Jack could only grunt. But she was right. And her attitude and her manner of speaking showed that she had matured far beyond her years. Perhaps the false experiences had had some effect after all.

"I suppose," he said, "that the brightness within the girl and the rays shining from it symbolize the Imago?"

"That's what the Latest believe. That's why the Integrator sent that honker to plant the egg-seed in me. The ability to do that, make the egg-seed, I mean, was within their powers long, long ago. They were just waiting for the right person to come along— me—and to do it. There's another burial chamber, miles from here, that gives instructions for doing that. It's in the characters of the alphabet used by the Makers, but with it are images that indicate how to do it."

Jack shook his head, and he said, "Too much, too much. I still think . . ."

"Think what?"

"Never mind. It doesn't bear thinking about."

He chewed on his upper lip before he spoke again.

"Why didn't the honkers lead us into the underground refuge as soon as we entered through the boulder-gate?"

"The Gaol were too close. Besides, it was evident to the honker spies that I was headed, being urged to head for, a destination north. They assumed that it was the pulsating vessel that had suddenly appeared. They tend not to interfere in certain situations. When we showed up near their underground entrance, the Integrator decided it was time to hide us."

She drew a deep breath.

"Also, when you and I appeared with Candy and Garth, they knew that the prophecy was being fulfilled. It was time to take us in no matter what the consequences might be for them."

"Anything else?"

"I almost forgot. The Integrator said he thought I was attracted to the boulder-gate on Earth because it led to this crater. The crater ring, he thinks, generates a weak field because it's rotating slowly. But the field was strong enough to attract me to it. I mean attract the Imago in me to it.

"The Makers theorized that the field or whatever should radiate from the Generator would attract the Imago. Like iron filings to a magnet."

"And . . . ?" Jack said.

"And what?"

"That pulsating ship Candy and the other androids manned: Why did it attract you more strongly than the crater ring? And who made the ship and the androids? Were they prepared millennia ago, too?"

"I don't know," she cried. "There's just too much to know, too many unanswered questions."

He embraced her and kissed her softly on the lips. "Take it easy. One thing at a time. You may feel as if you're about to crack up, fall apart. But you're really tough, Tappy, really strong. Just hang on."

He became aware that the shaman was silent. He looked toward him and saw him gesture for Tappy and him to follow him. He led them out of the muraled room and into another that also had wall paintings. Several yards into it, the shaman halted. He genuflected nine times before stepping ahead again. Then he halted again and genuflected seven times. When he went forward again, he made only three steps. The darkness shrank away from the lights of their torches. Not very far, though. The ceiling was so high that the lights did not touch them.

Now Jack saw, placed on the floor ahead of them, eleven twenty-foot-high globes made of some glittering crystalline material. When the shaman indicated that he and Tappy should come nearer to them, they got very close to the globes. Jack felt as awed and as seized with mystery as the archaeologists who had first entered King Tut's tomb. But this place was probably many thousands of years older than the tomb—older, indeed, than the very first Egyptian tombs or Stonehenge.

Each globe enclosed a body. Jack did not need to be told that each corpse was a Maker's.

They were six-limbed beings, quadrupeds with two arms. Centaurs, he thought, though not resembling much the half-man, half-horse of the Greek myths. Their lower part, the animal body, was shaggy with long red hair. The four legs were long but quite bearlike. The upright torso springing from the front of the quadrupedal form was covered with bright golden hair. Some of the corpses were female. The big, round, and thick-nippled breasts made that certain.

The heads were so flat above the eyes and so narrow from a side view that Jack deduced a similarity in this respect to the Gaol. Like them, the Makers' brains were in their bodies.

The eyes, like the beardless faces, were human, but they had epicanthic folds which would have made their faces Chinese-like if their lips had not been heavily everted like those of West African blacks. Their noses were very large and hawk-beaked.

The eyes, ranging in color from brown to blue, seemed to be magnets drawing eternity and infinity into them.

The Integrator brought eleven candles from his bag and placed them in their holders before the globes. After lighting them, he got down on his knees and began bowing and chanting while his right hand weaved unseen symbols in the air. The acrid stench from the candles made Jack and Tappy cough. They walked away to the nearest wall and studied some of the murals there. Most of those showed the Makers in their daily life—or so it seemed to Jack. The vegetation and some of the animals depicted were not those of Earth or of the honkers' planet.

He was just getting started on his study of the series when the Integrator suddenly quit chanting. He quickly put the candles out, placed them in his bag, and gestured that the humans should follow him.

Chapter 14

THEY were in the cavern headquarters of the Integrator. Two hours ago, he had given Jack and Tappy glasses of a thick and dark purplish fluid to drink. It was a mixture of berry juice and an amount, very small, of the venom of the fly called "quickdeath." By increasing the quantity every day, they should be immune to the venom after twenty days. Meanwhile, they could expect to feel somewhat sick during this period.

"One bite will semiparalyze a person of our body mass," Tappy had told him. "Two bites in rapid succession will kill. The whole honker population has been immunized."

The drinking skull of the shaman came from an upper-class ratcage who had died from the quickdeath's bites.

"The Gaol ruling class seldom leave their ships when they're on this world—in this area, anyway—unless they're wearing heavy nets. They send out their humans and lower-class warriors to do the work. The shaman says we were lucky we didn't get bitten while we were wandering around in the crater."

After swallowing the sweet but foul-smelling fluid, Jack and Tappy resumed their study of the crater-ring model. Jack picked up the page he had been writing on, but he put it down when a sharp pain struck his stomach. A few seconds later, he had a severe headache.

Tappy, who looked as sick as he felt, said, "It'll go away in an hour. But we shouldn't eat anything until suppertime."

Jack's vision blurred. Where there had been one piece of paper there were now two, one overlapping the other by a few inches. Moreover, his hands and feet felt numb. Both abandoned the study to lie down in their cave bedroom. But, as the shaman had said, after sixty minutes, they had recovered enough to go back to the model and their notes.

So far, he and Tappy, aided by a honker who interpreted the notes written by generations of honkers, had plenty of clues, too many. But they had no idea what any of them meant. In that case, as Tappy remarked, how did they know the items were clues? Jack had replied that everything on the ring had to be significant. So far, though, he had found nothing meaningful in the images and symbols on the ring or in their locations on it or their relationships to each other.

Some of the images were of the Makers; some, of the ratcage-bodied Gaol.

There were also representations of the pulsating in-and-out vessel in which he and Tappy had taken refuge. Red wavy-shafted arrows tipped by flames radiated from the ship.

"Maybe those indicate the magnetism which the shaman thought might've drawn you to the ship," Jack said. "Like you were a migratory bird following the Earth's lines of force."

He shook his head. "I just don't know. Our only explanations for all this stuff are just theories. Not even that. Just hypotheses."

"The crater's magnetism drew me through the boulder-gate," she said. "That means that it somehow, uh, leaked through the gate even though this planet must be many, many light-years from Earth."

"But you wouldn't have felt the attraction if you hadn't come near the boulder. That means—might mean, anyway—that your foster parents sent us there because they knew about the boulder."

"I suppose so," she said. "But if they knew about it, why didn't they take me there themselves?"

"They must've had a good reason."

"Why didn't they wait until I was mature enough for the Imago to develop fully?"

"Because," he said, "they knew the Gaol were getting close to finding out that you were on Earth. They had to get you away before the Gaol went any further in their investigation. They had to chance your finding your way to the boulder. Who knows what your foster parents did after I drove you away? Maybe they went through another gate to another world. I don't know."

He was wondering, though, if her foster parents had been agents of the persons who might be working to fulfill the prophecy. Those people could be organized as a cell system. Each cell knew very little about the others. The inferior agents worked in solitude and ignorance except when they received orders from a higher agent. On the other hand, the foster parents might be in the highest echelon.

A few seconds later, a tall rangy honker ran into the cave. He stopped before the Integrator. Though winded, he delivered a long series of honks. The shaman rose from the moss pile on which he had been sitting and began honking at Tappy. His eyes were wide, and he was gesticulating wildly. His excitement infected the beasts on him. The snake reared up and hissed. The dormouse growing from his navel yipped and squeaked and waved its paws. The hairy thing on his genitals split bilaterally, closed, split, and closed. It quivered violently. The hip tentacles thrashed around.

Tappy became pale. Her voice unsteady, she said, "A Gaol ship has landed in the crater. It's either the one that captured us or one just like it."

"The best defense is offense."

That was a cliché. But, like most clichés, it was often valid.

Jack, Tappy, the Imaget, the Integrator, Candy, and sixty honkers were deep under the ground. The large chamber they occupied had been excavated by the Makers. One wall was composed of an immense piece of nickel-iron, a fragment of the meteorite which had formed the crater long ago. Many times during the three-day underground journey to this place, the group had encountered large relics of the fiery falling star. The Integrator said that the Gaol's orbital geosurvey ships must have detected these and the cavern complex centuries or more ago. If they had ever gone down into the subterranean system, it had been so long ago that the honkers had no record of it.

Now, however, they knew, or thought they knew, that the Imago and its host were somewhere in the crater. Instead of trying to keep one step ahead of the Gaol, Jack had decided to attack.

After a conference, the Integrator had agreed that that was the best policy.

The war party was now directly beneath the Gaol ship that had landed several days ago. Sixty feet of earth and meteorite fragments were between the vessel and the chamber housing the Latest and the others.

A report about the Gaol had just been brought by a spy who had climbed down a series of ladders glued to the inside of a ventilator pipe. Its entrance was inside a hollowed-out tree. According to the spy, the Gaol had set up a camp inside the circle formed by the landing-support system beneath the ship. It was composed, so far, of humans and cyborg Gaol. But the cyborgs had gone back into the ship for the night.

"You can be sure," the Integrator said, "that a walking ratcage is in command. This is too important to leave to mere humans and cyborgs."

Jack wondered if Malva was in the crew. Though his empathy for others had gotten even stronger while he was with the honkers, it was not powerful enough to overcome his hatred for Malva. If he could get her neck between his hands, he would squeeze until she died. No way would he ever forgive her because he could feel the motives that drove her. She was as evil as the Gaol she worked for, and she must die.

"Jack," Tappy said, shearing off his detailed thoughts of the revenge he would inflict on Malva. "The Integrator says we should go up soon. It's after midnight."

"Not we. You don't go with us. You stay here where you'll be safe."

Tappy knew that he was right. The Imago was too precious to risk in battle. Despite this, she had been urging Jack and the chief shaman to take her along. Jack suspected that she was not so much intent on fighting with them as she was afraid of being alone. Though she had a bodyguard of four honkers, she was alone if Jack was not by her side.

Looking determined, Tappy honked at the Integrator. There followed a short but savage conversation. The honks could not convey emotion as a human voice could, but her facial expressions and the vigorous gestures of both showed that they were getting hot under the collar, as it were. Finally, the shaman threw up his hands in a quite-human gesture.

Tappy smiled, then turned to Jack. "He says I can go if I don't leave the exit in the hollow tree. Don't you dare try to argue with me."

"What'd you do? Threaten to rip his penis off?"

Instead of replying, she put on a heavy close-meshed net over her bone helmet. Jack also donned a net, and both slipped their hands into three-ply leather gloves. Since both were still not immune to the quickdeath-fly venom, they had had to be protected. Their clothing was thick enough to protect against the bites.

"You promise not to get into the fray?" Jack said.

She nodded. He hoped she would keep her promise.

The Integrator glanced around at the war party, seemed to be satisfied with what he saw, and blew three long blasts and one short one.

"The war cry," Tappy said.

The shaman went into the next room, Jack, Tappy, and Candy in single file behind him. The others followed. A moment later, the Integrator began climbing the ladders set up by an advance party. Most honkers were armed with blowguns and poisoned darts, bows and arrows, flint-tipped knives and short spears, and flint axes. Jack and Candy and two honkers carried beamers. Three of them and their batteries had been stolen over the years from Gaol expeditions. They were in soft thick bags strapped to their back. If a beamer should be banged against the shaft wall, it would make no sound.

Jack's big beamer and the small one in his holster had been brought with him from the Gaol ship captured before he came to the honker planet. He would have preferred the weapon he had used against the Gaol in their first encounter, the shadow-death weapon built into Tappy's leg brace. During their flight from the Gaol, he had wondered sometimes about the persons who had installed the radiator in the brace. Also, where had they gotten this weapon?

He had also speculated, fruitlessly as usual, on why Tappy had muttered about it while sleeping. How had the words gone?

"Alien menace . . . only chance is to use the radiator."

In what way could this weapon be the only thing to vanquish the Gaol?

He had asked Tappy about her other dream-begotten phrase, "Reality is a dream." She did not know what either meant.

Behind him were a dozen or so honkers with glass cages full of flies strapped to their backs. Behind them would be the rest of the party, including some bearing more cages. These would be swarming with insects with other deadly functions than poison. And some Latest were carrying boxes crammed with fungus.

Air was moving downward over Jack as he went up. According to the shaman, who was only guessing, the ventilating mechanism was part of the shaft wall and had no moving parts. Something magnetic in the metal kept the air moving. That was why the Makers' ventilation system never wore out. But the Integrator was great on magnetism. It explained just about everything for him.

The shaft was dark. Not until Jack got near the top of the shaft did he see illumination, and that was dim. When he was helped out of the shaft, he was in a large but crowded room, the hollow interior of a huge tree. The light was from the full moon, but it came through a big hole far up the trunk.

He was pushed gently forward until he was out of the tree trunk and in a grove of trees. He could see better now, though the moonbeams were filtered by the tangle of heavily leafed branches overhead.

Finally, the last warrior came out of the trunk. Tappy was behind him. In a low voice, he told her to go back into the hollow. "And if things go wrong for us, get the hell down the shaft as fast as you can."

"I will," she said softly. She kissed him on the mouth. "God bless you. May He keep you safe."

He hugged her quickly, then turned away, tears blurring his vision. He might never see her again.

"Forget that," he told himself. "Concentrate on what must be done if she's going to be safe."

Nobody except the humans had spoken. It was difficult for the honkers to whisper, if very soft honks could be called whispers. But everything had been planned; everybody had his or her instructions. They could make all the noise they wanted to when hell broke loose.

Straight in front of him, he could see a slice of the Gaol camp. Lights streamed from the windows of dark domed structures. Some of the light fell on a massive shadowy bulk some yards to the east of the camp. That would be the landing structure, a small section of it, anyway. He stepped out to a point just beyond two trees. Their branches kept him deep in their shade. Now he could see about thirty of the domes. They were so large they must be barracks. He could also hear human voices. A door opened in one of the domes, and a man stood in the doorway, the light strong behind him.

He was smoking a pipe, the pleasant but untobaccolike odor of which drifted to Jack. After a few minutes, the man stepped back and closed the door.

A group of machines, their function indeterminate at this distance, was parked in the center of the camp.

Unexpectedly, the camp had no walls. The Gaol did not fear attack. Besides, the landing structure, a vast ring from which pylons rose a hundred feet to the main body of the vessel, formed a very high wall. No lights came from the landing structure or the spheroid body of the spaceship.

The honker spies had reported that the Gaol had not as yet sent out scouts or exploratory parties. Whatever they were up to, they were taking their time. Probably, the technicians in the vessel were probing with their cavity detectors and also with the instruments that assumedly could detect the presence of the Imago. The latter instruments, he hoped, were directed outside of the radius of the landing structure. They would never imagine that the Imago and its host could be inside the structure. If, at the time of landing here, they had probed directly beneath the ship, they would have detected only a hollow beneath the huge meteorite fragments. If, that is, their instruments could penetrate through the nickel-iron pieces.

Jack stepped out to the edge of the shadows of the trees. Honkers followed him. Then the Integrator was standing by his side, his hip tentacles waving languidly like seaweed in a current.

The Integrator watched for a while. Then he bleeped softly, and he moved out into the moonlight. Jack and Candy and the two honkers ran swiftly to the doors of four domes near them. Each pulled out of a bag a small creature the bottom of which was a flesh suction pad. A long tuft of hair serving as a handle for the warriors projected from the back of each. Jack stuck his suckerbug, as it was called, onto the center of the door. Using his beamer, he cut a circular hole in the door. When he was close to completing the circular section, another warrior grabbed the creature's hair tuft. He pulled it and the section away from the door as soon as Jack had finished.

Another honker stuck the front of a glass cage against the hole. He pulled up a slide for a second or two, then closed it. At least two hundred flies, maybe more, had gone through the hole. Jack ran on to the next house while another honker put back the cut section and applied tape across it to hold it to the door.

Meanwhile, some honkers had gone to the parking lot. They had to make sure that none of the motionless machines there were actually cyborgs. In a few seconds, the Latest held clenched hands overhead. That was the signal that all was well in the lot.

Jack and Candy and the two honkers worked swiftly. Already, the first of the parties to enter the domes behind the cutters had made sure no one was alive in them. Now they were going into other domes, and most of them were carrying beamers appropriated from the dead Gaol.

Jack was on edge. He expected an automatic alarm to sound at any time or a Gaol in his death agonies to scream out. That did not happen. After an estimated fifteen minutes, the last warrior had reported to the Integrator. He held one hand up, turning this back and forth, a signal that he had completed his assignment.

Jack's beamer sliced through the thick outer wall of the curving landing structure. Three others also cut several large entrances near the one Jack had made. Then a number of suckers were applied to the wall sections just before they were completely cut. They dragged the pieces rather easily. Though thick, they were of very lightweight material.

The perilous ways were open. A dark corridor stretched before them. If an alarm was sounding in the main body of the ship, the war party could not hear it. But the Latest were going on the assumption that some would soon be activated. Jack was not so sure. The Gaol may not have thought it necessary to activate them.

The party was not in danger of getting lost in the vast maze of the ship. Garth had served on the same type of vessel. Through Candy, he had provided all the information needed to find the places to be invaded. The honkers had made diagrams of the passageways and the control center and where the crew was stationed when on duty and where it slept. While going through the tunnels to the chamber beneath the ship, the war party had studied these. Everyone knew exactly where to go and what he must do and how many he would have to fight.

Nevertheless, as in any battle, things could not only go wrong but doubtless would.

Chapter 15

JACK kept moving, knowing that time was critical. The Gaol captain had to know that the security of the ship had been breached. He would be ruthless in the defense of his command. The honkers were following a meandering trail around, over, and through the trusses and pipes of the skin of the ship, evidently seeking to lose themselves so that no guards inside could spot them. This was no innocent camping hike!

Yet now Jack was suffering significant second thoughts. Doubts which had been nagging him were now threatening to overwhelm him. It wasn't that he was afraid for his life, though he was, or that he was concerned that the odds were against this mission, though he was. It was that now, belatedly, the scattered bits of wrongness he had felt were coalescing into a more solid structure. He was no longer vaguely concerned; he was quite specifically alarmed.

He followed the honkers automatically while he put it together, making sure of his notion. Because if he was right, there might be worse trouble ahead than behind. Not physically, but in terms of Tappy's destiny.

Item: Tappy was the host of the Imago, an ethereal entity who could cause any living creature to have great empathy for all living things. The Imago could destroy the galactic empire of the Gaol by causing all living creatures, including the Gaol themselves, to have empathy for others, instead of oppressing them. Therefore the Gaol intended to capture Tappy and lock her away in isolation for life so that the Imago could not spread its harmony.

Item: Tappy had led Jack to the planet of the honkers, who were only vaguely manlike, and this planet had extensive ancient artifacts. These had been constructed by the Makers, who seemed to resemble centaurs whose nonhorselike portions were bearlike rather than human. Some of these artifacts were enormous, and seemed to be still operative, such as the metallic band around the crater wall, about fifty miles in diameter. What had happened to the Makers, whose power must once have shamed that of the present-day Gaol?

Item: A honker had somehow drugged both Jack and Tappy, and planted the egg-seed on Tappy's chest. Hormones or something similar from that egg had nullified the effect to the volition paralysis the Gaol had used on the two of them, so that Tappy was able to get them free, so that they could reach the Agents of the Imago and get help. This indicated that the honkers were not the primitives they had at first seemed to be.

Item: The egg had in due course hatched, producing the Imaget, a creature who could facilitate or enhance the qualities of the egg's host. The Imaget had the power to enhance or facilitate the powers of its original host, so that the effect of the Imago could be transferred in an hour instead of a day. It also was a telepathic transmitter, at least between creatures with whom it had had close physical association, or whom it had helped convert.

Item: Despite the empathy which had transformed him, cyborg-Gaol Garth had gone to his former ship and slain its living guards, equipment operators, and true-Gaol captain. He had shown no compassion; rather, the opposite, becoming an efficient killer. This could not have been because of reversion and loss of empathy in the absence of the Imaget, because both Tappy and the Imaget had been with him. Jack himself, just minutes ago, had participated in the honkers' savage attack on the human minions of the Gaol. Where was his empathy for those living creatures, which were his own kind? He should not have been able to do it. Only now, in retrospect, were his qualms manifesting. This suggested that the Imaget had another property: the ability to reverse what it had enhanced. It was a phenomenally potent little creature!

Put these items together, and what larger picture emerged? Imago, Makers, honkers, Imaget. All of them seemed to have powers beyond what first showed. All of them were working together to oppose the Gaol. But what were they working *for*? It wasn't enough merely to say that the empire of the Gaol was evil; one empire was probably similar to another, when it came down to it. Maybe it would be a better galaxy if every living creature in it had empathy for every other creature. But it might also be anarchy. Now, with this realization of what else the Imaget could do, Jack realized that he might not be working for a future utopia. He might be just another tool for some shadowy alien force whose ultimate purposes might be just as nefarious as those of the Gaol.

How could he be sure he was on the right side—assuming there *was* a right side? That he and Tappy were not mere patsies for some player in a galactic game of intrigue and power? That their honker allies were their friends and not their enemies? That they were not working for the restoration of the Makers to power, if any still existed, regardless of the welfare of the galaxy?

But his thoughts were cut off by an outside event: They had been walking through what appeared to be the space between the outer and inner shells of the ship. There was surely an aperture to the main portion. But the defenders of the ship must have located them, and were now counterattacking. There was a hiss of gas.

Jack and the honkers quickly donned simple gas masks that the honker leader passed around. These consisted of spongelike objects. They simply held them in their mouths and breathed through them. Jack realized that these could be living creatures, or could be infused with microscopic entities, that detoxified the gas biologically.

Similarly they plugged little pieces of sponge into their ears and nostrils and clapped flexible transparent shells over their eyes. None of Jack's senses seemed to be impaired by this. Then they brushed damp sponges over their bodies, covering them with somewhat sticky goop that quickly thickened. Jack painted his face, neck, arms, and ankles. They were now completely protected against poison gas—Jack hoped.

They moved on, breathing through their sponges. Jack found that the air through his was slightly flavored, not unpleasant. But his legs began to itch, and then his crotch.

He realized that he should not have assumed that his clothing would protect him. Of course it wouldn't! So he stopped to do what he should have done before. He ripped off his clothing and jammed the sponge into all the itchy areas, vigorously swabbing them. The discomfort eased immediately; the honkers did know what they were doing, here.

But his pause had caused him to fall behind; the honkers hadn't waited for him. They evidently did not suffer fools gladly. He would be lost in this labyrinth if he didn't catch up quickly. He didn't have time to put his clothing on again, so he settled for his shoes, and wadded the rest up into a knotted ball. Naked, he charged along the route he had seen them go.

For a while he feared he was lost anyway. Then he spied a honker, waiting for him. As he came up to it, the honker loped ahead, showing the way to the others. They had not after all left him to be lost. That was nice, since he was the nominal leader of this raiding party.

They came to a flat wall that might be the back side of a control panel. Many lumps and strands projected from it: the wiring of the ship? One honker brought out a little sac of paste. He rubbed this carefully on the metal wall, in a disk about two inches across. The wall became translucent, then transparent there. The honker peered through it. He nodded, then brought out a thin strawlike tube with a bulb on one end. He poked this at the transparent section, and it penetrated the metal. When it was through, he squeezed the bulb. There was a faint hiss of gas being forced through.

Then there was a thump on the other side of the wall, as of a guard falling to the floor. Gas was a two-edged weapon.

Another honker did something, and a panel swung open. They piled into the ship proper, jumping over the body of the guard or technician there. Jack saw that it was a human female, halfway pretty. But he felt no sympathy; she was a minion of the enemy. And realized that he could no longer trust his feelings; he carried the Imaget, which seemed to be immune to the gas, and it had reversed his emotion.

But now that he realized that things were not exactly as they seemed, he might be able to compensate. Regardless, he had to take this ship, because if he failed, it would soon attack and reduce the honker defenses on the planet, and Tappy would either be captured or killed. Of the two, capture was the worse risk. So his understanding could have little effect on his immediate actions, but perhaps much on his longer term strategy.

There were a number of creatures in sight, but they paid no attention to the intruders. Apparently they were androids, programmed for specific tasks, not for defense of the ship. However, when the authorities realized that their gas attack had not succeeded, they would send a more competent contingent to do the job.

The honkers had gone about as far as they could, without direction. They had breached the shell of the ship and gotten him inside. Now it was time for Jack to do his thing.

He had had a foolish notion of carving his way through the ship with a giant curving laser-edged sword, protected by some kind of magic armor, lopping the heads from any who opposed him. But of course that was unrealistic. The Gaol had lost one ship to a surprise attack, and would not allow another to go the same way. There would be attack robots marshaling right now, to come and cut him down. Sword and sorcery was not for this realm. There was a more subtle but effective procedure. He was prepared in a less foolish, less dramatic, but more realistic way.

He felt in his bundle of clothes and brought out a tiny tightly sealed jar the honkers had given him. He unscrewed the cap and lifted it off. There was a little puff of dark vapor that quickly dissipated in the air. That was all.

"Now find us a hole we can defend," Jack said around his sponge.

The honkers were already doing that. The interior of the ship was a labyrinth of passages and tubes ranging from twenty feet in diameter to less than an inch, and cables of many sizes twining like serpents through and between. Some seemed to be for air, others for mechanized delivery systems, and others for the passage of robots or living creatures. But spread around in it were glassy bubblelike chambers, evidently little command centers, which could be sealed off. Most of them contained creatures, but some were empty. The honkers brought him to one of these bubbles, sealed him in, then dispersed.

This ship was, Jack realized, like a giant living thing. He had seen it, or one like it, healing itself after he and Tappy had cut through its wall with the radiator. Now that he was inside it, he thought of the tubes as blood and lymph vessels, and the tunnels as part of a vast alimentary tract, and the cables as nerves. That would make the robots and androids and living creatures serve the function of the cells of the blood, circulating to every part of the whole. This chamber must be a temporary storage place for blood, so that it could be routed where needed in a hurry. Maybe antibodies were robot warriors with blasters.

Now a screen lighted in the bubble. The human woman Malva appeared. "So it is you, Jack," she said, eying his naked torso. He moved his bundle of clothes to cover what counted. "Evidently the job of disposing of you was bungled."

"So it seems," he agreed. He had to spit out his bit of sponge so as to talk clearly. It didn't seem to matter; there was no longer hostile gas here.

"But you are now sealed into a containment capsule. You will die when your air is exhausted."

"The ship will die soon after me," Jack replied evenly.

"You are of course bluffing. This ship has taken off and is now orbiting the planet. Your friends can not help you."

Jack had not felt the takeoff, but that meant nothing; the drive was inertialess. "I suggest that you put me into direct contact with the Gaol captain immediately, so that we can negotiate the surrender of the ship before it is destroyed."

"The Gaol do not surrender their ships. Nor do they negotiate with inferior life-forms."

"Have it your way. Meanwhile, let me clarify our threat. I have released a funguslike cloud of spores which is circulating throughout the ship. The spores' first priority is to multiply, which they do rapidly, feeding on the elements of the air and the substances of the ship. They are omnivorous, with appetite for metals, plastics, and organic things. Everything except living tissue. They even feed on poisonous things. Their effect is almost imperceptible at first, but increases exponentially as their number multiplies. Their life cycle is complete in a matter of seconds; they have a very high metabolic rate. Soon you will notice an impairment of the functioning of the ship, as they festoon and clog the smaller channels. Later you will notice that their waste products are highly corrosive, dissolving all the substances on which they feed. Indeed, that is part of their mode of operation: they dissolve things in order to feed on them. The effect will accelerate, until the ship is rendered inoperable and everything in it dies."

"You and your party along with it," she said.

"Yes. So no threats will prevail against us. We are a suicide mission. Only your surrender, in time for the antidote, will save any of us. Now put me in touch with the captain, because I will not negotiate with you. You have demonstrated your lack of integrity."

Malva's picture was replaced by that of the ratcage that was the captain. "What is your offer?" the Gaol's words came, translated.

So the Gaol did negotiate, when they had to! The captain must have verified the effect of the fungus, and realized that there was not time to bring an antidote from a far system, assuming they were able to devise one. Of course he could not trust the captain any more than Malva. But he didn't need to. *Orient,* he thought to the Imaget. *Convert.*

Suddenly Jack remembered the body of the young human woman the honker gas had killed. He had never known her in life, but he knew she had been a living, feeling creature who had done what she had to do to survive. If she served the Gaol, it was because they were the available employers, not because she was a bad person. In fact, there were no bad people, only differing agendas. There were no bad living creatures. Everything deserved its chance. He felt grief for all whose chances were denied.

The Imaget had focused on the captain, channeling its full power, as Jack had told it to. It was bringing empathy to the Gaol. But that meant it could no longer serve Jack, and so the full force of his empathy for all living things had returned. He had never lost it, only had it temporarily blotted out so that he could perform ruthlessly. Just as the Gaol cyborg had performed when taking over the other ship.

However, he had to hold the captain's attention while the Imaget made enough of an impression to maintain the contact. After a while, the captain would not object to the conversion, if he was even aware of it. It hardly mattered what Jack said, as long as it kept the dialogue going. "Surrender your ship to me. Then I will arrange to have the counteragent delivered, so that the ship survives without crippling damage."

"This is not acceptable. Make another offer."

"Wait it out. Then the ship will crash, and all of us will die. But you will not have the Imago or its host, and so your mission will be lost."

"There is always an intermediary course. Make another offer."

"I don't seem to be getting through to you," Jack said. "I don't have to dicker for terms. I have the controlling hand. Your only choices are to surrender the ship or die. I will let you live if you yield." Because he had empathy even for the Gaol. He did not like the idea of hurting any living thing, but knew that he had to to win this encounter or many more would suffer.

"I will demonstrate the intermediary course. You will save yourself considerable distress if you issue a message for your associates, to the effect that the situation is in order and you require the antidote immediately. If you do not, you will be captured and required to do so under duress."

"Fat chance, ratcage."

"This is negation?"

"Right."

The screen faded to blank. Then fully mechanical robots appeared around the bubble, using tool appendages to sever and seal off the various tubular connections it had to other parts of the ship.

The captain had distracted him with the dialogue while he set up his attack on the bubble! Who had been fooling whom? It was ploy and counterploy, in a deadly game. But the Imaget was still oriented on the Gaol. How long would it take, telepathically? If they broke in and killed him and the Imaget, the fungus would still disable the ship. But they did not intend to kill him. They were going to torture him to make him give their message. Could he resist that?

The robots severed and sealed the last outside connection. Then they simply rolled the bubble to a larger chamber. A coating of dirt was forming on the outside, which was odd; where would there be dirt in a sealed ship like this? Now Jack saw that similar bubbles enclosed the honkers who had accompanied him. All of them had been captured.

They were going to have him out and under duress very quickly. Too quickly? Time was his ally, but how much time did he need? Did the process of conversion take longer by telepathy? How could he stall, to get enough time?

The robots used what looked like lipstick applicators to mark lines on the outside of the bubble. But when they completed a circle, a panel fell out. Jack's protection was gone.

But he refused to give them any help. When a robot reached an appendage in, he knocked it aside. It was a futile gesture, but one that had to be made.

The robot swung its appendage back toward Jack, but slowly. Now he saw that it was encrusted with furry growths. The fungus!

Jack avoided the appendage, and it was unable to catch him, even in this confined region, because the fungus interfered with its mechanism. Now he saw that the other robots were similarly overgrown. They might be able to ignore fungus on their exteriors, but it probably was growing in the joints, too, and inside. Wherever it could reach. The same thing would be happening all over the ship.

Now he realized that the dirt on the bubble was also fungus. It was on the walls and floor, too. It was doing its job of spreading. How long would it be before it interfered with the major systems of the ship, bringing it down?

Then another robot came. This one was spraying something. A fungicide! It sprayed the other robots, and they then resumed faster motion. Maybe there wasn't enough of the stuff to douse the whole ship, but that wouldn't help Jack.

Then the motion slowed again. The fungus was growing even faster; he could see it appearing as a thickening film on all the sprayed surfaces. The fungus was now feeding on the fungicide!

But Jack was not yet out of trouble. Human minions came. Fungus was growing on them, too, or at least on their clothing, but they were functioning. They spoke to Jack in the highly accented English that seemed to be the class-taught second or third language here. "Come out! Or we drag you out!"

Jack was about ready to come out anyway. He climbed through the hole in the bubble. "Now what?" He noticed that there was no fungus on him, not even his inanimate portions, such as hair and nails. It seemed that the same paint that had protected him from the gas was effective against the fungus. The honkers were not about to be hoist in their own petard.

But coated or not, these human minions meant business. One brought out what looked like a set of electric probes. Jack felt a chill; that could be exactly what they were. He knew that electric shock could make a lot of pain that didn't show. He didn't know whether he could handle it.

So he made a break for it. He shoved the man with the probes against the one beside him, and charged through the gap in their circle this made. He had no idea where he was going. Just so long as it was anywhere but here.

There was a faint flash. Then he lost his volition. The honker paint did not protect against that device! But why hadn't they used it before?

Jack had stopped where he was, not losing his balance, just having no power to go anywhere on his own initiative. He stood facing away from the other men.

"Turn," a voice said from a hidden speaker.

Jack turned to face the others—and saw that all of them were turning away from him. What was going on?

"The intruding human being only will respond," the voice said.

Then Jack understood: the flash had nulled the willpower of all of them! That was why they hadn't wanted to use it. It did not differentiate; it affected any human being in the vicinity, making them almost useless. He had forced them to use it, and that had been a reasonably good move.

"Walk. Follow the blue line." A line appeared before him.

Jack walked. The line wound a devious course through the ship. Soon Jack was lost; he would never be able to find his way out on his own, even with the good chart of the ship the honkers had provided. Not that he was likely to be given the chance. There was a lot of walking, in a mile-diameter ship! But if he did get his will back, then he could follow the line back to his starting point.

Was there any way to break the hold of the null-volition? Before, Tappy had been immune, because of the Imaget egg, and then she had gotten him free of it by writing Malva's name as a Gaol symbol on a piece of paper and having him eat it. He still wasn't sure how that worked. But he couldn't do that now. No pencil. No paper. No Tappy.

But wait! Tappy had been free because of the Imaget egg she carried. Surely the Imaget itself had the same power! So why wasn't he free?

Because the Imaget was otherwise occupied at the moment. But when it finished that job, it would revert its attention to Jack, and then he should be free. Probably he could get its attention with a strong thought, if he had to. So he had a secret weapon. Maybe.

Meanwhile, he followed the blue line. At one point it spiraled up a curving ramp, and he happened to see behind him. The line had disappeared. It faded out as he moved along it, being clear only ahead. So much for following it back! However, he also saw his footprints in the furry gray coating of fungus on the floor. Maybe he could follow them instead, if they didn't disappear too rapidly under new growth.

Finally he reached a region he judged to be somewhere in the center of the ship. There was a huge bubble, opaque because of its coating, with an enormous number of connections. It was as if this were the central cell of a living entity, to which all others reported.

And of course it was, he realized. This was the abode of the Gaol captain! He was about to face his reckoning.

"Wipe a section clear," a loudspeaker said.

Jack realized that he was still carrying his bundled clothing. He used this to rub on the available surface of the sphere. It was like scraping snow off a windshield. Now a window of clarity appeared.

Inside the bubble was the Gaol captain. For the first time Jack saw such a creature with his own eyes, from up close, instead of by telepathic projection through other eyes.

The thing was horrible. All the details were as he had been shown before, but now they were in sharp ugly focus. The great external rib cage, as if it had once been fleshed but now was a carcass. The sacful of body organs, as if the guts had been wrapped in membrane and hung inside the stripped rib cage to cure. The legs and neck projecting from the general region of that internal mass, emerging from the cage. What a monster!

Yet perhaps it was in keeping with the spaceship the Gaol used. For this huge ship had riblike projections reaching up to join at the top. It was surely the kind of structure the Gaol would feel comfortable with, because of their own skeletal structure. Just as human beings felt comfortable with devices that had their controls at the top and their propulsion at the bottom, emulating the human head and feet. Maybe the nature of the originating species could be derived by inspecting their spaceships, if one knew how to interpret the signals.

"I did not know that the Imago could strike at this range," the speaker said. It was obviously translating for the Gaol inside the sphere.

Jack did not reply, because he had not been directed to. But he felt a thrill of excitement. Had the Gaol been converted?

"What is the mechanism?"

Now Jack could speak. But he did not *have* to speak, because the null effect did not extend to his mind. Would he be better off to refuse to, so that the Gaol would not learn what was going on? The null did not allow him to lie; he had either to tell the truth or say nothing.

He decided to respond with limited candor. "The Imago's power extends beyond its host. This enabled the minions of the Imago to take charge of the other Gaol ship."

"This one, too. But our tracers show the host of the Imago to be on the surface of the planet, and our experience of prior millennia indicates that the direct range of the Imago does not extend to interplanetary distances, and that of the Imago's converts does not extend beyond immediate personal contact. How has the Imago reached me?"

Had the Imago reached it—Jack assumed the creature was neuter for convenience—or was it merely saying so to fool Jack into betraying critical information? If he told of the Imaget, and the Gaol had not been converted, it could take the Imaget from him and destroy it, thereby achieving victory. But if the Gaol had been converted, the Imaget would be an even more useful tool for the conversion of other key entities aboard this craft, giving Jack the victory.

Jack decided not to gamble. He remained silent.

"We are at a temporary impasse," the Gaol's translated voice said. "I control your actions and can cause you to be extinguished. But you may be the only available creature who knows the agency by which the Imago is reaching me. If I do not ascertain this mechanism and abolish it promptly, I will be subverted by the Imago. Death is preferable. However, if I die without ascertaining the mechanism of corruption, there is a significant risk that the Imago will succeed in corrupting some other Gaol, as it did our cyborg, and that would put the empire at risk. This is not desirable. Speak."

"You are correct that the Imago is reaching you, but I do not regard that as subversion. I call it liberation. I prefer to wait for your conversion to be complete before giving you information that might enable you to interrupt it."

"I appreciate your point. But at the present rate of progression, my conversion will not be complete before the mold destroys the key mechanisms of this ship. Then all of us will die, regardless who is ascendant. This seems to be no more to your interest than to mine. Speak."

The fungus! Jack had forgotten about that. The Gaol was right; the ship was being destroyed while they talked. If they all died, so would the Imaget, depriving the Imago of its most useful immediate tool. It would also deprive Tappy of Jack, and that was apt to be a disaster of another kind. The Gaol empire might very well succeed in prevailing, if Jack and the Imaget perished together.

But the Gaol captain, by its own statement, had not yet been converted. He could not let it know about the Imaget yet! So what was he to do?

"I agree that we are at an impasse. I prefer to save the ship and all our lives. But I can not allow the Imago to be placed in jeopardy by trusting you. What is your offer?"

"Our loyalties are opposed. I must ascertain the detail nature of the Imago's threat, and survive to report it to my authority. You must subvert me so that you can eliminate the threat to the freedom of the Imago that I represent. We must come to a decision immediately. I offer a trade: give me the information so that I may relay it to my authority, and I will free your will, and turn myself and my ship over to you. Speak."

That was a considerable offer! The empire would know exactly what it faced, but this ship, under competent command, would be at the service of the Imago. That would allow a fair fight, as it were. It was devilishly tempting. But there was a flaw in it. "How can I trust you to keep the deal?"

"How can I trust you to provide accurate information?" the Gaol countered. "It is evident that neither of us has a guarantee, but that we can establish a guideline for action that will serve both our purposes. This must serve in lieu of trust. Speak."

Could he believe this? Jack wished he knew whether the Gaol were creatures of honor. Presumably they would not be able to maintain an enduring empire if they were not consistent in their statements and actions. But was that enough?

He flipped a mental coin and decided to gamble. "Agreed. The honkers provided the host of the Imago with an Imaget, which facilitates conversion. That Imaget is now facilitating your conversion."

"I restore your free will. Is this Imaget the creature Malva's projection perceived near the Imago host?"

Jack found that he could move and speak on his own. The Gaol had honored part of the deal. "Yes. It was planted on the host by a honker, and later developed and hatched. It identifies with her and enhances her power, which is that of the Imago."

"I will direct this ship as you command. I suggest that you take it aground so that the antidote can be obtained, or your life can be saved if the antidote is too late."

The Gaol was honoring more of the deal. "Do the four guard satellites have any living creatures on them?"

"None. They are robot controlled."

"Destroy them."

A screen lighted on a nearby wall. It showed the planet, with its satellite guard stations. Suddenly all four exploded.

"Where is the Imaget now, and how does it reach me?" the Gaol asked.

This was the critical point. If all this was a lie, and the satellites had not really been destroyed, the captain could renege and Jack would be lost. But the Gaol seemed to be playing it straight, and Jack had to do the same. "It is here on my body. It has been broadcasting telepathically to you."

"The ship is now descending to ground. We were not aware that this creature operated in such manner."

"Perhaps it's a new model," Jack said wryly.

"Where do you wish the ship to settle?"

Jack remembered how Tappy was waiting in the grove, hiding. He wanted to be back with her as soon as possible. "Right where it was before. Then open the hatch or whatever so the honkers and I can return to the ground. They'll get the fungus antidote."

"The ship will be at rest at that site by the time you have followed the blue line to an exit. I will hear any further directives you speak."

Jack looked around. There was the blue line again, leading away. "Good enough."

He followed the line. It was not the same route as before, but that could be because it was more direct. They had entered via the landing structure and would exit from a regular portal.

He turned a corner. There before him stood Malva, looking so real it was hard to believe she was a mere holograph. He stopped. He knew he should just walk through the image, but she was in a dress which revealed so much breast and thigh that he was afraid to touch it even vicariously. "What do you want?"

"The captain has made a deal with you," she said. "This places me in a precarious situation. I do not wish to be subverted by the Imago."

"You don't have much choice. All of the members of this ship's complement will be converted. I presume you will be useful in some way." He did not bother to conceal his distaste.

"Agreed. All will be subverted, unless they arrange to avoid it. That is what I wish to do. Agree to set me free, in mind and body, on the planet, and I will provide you with significant information of interest to you."

"No deal. I don't trust you. I may not trust you even after you're converted. Get out of my way."

She did not move. "Please, Jack. I am desperate. You have done what I thought impossible, and subverted the captain. The victory is yours. I will offer you anything you desire. Only guarantee my freedom."

"No." Now he resumed motion, intending to walk though her image, as he should have done before.

But he collided with her. Her lush torso pressed against him from breast to thigh as he tried to recover his balance, astonished. *She was here physically!*

Now he remembered that he was still naked.

He started to speak, but she cut him off with a kiss. "I can be extremely accommodating, if that is your desire," she murmured, glancing down. "I beg you to free me, whatever the price of it."

Jack got his hands up and pushed her away. "I don't want your body! I don't like you or trust you. I refuse to make any deal."

She disengaged, offering no resistance. "Will you at least listen? I believe you will find it worthwhile."

Jack started scrambling into his clothing. "Look: the captain is listening to everything we're saying. You must be guilty of treason already, trying to deal on your own. Anything you have to tell me, I'll learn when you are converted. This is pointless."

"The captain can not overhear us here; I selected this place because I know it is between monitors. Our dialogue is private. As for treason: he became guilty of it when he made his deal with you. I serve the empire, not the captain. I wish only to return to the empire, and to continue my opposition to the depredations of the Imago. Listen to me, then decide whether the information is worth the price of my freedom. Isn't that fair?"

Jack sighed. "All right. Tell me, and if I think it's worth it, I'll free you. You will be set loose on the surface of the planet and not pursued. But if you make any attempt to interfere with the Imago in any way—"

"Understood. Here is my information. Though the Imago you serve may be benign in principle, the tool it is presently using is not. The thing you call the Imaget has no necessary affinity for the Imago; it was pressed into service by the honkers for a reason of their own. I researched it, after spying it before. Bear in mind that I was the only person present at that encounter who was not subsequently corrupted, because I used the holo image. I alone remained objective. I discovered that the Imaget has gone by many names over the millennia, and that there is a pattern that is far from benign. It has formed empires in the past—"

"Now wait a minute!" Jack exclaimed. "This little thing could hardly—"

She glanced at his hair, where the Imaget nestled. "Do you suppose that any creature in its hatchling stage is the same as it is in its maturity? All babies are charming. What do you think its powers will be when it has grown to a mass greater than your own?"

She was making sense. He had been suspicious of the Imaget himself. Malva was independently confirming that suspicion. "Go on."

"The Imaget, by whatever name, enhances the properties of other creatures so effectively that they inevitably become dependent on it. It encourages this. When they can not function without it, the power passes from them to it, and they then serve the Imaget. Only the Imago has been proof against this, and in the past it has been the Imago who has brought down empires of the Imaget, as it has brought down those of the Gaol or other dominant entities. It is an irony that the Imaget is now serving the Imago itself, but perhaps the Imaget has found a way to add the power of the Imago to its own. If so, the empire that it forms this time will be truly impregnable."

Jack was appalled. "I can't believe—"

"Naturally, because you are already subverted. But you were subverted by the Imago before you encountered the Imaget, so you serve the Imago, and may be objective enough to appreciate the danger. The Imago itself is uncorrupted and uncorruptible, and this extends to its host. Perhaps the Imaget will simply cast the Imago aside when its usefulness is done, or confine it in the manner the Gaol wish to. One empire is very like another, in the acquisition and preservation of its power. If you are prepared to risk the exchange of one master for another and all that implies, ignore this threat."

Jack was silent, realizing that she had raised a question which he could not afford to leave unanswered. "Still, a single Imaget could hardly—"

"When the Imaget is grown, it will reproduce by having its minions plant its eggs on converted creatures, and these new hatchlings will ultimately serve the eldest one," Malva continued. "Once that stage is reached—"

"Enough!" Jack said. "I will give you your freedom. I will verify this by researching myself, and act as I see fit."

Malva smiled. "Thank you. May I take a weapon with me, to defend myself from wild creatures when I go into the wilderness?"

"Yes, take it," Jack said absently. The honkers—how much did they know of this? Were they working for the Imaget instead of the Imago? Could the Makers have been a benign empire, overthrown by the Imaget? Something like this was all too plausible.

Malva stepped to the side and reached into a recess in the wall. She brought out what looked like a twisted pistol and tucked it into her waistband. Then she followed Jack as he resumed progress along the blue line.

It led to a nether portal, with a ramp to the ground. The honkers of his raiding party were already there, waiting for him. Jack's dialogue with Malva had delayed him.

"Fetch the antidote," he told the honkers as he descended. Immediately one went to the ventilation shaft and picked up another small jar. "Release it inside the ship," Jack said, and the honker ascended the ramp and opened the jar.

Tappy emerged from hiding and ran to Jack's embrace as he reached the ground. "You won!" she exclaimed joyfully.

"Maybe," he agreed, hugging her. But he would have to do his research on the Imaget soon, because if what Malva had told him was true, they would have to get rid of the Imaget.

He turned to Malva. "You are free," he told her. "As long as you do no mischief on this planet."

"I think not," she said. There was a flash, and Jack lost volition.

Malva drew her pistol and pointed it at Jack and Tappy. "You are of course a fool," she said. "Did you think that if I researched the Imaget, I did not share my information with my master? We knew about the telepathy and were prepared. The Gaol captain simply compartmentalized his mind, so that only one section was subverted, while the dominant section remained independent. It was risky, letting you invade the ship, but it promised to lure the Imago into our control. So we landed the ship as bait, and waited for you to take it."

Jack could not answer, because she had not told him to. Tappy could tell him to—but she was covered by the pistol. In any event, mere words were pointless in the face of his disastrous misjudgment.

It hardly mattered at this stage, but he wondered whether she had told the truth about the Imaget. It seemed like a pretty involved story to make up, just to persuade him to accept her. It had a certain ring of authenticity. Maybe it was both true and false: true research, false motive.

Malva gestured with the weapon. "The two of you, enter the ship," she said.

Jack started walking toward the ramp. Tappy followed. The honkers remained unmoving. He did indeed feel like a fool. He should have known! Malva had never turned against the Gaol; she had been their agent throughout. She had used the pretext of her seeming wish for freedom to lull him into thinking it was safe for Tappy—and now Tappy and the Imago were prisoner of the Gaol again. What a cunning trap; they had even saved the ship from destruction by the fungus. But if they had anticipated the raid, they might have had it fungus-proofed anyway, and pretended to be suffering the effects so as to complete the deception. It was obvious that Jack was an amateur up against professionals.

But Malva had forgotten the Imaget! Whatever the truth about it, long-range, it served him and the Imago in the short range.

He concentrated, reverting it to orient on him. As he did so, he lost his stasis; it had nullified the null, as it were. He also lost his empathy for living things.

He acted immediately. He grabbed Malva's pistol and wrenched it from her hand as he shoved her back. Then he pointed it at her. It had a trigger, so he hoped he could fire it. If it had a safety, she had probably unlocked it, since she was not the kind to bluff. "Get to safety, Tappy!" he cried.

Tappy hesitated. He knew why: she didn't want to leave him.

"It's no good," Malva said. "Robots are coming. They will obey me, not you. They will break your bones if the host of the Imago does not obey me."

"You forget that I have the pistol," Jack said. Then, more urgently: "Tappy, get out of here!"

Tappy started to walk back down the ramp. But Malva went after her. "I'll be destroyed anyway, because of my contact with the Imago, but I can secure my mission. You won't fire, because of your empathy." She brushed by Jack.

"There may be something you don't know about the Imaget," Jack said. Then he fired the pistol at her chest.

A strike of lightning came from it. It bathed Malva in sparks. Then she fell, her face a mask of astonishment.

Jack turned and charged down the ramp after Tappy. But already the robots were arriving. They were roughly humanoid, except that they had three legs, so that they didn't have to worry about balance. They moved down the ramp in pursuit.

Jack started for the ventilation shaft. But already the robots were spreading out and forming a circle to close the two of them in. Jack fired at one, and scored, but the lightning had no effect on the metal. The robots were not likely to hurt either of them, just to immobilize them and carry them into the ship, because the Imago had to be alive and Jack was still a living lever to use against Tappy. But how could the robots be avoided?

Then he saw the stump of the ghosted tree, the one that the radiator had destroyed but whose upper structure remained as a shadow outline. The honkers had warned them not to go near that shadow. But it was within the closing circle of robots, and the alternative was to be captured by the Gaol. Maybe it was death to enter it, but it was their only chance.

"The tree!" Jack said. "Into the shadow!"

The two of them dived for the shadow.

Chapter 16

LIGHT dazzled Jack as his head passed through the faint dark of the shadow-tree. It blinded him and filled his head and his body. Every one of their cells seemed to glow as if they were thermite and had caught fire. He cried out with pain and terror as he fell forward and his hands and knees struck the ground. Behind him, Tappy shrieked. He had shut his eyes, but that did not help at all in making the light less intense.

He sat up and groped around, encountering nothing until he put his hands on the ground. Since the gloves hindered his sense of touch, he took them off and put them in a back pocket of the jeans given to him by Candy. The net over his head also went there.

The ground was fairly soft, as if it had rained recently. It was covered with a short thick grass. At least, the blades felt like grass, but they were softer than that which grew on Earth.

Something moved along his cheek, a gentle tickling thing which went down his neck, then was gone. It must be the Imaget. It had been on Tappy but, for some reason, had just leaped to him. Then it had crawled down from the top of his hair to his shoulder. Now that his shirt was between the creature and his skin, he no longer felt it. Or had it jumped back to Tappy?

The Imaget, he supposed, must be as blind as he. Unless its lack of eyes protected it. Whatever its state, it was not projecting telepathically so that he could see the land around him. If, that is, there was anything surrounding him. There might be nothing but this painful light here.

Here? A different "dimension"? Certainly, a different world, and one that might destroy him and Tappy. The warning the honkers had given them about the shadow had been short and simple. Do not enter! That was almost all the information the honkers could give. They had no idea of what would happen

218

if you did go through it. But they knew that the few who had
ventured through it had never returned. The last one to do so had,
like Jack and Tappy, used the shadow as an escape from deadly
enemies. That, however, had been over a generation ago.

Jack opened his eyes briefly, then closed them again. Though
it made no difference in the brightness whether or not he closed
his eyelids, he could not keep them open. His reflexes were ruling him.

He called out to Tappy as he groped around for her. He could
hear his own voice within his head, but it made no sound outside
of it. That swelled his fright. But it subsided somewhat when his
hand felt cloth and solid flesh beneath it. He ran his fingers over
the cloth until he felt a shoulder. The net covering her head and
shoulders had been removed. When he moved his hands down to
close over hers, he found that she had also taken off her gloves.

A second later, she was embracing and kissing him. Still in
their sitting position, they rocked back and forth, their arms
around each other. Her face, held against the side of his cheek,
was wet with tears.

He tried to tell her to take it easy, that they would be fine once
they mastered their terror and confusion. Again, he could hear his
voice circle around in his head without moving the air outside his
lips. Nor could he hear Tappy, though he could feel her body as it
was shaken by sobs. And when he released an arm to touch her
lips, he could feel them moving, surely trying to talk to him.

After a while, he got to his feet and pulled her up to stand by
him. He took her hand and pulled her along after him as he began
walking. He did not know where he was or where he was going,
but they just could not stay in one place. They would die of thirst
if they did. And if there was relief from this light or somebody
who could help them, they had to look—though "look" was not
the right word—for refuge and rescue. That would be slow going
since he had to slide his forward foot along and feel with its toe
for drop-offs.

His face felt as if it were in sunlight. Though he was sweating,
no doubt from stress, he was not too hot. The air was a mild
breeze, and it slightly cooled him.

They had gone perhaps a hundred yards when he jumped, and
he swore a soundless oath. Something had flicked against his
cheek. It was soft and momentary, but it had felt like the end
of a finger. The sensation was not caused by the Imaget moving
across his face. It had been too solid to be that. The Imaget had

been like lightweight velvet sliding across his skin. Also, its body had been too broad to be a fingertip.

Tappy squeezed his arm and moved so close to him that she seemed to be trying to melt her cells into his. She was no longer racked with sobs, but she was trembling. Had she felt that soft touch, too?

"For God's sake!" he said. "Whoever you are, whatever you are, speak to us!"

It was useless to speak; his words were imprisoned in his head.

He still had Malva's beamer-pistol, stuck in his belt, and the beamer-rifle, strapped to his back. But it would do no good to fire blindly. Besides, whoever had stroked his cheek probably did not intend to harm him. If the toucher did, he or she could have done so long before this. On the other hand, the person— or thing—might just be biding his time. For what?

It was then that he smelled a pleasant odor. Flowers? Wherever it came from, it was carried by the breeze from behind him. He turned around, sniffing, and then pulled Tappy along in the direction from which the odor seemed to come. I can't see, he thought, and I can't hear, but I can feel and smell. I'm not completely helpless.

Brave words. He was whistling in . . . not the dark, though this light was no better than complete blackness. If he tried to whistle, he probably wouldn't hear that.

The odor, which reminded him of tiger lilies, became stronger. He shuffled on until his leading foot suddenly felt a change in level. Carefully moving the foot, he determined that he was on the edge of a hill. Or a slight declivity. He began going down the gentle slope. After a hundred feet, he stopped. His left hand, held out at a downward angle before him, felt a stalk. He moved it around and encountered many stalks. The odor was so powerful that he knew he stood before a mass of flowers—if the stalks had flowers.

They did. His hand, sliding up a stalk, found the head. It was sunflower size, had nine big petals and a soft spongy center. Beneath the surface was a slight pulselike throbbing. Groping around, he found others like it. Then he let loose of them as something long and soft, too narrow to be the Imaget, slithered across the back of his hand. An insect? A caterpillarlike creature?

Though he had been startled by it, he was, in one sense, reassured. A world that had flowers and insects could not be entirely alien to him. And his sense of hearing was not completely gone. The rattling of the stalks as he moved them was clear.

He spoke again, hoping that his voice would project beyond his head.

"Tappy! Can you hear me?"

She could not do so. The question fluttered around inside his brain and could not escape.

He patted her shoulder, then took his hand from her and slapped his hands together. He jumped; his heart jumped. The clap was as loud as if it had been made on Earth. There was nothing wrong with his ears except that he could not hear his voice or Tappy's.

The echo of the hand-slapping had just died away when he jumped again.

A voice spoke from an unknown distance. It cried out, "Help! Help!" And then the woman—it was indeed an adult female's voice—began sobbing.

Jack shivered from a cold not caused by the breeze.

"My God!" he said, though no sound issued from his lips.

His panic, which had dwindled somewhat, roared back. He felt strange, strange, strange! This could not be!

The woman who had cried out and was now weeping was Malva!

It was her voice. No doubt about that.

But Malva was dead!

He reached out, touched Tappy, and took her hand. It felt clammy. She must have recognized the voice of the recently slain woman. He wished he could soothe her or, at least, talk to her. Then he turned to his right, his left side brushing against the flowers, his right shoulder brushing against her. After some seconds of slow progress, he could no longer detect the flowers except for the lessening odor behind him. Then he stopped. Malva was no longer crying out, but he could faintly hear other voices. They became stronger as he led Tappy toward them. But he halted once more. Silence had gripped his head again. It seemed to be squeezing him.

I can't take much more of this, he thought. And Tappy must be as close as I am to screaming with the pain of the brightness and a fear that tears the mind apart. A screaming only we can hear inside us. If this lasts much longer, I'll start running, stumbling around in the light that blinds, falling down, letting loose of Tappy, losing her because I'm so terrified I can only think of myself and of escaping this pain. But there is no escape.

Other voices, weak and distant at first, then stronger and closer, were brought by the breeze blowing against their backs. He stopped. Let them come to him. It was pointless to keep moving. They were going to die no matter where they were.

Then, an undercurrent to the approaching voices, the sound of running water came to him. That was followed by the splash of feet in the stream and, suddenly, more voices. He waited, though for what he did not know. Certainly, the voices did not seem hostile. They were low and murmurous. Again, he trembled. Soft fingers had brushed against his cheek. He felt Tappy become rigid as if she, too, had been touched.

Once more, he quivered, and his heart beat harder. Two hands had seized his face. Now they were running the tips over his face. Before they had withdrawn, he became bold enough to reach out and do the same thing to the person who was tracing his lineaments. The skin was almost as velvety as a baby's, and the bones below them were fine. It had to be a woman's. Then she spoke—he could feel her breath issuing from her mouth onto one hand—and she said, "Son."

"Mother!" Jack said.

He almost fainted.

It was not only her voice that told him that she was indeed his long-dead mother. His fingers, moving over her face, had evoked an artist's image. It would, if he painted it, be a portrait of her. But she was now a young woman. When she had died, she had been middle-aged, close to being old. She had borne him when she was forty-eight, her time of fertility almost gone. The wrinkles and the sags he was so familiar with had disappeared.

A whisper came to him. Someone must be speaking very softly to Tappy because she had suddenly begun shaking far more violently than before. He could not hear her reply, of course, any more than she would have heard him say, "Mother!" But she must have tried to utter something.

Things went swiftly after that. Hands turned them around so that they faced the direction from which they had come. They were pushed along, past the clusters of flowers, went up a long slope, were on level ground, and then began a long march. Jack was so numb with shock that he could not resist them. What sense was there in doing so, anyway? Yet . . . yet . . . he had met his dead mother; he could not speak to her; he was being sent away.

When Jack and Tappy became tired and slowed down or tried to halt, they were urged by gentle but firm hands to pick up the fast pace again. He had no idea how much time had passed. He became thirsty and wished that these people would give him water. Then he thought of the myths and fairy tales where the intruder from Earth drank the liquid offered for refreshment and of what happened to the intruder after that. He was doomed to live out the rest of his life in the domain of faery and to never see Earth again. It was better that he refuse water, no matter how much he craved it. Or was he just seized with superstitious dread?

Nothing superstitious about this place, he thought. It did exist. So did its citizens. Thus, he and Tappy were in a supernatural or infranatural world.

The numbness permeating him was good for one thing. It seemed to deaden the pain from the light and the pain of being united with his mother for a few seconds and then hurried off. But he was not so inwardly frozen that he did not guess that he was being sent away for his own good.

Abruptly, the hands held them back. Since he had heard his mother, he had heard no voices.

Now the hands pressed on them, and Jack finally got the idea. They wanted him to get down on all fours. He did so, feeling with one hand to make sure that Tappy was with him. For some time, he had feared that she had been left behind. But she was with him and also on her hands and knees.

Hands pushed on his buttocks. Tappy stayed where she was. For a moment, he thought of resisting. Then he thought that, if she were to remain here, she would not have been made to get down on all fours. He moved ahead until his head scraped against something hard. A hand pushed down on his neck. He got down lower and resumed crawling. The grass was gone. The floor seemed to be hard earth, then became mud. Presently, he had to go like a snake on his belly. If he tried to raise himself, his head bumped against stone or what seemed to be stone. That did not last long. All of a sudden, the floor dipped, and he was sliding downward on the soft mud.

Then that was behind him, and he was lying on hard earth. Something struck the bottom of his shoes, and somebody gasped and then cried, "Jack!" He turned over and sat up. Though thick mud coated Tappy's face, it did not conceal her strange expression.

"Mother and Father were there!"

Chapter 17

JACK did not reply at once. He rose, feeling tired, and looked around. It had been night when they had plunged through the shadow. Now it was just past dawn. The sky was bright and cloudless, but the sun had not come up above the crater wall.

Tappy sat in the mud like a statue shaped from it. Even the Imaget, crouched on her shoulder, was a hunk of water-soaked earth.

He did not know where they were on the crater floor. The Gaol spaceship was not visible, and there was no grove of trees like those under the ship, nor was there any Gaol camp. He turned slowly while he looked at the great figures on the crater ring, dim objects in the gray light.

After his survey, two things caught his mind's focus. One was the faint shadow through which they had just exited. A fan-shaped pile of mud, drying at its edge, extended from the base of the shadow. Here had once been a huge boulder which a radiator beam had disintegrated, no telling how long ago. The crumbled rock was in a heap beneath the death-shadow, the outline of which could be barely seen. It was close to fading away entirely. When it did, Jack thought, that gateway to the "other" world, the world of blinding light, would be closed.

He noted that more than people could enter and then leave that light-filled world on the other side of the darkness. Mud could also pass through the dark gate.

They had gone into that world through the tree-shadow beneath the spaceship. And they had left it through this boulder-shadow. They had been pushed back into the world to which they belonged. But they had reentered far from the point of entry.

Darkness implied light. There were no shadows without light, and the death-shadow was caused by the blinding light. At least, it seemed so to him.

This place was comparatively close to where he and Tappy had gone in. Probably, it was the first time that this had happened. He did not doubt that it had been no accident. Those people, the dead who were not really dead, had pushed them through this particular gate for a purpose. What the purpose was, he did not know.

But he wondered if the second object that had caught his attention was involved in the purpose.

That was a rose-red cut-quartz stone not sixty feet from where he stood. It was the model of the tiny stone Jack had seen centered in the model of the real crater-wall rings, the model he had seen on the table when he was in the underground complex. A seat and a back, a throne, had been carved out of the desk-sized quartz. According to the Integrator, the first honkers to enter the crater had found it. Though they did not know who had made it, they assumed that it was the work of the Makers. But it was obviously designed for a honker or a human and not for a quadruped.

By then, Tappy had risen shakily from her sitting position. Her tears were washing the mud from her face. Her hands were clasped just below her breasts. He did then what he would have done at once if he had not been so stunned. He went to her and held her while she wept. A few seconds later, he was weeping also.

"My mother . . . she spoke to me! And my father did, too! They only said my name, but I recognized their voices!"

"My mother," Jack said. "She spoke only one word to me, but I felt her face. And . . . you heard Malva, too!"

"What was that place?" she said.

"Some place where the dead live. Heaven, for all I know."

He had never believed that there was an afterlife. At times, he had hoped that there might be, but he had no faith that there was. It was a fairy tale which rational people knew was a fairy tale. But now . . .

"How could we have gotten there?" she said. Her sobs were tapering off. "There's only one way to get there, and we didn't die."

"I don't know," he said. "I could guess. It's possible that the radiator was designed to be a weapon but it had some unforeseen side effects, unexpected by-products. One was that the shadows created by the radiator accidentally opened the way to . . . what do I call it? Heaven? A parallel universe? I don't know what it is, but it exists.

"If the Makers made the radiators, they would have ignored the shadows after a few of them ventured into the shadows and didn't come back. Not to their knowledge, anyway. They would've had no idea they had serendipitously opened the gates of Heaven or whatever you want to call it. Anyway, what good would it have done them if they had known? Except maybe the certainty that death is not the end."

Even that, he thought, is not certain. What if the world into which we dived is just one that affects the minds of intruders? It's so alien to us that we can't comprehend it; its physical structure or whatever is beyond human understanding. So, the mind constructs something that can be understood, something it desires more than anything else. An afterlife. What the mind can't grasp, it interprets as something else.

If this was so, it would have to be an effect that all humans interpreted as the same. Otherwise, why would Tappy have shared his hallucinations, if they were such?

He was the ever-skeptical rationalist. Tappy, however, once over her tears, was certain that she had been, even if for a short time, in the place where the dead lived. Perhaps she was right. She might have a deeper rationality. Whatever "deeper rationality" meant. In any event, he was not going to try to invalidate her belief. She took great comfort in it, and she needed all she could get.

And . . . His thought was interrupted by a coldness thrilling through him. Wait a moment! Just hold up! How had he overlooked it? But he had been numb, still was somewhat, and he could be forgiven for forgetting.

"Tappy!" he said. "Your mother! How could you be sure that that woman is your dead mother? I was told by your relatives when I picked you up that you'd never known your mother! I didn't ask them why not. I just took their word. But if you'd never known her, if she died at birth or something, how would you know her?"

She stared at him, then said, "I remember her now. Those fingers on my face . . . her voice. I knew nothing of her until that moment. Then I remembered her, it all came back. I was three years old when I last saw her. I'd been sleeping . . . where was it? Our little house on the edge of the town called Tappuah. Tappuah means the place of apples. Something like that. I can still remember that wonderful smell from the orchards. The humans that lived there had come from another place, I don't know where. There were many honkers, too, traders mostly, but I played with their children, and I learned their language. I was happy there. Then, one night, I was awakened. My parents told me to keep quiet. I didn't know what was going on, but I was frightened. So scared that I didn't make a peep.

"Then I was being carried by my father through darkness. I think it was the forest up in the hills by the town. All of a sudden, a great light from above shone through the big trees. A very, very loud voice, must've been from a loudspeaker in an aircraft, said something about surrendering. But my parents kept on running, and then . . . then . . ."

She choked. It was a minute or so before she could continue.

"Then there was a different light, a scarlet-colored beam that swept through the forest and cut through trees. They fell with a terrible sound. By then, I was screaming despite my mother's commands to keep quiet. Then I heard shouts, men yelling. They must have been the Gaol humans who were hunting us. My father stopped and put me into a hole in a tree. He told me to stand still and not move an inch. Otherwise, I'd fall into the shaft behind me. I was standing on a very narrow ledge and hanging on with all my strength to the edge of the hole. The lights got brighter, but the scarlet ray quit coming. Maybe it had been turned off. And then my father turned to help my mother into the hole. But . . ."

She broke into a long and loud weeping. Jack put his arm around her and held her until she could talk again. Her face against his breast, she said, "Oh, God! Then there was a glare, and I could see that my mother had fallen onto the ground. Her legs were cut off. Her blood was spouting out of the stumps, spraying my father's legs. I was still screaming. Then my father grabbed me with one hand and lifted me up by my clothes and got halfway into the hole. He knew, I suppose, that the Gaol wouldn't shoot at him while he was very close to me. They didn't want to kill me and then have to start searching for the Imago again.

"My father held me in his arms, and he jumped. We fell down the shaft, not very far, I think, and then we were suddenly in bright daylight. He landed with his knees bent—strange how that little detail sticks in my mind—and he staggered. But he put me down and pulled a beamer from his belt and shot its ray upward. I remember just glimpsing a ledge projecting out over the top of the cliff. We must have dropped through a gate in the stone. He blew up the projection with the ray. There must've been explosives or something inside the shaft in the other world. Anyway, it exploded and, I suppose, destroyed the gate. The rocks and the dust rained over us, but my father covered me with his body. He was hurt protecting me, though not bad enough so he couldn't lift me and carry me off. I was still screaming with terror and with grief for my mother."

She paused, doubtless to scan the memories that had surged up from the unconscious, breaking loose through the barrier there. Then she spoke again, her voice less quivery.

"I remember now, though it's vague, being in a great cavern complex before we went to Tappuah. Maybe it was the same as the one we were in. I don't know. Anyway, it's coming back, part of it, anyway. It was there I first learned honkerese and English, the English which humans speak on the planet. After a while, we went to Tappuah. Maybe the pressure from the Gaol was off, and my parents thought it was safe to live with humans again. They must've been sick from being under the ground, must've longed for the open air and the sunlight. I know now that my parents and a few other humans and some honkers were part of a secret organization dedicated to fighting the Gaol. Plotting against them, anyway."

She was silent again. When she resumed speaking, she talked with a low voice and in broken phrases. It was as if she were sweeping the fragments of the life she remembered into a basket, then was picking up the pieces from the basket without regard to order.

"Once, I overheard my parents talking. They were saying something about the light that glowed from me when I was born, a light that lasted for an hour or so. By that, they knew that the Imago was inside me. Of course, I didn't know what the Imago was, and I forgot all about it when my mother was killed. That wiped out all my memory of my infancy and early childhood. Later, I forgot my life from the time my mother was killed to the time the airplane crashed and killed my father and crippled me. I could not talk after that. My tongue seemed frozen. Along with much else that was frozen. I lived, but I was half-dead.

"When you came along, you started the thawing out. I began to live again, though not fully. But I knew that you were the person I'd been waiting for to love me."

Father, mother, and lover squeezed into my person, Jack thought. Also, the knight in shining white armor who rode up to rescue her. In reality, the Doubtful Knight.

He said, "Your so-called relatives who raised you, Melvin and Michaela Daw, were they part of the anti-Gaol organization?"

She nodded, and she said, "They must have been. I think they're part of a very small band that went to Earth. They did so, probably, because they knew that I'd have to flee to someplace the Gaol didn't know much about or care about.

"The Gaol have probably been aware of Earth's existence for some time. But they didn't move in on it. They think that overpopulation and pollution will soon cause the collapse of civilization on Earth. Millions will die, and the Earthpeople will revert to savagery. Then they'll be easy pickings. At least, that's what I once heard my father say when he didn't know I was around.

"Anyway, to get back to the couple taking care of me, the Daws. They were in grave danger. And they knew I was the host for the Imago. That's why they were not as loving to me as they should have been. They couldn't treat me as if I were an ordinary child. Sometimes, though, they broke through their fear and awe and tried to love me. But I was a terrible burden to them. Of course, I didn't know that then."

"Still," he said, "they knew that the Chrysalis in you wouldn't become the Imago until you were mature. Why did they advertise for someone to take you to that institution when you were so young?"

He paused, then said, "And why did they pick me to do that?"

She pulled herself loose from his embrace and began pacing back and forth. He smiled. She carried the Imago within her, yet she looked as if she were the least likely vessel for such a great thing. No, not a thing. An entity of unprecedented and unparalleled importance. She was the very essence of the dirty and tattered waif of back alleys, of the most forlorn and rejected type of human.

Finally, she said, "I think that the Gaol may have been getting too close to the trail. They had to hide me someplace else before they fled. Or, I don't know, not really, they weren't going to send me to the institution. They knew that I didn't have time to mature. The Gaol would catch me before I did if I stayed on Earth. They had to take a chance, send me back to this planet. First, though, they advertised for someone to transport me to Vermont. I do know they interviewed at least a score of would-be drivers for me, and they rejected all. Until you came by, that is."

"Why me?"

"The paintings," she said, halting to look into his eyes. Beneath the mud was a face almost shining with exultance. Or exaltation.

"The paintings?"

But he knew before she spoke what she was going to say.

"The paintings in the Makers' burial chamber. They showed a male youth holding a painter's brush in his hand. You. You were a painter, and you were a young man. I think that they thought—maybe were absolutely sure—that you were the one the Makers prophesied. Predicted, anyway."

He snorted, and he said, "Prophecy! Prediction!"

She shrugged before speaking. "It seems farfetched. But who knows how much the Makers knew or how powerful their predictions could be. Maybe they figured out something on a probability basis. Maybe they counted on someone fulfilling the prophecy. Maybe they could see into the future. Or maybe the paintings have been wrongly read. They might've meant something other than the anti-Gaol honkers and humans thought it meant. But the anti-Gaols brought it about that what they thought had to happen did happen, even if they'd misread the paintings. After all, what we think is a painter's brush in the youth's hand in the Maker painting might be something else."

"You've gone a long way since I first met you," he said. "You've grown up fast. No thirteen-year-old I know could reason like you do."

"I'm fourteen now," she said. "Not counting the pseudo-years you implanted in my mind."

He had many more questions based on the fragments she'd muttered. But they had to get going. They walked toward a long double line of tall plants and found a creek between them. Though the water was very cold, they plunged into it and did not leave it until their bodies and clothes were clean. The Imaget stayed in the creek only long enough to wash the mud off. After that, it waited on the bank until the humans spread the wet garments out in the sun and then sprawled naked in its warmth. It crawled onto Tappy and snuggled between her beasts. After about twenty minutes, all three were dry and beginning to toast.

Jack was about to open his eyes and get up when he heard a honking. He jumped up, staring around. Tappy rose and stood by his side.

"We'd better find them," he said.

"But we'd better make sure they're friendly," she said. "There are traitors among the honkers just as there are among humans. Not many, I've been told. But we can't be too careful."

He listened, trying to determine the direction from which the honking came. Halfway around in his turning, he jumped with alarm. A honker had stepped out from behind a tree.

Tappy cried out with relief and welcome. She followed this with a series of blasts.

The honker was the Integrator but not in the condition he had been in at the Gaol spaceship. One eye had been gouged out. One hip tentacle was waving wildly, but the other was missing. A bandage concealed its stump. Dark bruises were scattered over his face and body, and his chest had long bright red rakemarks on it.

The snake around his neck bore a wound close to its head, though this did not keep it from extending part of its body toward Tappy and hissing loudly. The navel-beast's mouth and paws were caked with dried blood.

The shaman had suffered grievous wounds during some struggle, but he had not been defeated. Raised high in one hand was the severed head of a Gaol. He honked loudly, and Tappy murmured, "It's the head of the Gaol captain."

Behind him came Candy, then other Latest, some limping or being supported by their fellows.

A moment later, an aircraft, a vessel designed to carry a score or more, floated from the brush.

Chapter 18

JACK strode toward the shaman. "What happened?" he cried. "What happened?"

The Integrator, of course, did not understand him. Jack asked Tappy, who was behind him, to interpret for him. But the shaman dropped the Gaol head, hobbled to her, fell on his knees, and put his bloodied arms around her legs. His head was bent back as he stared up at her and honked loudly.

She said, "He's dumbfounded. How did we get out of the Land of the Shadow? He says that no one who goes through the death-shadow ever returns to this land. He cannot understand it."

The other Latest, fallen silent, listened while she told her story to the shaman. Then he got up to his feet, somewhat shakily, and he began to dance. The others joined him. Jack waited until the jubilation had died down somewhat.

"Now," he said, "ask him what happened back there."

She did so, but, first, the shaman had the head brought to him. While he issued a long series of blasts, he waved the ghastly head around and his tentacle thrashed. His one good eye glared, and the snake and the navel-beast twisted frenziedly. These two had aided the Integrator greatly in his struggle with the captain, and the shaman's tentacles had spurted poison into him. The Gaol must have felt as if he had been attacked by five people, not just one aged honker. Nevertheless, the captain had fought well.

The other honkers interspersed their comments or encouragement while the shaman "talked." Perhaps, these were their equivalent of "Right on!" or "Hallelujah! Amen!" Toward the end, the shaman's excitement swept through them, and they began a war dance, waving their spears, stomping their feet, mock-fighting, and whirling around and around. The sun glistened on the fungus-deterrent grease they had smeared on their bodies;

their feet, slamming onto the hard earth, made a primitive beat which echoed in the ears and the blood. Even Jack was not unaffected by it.

When the shaman had finished, his warriors continued making a hullabaloo. Candy had come up to Jack meanwhile but stood without speaking. Her right shoulder and left leg had been wounded, but these were healing swiftly.

"They saw us escape through the death-shadow," Tappy said. "However, they're too strongly conditioned against going through the shadows. Millennia of taboos keep them from even getting close to them, plus horror stories about them. They would die before they'd enter one."

And, dying, would go to that world, anyway, Jack thought.

The airboat, which the honkers had appropriated from the spaceship, was speeding across the plain. It contained only one person, the pilot. Apparently, it was simple to operate. Otherwise, the untrained honker wouldn't be able to handle it.

"As soon as we jumped through the shadow, they fled into the woods, only two of them being hit, one killed, one wounded," Tappy continued. "When they got there, they released the venomous flies they hadn't had a chance to let loose in the ship because the bubbles had enclosed them too swiftly. Then the three with beamers shot at the robots. The flies injected their venom in the human Gaol who followed the robots, and the Gaol dropped where they stood. Cyborgs came out, too, and the flies bit their metal coverings in vain. But enough stung the few areas of exposed flesh surface to paralyze them, too. This discouraged the few surviving Gaol.

"Candy and the Latest could have gotten away down the shaft inside the tree. But the shaman feared that the ship's heavy rays would be used to excavate the earth and pursue the warriors until they were caught and wiped out. So, he gave the order to charge. They lost a few, but they got all those who had come out of the ship. Then the Integrator had all the flies released inside the ship. He thinks that the detectors in the ship weren't set for anything which had a mass as small as the flies did. Or the detectors weren't working because the fungus had gotten to them. In any event, the flies swarmed all over the ship, barred only from entering rooms with closed hatches. There weren't many of those, and none of the crew except the captain was protected then by a bubble."

"But the captain still had his involition radiator," Jack said.

"Not by then!" Tappy said. She gave a short nervous laugh.

"The fungus was still working in some parts of the ship. It caused malfunctions in the involition radiator mechanism. It might've been quickly repaired if the technicians hadn't been paralyzed or killed or locked in rooms with closed hatches. The automatic mechanical-repair devices were also malfunctioning. But he did order robots to troubleshoot the circuits. They might've done the job in time to restore the radiator before the honkers entered. But they had a big task because so much equipment and so many cables were impaired."

"How did the Integrator know that?" Jack said. "I'd think he'd have been afraid to venture into the ship."

"He sent Candy to scout it. She isn't subject to the involition broadcaster. Why should she be? The Gaol had her programmed to do all they wanted her to do. It never occurred to them when they made her that she would resist their commands. They didn't figure on the Imago empathy affecting her."

"And?"

"And she went in and looked the situation over and then returned to report."

"And the honkers stormed on in?"

"Right. But by then the captain, who had been in the bubble, had managed to get a gas-supplier to him. By a still-functioning robot, I suppose. I don't think he could have communicated with the robot by radio or whatever means he normally used. The equipment for that would've been impaired by the fungus. He probably used hand signals or whatever to tell the robot to bring protective cloths and a gas-supplier to him. The supplier was some sort of scuba device, according to the Integrator. The captain was protected against the fly bites by heavy blankets thrown over his exterior skeleton, by gloves, and so forth, also brought by the robot. The captain was out of the bubble and just about to operate the ship controls manually when the Latest showed up. The Integrator said he doubts that the captain could have worked the controls because the fungus probably had wrecked all the electrical circuits.

"Anyway, the Integrator attacked the captain in the control room. Instead of just shooting the captain, who didn't have a weapon yet, he tackled him with bare hands."

"Why?" Jack said. "That was stupid!"

"Not by honker standards. It's something to do with their honor and prestige. Anyway, the shaman and the captain had an awful struggle while the other honkers stood by and watched. They'd been ordered not to interfere. Of course, if the Gaol won, then the honkers could shoot him. Despite losing an eye and a tentacle, the shaman strangled the captain and then cut off his head as a trophy. The honkers will sing a song about the epic fight for a long time."

"Sing? They can't sing."

"Their equivalent, anyway."

The Latest were jubilant and should be. They had, from their viewpoint, won a great victory. But it was really only a very small battle which did not affect the course of the war. The Gaol empire was set back a trifle, and it would not be long before their forces would be here. If, indeed, they were not already here. He looked at the sky. Only a few wispy clouds floated there. However, there could be hundreds of space-dreadnoughts assembled in a stationary orbit, and he would not be able to see them.

Tappy put her hand on his arm.

"Look!"

He turned. Here came the airboat shooting across the plain. Though he could not distinguish individual figures at this distance from it, he could see that the interior of the vessel was crowded with honkers. Something else had also been loaded into the airboat. By the time that it stopped about forty feet from him, he recognized the Gaol cyborg, Garth. It was partly exposed through the pile of honkers on it.

The canopy slid back. Honkers spilled out, reminding him of the tiny circus cars from which a seemingly unending line of clowns emerged. Other honkers had unloaded a collapsible wooden ramp—how had they crammed that into the vessel?—and had propped it up against the edge of the canopy.

Garth rolled out of the boat on his wheels. When it had gotten to the ground, the honkers pulled the ramp away. The Integrator spoke to an aide, and she hurried to the pilot and conversed with him. Then the canopy slid shut, the boat rose, turned, and accelerated away.

Garth came speedily to Tappy. It whistled a long series of dots and dashes. When it stopped, Candy said, "Garth says that it is ready to interpret for the commander of the fleet."

"Fleet?" Jack said, but he knew what she meant.

Candy pointed upward. He looked again at the sky and still saw only clouds.

"Garth has been receiving messages for the last half hour," Candy said.

Tappy spoke as if she were suddenly short of breath. "What did the commander say?"

"She wants to send down a negotiator. He'll come down in a small vessel, and he'll be alone and unarmed. He just wants to present the empire's demands."

"I thought he wanted to negotiate?"

"The Gaol don't know the difference between demanding and negotiating. You should know that, Jack."

"Yeah, I know. Candy, when does the commander want the meeting to take place?"

"As soon as possible."

"Tell Garth to tell the commander she'll get the time of the meeting shortly. We have to confer about it first."

While the android was whistling at the cyborg, Jack swiftly considered the possible consequences of permitting the Gaol to come down in the spaceboat. Why this face-to-face confrontation? Why not just talk via Garth? It could not be because the commander wanted a close look at the situation. She could see them as clearly through her instruments as if she were hovering just above them.

Maybe she thought that her demands would be much more powerful if they were delivered personally. Issuing from a scary-looking creature with its ratcage-body, its brutal face, and its lack of brainpan, the demands would have an impact that could not be matched by messages relayed via Garth.

But then the Gaol probably did not think of themselves as frighteningly alien and horrible. On the other hand, they must have observed that their appearance did nauseate the bipedal species they had encountered. See a Gaol; feel like throwing up.

It was an anthropocentric reaction, but it was natural.

The Gaol would not wish to destroy the Imago's host except as a last resort. Did the Gaol believe that this situation demanded that Tappy be killed? He did not think so. It had not developed to the point where they would say, "Screw it!" and then kill her. Not yet, anyway, though it could lead to that.

It was not likely that the negotiator's boat was armed or equipped with an atom bomb. The Gaol would not have to depend upon that to kill Tappy if the commander decided that that was the only solution to their problem. Missiles launched from the orbiting ships could do that work much more effectively and with no warning at all.

He told Candy and Tappy what he had been thinking.

"The Gaol boat might be equipped with remote-controlled machinery," he said. "Controlled either by the negotiator or, more likely, from the spaceship by the commander. She might have ideas about abducting you, Tappy. I don't know how, but I'm thinking of something like paralyzing gas sprayed from it, then the boat opening up and scooping you into it and taking off. The negotiator would be sacrificed, but they wouldn't care."

They agreed, and so did the Integrator when they explained what they had been talking about. Jack told Candy to send a message through Garth.

"The boat must land at least half a mile from us," Jack said. "The negotiator will walk to us. Just after he leaves the boat, it will ascend. When it's at least a hundred miles above the surface, the negotiator can start walking toward us. Tell the commander that you have radar capabilities and can ascertain that the boat rises to the agreed-upon altitude. And you'll know immediately if it starts to go below that height."

Garth whistled. Candy said, "He says he doesn't have long-range radar."

"The commander probably doesn't know that. Even if she checks up on the specs for Garth's type of cyborg and they don't indicate he has radar, she can't be sure we haven't installed the equipment in him."

The airboat had returned. It was as packed with passengers as during the first haul. They spilled out, the number of males being the same as the number of females. Now that he thought of it, the first load had been an equal division of the sexes. That was strange because the warriors who had attacked the ship had been mostly male.

The women and men were covered with war paint, black, white, and red stripes. Interspersed among these were stars and triple crosses. The women bore crimson six-pointed stars, and the men bore blue five-pointed stars. The triple crosses were all purple edged with yellow. The foreheads of both sexes were marked with three concentric circles. The outer circle was white; the next circle, black; the inner circle, blue. Around the women's navels were three similarly colored concentric circles. The navels were painted a bright rosy red.

The men's penises were decorated with three red wavy lines radiating from the longitudinal axis. The same number of wavy lines, colored blue, spread out from each side of the women's vaginas and across the upper thighs.

The second boatload had brought brushes and paint pots with them. They proceeded at once, in the midst of much honking and gesticulating, to paint the first boatload.

What were they up to? Jack thought. They certainly were not going to attack the Gaol negotiator. Probably, they were getting ready for some sort of magical ceremony. Though they were far advanced in biological science and technology, they were otherwise primitives. They believed in magic. That, at least, was the impression he had gotten during his brief but intense experiences with them.

But he could be mistaken.

Garth whistled. When he was done, Candy said, "The commander agrees to your terms. Everything will be done as you wish. The boat will land in approximately an hour."

"Ask the commander if we can get a preview of the offers that'll be made by the negotiator," Jack said. "We can think them over while we're waiting for him."

In less than a minute, the commander's reply was relayed by Candy.

"She prefers that the negotiator deliver the terms in person."

"Okay," Jack said. "We can't force her."

He wondered what the Gaol were planning. It would be nothing good for anybody in this camp and especially not for Tappy.

During the hour allotted, five more boatloads of honkers came. The sixth was jammed with cooking utensils and food. Jack asked Tappy to ask the Integrator about the reason for bringing in all these people. Also, she should ask him why they were all painted. By then, the shaman had also been decorated.

Tappy, after a brief exchange with the shaman, said, "He'll only say that this is all for, uh . . ."

She cocked her head as she did so often when thinking hard. "Uh, the best translation would be, 'for the big showdown.' "

"Showdown?" Jack said.

"Yes. And that's all he'll say."

"How the hell could this be a showdown? And how would he know it is?"

"He won't say anything more about it. Don't press him, Jack. It's not the honker way. He'd be offended."

"He knows or thinks he knows much more than I do. More than you, too, right, Tappy?"

"Yes, I think so. I hope so."

Jack strode back and forth, fuming and muttering to himself. Sometimes, he believed that he was the leader, the captain, the man with the ultimate authority. The Integrator had let him make decisions and so deluded him into believing that he was the leader. But when the shaman wanted to do certain things, he just ignored Jack.

Tappy was looking even more distraught than when they had first come to this place. In fact, she seemed to be coiling in on herself. She needed consolation, moral support, assurance, and love. He started toward her to give her what she needed. Garth's whistles halted him.

He stopped and went back to Candy. By the time he got there, the cyborg had quit speaking.

The android said, "The commander says that the spaceboat will soon be in sight."

Jack went to tell Tappy and the Integrator. But the shaman was busy marshaling his people into three still-ragged concentric circles which had the rose-red throne as its center. He was honking away, and his aides were pushing and pulling their charges into their places. Everybody had a short stick with a gourd at its end. These had come with the food and cooking utensils but had not been unloaded until a few minutes ago.

The commander, viewing this scene from her spaceship, must be as uncertain about this activity as he was, Jack thought.

Then the entire group of Latest blasted out a sustained sound. While doing this, they looked upward and lifted their sticks and rattled the gourds with a mighty noise. Jack also gazed upward.

The spaceboat was a black dot in the blue sky. It swelled quickly and became a small needle-shaped vessel. The honkers went back to their preparations for whatever they were going to do.

Chapter 19

JUST to make sure that the vessel would land at the distance indicated, a cross of stones had been laid out. Jack had not sent a message to this effect; he had assumed that the Gaol would figure it out. But the spaceboat settled down at a spot one hundred and eighty degrees north of the cross.

"Either he thinks there's a trap prepared under the cross or he's just contrary," Jack muttered to himself. It was also possible, however, that the negotiator was not as intelligent as he should be. Or that the cross symbol meant nothing in the Gaol culture.

A hatch on the side of the vessel opened, a ramp rolled out, and the negotiator walked out. The ramp slid back inside the hull, the hatch closed, and the vessel shot upward. It soon disappeared. About two minutes later, Garth whistled a message. Candy said, "The boat has now attained the agreed-upon altitude. If the commander is not lying."

Then the Gaol was walking across the plain, waddling a little because of its turtlelike underplate. His skin was much darker than that of the other Gaol Jack had seen. He had much higher cheekbones, and his eye sockets were square, not round. The Gaol, like humans, must have differentiated into races during their evolution.

Behind Jack, the honkers were still noisy as they organized the arrangement of the circles. A few seconds later, the Integrator joined Jack, Tappy, Candy, and Garth. He had turned over the directorship to an aide. Jack saw the shaman out of the corner of his eye. But when he turned his head toward him, he was startled. The severed head of the Gaol captain lay at the shaman's feet. Jack did not think that this defiant gesture was diplomatic. Surely, the negotiator would be offended. And so would the fleet commander, who would be looking at the head right now.

Jack started to ask Tappy to tell the shaman that he had acted untactfully. Then he closed his mouth. Why not show the ratcages that they were not quivering with fear of them?

"I wonder what the negotiator is going to say?" Tappy said nervously. Her hands were clasped on her stomach, and her face was even more drawn. He hugged her briefly and said, "We'll find out. It's going to be okay, Tappy. The Integrator is planning something bad, real bad, for the Gaol. I'm sure of that."

The words were for her. He did not feel as confident as he sounded.

Presently, the Gaol halted a few feet from them. He glanced at the head lying at the shaman's feet. If he was affected by it in any way, he did not show it. He lifted his hands above his head and locked the thumbs. Candy said, "That means he comes in peace, and he plans no treachery. With your permission, I'll reply for you."

Jack nodded. She imitated the Gaol's gesture. The Gaol lowered his hands and whistled for at least a minute. Candy interpreted.

"I'll condense his speech if it is your will. Much of it is bragging about the might of the empire."

Jack said, "Fine, as long as you don't omit anything important."

"He says that this business could have been settled long ago if we non-Gaol were not subject to irrationality. But the Emperor has taken this into account. Therefore, since irrationality makes us delay the inevitable and we are procrastinators, the Emperor gives us more time than is necessary to make up our minds to accept what must be.

"He says that we must deliver the Imago to the commander of the fleet. When we do that, no harm will come to those who have fought the empire. You, Jack, may live here as long as you wish. In fact, the Emperor, in his magnanimity, will leave this planet alone. The Gaol will stay away from it.

"You will have four hours to consider the terms and to decide what a Gaol would have decided within a minute. The Emperor is patient."

"And what if we still persist in being irrational?" Jack said harshly. "What if we refuse to surrender the Imago?"

Candy whistled. The negotiator's expression did not change. His "speech" this time was much shorter.

Candy said, "He says that the Emperor is patient, but his patience is almost at an end. This time, the Imago will not escape. Even if they have to search every square meter of the planet on or below its surface, they will do so. And they will find it.

"If, in our irrationality, we decide to kill the host and so release the Imago, we will all be killed. Indeed, all life on this planet will be destroyed. It will be so radioactive and so fragmented, nothing will ever again live here.

"Moreover, now that the empire has become aware of the native planet of the host's mate and it knows that there are gates to Earth, it will destroy Earth, too! He says to think of that, Earthman, before you defy the empire!"

Tappy gasped, and she gripped Jack's hand. Her hand felt very cold and damp.

The negotiator whistled. Candy said, "He says that the Emperor's terms have been delivered. There is no use continuing the meeting. He will be leaving as soon as his boat returns."

Jack thought of telling Candy to thank the Gaol for being such an excellent negotiator. Sarcasm, however, would probably ricochet off the Gaol's thick skull.

Presently, the boat landed. Before walking the half mile back to it, the negotiator whistled again. Then it turned and waddled away.

Candy said, "He said that the four hours allowed us start the moment he enters the boat."

The Integrator honked; Tappy replied; the shaman honked again. Then she spoke to Jack.

"I've told him what we and the Gaol said. He says that four hours should be enough. If, that is, all goes as he hopes it will, and if the Gaol don't break their word that we'll have that time. But it'll be, uh, how can I put it?"

After frowning for a moment, she said, "It'll be nip and tuck. It also will be chancy, iffy, but we have to do it!"

"Do what?" Jack said, close to snarling with frustration.

Tappy shrugged and lifted up her hands. "I don't know, and he won't tell me! But he says it'll be self-evident."

"The way of the honker," Jack said.

The shaman blasted again at Tappy. Then, his body movements expressing impatience, he took Tappy's hand and led her away. Jack, Candy, and Garth followed her. By then, he had become aware that the weather had changed. The sun was suddenly blocked. When he looked up, he saw that grayish clouds covered it. They scudded along, driven by a wind whose force was only beginning to be felt on the surface. The gentle breeze here had picked up a bit and hinted that it was going to get stronger. To the west, beyond the crater wall, black clouds towered. Lightning, very far away, flashed briefly and weakly. But the menacing-looking clouds would soon be over the crater floor itself, bringing with them the lightning.

He wondered if the Gaol's viewing instruments could penetrate electrical storms. If not, the honkers would be helped. They could do whatever they were going to do without alarming the Gaol.

By then, the honkers had completed making three perfect circles. They were standing still, listening to their group leaders. He supposed that they were still giving instructions or, maybe, a pep talk.

Then several leaders and a number of people in the lines began honking loudly and pointing up and outward. Jack said, "My God!"

The tops of the dark hemispheres rising above the crater wall startled him so much that he did not immediately recognize them. For a few numbing seconds, he was completely at a loss. As they continued to rise, their nature became evident. He said, again, "My God!"

They were Gaol spaceships.

He groaned. But, within seconds, he was yelling at Candy. "Tell Garth to ask the Gaol commander what's the meaning of this."

He waved at the spaceships. Candy whistled at the cyborg. While waiting, Jack, turning slowly, counted the vessels, as if it made any difference how many there were. There were fifteen, each stationed about a mile apart from each other. They had the same structure as the one which the honkers had invaded. That they could be seen at twenty-five miles distance and in this pale light meant that they were enormous indeed.

The empire was showing some of its awesome muscle.

Garth whistled then. Candy said, "The commander does not acknowledge the message."

But the ships did not move after they had risen in their entirety above the crater wall. They were going to hover there until . . . until when?

They might wait until the four hours are up, Jack thought. They have to. If we did intend to cave in to them and give Tappy up, they'd be screwing up by moving in now.

He relaxed somewhat.

The Integrator had quit staring at the ships. Now he was again leading Tappy by her hand. His obvious destination was the rose-red cut-quartz throne. Jack followed them. When the two went through the three lines of honkers toward the stone, he did the same. Behind him came Candy and Garth. Nobody tried to stop them. The moment he was inside the inner circle, however, the lines began moving. The Latest in them shuffled along, honking softly. The group leaders had taken the places left empty for them until now. Jack counted the number of people in each circle. Ninety in the inner ring. Ninety in the next ring. One hundred and eighty in the outer ring. Three hundred and sixty altogether. A compass card had three hundred and sixty points.

The numbers of honkers in the circles were directly related to the compass card points. Thus, since there were three hundred and sixty images and symbols (some groupings were counted as one) on the crater-wall ring, there had to be some relationship between the dancers and the paintings.

The images and symbols were still visible, though they would not be when the storm struck. They moved with majestic slowness, seeming to be as patient as eternity itself. Patient for what? he thought. They had not been set here without purpose.

The Integrator had led Tappy to the throne, which faced west. He made gestures that she should sit down in it. Before she had finished doing that, a honker handed the shaman a tall conical cap topped by a stiff paper model of the three crater rings. Then he gave him a crooked wooden staff at the end of which was a carving of a Maker's face.

Thus accoutered, the Integrator glared around him, his empty eye socket seeming even fiercer than the other eye. He gestured at Jack and his companions. When they came to him, he pushed and pulled until Candy was at the south end of the throne, Garth was at the north end, and Jack was at the east end. Though he was placed so he faced east, Jack did not keep his back to Tappy. He turned around to keep an eye on her. The shaman did not try to make him face eastward again. He was too busy dancing and honking and waving the staff in front of Tappy.

Meanwhile, the people in the three circles had stepped up their pace a little. The inner ring was moving counterclockwise; the middle ring, clockwise; the outer ring, counterclockwise.

The crater ring rotated counterclockwise. If there were indeed two other rings, as the models indicated, then these probably rotated in the same directions as the two outer circles of honkers.

Jack thought, What the hell is this? Magic? A form of sympathetic magic? Where things desired are simulated? Thus, the
primitive practice of trying to cause rainfall by pouring water.
In this case, simulating the operation of the three circles would
cause them to rotate. But they were already moving. At least, the
inner crater ring was moving, and he assumed that the other rings
were also rotating.

Why, then, were they performing a sympathetic magical rite?

The pace was being stepped up again. The stomping of feet
was faster and louder. The shaking of the gourds was faster. All
were honking the same "chant."

Of course, Jack thought, they're trying to make the great wheels
set in the crater go faster. Oh, God, what a waste of time!
We should be thinking about ideas to get Tappy away from
the Gaol!

But the Integrator knew that his world and Jack's would be
destroyed if an attempt was made to spirit her away. Moreover,
there was just no way of escape for her. None. None at all!

What about a gate? Not the boulder-gate to Earth but another
gate to another world.

No use. Even if they had one, and surely the Integrator would
have told them about it if one was available, the Gaol would ruin
forever the two planets. And they would keep on hounding Tappy
until they caught her.

The Integrator was using this magical ritual because it was
his only hope to save the Imago. Not to mention himself, Jack
thought.

But the shaman might know something that he and Tappy did
not know and for some reason should not know just now.

Maybe they were being kept ignorant because of the Gaol. If
these did catch him and Tappy, they might gouge out of them
the truth about the rings—whatever that was—and thus thwart
whatever it was that the Integrator planned.

Jack just did not know, and he was helpless to do anything but
watch this useless ritual. His mind was spinning like a centrifuge.
An empty centrifuge.

Suddenly, there was a silence. The shaman had lifted the staff
and shaken it three times. At that signal, the Latest had stopped
both their honking and their dancing. The Integrator spun around
to face Tappy. Jack could not see her face, but he imagined
that it reflected the terror and confusion she surely must be
feeling.

The shaman threw his staff up in the air, bent over, seized Tappy's blouse, and tore it open. One hand threw away the blouse and the other reached out—he did not even look—and caught the staff as it came down toward earth. It had whirled three times while aloft.

Tappy gasped. Then the honkers blew one long strong blast. Immediately, they began dancing and chanting again, stomping their feet more swiftly and harder. Jack could feel the earth tremble slightly beneath his feet.

The Integrator reached with his free hand and touched the Imaget, which was almost invisible in Tappy's brownish hair. It did not move. He gently picked it up and placed it over her left breast. At this, the honkers not only moved forward faster, they began whirling, and their honking was so loud that it hurt Jack's ears.

Jack thought, Is this going to go on for four hours? I'll go crazy. So will Tappy.

Then he cried out with horror. The Integrator had moved one step closer to Tappy. The tentacle had lifted, and it had plunged its poisonous tooth into her breast. It came out swiftly from the flesh, but some of the poison had been injected.

Tappy had not flinched when struck. She sat as stiffly as before, her head unmoving, staring at the west.

Jack came out of his numbness and started to crouch before jumping over the throne so that he could attack the shaman. He meant to kill him. But two very strong hands gripped him from behind. A blast of air ruffled the hair on the back of his head, and a blast of sound did deafen him for a second. He struggled and could not move.

Candy called out to him. He could barely hear her.

"He wouldn't harm her! It's all right! It's part of the ritual! She's just partly paralyzed for a little while! That makes her more open to the Imaget's channels!"

Candy must be guessing, but what she said made sense. He quit struggling. After a few seconds, the hands withdrew.

Open to the Imaget's channels? For what?

The shaman was bent over so that his head-nose almost touched hers. Jack could not hear what he was "saying," but he would not have understood it, anyway. Was the shaman speaking to her or to the Imago through her? Whatever he was telling her, his tense gestures made him look as if he were giving her instructions which he was repeating over and over. If she heard him, she did not respond with any body movements. But her lips might be moving.

The storm was coming closer. The dark clouds overhead, forerunners of the blacker and energy-shot body, were moving more swiftly. The breeze was a wind now, blowing his hair and Tappy's toward the east and raising dust clouds. The Integrator had lowered a chin strap to keep his conical hat from being blown off. The rains had passed over the western wall of the crater. Their drops looked like a solid silvery plate with discolorations running down here and there. The Gaol ships hovering there had disappeared behind the rain.

He turned back to watch Tappy. He caught his breath.

She was shining!

The glow was bright, about the strength of a dozen 100-watt light bulbs. But it was becoming brighter, spreading out from her as if the windows of her flesh were slowly opening.

That glow came from deep within her.

He shouted, "The Imago!"

And then he cried out again but uttered no words.

The fleet above the eastern wall was moving slowly toward the center of the crater.

Chapter 20

ABRUPTLY, the row of spaceships was veiled as rain struck. A few seconds later, the vessels faded away entirely. The downpour slashed into the center of the plain, drenching the area around the throne. The thunder boomed loudly as if it were a vast boulder rolling down a mountain. A lightning bolt like the flaming crooked cane of a blind god slammed into the earth nearby. A tree cracked into two parts, one of which toppled over.

Despite the drenching, the thunder, and the lightning, the honkers kept on dancing and chanting. Jack had jumped when the bolt had hit the tree, but he had been looking at Tappy's back when it happened. She had not moved. Nor did she seem affected by the rain and the cold. Her brownish hair had turned black with the water; that was the only change.

The light emanating from her was as bright as before the full rage of the storm. It pushed back the darkness brought by the clouds and the deluge.

Although he was shivering with fright and cold, Jack felt a tiny warmth deep inside him. The Integrator had done it! Somehow, he had evoked the Imago. But he could not have done it until Tappy had matured. Just when that had taken place, he did not know. Nor did he know the definition of "maturity." Somewhere along the line of time, she had passed from girlhood into full womanhood. It had happened very recently. Otherwise, the Integrator would have performed this ritual before now. He had been waiting for the unseen moment to occur. In fact, he must have been very nervous because he knew that the Gaol would be down on them like a lioness leaping on a zebra.

Maturity had come to her as silently and as unseen as the moment when a peach ripened and was ready for eating. Yet, the Integrator had felt it. Or had he been so desperate that he had started the ritual but had not known if she was ready for it?

It did not matter now. She had passed from human chrysalis into human imago just as the Imago—which had really been a chrysalis—was now an imago.

Jack, the eternal questioner, could not help wondering who had made the Imago. It seemed to him that the Makers had done it. They seemed to have been able to cross the bridge from the physical to the superphysical or the supernatural.

The infraphysical?

The death-shadow caused by the action of the radiator indicated that. Had the Makers been trying to find a gate into other worlds which were not physical worlds as Earthpeople defined such? And had they accidentally opened a gate into the afterlife itself? A gate they could not use.

Had this experimental project also revealed that the Makers could construct an entity such as the Imago? Though it was artificial, it was immortal. And it could be used only under certain conditions.

Either the Imago had been made because of the challenge of the Gaol or it been made before the Gaol had risen like the temperature of a malignant fever to spread through the universe. The latter event seemed more reasonable. Whatever the chronology, the Makers, despite their vast knowledge, had made the Imago a little bit too late. They had been vanquished. Not, however, before they had created a heritage that threatened the Gaol empire.

That heritage had been preserved by the Latest, the seemingly primitive species whom the Gaol did not fear. They had passed on this heritage—part of it, anyway—to a few human beings. And to who knew how many other species?

The honkers may have made the gates among many worlds so that the plot against the Gaol could spread. Or they may simply have used what they found in the Makers' burial chambers. The chamber which Jack and Tappy had seen was not the only one in the underground complex.

Lightning smashed the ground nearby again, though it was not as close as the tree-riving bolt. Its flash seemed to light up a previously hidden thought in Jack.

The prophetic paintings in that burial chamber had been recently repainted. The Integrator had told him that. But what if the Integrator had not repainted the ancient images? What if the walls had been blank or he had brushed over old works? Then he had painted the images which the two humans saw? They had been a pious fraud, a device to stimulate Tappy into a state where the Imago would manifest itself.

It was not so much physical maturity that had opened the gate in Tappy and allowed the Imago to be summoned. It was a maturity of the psyche.

He could get the answers to his questions later. If, that is, Tappy and he and the others survived. Just now the Gaol dreadnoughts were moving toward them through the storm. Why? He could only guess. But the commander must have been astonished to see them performing a savage's ritual when they should have been conferring about her demands. She may have decided that the four hours' grace was a waste of time for the Gaol. Had she given the order to move in and capture the Imago's host while they were deeply involved in their ritual? Or had she ordered the ships just to come closer to the group because the vast chaotic energies of the lightning were disrupting her observation capabilities?

But if she had seen the light issuing from Tappy, she must have known that the Imago was about to manifest itself.

Jack groaned, and the tiny hot coal of hope inside him darkened. All the commander had to do to stop the Imago was to order that all within the crater walls be destroyed at once.

He prayed to the God in whom he did not believe.

Then he cried out in wonder, though he had expected more wonders.

The brightness was a sphere extending from Tappy to about ten feet from her. It included himself, Candy, Garth, and the Integrator. It did not touch the people in the three circles, the honkers whose feet now struck the earth rapidly turning into mud with a mighty squishing sound. But, as suddenly as if someone had pushed a button, the sphere shot out many thin rays. At first, Jack thought that the sphere was doing it. But a much more intense ray was shooting out, laser bright, from Tappy's left breast through the bright sphere.

It had to issue from the Imaget upon her breast. It fell upon each of the dancers as each passed into and through it in his and her circuit. It made each of them glow as if each had swallowed a giant firefly. Or a saint's halo. Their lights paled the darkness among them. Despite the suddenness of this, they hesitated for only a second and then resumed their whirling and their forward progress.

Scarcely had Jack cried out than he did so again.

Now a ray shot out from each dancer into the black storm and toward the crater wall. The beams angled slightly upward.

If the Gaol commander knew of this, she must be whistling the equivalent of a human screeching into her communicator. "Destroy them! Destroy them!"

Now the dancers were whirling faster and had also speeded up their passage over the circles described in the mud by their feet. Somehow, despite the energy output that should have made them short of breath, they were still chanting. And their gourds were rattling even more furiously.

The thunder and the lightning had raced past the group. The rain quit as quickly as if a giant stagehand had cut it off. Though the clouds were still black above, the storm had quit for now. A few minutes later, the clouds took their darkness over the eastern wall. The sun sprang out as if from ambush.

But the sphere of light and the ray emanating from the Imaget and the rays shooting from the dancers were easily visible.

Jack saw that the beams from the dancers were impinging upon the images and the symbols on the crater-wall ring. He did not know until then that he had unconsciously expected this.

He cried out a third time.

The figures on the ring flashed as each passed through a ray. The ring was moving much faster. Though it was at least twenty-five miles from him and the figures were gigantic, they could be seen now only as almost unrecognizable smears. While he stood astonished, he saw them become even more blurred.

The outer rings, the two concealed within the crater wall, must also be rotating at an incredible velocity.

The Gaol spaceships were truly colossal now. They were poised halfway between the throne and the wall. Poised! Not moving!

He turned to look westward. The storm had hidden the fleet in that direction, but now he saw that it was also hovering halfway to the ritualists. In fact, the entire array of vessels formed a circle around them.

The Integrator blew a very loud and long blast. After a sustained single honk, the dancers became silent. They stopped their frenzied motion and turned to face the wall. Quickly, they broke up the circles and rearranged themselves in a long line facing the western wall. Their work was done, the wheels no longer needed them to spin them, and they were going to watch the results.

The ray from the Imaget had ceased. But the glow from Tappy spread out and sped across the plain until it filled the crater. Its brilliance was not diminished by being diluted. It was not, however, a photonic light. Glaring as it was, it did not make Jack close his eyes. Like the glare in that other world reached via the death-shadow, it seemed to fill every cell in his body. But this light did not hurt or blind. That other light had done so because he and Tappy were in a place where they should not be.

Soundlessly, lubricated by an unknown substance or field, the ring spun until the blur of the images and symbols became a single dark streak. The air near the ring was agitated, however. It quivered and shimmered. Vague figures flew around in it as if they were birds in a mirage.

"No!" Jack said aloud.

He realized suddenly that he had been mistaken. First, he had thought that the weapon which left a shadow like a bad aftertaste in Death's mouth was what Tappy had talked about in her dreams. "Alien menace . . . only chance is to use the radiator," she had muttered. Then, he had suspected that it was not the weapon but the Imaget. But now . . . he knew the truth.

The radiator—the Radiator!—was the crater-wall ring. The three rings, rather. They were pouring out radiations of empathy, the empathy which would conquer the Gaol. No, not just them. The entire universe of sentient beings. All, Gaol, honkers, humans, the multitude of language-speaking species which must be scattered throughout the single world made of many worlds.

If there was anything faster than light, it would be the empathy waves. These were infraphysical. At least, he assumed that they would be if they were going to affect a significant number of sapients.

Also, there were the gates such as the boulder-gate he and Tappy had passed through from Earth to this planet. There must be many throughout the cosmos. And the gates on this planet would be transmitting the waves to Earth and to gates on Earth which led to other worlds and to gates on this planet which led to other planets. The effect would spread much more quickly through them.

Was it already affecting the people of Earth? God knows that that planet needed it. But then every planet probably did.

The end of wars and of murder and of viciousness? The lessening of hate and greed and ruthlessness? The growth of love and compassion?

The spaceships had stopped in their advance toward the Imago and its host. He did not know, but he was sure that the Gaol in them had been overcome by an onslaught of empathy far more powerful than anything Tappy had radiated before the real Radiator, what the honkers called the Generator, had started to function. Its waves had reached up to the fleet in orbit and stunned the Gaol in it. And the waves were on their way, directly or through gates, to the rest of the empire and beyond it.

He got a flash of something. Then it was gone. But it would be back. For a second or two, he had been in a Gaol. Or, maybe, in every Gaol. He had been in the mind of a Gaol. In that fraction of a second of full comprehension and actually being a Gaol, he had been as frightened as he had ever been. But now he also understood what drove them. Despite their repulsive appearance and behavior, they were not unlike human beings. What was ugly in them (and also what was ugly in humans) would change into beauty.

He was surprised that he had not had this feeling before now. After all, he was standing in the very center of the radiation. But his location was similar to being in the eye of a hurricane. All around him was a gigantic surge of the force that had been, as it were, born and slain many times before it could get anywhere near full fruition. Now it was the mightiest force in the many universes. Compared to the combined energies of a trillion trillion stars, the Imago was a sun beside a candle.

He, however, was in a null area. Comparatively null, that is. Once he went to where he would be in the full force of the empathy, he would be as filled with it as the Gaol now were.

The rays from Tappy's breast and from the Imaget were fading now. Their work had been done, though they still lived and would again become as bright as angels if they were needed.

Jack hoped that they would never have to be invoked again, that their force would endure. Surely, they would not have to be used in Tappy's lifetime.

But he could see on Tappy's face a golden aura, faint but still evident. Evident to him, anyway. It was probably his imagination. No one else could see it, though he would ask others if they detected it. It was an afterimage of the holy light. Yes, the holy light. Though Jack was an agnostic and would have felt uncomfortable calling anything "holy," he now would think of the aura as, if not holy, the echo of holiness.

Tappy would be something to be worshipped by him.

Would that interfere with the union of their flesh? Would he always be inhibited somewhat when they made love or—a mundane thought but valid and realistic—when they argued about the budget or when they disagreed about disciplining their children? Would he always give in, even when he knew he was right?

He hoped not, but he would have to wait to find out.

They would have to get back to Earth first. Neither he nor Tappy wanted to stay here, no matter how pleasant it might be. Despite all the madnesses and hideousnesses that stalked Earth, it was their home. And, now that the Imago was flooding the souls of its people, Earth would become far better. Perhaps the Earth that all sane people wanted it to be.

How to get back? That should be no problem. The honkers would know of a gate to it. If they did not, the Gaol would.

He laughed. Whoever would have thought that he could ask the Gaol to help him? Or that they would do so willingly, even gladly?

There was still one question unanswered. What had Tappy meant in her sleep-talk when she had said, "Reality is a dream"?

Later, much later, when they were living on an Earth the societies of which were greatly changing for the better, he asked her about the phrase.

She had to probe her mind for some time before she remembered where she had heard it. So much was buried there, and so much was still difficult to find.

"My father," she said. "He told me that several times. I was so young, I did not ask him what it meant. Or, if I did, I've forgotten his explanation. Anyway, I did puzzle over it, then I forgot about it. So many bad things were happening then. But my unconscious evidently did not forget it. I really don't know what he meant by it."

"He must have meant that dreams shape reality," Jack said. "The Makers had a dream of the means whereby they could conquer the Gaol even after they, the Makers, were gone. Hence, the Imago. The honkers and the humans allied with them continued to dream the Makers' dream. They made the Imaget, and they dreamed of how they could use it to let the Imago come to full bloom.

"Dreams shape reality. Thus, dreams are reality."

"That must have been what he meant."

Authors' Notes

PIERS ANTHONY

This really started in 1963. Back then I was a hopeful writer, with one sale to my credit. I was taking one year to stay home and write, while my wife went out to earn our living, and the year had started in September 1962. If I didn't prove myself by September 1963, I would have to return to the mundane grind and give up my foolish dream of being a writer. As it happened, I did sell two stories in that year, for a total of $160, so was technically a success. But realism intruded when it came to paying the bills. I did return to mundane labor, but in 1966 tried writing full-time again, this time doing novels instead of stories, and that was the one that took. It was after all possible to earn a living doing novels. I have been writing ever since. The details of my life and career are too tedious to go into here; they are in my autobiography, *Bio of an Ogre*. What concerns me now is just one story written in that first year, and the story of that story.

The story was "Tappuah." I wrote it for God rather than Caesar; that is, for love instead of money. The name derived from the Bible; I am hardly a Bible scholar, but in a concordance or some such I had seen the name, and learned that it meant apple, and it intrigued me. The setting was the Green Mountains of Vermont, where I was raised. The character turned out to be the first of a type I have explored considerably since: a young and tortured girl. Critics accuse me of having nothing but luscious and sexy women; Tappy is the evidence that I tried other kinds, but without success on the market.

In February I completed the monster story "Quinquepedalian," and in March I would complete my farcical fantasy story "E van

S." Between them I fitted in "Tappuah." It moved better than anything else I had done up to that time. I wrote just over 2,000 words a day for three days, and had it complete at 7,000 words in February, my favorite. It had a fantasy theme: Tappy, lame and blind, nevertheless had an affinity for extinct creatures, and they tended to show up.

I was then in touch with several other hopeful writers, such as Robert E. Margroff, H. James Hotaling, and Frances T. Hall, with all of whom I subsequently published collaborations. I sent "Tappuah" to them for comment. They liked it; they felt it was the best I had done. That was my own sentiment.

I tried it on the market. It bounced at *Playboy* (as I said: about non-luscious girls and the market . . .), and at *Cosmopolitan, Ladies' Home Journal, Redbook* (probably they didn't like the fantasy element), *The Magazine of Fantasy and Science Fiction,* and *Fantastic.* Evidently the genre magazines didn't want it either; one of them sent a scribbled note suggesting that I try it on the "straight" market. So I tried it on a mainstream literary magazine, *The Atlantic Monthly,* and it bounced there too. So much for that; seven markets had rejected it, and I had to retire it. For a while. But I did not forget it.

Meanwhile I went back to college to get my certificate to teach English, and I became an English teacher. It was a poor substitute for the real thing, creative writing. But I took advantage of the interim to show the story to my literature professor there, Wesley Ford Davis, himself a published novelist. Intrigued, he read it to one of his classes, and relayed the students' comments to me. They liked it, but felt that the human element of Tappy's situation warred with the fantasy of the extinct animals; it might be better as one type or the other.

When I taught English at the Admiral Farragut Academy in St. Petersburg, Florida, I read the story to my tenth graders. They liked it, and offered thoughtful comments. I hope that they profited from this examination of an actual piece in the throes of revision; I was trying to teach them meaningful things, as well as the required material. (If you suspect that I am implying a disparagement of the standard material, you are on target; I feel that much of American education is wasted on irrelevancies.)

So I rewrote it, eliminating the fantasy element, and put it in for comment when I attended the 1966 Milford Writer's Conference. There were a number of comments there; I remember Harlan Ellison advising me that women didn't talk the way Tappy's mother did, condemning her crippled child. Damon Knight criticized Tappy's leg brace, thinking it was inconsistent to mention it once as being on her foot and another time as on her leg. Was it on her foot or her leg? he asked. It was on both, of course; apparently he had not seen such a brace. Gordon Dickson had no problem with his critique, but took time out to walk by himself in order to figure out how to present it in such a way that I would not freak out. That sort of thing makes me wonder just how I come across to others, but I appreciated his sensitivity. I don't remember the critique itself, except that it seemed reasonable. So I eliminated Tappy's mother and tightened the story up in various other suggested ways and clarified references. Then I tried it on the market again.

No luck. *Knight* rejected it in late 1966, and in 1967 so did *Good Housekeeping, Playboy* (after four years, changed editors might make a difference), *Cosmopolitan, Redbook, McCall's, Atlantic,* and *Mademoiselle.* Tappy had now been rejected fifteen times. But I didn't give up; I included the story along with all my other rejected stories in a volume titled *Anthonology* and tried that on the market in 1970. You guessed it: that, too, was solidly rejected. Later I used the title for a collection of previously published stories, and that was published in 1986, but it's not the same volume unless you count two unsold stories I slipped in. But "Tappuah" was not one of them. She still languished.

Then in late 1986, I believe, I received a proposal from Hank Stein for a round-robin novel titled *Lightyears.* It was to have ten or twelve established genre writers, each doing one chapter. A number of noted genre figures were interested, such as Poul Anderson, Robert Silverberg, and Philip José Farmer. In fact, this had the potential of being one of the most star-studded genre novels ever. Naturally I agreed to participate. Then, early in 1987, the word came that I was to do the lead-off entry. This surprised me; I had expected to be buried somewhere in the middle. I was of course jammed for time—this is a chronic condition with me, perhaps typical of workaholics. How could I start a novel which others would finish, and do it rapidly and well?

Then I thought of Tappy. I reasoned that to achieve bestseller status, this volume should at least start in the contemporary mainstream. Later it would get into the deep space, alien monsters, universe-destroying elements, but it needed to have one or two main characters with whom the average mainstream reader could identify. I remembered how *The Wizard of Oz* started with an ordinary Kansas girl, then got into full-scale fantasy, and was successful. My story of Tappy fit the criterion. Also, and by no means incidentally, I very much wanted Tappy to have her place in the sun. My characters are real to me, and I hurt when they hurt; I did not want to allow Tappy to be as brutally treated by the market as she had been by her folks.

So I adapted the story in two ways. First I changed it from first person, Jack's viewpoint, to third person. This was because I did not think it was fair to lock other writers into the first person mode. I regretted the necessity, because there was a certain cadence in first person that third person lacked. Such as the line "My mind meanders when I paint." That has a poetic beat and alliteration. "His mind meandered when he painted" just doesn't do it. I do write for sound as well as sight; when I edit my material, I often read it aloud. But it had to be. Second, I added back in some hints of the fantastic, so as to give following writers something to work from. I made it evident that there was more to Tappy than her mundane existence.

I turned it in to the editor, and he loved it. In due course I was paid for it. I had succeeded in finding a place for Tappy. The second chapter was written by Phil Farmer, and the following chapters by other writers.

But there were problems, and the project foundered. Oh, no! Once again Tappy was cast into the street.

Then Charles Platt, who had been editorially involved with the project, made a suggestion: suppose I worked with Phil Farmer, taking our first two chapters and continuing as a two-writer collaboration? That way we could eliminate the major problem of the first attempt, which was such a diversity of styles and directions that there came a point when no other writers would tackle the later chapters. The notion appealed to me, for three reasons. First, I don't like to have anything I start go unfinished; I'm ornery and don't quit readily, as you may have gathered. Second, I have admired Phil Farmer's work since seeing his 1952 novel *The Lovers;* I am not alone in regarding it as a classic of the genre. That's by no means the only significant writing he has done; I believe it is fair to say that he is regarded as one of the outstanding figures of the genre. (In case you are curious, the consensus of the critical establishment seems to be that I am pedestrian in style and theme, and not a credit to the genre. It has been suggested that I owe my commercial success to the fact that my pseudonym begins with the letter "A.") I have done seventeen collaborative novels, but never with a writer of Phil's stature. I was eager for this chance to work with him. Third, I wanted to save Tappy, and this was a way.

But there were complications. The rights to the material in the *Lightyears* project were not clear. I finally clarified them the hard way: I bought the project and returned the rights of the entries to the authors. Phil Farmer and I had different literary agents. I settled that with the finesse and politeness for which I somehow seem not to be known: *My agent* will handle it, I said, refusing to negotiate. I had reasons which made sense to me, and Phil, being a nicer person than I am, yielded gracefully.

We moved on with it, at first alternating chapters, then—well, if you can tell who wrote what, more power to you, but you're probably wrong. Our styles and notions meshed nicely, and I think we have a good book. It was of course impossible to have it absolutely smooth, because each of us had to read the other's latest chapter before deciding where to proceed. This is the first collaboration I have done this way, and I suspect it's not the best way. But it was set by its genesis; we had alternated at the beginning, so we continued.

There is a round-robin story game, done either verbally or in writing, in which each participant tells a segment of the story, setting it up for the next one. Person A may have Boy meets Girl, but as they are indulging in their first kiss, the barricade at the edge of Lover's Leap gives way and they plunge down a thousand-foot cliff. Now it is Person B's turn. He establishes that there is a deep lake at the base, somehow not mentioned before. The lovers plunge in, bob to the surface, finally break their kiss, and realize that something is amiss. So they swim to shore, but are in a strange region uninhabited by man. They make a fire and dry their clothing, then spend the night, preparing for an arduous trek in the morning. But great eyes loom out of the darkness, and an enormous hand reaches down to pick them up, screaming. Oops— it's Person C's turn. And so on, in a gentle contest to see who can mess up whom the worst.

Naturally professionals such as Anthony and Farmer would not stoop to such one-upmanship. Or would they? Well, maybe on a subtler level. We had a mutual interest in having a good novel, because we were not doing this for our health. Amateurs may write just for fun, but professionals write for money. Fun, too, but the professional who does not keep an eye on commercial prospects does not remain professional long. So we tended to be conservative, making sure there was a reasonable continuation. When each of us forwarded his latest chapter to the other, he also sent a few notes indicating what he had in mind and where he thought it might proceed, and what baffled him. Thus, had I been the one to drop my lovers off the cliff, I would have indicated that there indeed was water below, while allowing my collaborator the option of having them go splat on the rocky shore instead if he preferred. As with chess: you don't just wipe your opponent's king off the board, you announce your intention by saying "Check" and giving him a turn to respond. Not that this was any contest; we were going to win or lose together, by the success or failure of the final novel.

Still, there was a current. I hoped that Phil would make contributions with the imagination and vigor of *The Lovers* or one of his "Mother" stories, or maybe like *The Night of Light,* in which good wars with evil in a religious setting and at one point the Boy cracks the Girl's head open and a snake jumps out from the shell of the skull. What he hoped for from me I'm not sure; perhaps that I just manage not to drop the ball before scoring. So I did set him up with some brinks to hurdle (or whatever)—which he neatly finessed and tossed back to me. Meanwhile, it seems to me that our approaches melded nicely, so that there really wasn't much jerkiness in the progress of the story. That's one reason I prefer to be slightly ambiguous on exactly who wrote what: so that armchair critics can't say, "It's plain that we had one superior writer and one hack; the Farmer chapters are outstanding. Too bad he didn't have a better collaborator." They are going to have to figure it out without merely checking off every second chapter. (If you get the impression that I don't have any more respect for critics than they have for me, you're two for two.)

We brought the novel to the halfway point, and my agent marketed it. It was just in time for what appears to have been the worst slump in novels sales and prices in a decade or two. This is the inevitable luck of writers. Nevertheless two or three publishers were interested, and we finally landed a satisfactory contract. Now all we had to do was complete the novel.

I mentioned the luck of writers. Well, about the time we were heading into the home stretch, Phil Farmer's wife, Bette, had to have surgery. They went from Illinois to California for two weeks to take care of it. Right: it took longer than anticipated, and Phil was stuck for months without his notes, prior text, or computer as the deadline loomed. He had to write out his material longhand

and type it manually. I'd hate to see the color of the air around his working place while he commented on the situation! So he summarized what he had written for me, so that I could start my section without waiting to receive his. In this manner we moved it along despite his situation.

And so we completed the collaboration. I think its full history is unusual, even for a genre in which the unusual predominates. The result will be for you, the reader, to judge.

Meanwhile, anyone interested in a source for my other titles or newsletter may call my "troll–free" number, 1-800 HI PIERS.

PHILIP JOSÉ FARMER

My first collaboration was thirty-eight years ago. Up until recently, it was my only one. That is, it's been that long since I wrote a story in partnership with a real person. I have collaborated with some fictional writers derived from one of my schizophrenic personae. The last one, I think, was with Leo Queequeg Tincrowdor. But that's another story.

Other than Piers Anthony, my only partner in the felonious deed of writing fiction was Randall Garrett. If humankind has North and South Poles, Randall was the South and Piers is the North. Or vice versa. I'm somewhere between the two, a sort of Equator. Or perhaps the Tropic of Capricorn.

Inherently a loner, I've never thought, "Hey, I feel like collaborating with someone!" When I did, I did so because someone asked me to do it and it seemed like a good idea at the time. Randall Garrett was residing with my family and me in 1953 when he talked me into writing a novel, *The Ballad of Hilary Boone,* with him. This was based on a poem which Charlie Tanner had written. Charlie was an old-time science-fiction author whose heyday was in the Gernsback era. His "Tumithak of the Corridors" delighted me when it came out in *Amazing Stories* in 1932. It's still a good read. He was also a master at composing satirical poems based on s-f motifs.

Hilary Boone, hero of Charlie Tanner's song, "The Ballad of Hilary Boone," was a space pirate who fought—I think—the evil empire of Earth. Or maybe it was some vast monopolistic business corporation. I can't recall the details. One day, while Randall was singing the ballad and both of us had had too much beer (we couldn't afford Wild Turkey in those days), he suddenly broke off and said, "It'd be a great idea if we'd write a novel based on Charlie's song!"

So, we did. In those hoary old days, stories about space pirates and individuals building their own rockets were believed by the readers and purchased by editors. Most of them, anyway. And Randall and I were naive enough to believe in space pirates. Randall would write one chapter, and I'd write the next. So, without really knowing where we were going except for the story outlined in the ballad, we launched into the collaboration. I don't think our styles or approaches melded too well, but we did have a good old-fashioned rousing story. We sold it to *Startling Stories* magazine, which intended to publish it as a serial. If I remember correctly, it would have been the first serial ever in *Startling Stories*.

We got paid. But the magazine, which had been around for years, suddenly folded. The novel was returned to us. We sent it to a new agent I had just started with. Then she died, and the ms. was lost. It might yet be floating somewhere out there, or it might be lost forever. Probably the latter.

It was fun, but it was no classic. In fact, it's probably better that it was never published. Randall and I wrote at a breakneck pace. However, I still hope that it will turn up. I might rewrite it and send it out again.

Until Piers suggested that we coauthor the work at hand, I politely turned down the requests of various people (not many) that I collaborate with them. In his Author's Note, Piers has told you somewhat of the circumstances of the round-robin writing of the novel. That procedure failed because those who followed us tended to go off in directions too wild. They also did not develop the ideas Piers and I had planted in the first two sections. Thus, when he suggested that we do it as a twain, I was enthusiastic.

Piers is generally regarded as a sort of ogre. In fact, his autobiography is titled *Bio of an Ogre*. However, if you've read it, you can see that there's far more to him than being an "ogre." He's a writer who won't take any crap from anybody, especially certain publishers, editors, and agents. He fights fiercely for what he believes is right. He is very compassionate and honest. He is also highly imaginative and inventive.

I admire him as a person and as a writer.

There are many good writers around. There are not many people who embody the old-fashioned but still viable principles of honesty, integrity, and high courage.

We melded well in style and inspired each other with challenging ideas and turns of plot. At least, I like to think so.

When the end of the novel was nearing, I had to fight my inborn pessimism (or clear view of reality) to conclude with a tragedy. It seemed to me that the Imago would take over Tappy so completely that she would become alienated from Jack. As the host for the Imago, she would indeed become a goddess; she would be worshipped. Though Tappy would resist that, she would inevitably be a victim of this deification. Thus, Jack would lose her and have no hope of ever getting her back.

Also, the spreading of empathy throughout the universe would not be all good. Every good has its disadvantages and flaws. And vice versa.

But the extrapolation of the full effect of the Imago and Tappy's sufferings is another story. When the novel ends, she and Jack are happy and the good times have come to the sentients of all worlds. Let it end there.